THE
LORD OF WENSLEY

by

ERNEST RAYMOND

CASSELL · LONDON

CASSELL & COMPANY LTD
35 Red Lion Square, London WC1R 4SG
Sydney, Auckland
Toronto, Johannesburg

First edition 1956
First edition, second impression 1974

ISBN: 0 304 29277 X

Printed in Great Britain by
Fletcher & Son Ltd, Norwich
873

AUTHOR'S NOTE

The two prisons in the latter part of this story are given the names of Brixton and Wandsworth and are, in the main, true pictures of those prisons, but I have incorporated into them, for the purposes of the story, and to avoid any risks of character-identification, one or two features from other London gaols. They may thus be considered as composite pictures.

PART I

CHAPTER ONE

My own club is in Piccadilly, fronting the Green Park, but sometimes when it is closed for a staff holiday we are given the hospitality of the Old Universities Club in St. James's Street. I always like to go to the Old Universities as a temporary guest and I was there one Easter morning last year. Very empty it was that holiday morning, though the skies over London were grey and promised no comfort to those who sought the fields or the sea. I walked up empty stairs and along empty corridors to the Great Library, which is a room in which a man may sit with every comfort to read—or sleep.

It is a beautiful room, long, with tall windows between whose glazing bars you can look across St. James's Street either at the charming eighteenth-century front and Thackerayan bow-window of Boodle's or at the less charming but perhaps even more exclusive walls of White's. All round the room the book-shelves rise to the cornice of the ceiling, the books getting smaller and smaller as the shelves mount higher and higher. Four head-lands of bookshelves advance into the room and make five quiet bays. Black leather armchairs stretch the whole length of the room, facing each other *decani* and *cantoris*. In the centre is an oval table, large as a pond, on which rest all the journals in the world—or, at least, most of them. And the final satisfaction, the last comfort, is assured by a notice which stands framed on the big marble mantelshelf. It is brown with years but still says firmly

SILENCE

Conversation is strictly forbidden in the
Library

By order of the Committee,
J. A. Thomasy, Lt.-Col.

7th February, 1905   Secretary.

1905! Fifty years ago, and since the Secretary was a colonel then, I assume that he has long ago gone hence and been admitted to that great club of the dead which is so little exclusive that it blackballs no one at all. Dead too, I surmise, the hand that typed that notice. But there your notice still stands, gentlemen, and thank you both for this great silence. Nothing can be heard in that room but the surge and sighing of the traffic in St. James's Street.

Or nothing but the creaking of a chair. Thinking I was quite alone in that room, and blessing Heaven for this favour, I had dropped into a deep chair and opened my book. But I had not read two pages of it before a chair creaked by the fireplace far away. Here high mahogany screens made a kind of ingleside free of draughts for old gentlemen who shiver within their woollens. I looked that way and saw a figure rise from a chair under a screen. He did not stoop, but his clothes hung straight and loosely on a shrivelled frame, and his head hung forward as he came from the fireside to the big oval table. His face was turned from me as he picked up this journal or that, looked idly through its pages, and laid it down. None holding his interest, he walked round the table, searching relief for his boredom and so brought his face into the light of the windows.

I started. That famous face! It was the face of perhaps the most famous living judge, one who had sat on the Bench for a quarter of a century, hearing cases and appeals till he was over eighty. As a Treasury counsel, he had prosecuted in some of the most notorious trials of this century; and as a judge he had heard more of them. I was fascinated to study that old dried face with its pendulous cheeks that almost touched the lapels of his coat as he bent over the table. Not a handsome face, but the brow beneath the thin silver hair was fine, and (thought I, gazing at it) what memories of dreadful occasions lodged there—what recollections of white faces that had stared at him in bewilderment as he pronounced the last words they would hear from an offended world.

Perhaps he was not well off in his retirement, or he had grown careless in the weakness of his eighty-six years, but his black suit was shiny and dusty with tobacco ash, and his stiff collar and cuffs, so old-fashioned to my eye, were cracked and frayed. I could not help contrasting these tired garments with the majesty of his robes when he walked, a 'red' Judge, to his throne at the Old Bailey.

Having at last chosen a journal, he took it and sank heavily into a chair almost opposite me. I pretended to read but could not take my eyes off him as he carelessly turned its pages. So little did they interest him that he rose again and replaced the journal and, wandering to another table, sought something there that might fill up an hour or two in a life that was widowed now of all its greatness. He picked up some shining weeklies, looked at their pictures, and put them down again. He wandered into the bays between the bookshelves and glanced along the titles, but found nothing to divert him. And he prowled on, from bay to bay, like an old worn leopard.

At length, but not enthusiastically, he selected a book and brought it to the chair before me. And for some eight or ten minutes he read in it. But no, it could not dispel the boredom, and with a sigh he went again to the table, and gathered up *The Times*, as a publication which must surely hold somewhere *something* of interest. This he studied in his chair for a half hour or so, but then the old eyes asked for sleep and he laid the paper on his lap. He joined his veiny and thin-wristed hands across his stomach, let his head fall towards his jacket, and his underlip protrude. He was waiting with closed eyes for sleep.

§

I was to learn later that before he closed his eyes he had been reading about the escape of a Russian official from the Soviet sector of Berlin into the western sector where he had asked the western Allies for political asylum and offered them his services and his knowledge. And now, in the deepening twilight behind his shut eyes, he was thinking, 'To us of the West this fellow seems a brave man who has defied a government of which he disapproves, and sought a place where he can act according to his convictions and fight it. To us a hero, but to his own people—what? A traitor. A traitor whom, could they get him, they would assuredly convict of treason and lead out to slaughter.'

And this, of course, made him think of many whom he'd tried for treason and sent to death, ten years before, after the second of the German wars. Especially he thought of one: his last thoughts were of this one before sleep quenched all. That had been the briefest trial of his whole career but within its short spell he had suffered two sharp pangs of pity: one when he first saw the sad young face in the dock before him, and another when, glancing round the court he saw a look of utter love and helpless encouragement pass from an elderly, corpulent man to the young prisoner who had turned his face that way. By the side of this man sat two women, one elderly like him and dressed in her best for this hour of her public agony; the other younger, forever watching, watching the prisoner; and they too sent their glances of love if for a moment they caught his eyes. Manifestly father, mother, and sister of the accused; and if ever the judge had seen a dead misery in a man's face, it was in a father's then. It was the way this large, heavy, coarse-featured man hid his despair behind an encouraging smile for his son's sake that so disturbed the judge on his bench and hurt in his memory still. 'Seventy-six. I must be getting old and soft for a smile to shake me so,' he had thought on his throne. And he had bent his head over his desk and recalled all the depositions in the case which were surely shameful and shocking, rather than glance towards that family again. The desperate courage on the younger woman's face as she watched and watched her brother —one dared not look at that again.

What a queer life, what a life built on fantasies, that boy had led; but——

But now the judge, drooping before me in that chair, was no longer in a court-room of the Old Bailey but in a train as it thundered over the viaducts past Balham and Tooting and Streatham. Because he could never remember that boy in the dock without thinking of Balham and all the crowded regions round about; nor could he ever look from a train as it flew above Balham and see those streets of small houses stretching to the horizon on every side without thinking of the boy who had come from somewhere among them. The boy had lived in his father's public house till he set forth on his ridiculous and baleful road. Where was that public house? On Balham Hill was it? Or in Balham High Road? And what was its name? One forgot everything—everything—as one grew old. No, not a hint of its name came back into memory. That father in the court must have been the publican—yes, large and generously built he could well have been, in happy days, the jovial and popular landlord of a friendly house—the captain of a happy ship.

'Michael Townes, you are charged in this indictment with high treason, in that you, being a person owing allegiance to our lord the King, and while a war was being carried on by the German realm against our King did traitorously adhere to the King's enemies in parts beyond the seas. . . .'

'Members of the jury, are you agreed upon your verdict?'

'We are.'

'Do you find the prisoner Michael Townes guilty or not guilty?'

'Guilty.'

'You say he is guilty, and that is the verdict of you all?'

'That is.'

'Prisoner at the bar, you stand convicted of high treason. Have you anything to say why the court should not give judgment of death according to law?'

But it had not been like that. Not at all like that. It had been different from any trial he'd ever known. Only the judgment of death had been the same—the words, spoken by him, which sent that young man away from father, mother and sister and straight to the antechambers of death. One impulsive, unavoidable look at that father whose blunt-featured face was now bloated with unshed tears, and then the words. And the chaplain's Amen. The boy goes down below and out of the world's view for ever. Down to the cells beneath the dock which for him were the first of the tombs. 'Amen . . . amen . . . amen. . . .' So one repeats a word or phrase till it becomes meaningless, a mere incantation, as one drifts down through the darkness into sleep.

CHAPTER TWO

THERE was a sound of singing in the Balham High Road. It was fifteen minutes to midnight at the Lord of Wensley, on New Year's Eve, and Saloon Bar, Public Bar, and Private Bar were all loud with song. For, on New Year's Eve, not only had the Lord of Wensley a licence to stay open till after midnight, but its customers had a licence from the landlord to fling back their heads and open their jaws and sing. As a rule, Captain Harry Townes, licensee of the Lord of Wensley, did not like singing in his bars and would stop it with a 'That'll do, me lord. Thank you, old son, but that's enough to be going on with.' Not because he was an unlively soul—one glance at his face and habit showed that he was anything but that—but because his more gentlemanly patrons in the Saloon might like to enjoy their drinks with their ears unbruised, and he had no desire to lose these customers of refinement; and, in the second place, because all over England the Licensing Justices (a most curious race of men whose blood must be largely composed of distrust and water) seemed to hold that beer should be drunk without frivolity—and he had no desire to lose his licence.

But on New Year's Eve everything was different. Everyone who held glass or tankard or can—in Saloon Bar, Public Bar or Private—expected to sing and was allowed to sing. They were singing now, in unison, and very loudly. When we say 'in unison' we mean that each separate choir sang in unison, untroubled by neighbouring groups who were rendering different songs. Sometimes the songs were lively such as 'My old man said Follow the van,' but more often they were sentimental, and the sentimental ones were the most popular, because the death of the old year is an affecting time. They were also the best sung, because sentimental words demand the utmost expression from your voice, your eyes, and your tankard. Indeed the sentimental songs tended to unite all the competing choirs in one mass festival. Thus in the Saloon Bar—with some support from the Public Bar—they were soon roaring all together, and with deep feeling, 'There's an old mill by the stream, Nellie Dean, Where we used to sit and dream, Nellie Dean'; and they followed it with 'Love's Old Sweet Song.'

Then one man turned towards Captain Townes, who stood behind his counter wiping his tumblers, and sang to him alone. This was an enormous man with eyes so moist that it seemed the liquid he had drunk had reached their level, and if this was so, he must have tossed it back in enormous quantities. On his head he wore a tartan tam o' shanter, made of paper, which he had brought into the pub from some Hogmanay celebration in a street near by. The Scotch bonnet looked wonderfully out of place on the top of his head because his hair was black and crimped and silken, and his little eyes and heavy drooping nose were palpably Jewish.

And now throwing back the great black head (at some risk to the tam o'shanter) he serenaded his host with

> When you are happy, friend o' mine,
> And all your skies are blue . . .

and because the Captain was a popular host, and this an exceedingly sentimental song, soon all the rest were singing it with him.

> Tell me the hopes that spur you on,
> The deeds you mean to do,
> The gold you've struck, the fame you've won
> And let me joy with you.

The Captain smiled back at them and conducted their serenade with his festival cigar. (He allowed himself a cigar on all festivals.) He lifted his own glass to them in acknowledgment when all were moistening their throats after a strenuous song. And to the huge plump Jew in the Scotch bonnet he he said, 'Thank you, Jehoram. A filthy row, but well meant.'

Jehoram he called him, because his name was Joseph Henry Oram, and he could have stepped out of the Bible,' and because he was a regular arrival in the bar and fairly popular with all, and so worth the accolade of a nickname. True that, out of his hearing, he was generally called Bossy Jehoram, because he must always if possible, get command of proceedings, and get it by pitching his voice higher than any other. He must boss every festival as he was bossing this one now. Having produced a popular number in 'Friend o' Mine,' he tried to lead his disciples in 'Mademoiselle from Armenteers.'

> Mademoiselle from Armenteers,
>   Parlez-vous!
> She hasn't been . . . *mmm'd* . . . for forty years,
>   Inky-pinky parlez-vous.

And as they sang this song the Captain ceased to swab his counter, and stood listening, while gently drawing at his cigar. For he loved these songs of the old war. He had joined the army in August 1914 within one day of the outbreak of war, and since he was then over thirty and a big, heavy, well-set-up-man with a strong and combative chin like a door-knob, and since he had been a foreman in a brewery with the habit of command and a ready choler, he was patently the substance for a sergeant. In France, after leading many a bold raid into the enemy's trenches, he was given the Military Medal and later, after swatting a whole machine-gun crew with a single bomb as one swats an assembly of flies, he was offered the choice between a Distinguished Conduct Medal and a commission. For the sake of his future career, and because (as he said) 'the D.C.M. might never come up with the rations,' he chose the commission, and in 1919, the war won, he was released with the honorary rank of captain and the right to call himself Captain Townes, if he liked to do so. He liked very well to do so, both because it kept him among the gentlemen and gave a 'tone' to his pub, and because he loved his memories of those old heroic days.

In the Public Bar they might speak of him as 'the Guv'nor', but it was quite the fashion in the Saloon to call him 'the Captain', though the regulars here, when in bantering mood, did not let him forget that he had once been that most raucous and disquieting and fundamentally ludicrous thing, a sergeant-major. To be sure, Bossy Jehoram, fixing his aqueous eyes on his host, had now changed the words of 'Mademoiselle from Armenteers' into those of 'The Sergeant-Major's Having a Time.'

> The Sergeant-Major's having a time
> Swigging the beer behind the Line,
>   Inky-pinky parlez-vous.

But the tune was the same, and since there is no better tune, almost the whole company had joined in.

> The Sergeant-Major's having a time
> Kissing the girls behind the Line.

And the Captain listened, sometimes guiding them with helpful wavings of his cigar, while behind the cigar's blue smoke, he saw the faces of half-forgotten comrades, familiar once as household friends—men in uniform who had sat with him in French estaminets or billets, singing this song. And as the faces faded, he saw the long French roads going on and on between the poplars, and himself as a company sergeant-major marching at the head of his company, on and on, while the boys behind him sang.

> Madame, have you a daughter fine,
> Parlez-vous,
> Fit for a soldier of the Line,
> Inky-pinky parlez-vous.

Good memories of a simple life among a migrant people; of marching along the flat roads under a wide sky and resting at night in the heart of a green landscape with the promise of new scenes and new adventures in the morning. Your body a vessel so charged with vigour that you could drain it to the utmost, in trench or attack or forced march, and it gave you all. Your heart strangely at ease because for once it beat in community with a million others, and deep down in it, far beneath avowal, lay a consecration to something larger than your own little desires. Yes, that had been a full life, under the French skies; a life of strains and pains, often, and of many fears; but a man's life; larger, wider and better than he would ever find again among the endless pavements of South London.

The song ended with a grand vocal chord, and Jehoram, glass on high, cried, 'Captain Townes. To you, sir. My last drink this year is to you. Cheerioh and chink-pot.'

'Ta, Jehoram. Here's Happy Days.'

'The Captain! Come on, all. You've got to drink to the Captain Gob'less him. May his shadow never grow less. And to his good lady. Gob'less her.' Mrs. Townes, drawn by powerful singing of Jehoram's glee society, had come from the Public Bar counter to her husband's side, saying, 'What is it,

Harry?' And when Harry answered simply, 'It's Mr. Jehoram, ducks,' that impresario called out: 'Come on, all of you. To our dear landlady—' here a slight hiccup—'Beg pardon, everybody. Ida, my angel, your very good health. May your shadow——'

But here the voice of Jehoram plunged into his tankard and was heard no more. Only his black eyes, over its brim, flashed a signal of alarm at Captain Townes. Misguided words, his last. For Mrs. Townes threw a shadow of very large proportions, and it was obvious from the elaboration of her coiffure, the efflorescence of her dress, and the brilliant ornament on the long slope of her bosom that her appearance was a major interest in her life. She must have been exceedingly handsome say twenty odd years ago, in 1914, when the war started and she was but thirty. And she was a fine vessel now when dressed over-all for her bars. Her eyes were large and dark and showed to advantage beneath the masses of her bronze and silver hair. Her nose, well curved, was an aristocratic feature when powdered; less so when the powder was off, for then it had a purple tinge. This faint purple, however, was simply the imprint of her geniality, for she delighted in good fellowship with all her customers, and drank readily with them all.

And purple, white, or dustily grey, the Captain was proud of that nose, because it proved, in his view, that she was of aristocratic stock. Even now he mentioned her ancestry to Jehoram, who'd heard all about it many times before. Jehoram had whispered, as Ida drew away to attend to a call from the Public Bar, 'The devil, Harry! I nearly said the wrong thing then.' And Harry answered, 'Yes, our Ida doesn't like to be reminded how fat she's getting. And it's understandable, you know, because she was a bit of a knock-out for beauty when she was a girl. She looked like a young duchess then—everyone said so. And there was no reason why she shouldn't. She comes of much better stock than I do, you see. The Cawdors are a famous Scotch family. Descended from the old kings of Scotland, believe it or not.' Saying this, Harry threw a glance at the picture of the King where it hung like an ikon on his wall. 'The Campbells of Cawdor are descended from Macbeth. Shakespeare's Macbeth, you know. My lad found it all out. Yes, she's got Macbeth's blood in her. And Lady Macbeth's too, I suppose. Gor-lummy, that makes you think!'

'Yes, watch out that she doesn't start stabbing someone in their beds.'

'Ida'd never stab anyone, except with her tongue. She can use that a bit violently sometimes on her old man and the children. Those two children, by the way, must have the Cawdor blood in them too—Michael and Beth. Yes, their old dad's the only common one in this family. Nothing distinguished about me. I believe one of my forbears was hung for sheep-stealing; that's all.'

Harry had an immense pride in ancestry, but in his wife's, not in his own. He always depreciated his own so as to exalt hers.

'I make no pretence to be of good family, like Ida. Just ordinary, I am. And pure English. The only Scotch in me came out of a bottle. It's her that's the goods, and I think you can see it in her face. I'm glad she's like that because it means she doesn't talk common like so many barmaids do.' As a rule Harry, an ex-officer, didn't talk common either, but now and again when enthusiastic about Ida, or about something else, he could slide back into the old Cockney of the brewhouse. 'Yes, she's got good blood in her, has Ida. Royal blood, as you might say.'

'Well, make her come over and mix a little gin with it. She's got to have a last drink with me. Get her across.'

'Ida! Ida, ducks!' Harry pronounced her name to rhyme with Cider, even to the point of sounding a final 'r' when shouting for her. 'Ider, ducks. I-*derr*! Come here. Jehoram wants to treat you. Come and let him. It's good for business. There she is, and plenty of her. All yours, Jehoram.'

To call her 'Ida, duck' was a standard joke with Harry, and a whole litter of smaller jokes did he produce from this big one. He had learned from a bird book, studied for this purpose, the habits of the eider duck, and he was charmed to find that many of them could be applied very happily to Ida herself. He would remind the children in her presence that the eider duck had a wailing cry; that its call was harsh and grating; that it was resident in Scotland; that it was considered a beautiful and picturesque bird; and that it was a devoted mother, sitting on its eggs for weeks. 'Get along with you!' Ida would say. 'Such nonsense I never heard. Talking to the children like that!' But she was quite pleased with some of it, and Harry, knowing this, might add 'What's more, children, it has a breast like a pouter pigeon, and that goes for your mother too, eh what? That's a bosom to be proud of: it's largely made of my best four-ale and gin.' Then, lest he'd hurt her, he'd pick up her be-ringed hand and, saying 'Never mind, my dear, we all love you,' kiss it.

'Ida, beloved,' said Jehoram, 'what'll you have? You've promised me for the last ten weeks that you'd have a drink with your Uncle Oram on New Year's Eve.'

'No, ta, Jehoram. I've had quite enough for tonight.'

'Cut that out, Ida. Fill up her glass, Harry. If you're not quick, Ida, you won't get another drink from your Unkelorum till next year.'

'Well, if you insist, Mr. Oram. . . . Yes, thank you.'

Ida's initial refusal of a drink was seldom more than a formality, genteel and coy.

§

Nine minutes to twelve, and slowly the saloon door opened. Slowly, because the visitor from the street was pushing it open against the resistance of several backs and against the heedlessness of fifty singers. But he managed to effect his entry and to thread and inch his way through the crush to the counter. Some turned to look at him: a slender grey-haired man with a thin face, thatchy grey eyebrows over gentle, simple eyes, and a crisp grey moustache. In his grey suit, and with a rolled umbrella as neat as the moustache, he looked exactly the 'typical English gentleman' you pass so easily in Piccadilly or Pall Mall.

'Hallo, Harry,' he said, and his utterance was as brief and clipped as his moustache. 'Good evening.' His voice was as low as Jehoram's was loud.

'Dick! Mother, here's Dick!' Ida waved from the distance where she was serving a customer. 'I said he'd be here. Has he ever failed?'

'Yes, I think I'm just in time,' Dick said.

'Only just. Where've you been?'

'At a party. But I insisted on coming away to see the old year out with you. What'll you have?'

'No, this is with me, Dick. I'll have one with you next year. George, this is Dick Templer. My oldest and best friend.'

'Pleased to meet you, sir,' said George, a tall youth, who as a newcomer to the Saloon had not seen Dick Templer before. Jehoram, standing by, his hands in his trouser pockets so that they pushed his overcoat open, smiled down upon the introduction. *He* knew Mr. Templer well, for Dick was a familiar

18

figure in the pub, though generally a very silent one, being no 'mixer' like Jehoram.

'He's not only my best friend, George; he's my lawyer too. And an honest one, believe it or not. I say there are two Honest Lawyers in London, and one's a pub in the King's Road, and the other's Dick Templer here. More'n twenty-two years he's been my best pal—eh, Dick?'

'About that,' said Dick, with his clipped utterance.

'Yes, ever since we came together in the old war. Remember New Year's Eve behind La Bassée, Dick—what, twenty-two years ago?'

'Something like that.'

'And you as tight as a lord, and wanting to get on with the war at just about this time, ten to twelve? Wanting to give old Jerry your best wishes in the form of a few cricket-ball bombs? I'll tell these boys all about that some time.'

'Well, as long as they only believe half of it.'

'No, but it's true, George. It's true, Jehoram. He was the biggest fire-eater in our battalion. You wouldn't think it, to look at him now, would you?'

'If there was a fire-eater in our battalion, gentlemen, it was Harry himself.'

'I'll believe *that*,' said Ida, who'd come close, bringing a small goblet to the optic beneath a whisky bottle.

Harry did not dispute it. Instead, proud of it, he said, 'Ah well, I've quietened down now, like Dick. Just a quiet old man now.'

'You think so?' asked Dick.

'Yes; and I'll tell you for why. Ida's seen to it. I'm kept under, I am.' And he held a broad flat thumb an inch above the counter to show the position a married man occupied, if Ida was his wife. 'It's a very formidable woman I've married. She's the boss.'

'Oh, give over, Harry!' Ida scoffed. 'I like that! If ever a man had to be boss in his own house, it's this man here.'

'The lies women'll tell,' sighed Harry, and as Ida went back to her customer, he turned again to George. 'Dick's also my boy's godfather. And my girl, Beth's, adopted uncle. She adores her Uncle Dick. Thinks he's worth twenty of her father, and she's quite right.'

'Where's the boy?' asked Dick.

Harry took his cigar from his mouth, spat a tobacco flake from his lips to the floor; then stooped down and picked it up, because he liked his bars clean. He took his reading glasses from a breast pocket, breathed on them, wiped them, held them up to the light, and put them back in the pocket. 'Where's Michael? Where do you suppose? Not with his family. Not giving his old man a lift on New Year's Eve, like Beth's been doing till she went off to her Watch Night service to pray for us all. He's with all the other young fools in his so-called Black House. Of all the darn-silly nonsense! Calling himself a Blackshirt! Dressing up like a demon king or something, and marching about London with a thousand other idiots, and his chest out.'

Dick nodded as if he understood the father's irritation but he only said briefly, 'Well, why not?'

'Why not? Because it's un-English. Because it's just being a copy-cat of the Italians and the Germans. According to him everything's wrong with England, and the only person who can set her to rights is his precious Leader. Argue? Good God, he drives me scats with his arguing! Argue, argue, argue. Good *lord*!' Harry seized a swab and wiped his counter angrily and unnecessarily. It was no overspill on the counter but a sadness in his life that he was trying to wipe away. 'He's gone crazy about what he calls The New World Movement, which simply means him and the other dressed-up louts, and their Leader.'

Dick did not at once answer. He drank, thought, and said, 'Isn't something like that inevitable in a lad of twenty-two? When I was at Cambridge before the war, most of the boys were Anglo-Catholics. They liked to dress up in lace cottas and serve at mass; and they had statuettes of the Blessed Virgin all over their mantelpieces. Now I'm told they have busts of Marx and Lenin.'

'Good *Christ*!' muttered Harry.

'They like a cause to fight for. If it's not religion or politics, it's the latest rebellion in literature.'

'Yes, at one time I rather thought that was the way Mike would go. I thought he'd take to poetry or art and wear long hair and smell. Instead of that, it's this present nonsense. Talk about statuettes! Instead of statuettes on his mantel-piece of the Blessed Virgin and Jesus Christ—Beth's got those—he's got a picture of his Leader, as he calls him—there in the place of honour. No picture of the Old Man, bless you. The Leader—did you ever hear such stuff?'

'Yes,' said Dick with a grin designed to disarm. 'Heard it since the beginning of time.'

Harry let his anger die down. 'Old Dick here always stands up for his godson, George. Won't hear a word against him. But then, mind you, he hasn't got to live with him. Forgot to tell you, Dick, that he's thrown up his perfectly good job with the *Balham and Tooting News*, which I got for him because he liked literature and poetry and all that, and he's taken on a job with his dam' Movement which he's pleased to call Assistant Editor of Publications. And what does he get for it? Three pounds a week. Less than he got with the *News*.'

'Well, that at least shows that he's not gone into it for what he can get out of it.'

'He also calls himself Assistant Director of Propaganda,' said Harry, refusing to listen to any pleas. 'He's their Dr. Goebbels. Speaks at street-corner meetings, and Lord knows what.'

'Well, why not? Was there ever an imaginative boy who didn't want to think himself the member of a camarilla, plotting some rebellion or other?'

'Rebellion.' Harry heard this all right. 'That's just it. It's discipline these boys want, not rebellion. Maybe if I'd given him a few more hidings when he was a kid——'

'Or a few less,' interrupted Dick, with a small smile so that the words shouldn't hurt. 'My dear Harry—look—can't you see that nearly every young boy, just because he's really so insecure at twenty, is driven to think himself intellectually superior to his parents——'

'Intellectually superior? Damn his eyes!'

'Give him time. He's only twenty-two.'

'Twenty-one,' corrected Harry, as if this extra year increased the slight hope of improvement.

'Twenty-one. Well, with all that eagerness in him he should turn into something very good in the end. You'll see.'

'Dammit,' laughed Harry, all spleen gone. 'Dick's a lawyer and can always put a case for the Defence. He could have argued that Crippen was innocent and ought to have been commended by the Judge and sent home.'

'I'll go and argue before Ida for a change,' laughed Dick in return. 'She's not quite so ready to damn the boy as you are.'

§

When he was gone a sufficient distance, Harry began to speak of him to the newcomer, George, with no less enthusiasm than he had spoken of his wife to Jehoram. And Jehoram stood by (having heard most of it before) watching benevolently, with his hands in his pockets pushing back his overcoat and his cigarette dancing up and down in his lips.

'Ah, a great fellow, Dick Templer. He really is a gentleman: public school and all. Westminster School—used to go there with a top hat on the back of his little head. And Cambridge University and all. And yet he's quite glad to have an ordinary chap like me for his best friend. That's true what I said: he was quite different twenty years ago. Believe it or not, he was the wildest and rowdiest member of our mess. And don't forget he was older than any of them, except the Colonel. Just on forty, and ought to have known better. The boys used to call him Uncle Dick. Blast them; they're forty themselves now. And on that New Year's Eve, twenty years ago, after we'd been toasting the good old war for a couple of hours he decided that it was Hogmanay and it'd be friendly to go out and visit the Germans across the way. And he staggers across No-man's-Land and lobs a bomb with his love into Jerry's trench—quite a good shot for a fellow half-seas-over. Of course they put him under arrest for getting on with the war without orders, and when they had time to spare they court martialled him. But Uncle Dick was a lawyer, and he got the old buffers on the court so tied up that they began to wonder if they oughtn't to give him ten pounds instead of shooting him. That was Dick twenty years ago. And then' Harry's voice dropped into the low tones of reverence—'in the very last month of the war his own boy was killed—a lad of nineteen and his only child. It broke poor old Dick's heart, and his wife's too, so that she went and died in the 'flu epidemic of that year. That was the end of the rowdy Dick. He gave way to grief for a year or so—I remember him saying to me "All meaning's gone out of my life, Harry"—but his religion or something helped him, and he turned into the quiet old thing you see now. Mind you, he's not as young as he was. Must be sixty-two now; five years older than I am. We were a pair, you see, in the old company. The two old ones. That's why he came to live at Streatham: so as to be near me. It was always our dream in the trenches that I'd have a pub after the war and he'd have a house somewhere

near. And here we are tonight. Here's the old Lord of
Wensley. A first-class house, not large, but good—like our pay
in the army.'

§

Where Balham Hill slopes gently down to become Balham
High Road—there, near the viaduct, stands the Lord of Wensley.
It is not an imposing tavern; no glittering corner palace; but
merely a single-fronted house with windows and doors of engraved glass between pilasters of brown marble. From between
its first-floor windows its sign-board creaks and sways in the
southerly wind that wanders nearly always up the long straight
channel of the road. The sign shows a baronial figure gazing
from his battlements at a broad green lap of England. Skilfully
the artist has painted this hooded mediæval lord full in the fore-
ground but with his back to the street (no one knowing the true
face of this Seignior of Wensley) and his green and wooded acres
stretching beyond the battlements into the distance, far away
from Balham.

An unremarkable house outside, except for this sign; but what
Captain Townes looked at, from his place behind his counter,
on that New Year's Eve some years since, was dazzling enough.
Within doors the Lord of Wensley, a Victorian house, was
splendid with carved mahogany and brilliant-cut glass. Its four
bars, Saloon, Public, Private, and Jug-and-Bottle, were at once
separated by handsome partitions of mahogany and united by the
single ceiling of embossed Lincrusta. This ceiling sought to be
worthy of the flamboyant mahogany and glass, and we assert that
it succeeded, so ornate its pattern. Once it had been painted a
shining cream, but the smoke of a hundred pipers (and all) had
stained it to the tawny hue of a pale tobacco—a warm and
friendly varnish with which no stickler for original texts should
interfere. It was a rectangular ceiling but you hardly realised
this, no matter in what bar you stood, for the partitions radiated from the service counter at strange angles—again an
admirable arrangement, because wherever you stood to drink,
you got an impression of oddly shaped enclosures beside and
beyond you, and of unbeknown persons speaking together in their
cabined and smoky haze, and thus there were elements of
mystery and poetry within four walls that were not really far
apart.

These partitions may have been made of carved mahogany and etched glass, but they were also built of tribal custom. Their root substance was Caste. The Saloon Bar on one side of a partition was very different from the Public on the other. The walls of the Saloon were aglow with bevelled mirrors which doubled the ferns and flowers with which the Captain and his lady loved to embellish it. In the Public Bar were no mirrors, possibly because its patrons were seldom dressed for self-esteem. It had only its ration of flowers and the glory of the ceiling, but it may be doubted if its habitués resented the mahogany demarcation between them and the company in the Saloon; if a black-jacketed gent from the Saloon had come to their counter, they would probably have stared at him somewhat sourly as at a tight-wad who wanted to save a penny on his beer.

The Jug-and-Bottle was a narrow, nasty, secretive little cubby-hole, from which a man who would not drink his ale in the face of all men, and honestly, took it home in sly jugs. It was no part of the genial pub; it remained a part of the Balham High Road out of which it came sidling so shamefully.

One other thing besides the ceiling linked all the bars together, and that was the service counter which, in the shape of a long U, commanded all the compartments that radiated from it. In the midst of this U a long island fitment or 'wagon' expressed the very essence and meaning of the house, its mahogany shelves a-glitter with bottles of all sizes, shapes, colours and contents, and with wine glasses of every build and design, each of them as clean and aglow as only a well-trained bar-tender could make them. This bar-back was the brightly illumined background against which, on most evenings after six or seven, you could see Captain Harry Townes, with probably his large and largely adorned lady at his side, and Walter his barman not far off, and possibly his plump little daughter Beth too, with Old Agnes and Mrs. Bensky, his part-time barmaids, if it was a crowded occasion such as New Year's Eve.

§

'Just on time, people!' Harry roared it to all his bars at once. 'One minute to go.' After a glance at the saloon clock, he had switched on the radio set. This little box did not stand among the bottles or glasses on the bar-back, for the display there was sacred and Harry would allow nothing profane to

24

mar it; the radio had a bracket to itself on a side wall. 'Shut that ghastly row, Jehoram, and let us listen.'

Jehoram's male voice choir, which had been rendering 'Shenandoah,' obeyed rather raggedly, one member insisting on completing his statement, 'Away I'm bound to go 'Cross the wide Missouri.' Everyone else stopped talking or singing; they even stopped moving; and there was silence in the bars.

From the wireless set came the first notes of Big Ben.

Some cheered. Others yelled, 'Happy New Year!' Harry shouted, 'Come on, Mother. Come on, Walter and Agnes. Come on Dick, Mr. Templer, sir.' And he and Ida, and his barman and old barmaid, all came from behind the counter to join their crossed arms with the others and sing 'Auld Lang Syne.' When this had been sung they all broke apart to kiss. Every man kissed every woman he could reach. 'Oh, dear, oh dear!' Ida laughed breathlessly and tried to pat back her hair and rearrange her dress, but she had little time for this, since one man after another was giving her the New Year kiss. 'Ah well,' she said. 'It's nice to let oneself go sometimes.'

Then, since linking hands was the mood and the New Year was with them, they willingly accepted the loud orders of the self-appointed Master of Ceremonies, Jehoram, and, linking arms again roared, 'Knees up, Mother Brown.'

> Knees up, Mother Brown,
> Under the table you must go,
> E-I-E-I-E-I-O.

Ida, very happy, jumped her knees as high as any of the other women, and, indeed, nearly as high as the man next to her. Her performance was perhaps the most remarkable of all, not only because her body was so large, her dress so fine and her bronze and silver coiffure so elaborate, but because Harry spoke so often of her natural refinement. But as soon as this boisterous business was finished the normal refinement was promptly underlined again as she reiterated breathlessly, 'Ah well, it's good to let oneself go once in a way. It's not natural, I always say, to keep oneself bottled up for ever.'

It was stressed even more emphatically a second later when Harry, much uplifted by the general good-fellowship, enjoined Jehoram to kiss her again and, after giving her another hug himself, said to a customer beside him (whom they hardly knew at all), 'What do you think of my brood mare, eh?'

'Really, Harry!' Ida protested.

'She's worth her weight in gold, is Mrs. Townes: twenty-bob a pound, live weight—and that's saying something.'

'Stop it, Harry! You're being very vulgar.'

'Nonsense, Mum! Nothing of the sort.'

'Well, I think you are. And I don't like vulgarity. I never did.'

'I know you don't, love. Okay, I'll put my threepence in the blind box. Utter a bad word in the bar in Ida's presence and she hollers out, "Threepence for the blind, please." She's a very refined lady, my wife.' And he punched her behind, murmuring with a wink to the customer, 'Prime Scotch beef, that.'

She squealed at the pain and knocked his hand away, saying really angrily, 'That'll do. Give over, Harry. You're impossible sometimes.'

'See?' he demanded, as he walked away. 'See how I'm made to behave? It's plain who's the C.O. here.'

The men were now singing, 'Take me back to dear old Blighty,' and of a sudden Harry saw the old half-forgotten faces again and, falling serious for a moment thought how, in a few years all these friendly faces would be half forgotten too. This sank him into a sentimental mood, with a result that mention of dear old Blighty stirred his patriotic loyalty; and since his patriotism was often assertive enough to embarrass people—and, furthermore, since it had been recently inflamed by that talk about Michael's criticism of England—he now cried out, 'Gentlemen, *please* . . . *if* you please. . . . Gentlemen, the King.' And, taking up his glass which still stood upon the bar, he raised it towards that portrait of the King which hung like an ikon on his wall.

Willing to please him, all raised their glasses and drank and said, 'The King. God bless him.' One merry fool started to sing 'God save the King,' but no one joined in and his song dwindled to an untimely end. Nevertheless at the first notes of the National Anthem the Captain came smartly to attention; and stood rigidly so till the hymn's unfortunate demise. Some of the other men copied him—in a shamefaced way, mostly, and explaining afterwards, 'The Guv always does it, so it's best to please him.'

'Good-bye.' The people began to go. 'God save the King means Hop it. 'Bye, Guv. 'Bye, Ida. 'Bye, Guv.' And they drifted into the cold night and the new year. The bars were emptying.

Soon no one was left but the Captain, Ida, Walter, the barman, Old Agnes the barmaid and Dick—for Harry had begged, 'Don't go, Dick.'

§

The Captain shut his street doors, and instantly everyone, as if his touch on the door-handles had switched on this new activity, set about an allotted task. Captain Townes opened the windows to let the clean air in. 'And the stink out,' he said. Dishcloth on shoulder, he collected all the discarded glasses and put them on the counter. The women washed and polished the glasses to a diamond brilliance and arrayed them in regimented rows. Then they washed out swabs, and Ida checked the till. Walter swept up the cigarette stubs, match ends, bus tickets, biscuit crumbs, and tobacco ash from the floors, and Old Agnes came from behind the counter and cleaned ash-trays, tables, chairs, and stools. Harry told Walter what he would want up from the cellar to restock the bar, and nipped down and helped him up with these supplies. Together they polished the new bottles and arrayed them on or under the dispense. And all the time Harry, cigar-butt in mouth, was chatting to Dick. 'Have a look at that display my boy. There are not many pubs in London that maintain the standards I insist on. A word of advice: never drink beer in a pub without looking first at the display. If the bottles and glasses shine to high heaven, it's a good pub; its cellars and pipes are clean, and its beer's properly cared for.'

'I see,' said Dick with his quiet smile.

'And if you've half a chance, take a look at its cellar. A pub is as good as its cellar, and no more, my boy. Same with the Gents. If that's clean and shines to heaven, you can come back and drink your beer in peace.'

'Is that so?'

'That is so. Absolutely.'

He stooped down to stack a bottle below, and just then, the street door, still unlocked, was pushed open, and into the Saloon, as silent now as it had been noisy half-an-hour before, a figure entered. A figure all in black. Black high-necked jersey, black cummerbund, black trousers. A figure that, but for its youthful grace, might have suggested an executioner of Tudor times. 'Enter the Man in Black,' laughed Harry. And stretching forth his right hand in the fascist salute, he said, 'Heil Hitler.'

Wishing to begin the New Year well and be merry with his son instead of critical of him, he kept the arm extended and added, 'Duce, Duce, Duce.'

A very slight sideways fling of Michael's head showed that he didn't altogether like this salutation.

The boy's overcoat was hung across his arm, and Dick wondered why he should have come through the cold night carrying it thus. Then he guessed. Michael had removed the coat before coming through the door so as to flaunt the black uniform in his father's eyes.

And a pity rose in Dick for this good-looking youth with his fair hair, clear skin and small boyish features—his face a smoother but weaker edition of his father's. It would have been a completely attractive face, were the brow not printed with symptoms of some inner ferment, and if the blue eyes—his father's eyes—did not hold those signs of strain. Here, thought Dick, gazing at him, was a boy of bright imagination but ill-tutored brain; a boy who, though aware of his own diffidence and shortcomings, passionately desired to be something in the world; who, refusing to believe in his own weaknesses, proposed to conquer the world.

He spoke guiltily. 'Well, Dad . . . Happy new year. Happy new year, Mum darling. Oh, there's Uncle Dick. Happy new year.'

His voice, like his face, had all the charm of its youth, thought Dick. Indeed, it was a singularly beautiful voice, but flawed just now by those faint notes of guilt and defiance.

'Delighted to see you, sir,' said the father, still trying to jest. 'Where've you been? At church, I hope, like your sister, praying for the family?'

'I've been at the Black House with the lads. You know I have.'

'Oh, well, each to his choice. So long as everyone's happy.'

'Any objection to my going there?' demanded the boy, instantly on the defensive.

'None at all. Only, perhaps, to your slipping out of the house without a word to anyone.'

'Did I do that? I'd forgotten.' This was inescapably untrue. 'I'm sorry.'

'And I must say I'd have thought you'd like to be with your family on New Year's Eve.'

'Now, don't start going on at him directly he comes in,' said Ida.

This was a fatal interposition. Harry had wanted to behave well, but he loved contention and argument, and this combativeness, like fumes of buried petroleum, could ignite at a spark. And to chide him when he deserved praise was less a spark than a flame. 'Who the hell's going on at him? I was trying to be nice. God, I wish someone were on my side sometimes. I merely suggested that he might have stayed and given the family a helping hand on New Year's Eve. Instead he has to go off with that wretched Dermot. It's Dermot who leads him by the nose everywhere. His family's absolutely nothing compared with that ridiculous young man. We might as well not exist. And I've never concealed my opinion of that Dermot. A thoroughgoing wrong 'un, if you ask me. A most dangerous young man.'

'He's nothing of the sort! You know nothing about him. I know him as you can't possibly know him.' Michael's round face was white. Dick could see a fury vibrating his limbs and his lips like a current of electricity. This current had run the blood from his face, leaving it to look as it would one day in death. 'Dermot's easily the cleverest person I know. And— I think—the best. I take it I'm not a fool and can tell who's a fraud and who's genuine—I take it I've some right to choose my own friends. Dermot's the best read person I've ever met, which means that at last I'm able to associate with someone who knows something about literature and music——'

'What do you mean by that—?' Harry's eyes were no less furious now than his son's.

'Michael . . . Michael . . . don't go riling your father,' Ida pleaded.

But Michael was determined to go on '—someone who reads something else than his newspaper and whose taste in music rises above "Little Brown Jug" and "Land of Hope and Glory".'

'My God, will you shut your insolent face!' This was a roar. It was the roar of a sergeant at a recruit.

Michael started back at the shout like a frightened child. And Dick saw with a sharp pity a leap of childish tears into the eyes of this young man full-grown.

Harry too, saw that backward start and that leap of tears, and now the sullenness and sadness in the young face. He too felt a heart-searing pity and a dislike of his own inflammable temper; but pride would not suffer him to make any amends; and all he said, very sadly, was, 'So we begin the new year.'

CHAPTER THREE

THE new year was barely a month old when Michael became twenty-two. Always on a birthday the Townes People, as some of their friends called them, had a family feast, all sitting at table together. This eating together was rare because as a rule Ida had to snatch her dinner at about two o'clock when the lunch-hour influx of customers was dwindling, and then relieve Harry in the bars when the influx was an efflux. They were hearty eaters in the Lord of Wensley; at least host and hostess were. By half past two the Captain had raised an appetite, and he sat down with application to a packed plate, hot from the oven, of meat and vegetables which Ida had laid in front him before skipping downstairs to take his place in the bars. He liked eating alone on these non-festal occasions, because it meant he could eat at speed, and not at all nicely, if he didn't care to. He wolfed the food happily, with his newspaper on one side of him and his pint of bitter on the other to wash it all down, meat, news, and bread. 'Nothing like the roast beef of old England,' he would say, dabbing at his lips with a napkin, when Ida came skipping up the stairs to give him his pudding. 'And there's no doubt that in this Townes woman I have the best cook I ever had.' To which Ida would retort, bringing a steaming suet pudding from the stove, 'Well, that's easy, being as how she's the only one you ever had.'

But it was nothing like this on a birthday. Then the Captain insisted that they must all sit down together and, if it was Mike's birthday, that Dick, the lad's godfather, must sit with them. He had arranged his children's birthdays well, he said; taking care that they should be born in those months when business was slack in the bars: Beth in December, Mike in February. 'A little arithmetic, and one can arrange these things,' he would affirm with a wink. 'December's a slack month because in the first three weeks all the lads are saving their money for Christmas; and in the last week they've spent it all. And February's a slack month because the weather's always foul, so the gardening season hasn't begun.   In April, on Sundays, the lads are all out in their little back gardens, and by mid-day a most terrible great thirst spreads over Balham.'

It was always on the Sunday after the birthday that the family feast was held, because on Sunday the pub shut its doors early and all could be round the table by two-thirty.   On such a feast day the food was distinguished.   The Captain (whose writ ran unopposed in this household) prescribed a roast bird with tasty stuffing, a Christmas pudding drenched with rum, and instead of the usual jugs of beer, plenty of bottles of Barley Wine No. 1, which, he declared, was the quickest to enrich your guts and enlarge your love for all.   Then nuts and port till such time as the food and drink completed their noble job on you, and you took to a deep chair, and joining your hands on a comfortable stomach, went to sleep.

'Good-bye, all; lock all doors; it's our Mike's birthday, and we have drinks in the bar before we all go upstairs and really eat.'

In the Saloon, now emptied of customers, stood Harry and Ida, their two children, and Dick, and Walter the barman, who would be an honoured guest like any other, since, as Harry said, slapping him on the back, he was one of the family—like hell he was.

'Come on, Walter.   Do your stuff as barman.   Serve us all round and yourself too.   Jump to it.'

'Indeed I will, sir.'

Walter Gillies, a young man in his thirties, was a barman of some rarity, in that he was also an intellectual and a most gentlemanly one.   It was a pity that his body was short and unimpressive because his features beneath fine waving brown hair had a classical regularity.   It was possibly the regularity of his features that turned him into an intellectual.   A face so Greek demanded an intelligence to match it, and a gentlemanly vocabulary and accent.   The son of a barman, he'd had no schooling after fourteen; and even at school he'd been no exemplary student; because it was not till he was about eighteen that he awoke to the classical quality of his features and to the obligations they thrust upon him.   From that time onwards he set about educating himself.   Often, when the Public Bar was empty or very quiet, you might have seen him with his elbows on the counter, and a book between them, and his head bent over it.   Did you peep over his shoulder you might have discovered that the book was Davies' *Man and His Universe*, or Singer's *History and Method of Science*, or perhaps Emden's *Philosophy from Thales to Hegel*. Sometimes Harry looked over his shoulder and down at the title and exclaimed, 'Good lord on high!'

The effect of all this reading on his vocabulary and accent was remarkable. He spoke no slang, coarse words, or lewd jests like Harry; or fell into grammatical errors like Ida; and he even found it impossible to approach so near inelegance as to speak of his master, in the manner of the Public Bar as 'The Guv'nor' or 'The Old Man.' He always referred to Harry as 'The Captain'; to Ida as 'Madam'; to Beth as 'Miss Beth'. Perhaps his language was a little too ornate. If one might liken it to architecture, and if one agrees that Early English with its simple lancet windows was England's best period, and the Decorated and Perpendicular which followed it something less good because a trifle too showy, then Walter's English was certainly Decorated and Perpendicular. You could even say that at times it had the free-flowing tracery of the French Flamboyant.

For some reason or other his favourite word was 'Indeed.' If asked, 'Got a pint for one of the world's workers, mate?' he would go to his beer-handle saying, 'Indeed, yes, sir.' If asked Did he approve of such and such, he would reply 'Indeed I don't,' or 'Indeed I do.' And if a hearty entered the bar halloo'ing, 'May I wish you a very good evening, Mr. Walter Gillies?' he would assure the man, 'Indeed you may, sir.' And if a woman came in to inquire if he was still a bachelor, he said, 'Yes, indeed.'

'Walter's dishing it out now,' cried Harry above the talk. 'What'll you have, all of you?'

Dick had a sherry; the two children, modern young people, had cocktails which Walter shook up for them, and their father deplored; Harry himself had a light ale since he intended drinking deep of Barley Wine later; and Ida had a glass of Red Biddy —a shocking mixture, so her husband said, of red wine and spirit. 'They learned her to drink it in her days as a barmaid, and now, given half a chance, she asks for it. Good *gracious!* Red Biddy?'

'Ah, well,' said Ida. 'It's good to let oneself go sometimes.'

'I wouldn't let her have it,' Harry explained to Dick, 'if she hadn't a head that'll stand up to anything. She's been stood so many fiery drinks in her time that now her head's lined with asbestos. You can't make her tight. Chatty, yes. Bossy, yes. Damned argumentative, certainly. But not blotto.'

'Oh, give over all that nonsense, Harry,' begged Ida. 'Draw it mild, for a change.'

Harry grinned and, as she walked away to speak with Walter, expounded his good fortune in having a wife who'd been a barmaid. 'It's a job that needs character and tact and good temper, Dick, with a plentiful mixture of firmness; and believe you me, Ida's got 'em all. She was just about the ideal wife for a chap starting a pub. God bless me, I was little more than her pupil at one time. And, all said and done, it was a good thing they learned her to drink a lot without puking; the chaps like her to drink with them. Mike, son.' Now that all glasses were filled, his father toasted the boy. 'Twenty-two! May you reach eighty-eight—though your old man won't be there to see. But you'll do it, provided you don't drink too much like your mother. Here's to you.'

'Thank you, Dad.'

'Michael darling,' toasted his mother. 'Bless you always.'

'Ta, Mum.'

Dick said only, 'Your health, Michael;' and Walter: 'Mr. Michael, sir. *Prosit*;' adding after he'd sipped, '*A vous, Monsieur le Capitaine. A votre bonne santé;*' at which Harry exclaimed 'Good *God*!'

Continuing in the grand manner, Walter turned again to Michael. 'May I offer you my heartiest congratulations, sir, if they are not too belated.'

'Ta, old boy,' Michael acknowledged with less distinction.

Then, of course, Harry must sing 'Happy birthday to you,' and Michael protest, 'Oh, shut up, Dad'; but his father didn't spare him, bellowing above all the others, 'Happy birthday, dear Michael, happy birthday to you.'

After which he drank, wiped his lips with the edge of his hand, and said, 'There you are, Dick. There he is, your godson. Not bad to look at, but not all that good inside. He's your spiritual responsibility, thank God, not mine. Ida ducks, your health. *I-derr!* I'm trying to say I love you, damn you; why the hell can't you listen? Dick, Mr. Richard Templer, sir, your health. Who's ready for some more? No one? Thank the lord. Saves money. Let's all get upstairs then. Lead on, Mike; it's your party.'

So Michael went first, and all followed him, the Captain thrusting Ida's arm through his, since this was a ceremonial banquet.

§

Last of all, and alone, walked Beth. And, in so doing, expressed the state of her heart. For Beth Townes, in these days, though apparently as ready with family jokes as any of them, was really walking through the world alone—surrounded and enclosed by an invisible essence which she created daily out of her dreams, disappointments and shames, and out of a love that could never be confessed.

She had become thirty in December, and that was an hour in which her lifelong, if often laughing, disappointment in her appearance changed into a real and ever-aching sadness. It was cruel, she would think, that she should be so obviously her father's daughter instead of her mother's. Instead of her mother's fine features, she had her father's brief nose, small blue eyes, and deep upper lip. Like him she was full-fleshed, but while his good masculine height carried the plumpness well and even made it impressive, her shortness only made it dumpy. Because of this dumpiness Michael had always called her 'Podge,' and for a while she had not minded this, but now she never heard it from his lips without pain. She had two beauties: her hair and her skin, the one gold and silky, the other fresh, flawless, and pink; but what could you do with them, if you had small, blunt features like hers? With her lip-stick she made a red cupid's bow of her mouth; she kept her eyebrows plucked and her hair waved; but she feared, and justly, that these efforts after beauty could only strike people as pathetic. Once she had affixed a beauty spot near her left eye, but Michael had so roared with laughter at it, and had found such pleasure in calling her 'Spot' thereafter, that the memory of that little black patch was now a permanent centre of pain. The prick of pain which it always gave her lost none of its sharpness with the years, and it seemed, accordingly, that it must spoil Heaven and Eternity for her. Every time she thought of it she had to toss her head to toss the memory away.

Thirty now, and because her plump body and heavy legs were worthless possessions, no love had come into her life. Nothing but occasional gallantries, arch and meaningless, from beery men on the other side of the bar. And out of this dearth sprang her secret shames. Let nobody ever know the hungers that racked her in her bed. Often she got into her bed knowing that she would have to wrestle with the devil there, her only bed-mate. Possessed by these hungers, she felt that she could give herself to anyone, if anyone came. She allowed that she would not be happy with 'just anyone', but at least she would have experience of a man and the chance of becoming a mother. She would toss in bed thinking of, envying, women she'd seen in maternity gowns, some of whom were surely uglier or dumpier than she. For with her physical hunger went a spiritual hunger to devote herself to another; and now this need had flowered into the love of which she could never speak. All her love—and it was a passionate love, the love of a lover—had fallen like a spotlight on her brother and fixed itself there. Michael, eight years younger than she, had the good looks that she would have liked. What he had taken from his father he had converted into charm. She loved his light blue eyes, thick plumy hair, and coltish habit of tossing a tumbled forelock from his brow. She loved his boyish profile and would stare at it for hours. She loved his young masculine body, and accordingly longed to kiss him. She would have liked to hug him as a woman hugs her man. It seemed a miracle that he was her brother, flesh and bone—and a man.

Her love was maternal too: it had been so ever since she was twelve and he four. And now if his father bawled at him and he shrank away in a childish fear and then looked sad or sullen she wanted to hug him to the comfort of her breast as a mother hugs a child. But all she could ever give him was a peck on the cheek, and all she ever got from him in return was a brother's flat, damp, uneager kiss.

Naturally she turned to religion, and now she was only really happy when she was secretly overcoming herself; when with a mighty effort she was doing exactly the opposite of what she would have liked to do. And so she was very often in the bars helping her father and mother, or Walter and Old Agnes; and sometimes as she pulled her beer handles, amid all the confusion of voices and laughter, she was thinking how much she would like to be a saint and wondering if she would become one. But even in this desire she was puzzled and worried, because there seemed so generous a dose of selfishness in it. For example, she could be quite pleased if bad news came to the Lord of Wensley, or to a customer, because it gave her a chance to sacrifice herself and behave like a saint.

§

Her real name was Elspeth, because her father thought a daughter with the blood of Scotch kings in her veins ought to have an unusual name, and Elspeth was both Scotch and unusual; but after a year's experience of it he declared that few could utter it without spitting; and henceforth he was going to call her Beth. Since then everyone in the Lord of Wensley had called her Beth, for, speaking generally, whithersoever the Captain turned his steps his company, as in the Army, followed obediently behind.

§

The room upstairs, being the family's only sitting room, was both drawing and dining room. The heavy Victorian dining room suite stood between the upright piano against one wall and the fireplace in the other. Before the fireplace were huge deep corpulent leather chairs, for 'I love comfort,' Harry used to say.

The lid of the piano supported two relics of the old war: a small glass-fronted case holding Harry's war medals, his five service chevrons, and his single gold wound stripe, all a little tarnished now; and a silver-framed photograph of Harry in uniform (officer's uniform and very new), and this was inscribed, 'For Ida, with all the love in the world—and then some.' The only other picture to catch the eye, because it hung on the wall so incongruously among water colours and steel engravings, was an enlarged photograph of a column of fat happy men, laughing women, and grinning youths, all with their cycles in front of the Lord of Wensley. These grinning people were the Balham and Graveney Wheelers about to start down the Balham High Road, on their run to Brighton in the year '21.

This birthday meal was very merry to begin with, since all had drunk before it, and Barley Wine is a powerful brew. After the first course the Captain shamelessly (was it not all in the Family?) undid the two lower buttons of his waistcoat and the top button of his trousers, and announced with satisfaction,

'I wouldn't wish to be coarse, but I feel like a kilderkin of the best.'

'A kilderkin!' laughed Ida loudly. 'I should have said a barrel. A kil only holds eighteen gallons.'

'Well, you haven't done so badly yourself,' he rejoined. And this was true enough. For Ida, a simple, natural, large-breasted woman, one of Earth's female creations not over-given to intro-spection or self-criticism, was a natural-born sybarite and on lively occasions like this ate and drank voluputously. All she said now, while continuing to eat, was, 'You've got gravy all over your mouth.' To which Harry retorted, 'Well, you don't look so good, either.'

All very merry, but the Captain, when he had eaten of the pudding soused in rum, and was putting a fine old port on top of that, became loquacious above all, his voice growing brighter as he delighted in his jokes, and his laugh rising to an enormous 'ha, ha' when his jokes seemed to him funnier than they were.

For a time hardly anyone else's voice was heard at all. Dick had been silent from the start; Beth was not talkative today nor Michael argumentative—as yet; Walter when addressed said little but 'Indeed yes,' and 'Indeed no'; and Ida was still busy with her spoon and fork.

But any threat of a silence, and Harry filled it up like an empty glass. He was in the mood to tease everybody. 'What's time, folks? Hah' past three. Beth, it's Sunday, and you've missed your Children's Service. Dick, she's neglecting her duties; you must take her in hand. Who's going to pray for her old man? And for her mum? Good Crikes, Ida needs a lot of praying for, but she doesn't know it. Poor old Mike's past praying for, ha, *ha*! The old man's your best bet, Beth, because he knows he ought to be better—and would like to be, dammit.'

'Don't rag the child, Harry,' said Ida, her mouth rather full and her voice a little embarrassed, because she was always un-comfortable when Harry was drinking too much.

'I'm not ragging her. Pass the port round, Dick. I, wish I could go to church myself—Hell, I got a prize for Scripture once—but I can't quite manage to. Too much to do in the cellar of a Sunday morning. I like church, and I get on fine with padres; always have. My old man was a power at St. Mary's, and he made me say my prayers every night; gave me the flat of his hand, if I didn't. And I say them still, don't

I, Ida?' He turned to Michael and, well permeated with his port, gave the company the advantage of his views on Prayer. 'You young men don't believe in Prayer; I bloody well do, and I'm not ashamed to say so. If I hadn't believed in Prayer, and said my prayers every night, I should never have been able to lead the fairly decent life—if I may say so, Dick—that I have done. No, I'm sure o' that. But there's young Walter there; *he* doesn't believe in Prayer. No, much too clever.'

'Indeed I do—sometimes. But I take the view that a prayer is less an appeal to the Power behind the Cosmos to suspend in one's favour the laws of cause and effect than a method of calling upon the divinity in oneself and drawing from it a supply of new power to meet the trials——'

'Kind of beer-engine, you mean?'

Walter, head to one side, met this with a well-controlled smile. 'Well, that's a rather homely simile, but it's by no means an inapt one. And considered in that aspect, prayer might be regarded as a perfectly legitimate and profitable exercise in auto-hypnotism.'

Not at all clear what all this rigmarole meant, Harry gazed through his mists at Walter and said, 'Well, I'm glad he prays, Ida. I'm glad there's a divinity in him that he can syphon up at call. It'll make him a better barman, and we needn't worry about the till. All I know is that, gawd lummy, I'd no more not say my prayers at night than not brush my teeth. If I haven't said 'em, I feel all adrift and have to get up and say 'em. *You* know that, don't you, Ida?'

'Do I not? And don't I wish he wouldn't get up sometimes. He wakes me, getting up after half an hour to say them. Surely he could say them, lying where he is.'

'Oh, no. *No.*' Harry said it with conviction. He could not but believe that prayers, to be any good, must be said on the knees. 'Hear that, Dick? I tell you I'm much more religious than Ida.'

'That's all you know,' Ida hinted; and she was justified in her words. For Ida, secretly but not lightly impressed by Beth's new church-going, and by the talks they'd enjoyed together about it, had once or twice of late, simple woman as she was, slipped off to church to see if she could get from it what Beth got. She had gone there dressed as for a King's garden party but saying nothing to the family lest they made fun of her. Michael on that New Year's Eve had not slipped from the house

38

more guiltily than she, when, for his part he was seeking comfort and a religion among his black-shirted friends.

§

Dick, listening to his friend, Captain Harry Townes, on Prayer, had a vision of the Battle of Hastings. Why this should ensue on a picture of Harry getting out of bed to say his forgotten prayers because in that posture only could they be trusted to work, may not be clear; but it happened because, looking at Harry, red with wine, he thought, first, that he had never seen a more Saxon face, and then that the thousand years since Harold fell at Hastings had really done little to change the simple beliefs of such as Harry Townes. The Saxons believed in God and His Merciful Son, and knelt down and prayed to them, but when they were risen from their knees, their prayer, though it kept them large-hearted and hospitable, did nothing whatever to curb their natural belligerence and vindictiveness or their faith in violence and punishment. And, still looking at Harry, he thought how a supply of drink, like a developer washing over a camera plate brought into definition the real truth of him, namely that he was just such another loving, laughing, generous, but obstinate, harsh and combative man.

Continuing with his nuts and wine and listening, he thought in a quiet dream how, sitting here at Harry's table twenty years later, he was bound to him for ever by the thin trenches this side of Thiepval Wood: by that long, straight road that led between the blasted tree-trunks to the rubble and dust that had once been Pozières; and by all the rain and mud of those days; and the oaths and the French wine and . . . the women of Amiens.

There were not many who'd been together in those days of hissing shells, chattering machine-guns, and pounding bombs, of laughter and blasphemy and endurance, who, twenty years after, were still side by side.

§

Yes, Harry was in truth a combative man and an obstinate, and he was feeling now that he could do with an argument. On politics perhaps. On some point on which Dick, or young Mike, must disagree with him. Now one way to open old

Dick's lips and get him gently arguing was to suggest that Britain was better than any other country in the world, for Dick called himself a Liberal and Internationalist, which, in Harry's view (whose politics were still stamped with the date 1906), was little better than being a Socialist or a Bolshevik. And as for Mike, he might stand at the opposite end of the scale from Dick and pretend to be one of these filthy Fascists, but he wanted no less to muck about with the Capitalist System, which his father didn't wish altered in the least. So one or other of these exasperating revolutionaries must now be provoked—probably Michael. Harry lifted his glass with fingers that shook and said, 'England, the Land of the Free.'

'Ha!' laughed Michael, and there was a half-hidden sneer in his tone like the kernel in a nut. Just as his father had hoped. 'Free!'

'Certainly. The Land of the Free.' Harry stared at Michael truculently.

Michael looked down at his walnuts. Always a little afraid of his father, he did not return the stare. But he said to the plate loud enough for Harry to hear, 'The Land of the Fooled and the Tricked.'

'Whatter you mean?' Harry paused in his eating and rested his fists on the table. 'I know things are not perfect in England, but at least we've none of your filthy dictators here, have we, Dick?' Dick, the Liberal, should be on his side here.

'Oh, yes, we have,' declared Michael, since Dick had only shrugged. 'Poor old Britain's allowed to think she's a democracy, but she's really an oligarchy run by a minority of greedy, grasping old men. They may be peers of the realm, many of them, but they're predatory old rogues, for the most part, just the same.'

'Will you only listen to him, Ida? And who are these old rogues, pray?'

'That's simple: the big financiers and the bosses of the big combines. In a word, those who hold the Money Power.'

'J'ever hear such crap? The big financiers and industrialists can do nothing that Parliament doesn't let 'em do.'

'How right you are; and so they see to it that the parties and the Government are merely their paid puppets. And the Press their own instrument.'

'Gaw . . . Lawd. . . .' Never such indignation. 'Stuff and nonsense! They could never get English politicians in their

40

pay. English politicians may be fools sometimes, but they're incorruptible. I'll say that for them. Incorruptible.'

'Oh, they get them in their pay all right. Or their power. There are such things as party funds, you know——'

'Of *course* I know!'

'—and such a thing as the power of blackmail by threatening a flight of capital. Oh, they've got them where they want 'em; where they can't move without their Masters' consent——'

'Well, at least we've got freedom of expression in this country, which is more than they've got in your god-damned Nazi Germany.'

'Yes, freedom to come into your Saloon Bar and grouse till we're black in the face. They allow us that as a safety-valve——'

'Glad my poor little Saloon means something——'

'—yes, and neither that nor our votes are worth anything at all, because it's they, not we, who control the instruments of power.'

'Hell, the instruments of power are not doing so badly for us, are they, Dick?'

'Good God, Dad!—three million unemployed, which means about twelve million frustrated human beings, all more or less starving in the midst of plenty. It's a crime against God and Heaven, and we're determined to end it——'

'Who's "we"?'

'You know well enough who "we" are. Some of our lads are sufferers from it and have had enough of it. And I'm on their side. You bet they join a Leader with vision and vigour who'll exchange their present freedom to starve into freedom to live. It's happening the whole world over. Call him a dictator, if you like.'

Dick, listening, thought, 'Poor Michael: is he really fighting for these, his three million brothers, or fighting his father?'

'I'll call him something else than a dictator. I'll——'

'But, Dad, how can you be so blind to what's going on? How can you go on believing in these old men's lies and humbug? It's all a pretty camouflage to hide their profiteering or their usury. How can you be so simple-minded?'

'Me? *Simple-minded?* My God!'

'Michael, don't rile your father,' Ida begged.

'Oh, yes, stow it,' agreed Beth. 'This is a party, isn't it?' Always Beth hid her love behind a mask of satire.

'You know how hot he gets,' Ida added in a lower tone.

But Michael was too like his father to break off a battle with an enemy still undefeated. He pursued his attack, spitting a little in his excitement. 'Surely you can see that your poor old Tory party depends on the support of the men with the money and jolly well has to do what *they* want and not what we poor coves in Balham tell 'em.'

'Well, what about the Socialist Party—eh, what about *them*?'

'They're no better because they're in the pay of the big Trade Unions and are certainly not the servants of you and me, who're silly enough to vote for them. What's more, the political parties come and go, but these old boys are there for ever, like the King.'

'I'll have nothing against the King.'

'I've nothing against him either——'

'Thank you, my lord. That's good of you.'

'——because we took away his power long ago. But now these old bounders have bagged it and we're going to get it away from them. It's got to go because it's a greater power than ever any king enjoyed because it operates all over the world. And we're going to end it. There's a New World coming. Either the Reds'll bring it, or we will. You can choose.'

'Oh, my God, you make me tired! Lot of crackpot nonsense. He's simply dishing out the hogwash that Leader of his pours forth.'

'Certainly I am. And I'm not ashamed to be doing so. He's the one man in England with the courage to defy the Party Machines and the Press, and stand alone.'

'An ambitious careerist: that's all he is.'

'That's a lie! A *lie*!' Wild anger washed the boy's eyes. 'He's the only man who dares to tell the truth in the face of them all, and I'm proud to serve under him.'

'And everything he says is right, I suppose, and everything your old father says is wrong.'

Not wanting to hurt his father too much, or infuriate him too much, Michael paused before saying with face turned away, 'I'm afraid I must say so, if that's what I believe.'

'Oh.' Some pain stood now in the father's eyes. 'I see. I see. These are nice things to hear from one's son.'

'Well, then, could we call it all off?' pleaded Beth.

'Is there nothing right in your country? It defeats me how

a son of mine can be so disloyal. Have you no loyalty to England at all?'

'Not much to England as it is, but a very great deal to the England I want to see.'

'Well, there!' Ida sought to mediate. 'You see? The boy's all right. I'm sure that sounds fair enough.'

'Yes,' said Beth. 'And now could we stop?' She spoke sarcastically but her heart was aching, throbbing, to see Michael looking so miserable. She would have loved to run to him and put an arm along his shoulder and draw him against her, and lay a kiss on his hair. But she sat still and said only: 'It gets so wearisome.'

Ida, encouraged by this support, continued sentimentally: 'I'm sure at his age he should want to put the world to rights, shouldn't he, Dick?'

Dick, looking up from under his thick and wiry grey eyebrows, tried to soften his answer with a tenuous smile. 'I've often said something of the sort to Harry, but he never listens.'

Whereat Harry's temper, like a horse stung on the rump, bolted away with him. He flung down his nutcrackers and stood up. 'Oh God in His mercy, I wish someone were on my side sometimes. You all take his part. The boy can be as rude to me as he likes, he can call me simple, and I'm to sit down under it, I suppose?'

'You roared at him,' Ida reminded him.

'And I'll roar again next time. He said that everything I said was wrong, and all you do is to encourage him—all of you.'

Ida sighed and prepared to rise from the table too. 'Oh, my gracious, you are difficult sometimes,' she said.

'Me? Difficult? Simple-minded. Difficult. Is anything right about me at all?'

'Oh, don't be absurd, Harry. You do lose your temper so easily.' With that she rose and began to pile up the plates. 'It spoils everything.'

'All right, all right, all right. I know that I'm invariably wrong and the children invariably right.' Snatching at a cigar, he cut it (since this was a festival) while he walked about the room, like a panther circling a cage unhappily. 'You needn't go on at me.'

'*I* go on!' Indignant at such a suggestion, Ida stood with four plates in her hand and went on. It was he who went on,

43

she declared; he went on and on at the boy. Why couldn't he let the poor lad alone? Let him have his enthusiasms and his heroes. He could be young but once——

But at this point in the address Harry staged a dramatic act. He walked along a dead-straight line to the door, opened it, and said, 'Kindly stop going on at me. When you've decided to stop, I'll come back. Meantime I go.'

'Oh, well, *go*. Go, go, go!' Ida screamed it, whipping more plates together. She intended now to put on a scene that would completely overwhelm any drama of Harry's. It would be a paroxysm of tears and tempestuous words and desperate head-shakings. For Ida, just as she believed it was 'nice to let oneself go once in a way,' in the matter of gaiety, so she fully believed in letting herself go now and then in the matter of misery. A favourite remark of hers was 'It's not natural to bottle things up like Beth does.' But she would never have admitted—possibly because she would never have known—how much she enjoyed a real, all-out, thoroughgoing tempest of misery and hysterical words. Had she been able to speak the truth about these indulgences she must have said, 'Why is one provided with tears if not to use them for all they're worth? With a voice if not to lift it high? With a foot if not to stamp it? With a head if not to shake it in despair?' And all of these properties she now put to their full use, concluding a storm of declamations with, 'Come and help me clear up, Beth. I can't do everything. Look, you've made Beth cry now. On Mike's birthday. And what Dick and Walter are thinking of us I can't imagine.'

'I'm all right, Mum,' said Beth, which, of course, was untrue. But Beth's tears, unlike her mother's, were always controlled—held back behind a tight quivering mouth—or taken out of view, far away.

'If he wants to go, let him go,' Ida shouted at the plates and the table. 'That's what I say.'

But Harry, at the door, didn't want to go at all. He wanted to continue the battle, and he was glad that those words about Dick and Walter gave him an excuse for coming back into the room. 'I'm not afraid of what Dick and Walter think. I'm not afraid of what anybody in the whole damned world thinks. They know I do my duty——'

'Who said you didn't?' interrupted Ida.

But Harry wasn't available for interruptions. 'They know

how I slave to keep the family and to put money by for you all, in case I die—which might happen any day, and I'm not sure that I'd mind if it did.'

'The trouble with you,' said Ida, wilfully noisy with plates and cutlery, 'is that you'll never admit you're in the wrong. Here you've fired up and spoiled Mike's party. Can't you even say you're sorry?'

'No, I can't. Becasue I don't *feel* sorry. The boy was bloody rude—and what the damned hell—am I to put up with that? I should think you might be on my side for once. I can understand the children having no thought for what it costs in endless bloody work to bring them up in nice cultivated surroundings, but——' and here he saw before him some words that would strike like an assagai through Ida's heart. He saw that it would be cruel to use them; and he used them. 'But I should have thought *you* would have been able to feel with me sometimes. Upon my soul, there are times when I wish I'd married someone with some imagination.'

That finished Ida. She put down the pile of plates with a bang and went out through the open door, straight as a draught of chilled air.

§

Michael turned to follow her. But his face was so sad, his whole attitude so forlorn, that his father, conscience-striken, proffered his cigarette case like a peace offering. 'Cigarette, son?'

'No, thank you, Dad,' said the boy, and sauntered out, while Harry sought a speck of comfort in the thought that at least the boy had said 'Dad.'

For two minutes Beth stood in secret thought, gazing down, without sight, at a bill-head on her father's desk; then she ran out of the room after Michael. In the dusk of the passage outside, keeping statue-still and silent, she listened to his movements in his bedroom and guessed that he was making ready to go from the house and lose his dejection and loneliness in the company of his blackshirt friends. On tip-toe she walked down the stairs and stood in the dark narrow hallway behind the private door of the Lord of Wensley. Here she waited and waited, listening and peering for him: not otherwise does a girl linger in secret for an encounter with her lover. At last

45

Michael came down in his taut black jersey and black trousers, with a belted grey overcoat covering, rather ridiculously, this headsman's uniform. Instantly Beth pretended that she'd picked up a slip from the hall mat and was reading it. It was an advertisement she'd snatched from among the piled papers on the hall table.

'Oh, hallo, Mike,' she said, as if surprised.

'Hallo, Podge.' As always the nickname, meant affectionately, was a knife-stab.

'Going out?'

'Sure thing.'

'To the Black House?'

'Yes. Things aren't too jolly here, are they?'

'I'm sorry there was that row.'

'Oh, it can't be helped. I understand Dad all right, but he'll never understand me; that's the trouble.'

'*I* understand you—I understand all you want to do—at least I think I do.'

'That's a good Podge. Well, hurray; thank God some-one——'

'I understand your love for your Leader, though I've never seen him. I'm sure he's wonderful. And for that Dermot. I quite liked your Dermot. And I think you were perfectly right to give up that reporter's job if you felt you'd be happier in your present work.'

'Splendid, Podge. Thank God someone understands something.'

'Good-bye.' Her plan had been to put her arms around him and kiss him good-bye in his sadness even though she received in reward only his flat, damp, uneager kiss; but now she had no courage to touch him. And perhaps this was as well, because all too often the flat, damp, uneager kiss touched a spring of tears which must not flow—not, anyhow, until he had turned and was gone.

''Bye, Podge. God bless.'

'God bless.'

She opened the door and he went out, turning in the street to give her a smile—and this smile was *her* only speck of comfort, like the 'Dad' he'd given his father.

'Podge.' Now that her angry sadness could express itself unseen, she let a sob climb up her, but wretchedly it concluded with an embarrassing snort in her nose, which surely could be heard all over the house. Nothing ever seemed to happen romantically with Beth, and she tossed her head angrily.

§

'Now I'm in bad odour. Shocking bad odour.'

Harry and Dick were sitting alone among the ruins of the party, for Walter had quickly and discreetly withdrawn, saying to Harry, 'Thank you for the most excellent entertainment, Captain Townes, sir,' and to Dick, 'Good afternoon to you, Mr. Templer, sir,' and comprehending both in a small, grateful bow.

Harry pulled at his cigar. Dick drew at his pipe. For a time neither spoke. Then Harry said, 'Oh dear, I wish I didn't always quarrel with the boy so. Can't imagine how it's all come about. Where have we got it wrong, Dicky?'

But Dick only shook his head and watched the smoke clouding up from his pipe. And Harry wondered what thoughts might be shaping in that smoke. He sighed and spoke again.

'We were always such pals when he was a kid. I love kids. I've always said a man's life isn't complete without kids about. It's lovely to tease 'em and tickle 'em and hear them laugh. And I think the greatest day of my life was when Mike was born—do you remember, Dick: we were in the Line at Beaumont Hamel? The dreams I had about him in those trenches: someone to work for; someone to hand the old pub to, if I succeeded in getting a pub. And when I came on leave I was ready to do anything for him: change his nappy, wipe his arse, bath him, put him to bed. . . . When he was older, I used to tell him bed-time yarns. Good times those. Yes . . . yes . . . he'd sauce me, and I loved it. As sure as I bent over to pick up something he'd smack my bottom for me and then I'd chase him all over the house. Sometimes we changed that round and played "Follow my Leader" all through the bars and down into the cellar and out into the Gents—even into the Ladies, bless you, giggling like hell. He used to call me "The Captain," damn his eyes. He'd come home from school and ask "Where's the Captain, Mum?" as if he wanted me. Wanted me to play with him. And I would nip from the bar to teach him cricket in the back garden or on the Common. We used to go to the Oval together whenever possible—hot Surrey supporters, both of us—and let me tell you, there's no companion at a cricket

47

match like a twelve-year-old. When the pavilion bell went he'd elbow me in the ribs with excitement and say, "Fifteen minutes bell, Dad," or "Five minutes bell. . . ." Ah, I wonder if he remembers all that . . . sometimes. . . .'

He waited for a comment from Dick; but Dick only knocked out his pipe on the fender, and filled it again. And lit it.

'I'm a sentimental idiot, I suppose, but I shall always say that the loveliest sound in all the world is when your kid first says "Dad" at you with a smile. But they give you other thrills too. I shall never forget when I first saw Mike in long trousers and school blazer, with his pink round-cheeked dial on top of it all, like he was still only eight. . . . And always that mop of hair falling over his eyes, and him tossing it off. . . . Yes, it's wonderful to watch 'em blossoming—wonderful —till they blossom all wrong.'

Dick nodded to himself, and Harry hoped this meant agreement, but feared it meant something else.

'He began to turn funny about fourteen. I guess it was partly his mother's fault because she always took his part if I gave him a hiding—as one has to do sometimes with any boy. Perhaps I ought to have taken a stick to him more often.'

'Or less often.' This was exactly the answer Harry expected —and wanted. He'd prised it out of old Dick many times before. And now, just as he had provoked Michael into an argument on Politics, he was disposed to stir up an argument on Corporal Punishment with Dick. 'What do you mean: "Less often"?'

'You know what I tend to think about any punishment that takes the form of violence.'

'Yes, and you know that I don't agree with you. I'll never believe a bit of the stick hurt a decent lad yet. It helps to make a man of him.'

'Depends what you mean by a man.' The first warmth of asperity could be heard in the words; but Dick quickly damped it down, and offered instead, 'Maybe it doesn't do some boys any harm, but children vary.'

'Well, I can't see why Michael should vary from what his dad was. I had plenty of the stick when I was a boy—much more than ever Mike had—and it did me no harm.'

Dick looked up, and the blue eyes beneath the thatchy grey eyebrows, the lips beneath the clipped grey moustache, held a mocking smile. 'Are you perfect then?'

'No.' Harry was ready to admit he was not perfect. 'No, certainly not.' He removed his cigar, now a chewed butt, and spat a flake into the fire. 'Not perfect; but I'll never believe my old man's hidings did me any harm. They learned me obedience, anyhow. . . . Well? . . .' This was a query because Dick had answered nothing in refutation. 'For a lawyer accustomed to pleading, you say mighty little. I don't like a son of mine going about in a dam-silly black shirt like some dam-silly hokey-pokey Italian. He's an Englishman, and half a Scotsman. Dammit, he's descended from Macbeth!'

'Harry.' Dick leaned forward, rested his elbows on his knees, and tapped the palm of one hand with his pipe, which was now out. 'Have you ever really looked down on South London, say from the tower of Wandsworth Prison? Or, better, Brixton Prison, because it stands on high ground? Nothing but streets of dreary little houses going on and on to the very edges of the world, with only a torn common or two to play on——'

'I know, I know,' Harry interrupted. 'I always say Balham and Tooting are graveyards because the people only come there to sleep. But thank God they come in here for a night-cap sometimes.'

'And have you ever thought that in all that dreary sea of houses the only really big buildings are two mental hospitals and two prisons?'

'That's right. Tooting Bec Mental Hospital and Brixton and Wandsworth Prisons—good lord!' Harry had always been fascinated by the great grey prisons. 'Ah, well, Tooting Bec Mental for me.'

'And have you ever asked yourself, what is there for lively and imaginative boys born in those streets? What does a boy want? Pageantry and colour and adventure; and, perhaps above all, devotion to some Cause. Unfortunately they also like a spot of fighting—and don't forget Michael Townes is a son of Harry Townes. Harry Townes of Thiepval Wood. I remember that old fighter.'

This was to touch Harry in a tender place and plunge him into memories, so that he softened.

And Dick went on, 'It must seem a fine thing to march away from Balham to where the Reds wait and there fight them along the streets for the honour of England.'

'Fine! I call it damned hooliganism.'

'So do I, but they don't. Michael probably thinks himself a kind of follower of Garibaldi; this new and exciting crusade has made his life worth living for him. That Leader of his is an impressive person, tall, dark and handsome, and no small orator—I've heard him. I can understand his boys worshipping him.'

'He ought to be locked up.'

'No, Harry. Come! For my part, as Mike's godfather, I'm glad he's turned to Politics instead of Crime. Just think: if he'd been a step or two lower in the social scale he might easily have sought adventure and escape in petty crime. We've *real* hooligans in Balham and I don't wonder. I've had to defend many of them in my time—and often I've done it with quite a good heart. A boy in Clapham or Balham who doesn't break out in one way or another, it seems to me, is either a saint or a dullard or a tamed creature.'

'Well, our Mike's no saint,' laughed Harry. And having no brain to cope with Dick's (whose headpiece he always described to his pals, with pride, as 'worth ten of mine') he chose now to be cheerful and conciliatory. 'Well, you've certainly said your piece now. And I hope there's something in it. Dare say there is. I always say to the chaps that you're my window cleaner. I can clean my lower windows but not the upper ones. Have to call in old Dick for them. And I expect he finds it a tough job, because they're pretty damned murky.'

§

When Dick was gone Harry stayed in his deep chair by an ageing fire, and his only companions were melancholy and remorse—the remorse much the smaller friend, but a fine growing fellow, with more and more to say, if you'd listen to him. The house from ground-floor to roof was as silent as a hurt man's disapproval, or as the condemnation of God on high. No doubt Michael had gone in displeasure from his father's house (and it was his birthday) and Beth had sought peace among her church friends, and Ida was sitting in deliberate and determined loneliness in her kitchen. She hadn't even turned on her wireless, lest he should suppose her capable of enjoyments. Every wall in the house was registering his disgrace.

50

At length, with a heavy sigh, he rose and walked to a window. The February day was bright, and the late afternoon sun invited him to come out and get its healing on the Common. He obeyed it. He went down the stairs to the street door, and not a sound from any part of the house suggested that anyone cared where he went or what he did. Snatching his thick cherrywood stick, he went out. By Elmfield Road and Cloudesdale Road and Bushnell Road he strolled towards the Common, and all the way he thought of what Dick had said about these endless streets of little houses. Small red-brick two-storied houses they were, in long monotonous row upon row; all with butter-coloured ornamental dressings, and some with names like Lochinvar and Fernbank and Elmhurst, though they had nothing but fringes of dusty privets behind the railings of their narrow forecourts. Huron Road, Streathbourne Road, Drakefield Road—all of them as straight and quiet as lower-middle-class propriety, and they and their sisters went on and on, as old Dick had said, to the ends of the visible world.

He came to the Common and, finding a seat under a great chestnut tree, sat himself down in this sham countryside. And something in him, some deep and ancient craving for the lost landscapes of men which they enjoyed before they imprisoned themselves in towns, was bruised and disappointed as he gazed at the avenue of old sooted elms, at the clusters of young, tired trees, and at the dark drab clumps of gorse. And he thought again of happy days when he had been a nomad once more and wandered with his men among the lush landscapes of the Somme, or over the rolling green plains behind Gheluvelt and Ypres.

It was fairly warm, though the sun was now low, so he stayed there on the seat, beating his stick on the foot-worn path between his shoes. And while he sat there he suddenly saw Ida walking along the broad avenue between the old elms. He guessed where she was going, for that road led across the Common to the numberless small streets of Streatham, among which her sister lived. She was dressed in her very finest Sunday affairs, and her neat little hat supported a feathery spray of some kind which stood erect and trembled in its upper air. Seldom, it seemed to him, had she carried her big bust and her small hat so high. That spray up there might have been her undefeated flag flying above her citadel or, better perhaps, the broom at her masthead with which, like Admiral Van Tromp, she proposed to sweep from her path all who were rude to her. The sight of her sad dignity filled him with a pity almost unbearable. But his pride would not suffer him to move from his seat, and reveal himself, and comfort her. That would be to admit he'd been wrong; and at all costs his show must go on. So he just sat there and watched her sail along the avenue, a broad-bowed galleon with her crest aloft, till she was out of sight. His own sadness was probably greater than hers, and his consciousness of sin certainly greater. 'She means so much to me,' he thought, and, longing to embrace and comfort her, he sat there looking forward to the hour of reconciliation when they would both be happy again, and more loving than ever, for a little while.

CHAPTER FOUR

In the old days when Michael was a child, Harry was always very unhappy in secret, for twenty-four hours at least, after he'd bellowed at the boy or struck him. He would spend much of that twenty-four hours walking about the house and wondering how he could invent an excuse for buying the child a toy or treating him to the Pictures, or taking him to the Oval, but an excuse that would seem quite natural and not in the least like an amends. On the day after a noisy row he would seize upon every opportunity for praising the boy and every opportunity for agreeing with his very silly remarks. He imagined that no one perceived this hidden penitence, this craving to 'make it up' to the boy who was his son, but Ida perceived it well and snatched at any such favourable moment for getting from him the new clothes which Michael needed. She knew that when Harry was in this chastened mood he might well leap at the idea of taking the boy to the outfitter's and spending pounds on shorts and shoes and jerseys so that the child could see that his father was always ready to do his duty by him, and in no niggardly way either.

It was not greatly different now, when the boy was in his twenties: Harry Townes experienced all these emotions the day after that birthday quarrel. He paced about, wondering 'how to make it up to the boy.' He had offered no words or deeds of appeasement on the day itself, because that might savour of apology (and to hell with that!), but all the next day, while Michael was at his Black House, his father was longing for him to come home that he might agree with him about something. He was longing also for Dick to come in, because Dick was the one person to whom he could tell everything in his heart—everything, that is, except those things of which he was too much ashamed to tell them to any man.

But the day passed, Michael did not return till late, Dick did not come in at all, and so an opportunity for all he desired to do was not granted him. But one evening in the early summer of that year the situation was much what he'd had in mind. There had been a boisterous quarrel with Michael the evening before; Harry was feeling sorry for his part in it and determined not to say he was sorry (to his victim, at any rate); thus only a patched-up peace hovered between him and the boy, and the 'making it up' to him had still to be achieved; and here were Dick and he sitting in opposite chairs, with their whiskies beside them, Dick's on the mantelpiece, and his on the carpet. There was old Dick yonder, seated beneath his blue drifts of pipe-smoke, and ready as always to listen; there he was, an old and most friendly receptacle, which, as the confessions dropped into it, rang with no blame.

It was early summer, we say, and in early summer the street-fighting season opened.

Harry was busy expounding the quarrel and his own lamentable weaknesses to Dick; he was asking for Dick's advice and not listening to it, when he heard a sound of footsteps springing down the stairs from the room above. Young steps. And a young, happy voice. ''Bye, Mum. 'Bye Beth. Lord knows when I'll be home.' A voice, as Harry always thought, of great, unconscious, charm.'

'Hush!' he said. 'Here he is.'

Michael entered in his full black uniform. 'Good-bye, Dad. Oh—Uncle Dick—hallo!'

The sight of the uniform pierced Harry like a thrown knife, but he determined to rein back the annoyance and be nice to the boy; if possible to agree with him about something; so he kept his eyes off that black breast and gave him a jocular greeting. 'Heil Hitler. Sieg heil. Where are you off to now, son?'

'Bethnal Green,' said Michael, a light in his eyes.

'Bethnal Green. And what's afoot there?'

'The Leader's going to speak there in Three Colts Lane, and we're jolly well going to see that, if he wants to speak, he shall. We're going there a thousand strong. Rather more, probably. We're forming up on the Embankment in an hour's time and marching off behind him. They know we're coming, and they're waiting for us.' Plain from the light in his eyes that the hope of danger and excitement was like a wine in his veins. 'There should be some fun.'

'What do you suppose'll happen?' asked Dick, taking his pipe from his mouth and pressing down its sparking contents with a thumb.

'Oh, that's simple. Anyone who tries any funny stuff will be very promptly dealt with. We've got our Strong-Arm Boys marching at the head of the column. Picked lads.' Michael bent his right arm and, tautening its biceps by closing his fist, tried the fine swell of it with his hand. 'Powerful lads.'

Scoffing words jumped to his father's lips, but he kept the lips tight and let nothing pass. Tonight—for once—let there be nothing but affection between him and his son.

But Dick, having no memories of quarrels to act as gyves upon his tongue, continued to make fun of him. 'And it'll need a thousand of you to keep order, will it?'

'No,' laughed Michael. 'I don't suppose it'll need much more than our Strong-Arm Boys. No one argues twice with them. The rest is merely a demonstration. Nothing like showing the Bolshie boys we mean business. Now they can see what they've stirred up. They used to wait for us and smash up our meetings if we were only a few. Never again. And they've threatened the Leader's life more than once. Okay, but they'll only get to him over our dead bodies.'

'That's the spirit!' Dick replaced his pipe; his eyes smiled above it. 'And you've no feeling that this parade in force is really designed to provoke them and stir up trouble. You don't, eh?'

'No.' Michael had his answer pat. 'Because we go un-armed. So far the Leader's insisted on that. They have all the weapons—razors and knuckle-dusters and stockings filled with glass—a charming selection—but we've only what the Leader calls The Good Old British Fist.' Michael raised his fist breast high and shook it merrily. 'But, my God, we shall have two thousand of them.'

A tut-tut behind his father's lips almost got through, but not quite. Instead he drank from his whisky glass and, wiping the lips with a finger, saw a chance of agreeing with the boy. 'Well, if it's only the Red bullies you're welcome to do what you like with them, so far as I'm concerned. Give 'em some of their own poison.'

'But, Michael,' Dick pursued, 'honestly now: isn't it the truth that you go there, not really wanting to keep order, but spoiling for a fight?'

The father's head nodded 'Yes, yes,' but his head only; and the boy was not looking at him. He was looking at Dick with gay, mischievous eyes. 'Well, Uncle Dick, to be absolutely honest, there's the tiniest touch of truth in what you say.'

'In other words, you enjoy fighting in the streets under the plea that you're establishing order?'

'He's a good cross-examiner, isn't he, Dad? I think I can answer learned counsel by saying that, yes, I enjoy giving the Bolshies an occasional reminder that we stand for freedom of speech. Why it's we who broke political violence in the East End. Only one man in England had the courage and forged the instrument to break it—and you know who that was. I say you ought to be grateful to us, Dad, because, before we took the business in hand, none of your Tories could hold an open-air meeting east of Aldgate. But we had every intention of holding meetings east of Aldgate. We shall hold ours tonight.'

'Well, have a good fight.' Taking out his pipe Dick lifted his whisky glass and toasted the fight. 'Here's to it. Enjoy yourself.'

'I will.' Perhaps the boy discerned in his father's silence an effort at friendliness and tried to respond to it, for he suddenly said, 'After all Dad used to enjoy fighting. And the only difference now is that the war's no longer between nations but between world-wide movements. Between us and the Commies. The old order is rotting to death. A new order, ours or theirs, is coming fast; and I guess I know which it is. It began in Italy; it spread to Germany, and now——'

'Is all this a quotation from your Leader?' murmured Dick, holding his pipe bowl with both hands.

'Certainly it is. And why not? He's the only man, so far as I can see, with a fighting faith, in a world of impending catastrophe. The trouble is, he's a portent; he threatens the overthrow of all profiteers and exploiters and enslavers, and that's why they revile him.'

'Der Fuehrer again?'

'No. Der Dermot that time,' Michael laughed. 'Dermot's a thundering good speaker too.'

'And how, precisely, do you boys propose to overthrow all these Mighty Men of Money?'

'With a disciplined party that's an instrument of steel. An iron instrument that'll shape, not the will of these old grabbers to exploit the people, but the people's will not to be exploited!' The light sprang again into his eyes as he heard his fine words.

'All of which means,' put in his father, unable to hold his peace any longer, 'that you propose to set up a dictatorship here like—— Not in Britain, I think.'

'My dear father.' Michael addressed him almost pityingly, and Harry didn't at all like his 'damned superior' tone. 'There's a dictatorship here already, beautifully concealed behind the shams of party politics. The dictatorship of the Big Paymasters. They're the real enemies of Britain—not the German people. Our war is against them.'

'I thought you said,' Dick submitted, 'that it was against the Communists.'

'Oh . . . well. . . .' For a moment the boy's stance was shaken. 'Yes . . . it's a war on two fronts, if you like. Against Big Business on the one hand and the Commies on the other.'

'I can never tell the difference between you Fascists and the Communists,' said his father. 'What is it?'

'Oh, a hell of a big difference. I'll explain one day. I'll tell you one day. But I must go now. Good-bye, Uncle Dick. 'Bye, Dad.'

Pleased to have controlled his temper fairly well, Harry projected the resulting goodwill on the boy. 'Good-bye, son. Go out the back way in that kit, so that no one can see you.'

'Okay, Dad. Don't worry. I won't spoil your business for you.' He waved at the door and was gone.

'Did you hear ever such poppycock as he talks?' Harry asked of Dick. 'But I say: didn't he look handsome in that get-up? You *must* say it's damned becoming to a young figure. I say, Dick!' He leaned forward with his hands on his chair arms. 'Let's go and see them! *Come* on.'

'See whom?'

'All these silly lads on parade. Saint Michael and all his angels. And their precious Leader. The whole damned circus. I've never seen this Leader of his.' Harry was fascinated by his hostility to this man who not only stood for things that alarmed and exasperated him but had supplanted him in the loyalties of his son. 'Come. I'll get out the little old van and we'll be there as soon as Mike is.'

'No. Like Mike, I'm a man under discipline, and I do what my housekeeper orders. And she says "Dinner at seven." But where do you propose to go? Bethnal Green?'

'No; only to the Embankment where he said they'd parade. I can't go the whole way, more's the pity, because I'd have liked to see the scrapping. But I must be back in the bar by eight when the rush begins. That's the worst of being one of the Bung Boys; one can hardly ever have a night off for a bit of real fun. Sorry, old boy, but good-bye. I'm off.'

Once in the street he hurried to Cannings Yard where he kept his little blue Huntingdon van. This was a shabby little vehicle that he'd bought second-hand as a means of fetching extra stock from the brewery, or taking supplies to some Annual Dinner which he'd a special licence to serve, or for taking the family into the peace of the country on a Sunday afternoon.

This evening Harry drove it off alone, and rather quickly as he passed the windows of the Lord of Wensley.

§

Approaching the Embankment that sunny evening, having hidden the van in a side-street, Harry saw a large crowd on the pavement between him and the parade and heard a hubbub of many voices—cheering voices, jeering voices, angry, arguing or laughing voices—and like a child he hurried his steps to miss nothing of the show. But as he got among the standing crowd he bent his head that his hat-brim might curtain the top of his face, and pulled at his upper lip that his hand might cover the lower part of it. Taller than many, he walked along the back of the crowd to survey the parade.

It was impressive—more impressive than he wanted to admit. Sinister indeed, because there were all of a thousand of them, and all in black. At the head of the column was a squad of some twenty exceedingly powerful-looking bruisers—the Strong-Arm men, no doubt; then a band of twelve black drums with fifes and a bagpiper; then the massed flags—huge black flags and Union Jacks; then an empty space, presumably for the Great Man Himself; then contingents from all parts of London; and then, God save the mark! a contingent of women in black blouses and grey skirts with their own drums and drum major—good heavens!

He could not espy Michael for some time, but at last discerned him near the head of the column, apparently among the principal officers, and, against his desires, he felt a touch of pride at this unforeseen importance in his son. But then a touch of annoyance for there at his side, talking and laughing with him was a short young man with broad shoulders, a flat Irish face, and a horrid scar across one cheek from mouth to ear—the brand from a street battle, so Harry guessed, when a

Red boy's arm had been twisted in a back alley and a Jew boy, perhaps, had dashed up to avenge him. Dermot. Dermot O'Neill.

Now he crossed over to the south side of the Embankment, for the parade was facing the river. From behind the jeering crowd on this pavement he scanned the faces of these, Michael's friends. Some were grey-haired veterans, but most were youths, and of these some had ordinary, pleasant, eager-eyed faces like Michael's, but others were palpable toughs with dull eyes and sour or cruel mouths; and Harry was relieved to see these repellent types because they justified his condemnation. Many of the older men also had hard faces in which it was difficult to see any symptoms of the dedicated self-sacrifice that Michael proclaimed. And again Harry was glad to note this, and to feel justified. But then, considering anew the younger faces, some sallow and hollow and angry, he remembered Michael's words about the three million unemployed and, for a second, saw them with new eyes as faces of the defeated—and he suddenly felt frightened. Was this, then, young England to-day? Young England on the march? Some sympathy mingled with his fear, but this sympathy vanished like vapour down the wind when he saw, for the first time, a squad of lads in peaked caps, black tunics and black top-boots with brassards on their left arms, deliberately reminiscent of the brassards of the Nazis.

This disgusted and therefore pleased him. 'Bah!' he muttered. 'Copy-cats!' and felt more than ever justified.

Where he now stood the crowd was thickest, and he soon gathered that they, like him, were eager to see the Leader. Dick had said that he was a striking figure in his own right but, beyond this, he had around him the dark aura of the German dictator, who was his friend; and Harry could feel in these watchers the same fascination, compounded of hostility and reluctant admiration, which this portentous person could arouse in him. Some were calling out, 'Where's your pocket Hitler?' and, mockingly, 'We . . . want . . . the . . . Leader . . . L.E.A.D.E.R.' or angrily, 'Why don't you pack up and go to Germany? We don't want you here. . . . Who do you think you are? Al Capone's body-guard? . . . Nah! Them's the Church Lads Brigade. . . . Yes, and in half a mo' their blasted Pope'll be along.'

But they did not molest them, for mounted and foot police stood waiting to march with the column.

One more minute, and then to a great roar, nine-tenths jeers and one-tenth cheers, a tall figure, slim and erect, in black fencing shirt, grey breeches and top boots, came from round a corner where presumably he had left a car. He might have been forty, but he had the figure of an athlete and the carriage of a swordsman as he walked scornfully and with head high, towards the storm of booing. Immediately a voice yelled (as Harry had done many a time, so that he was annoyed to see an amateur attempting it) 'Parade. . . . *Shun!*'

A battalion of the Guards could hardly have responded more sharply to a word of command or stood more severely and incorruptibly at attention. The women's ultra-vertical and chest-out posture was even better, some said, than the men's. It was so splendid as to be comic.

The crowd thought so and shouted their ribald approval. 'Smarten up now, girls!' 'Come on: elbows back; hands at the seams of your trousers.' 'You there—number three—keep your belly in!' 'Nothing wrong with her belly. Very nice!'

Meanwhile the Leader was walking along the ranks like a king inspecting his guard of honour.

Harry, with all the others, studied his face as he went by. It was a face to draw your glance again and again: youthful, handsome, with a commanding nose, dark eyes, and stern, unsmiling, melancholy mouth; the face of a young condottiere or conquistador whose trust was in his sword. Some might have found a harder term than 'stern' for those eyes and that mouth; nevertheless the very ruthlessness in them fascinated. Harry understood why youths like Michael and Dermot could make a hero of this handsome man, but at the same time he thought that staring, unsmiling countenance the most frustrated and lonely face he had ever seen.

Now, as Leader, he went to his place behind the massed flags, whereupon the second-in-command, or whoever he was, bawled out in full military fashion (which further galled Harry) 'Move to the left in threes. . . . Left . . . *turn*. . . . Quick . . . MARCH!'

Straightway the column, shepherded by the police, moved eastward, tramp, tramp, behind its Leader, whose head, fittingly enough, was inches higher than any other. His tall dark figure marched in the place of command, straight and stern as the shaft of a spear. At intervals, between the contingents, youths were carrying placards on poles, and as they went by Harry read 'Britain Shall be Great Again,' 'All for the State and None for the Faction,' 'We Fight for Freedom and for Bread,' 'Tomorrow We Live.'

At first they tramped along to the beat of a drum, but then the band started up, and all the thousand of them began to sing. Harry knew their song, because it was much spoken of and Michael had once, at his request, sung it for him.

Comrades, the voices of the dead battalions,
Of those who fell that Britain might be great,
Join in our song, for they march in spirit with us,
And urge us on to gain the Fascist state.

Blood of our blood and spirit of our spirit . . .

It was the Horst Wessel song, which their German brothers were singing across the way.

Harry, looking for Michael's head, discerned it at the front of the procession, near the Leader's. Staying in his place behind the crowd, he did not take his eyes off it, but watched his son march out of sight, with those massed flags in front of him and this stream of song behind.

CHAPTER FIVE

THE two master interests of Michael's life in these days were his devotion to his Leader who had brought this new Gospel to the world, and his affection for the pale young man with the scar whom Harry had seen at his side.

These two emotions satisfied his young needs so that there was no room in his life for flirting, or loafing after girls, or gambling in amusement arcades, which seemed the chief pastimes of the youths in the Balham High Road.

His romantic attachment to Dermot was Elizabethan in its ardour; an affection akin to that of Philip Sidney for Fulke Greville, though much less articulate. He did not call Dermot his 'heart's brother', but he might have done so in a more lyrical age. Their lyricism got no further than enthusiastic plans for working together, travelling together, and living together. Sometimes they even chose the West End house in whose lower rooms they would work 'with their staff officers' for the Movement, and in whose upper rooms they would share a flat (neither having any interest in women).

Michael first encountered Dermot by being pressed against him, elbow to elbow, in the front row of the standing 'promenaders' at a symphony concert. Michael had taken to attending concerts largely because his father proclaimed so noisily that he'd 'no use for this classical music' and that he suspected that most of the 'long-haired ninnies' to be found in concert halls only pretended to enjoy the meaningless row. So Michael, soon after hearing this, announced with pleasure that he was going to attend at least a dozen concerts this year, and Harry maintained to Ida that it was all a new pose on the boy's part, adopted to irritate his father—as indeed it was, till the music, by its gradual assaults and its occasional caresses and its sudden splendid violences, won him as its thrall for ever, and he could rejoice that his love was sincere.

It was exactly at this hour of joyous surrender that he found himself pressed by the crowd against a short, broad, rather sickly-faced young man with an extraordinary scar. More than once he had to apologise for the pressure and the bumping, and so they got to laughing and talking together. And often when Michael's rapture in the music slackened, his eyes returned to that strange scar stretching from lips to ear. In the interval, after being thus clapped together and moulded together like butter, they went out as friends for ginger beers (neither being interested in alcohol).

That was the beginning: Sidney had met his Greville, David his Jonathan. In snack bars or at coffee stalls after the concerts, and later in Dermot's basement bed-sitting room, they would talk and talk—and how brilliant, how ebullient, how sparkling a talker was Dermot; how caustic his wit; how ruthless his logic and, accordingly, how shocking—thrillingly shocking—some of his conclusions. Michael, from a conventional Tory home, listened, rapt, to this daringly revolutionary stuff, and to the experiences in Dermot's past by which he justified it. His name, Dermot said, was O'Néill, with an accent on the 'e', if you would kindly oblige. O'Néill, because he claimed to be descended from Diarmait of the Húi Néill, who were kings in Ireland centuries ago. (It was Dermot who set Michael raking in the history of the Clans for the origins of the Campbells of Cawdor, who, he exulted to find, had connections with Macbeth, a king in Scotland, if a scoundrelly one.)

'I'm no Londoner like you,' declared Dermot. 'I'm not even an Englishman. My dad, Kevin O'Néill, was the son of a poor Irish immigrant in Liverpool, but he was a pretty brilliant chap, and they thought the world of him at Crase and Paton's, the great engineering firm where he worked. At least they said so, as long as it suited them.'

When he said this, they were sitting in Dermot's basement lodging, a long narrow room under a tall red house in West Kensington; a place which had probably been a maids' room in the days of the house's prosperity. Dermot was sitting on the narrow bed with a knee cocked up and his hands intertwined around it; Michael on a cane chair with his elbow resting on the wash-stand, over against a pink-flowered basin and ewer, and his rapt eyes staring at the talker.

And Dermot talked on. How proud he'd been when he was accepted as an apprentice at Crase and Paton's directly after he left his council school at fourteen; how he'd loved to speak of himself as an 'engineer'; how secretly he'd thought of Crase and Paton's with its shops and foundries and its ten thousand skilled workmen as his university—his Oxford! But then, just when he'd done six years of his apprenticeship, came the Great Depression, and his father who'd served the firm for twenty-three years and long since risen to be a foreman, was cast out—discharged—left at fifty without hope of other work and bidden live on the dole. Dermot's work was secure till his seventh year expired—and then out he went too. Out on his ear. Out with the Freedom of the Street. Any other work for him anywhere? In the pride of his youth? No. Give up all hope of that forever and live on the dole.

'What sense is there in a system which couldn't use a man of Dad's skill and decency? In his way, there's no cleverer or better bloke anywhere. Or me, a fully trained engineer and a nice lad, too. They couldn't use me anywhere. And I reckon I'm able enough; and up till then I was willing and law-abiding enough. The whole rotten system, Mike, is just damned bad engineering. It offends me. We need a wholly different machine as quickly as possible, and, by God, I'll do what I can to build it.'

So it was that Michael, that evening, learned of Dermot's activities in the Blackshirt Movement. He was shocked at first because he'd heard nothing but abuse, especially from his father, of these people. But Dermot, the exuberant and dazzling arguer—his words pouring forth in a cataract and his eyes sparkling because of the lightnings in his breast—soon broke down these resistances and planted in Michael the first seeds of his own hates and dreams—not a little to Michael's pleasure, because all this fine argument was on the opposite side of the net to his father's.

'Look at it! Look at it all!' cried Dermot, springing from the bed and spreading his hands in exposition. 'Look at our present free-for-all system, with its roguery and cheating everywhere—everyone trying to bloodsuck wherever possible an unfair profit out of everyone else—the little men in little pettifogging ways and the big boys on a large scale with their price-rings and trusts and cartels. Bleed the blind consumer for all he'll stand! And then the insolent arrogance, the insufferable, blown-up pride of those who've climbed to high social position by these methods of banditry and cheating—either their fathers' or their own. Especially the women. And the Jew boys. Damn them with their long cigars in their long limousines for which you and I have paid. Damn their mink and their ermine and the tiaras in their hair!'

§

After that night of initiation Michael listened to his friend's oratory, not only in that basement, but at street corners when Dermot stood on the roof of the Blackshirts' van and harangued a noisy crowd, his voice amplified by three loud-speakers whose great trumpet-mouths gaped east, west and north. The crowd might jeer and hoot as it liked; the loud-speakers could always lift his voice above theirs. Dermot, having none of Michael's diffidence, was a natural orator, and Michael, selling, or trying to sell, Blackshirt literature on the fringes of the crowd, would listen with envy of his ease and fluency. For Michael, when he too spoke from the top of the van, had secretly to write his speech beforehand, learn it by heart, and deliver it nervously with gestures and accents that he'd rehearsed at home; his an actor's, not an orator's, part.

'Revolution of some sort is bound to come,' shouts Dermot from the top of the van, and the loud-speakers bellow the words for him, under a night sky that arches over the world of low roofs and little chimneys that is East London. 'Bound to come because the present system no longer meets the needs and aspirations of men. It imprisons them in great cities of sprawling streets and allows only a minority of grabbers to live their lives to the full. Bound to come—either from us or from the Reds—and God save you from *them*! We Blackshirts are hated and slandered. Why? Because we've detected the swindle. And because we're publishing it from the housetops. We tell you all about the wires that work the idols which they set up in front of you—and two of those idols are your Free Press and your Freely Elected Political Parties. *We* know who holds the strings of those two giant shams. We're rebels, if you please—traitors even. Good! If it's disloyal to want the emancipation of the weak from the exploitation of the International Financiers and Monopolists everywhere, then we accept the definition. Let it stand.'

§

So he would bawl to the crowd around the van. But he did not frighten them with some of the ruthless conclusions which, in his basement, he was ready to proclaim, and rejoiced to proclaim, to Michael, for his shock and his education. Such as these: that he longed for a revolutionary faith which would destroy all frontiers; that this faith might have to be imposed upon Europe by top-down control instead of by bottom-upward choice; that, if this were so, Germany would probably be seen as the centre of the world after the tides of revolution had passed; and that he was ready to accept such an issue, because he wanted to have done with the old limited patriotisms and to be a citizen of the world.

As in the street, so in the basement room, Michael listened with some admiration because hitherto he'd had no such toughness of nature as this, nor such boldness in thought. He saw that he'd have to force his nature quite a way, if he was to be like Dermot and something more than a mere dilettante of revolution.

§

The coming revolution was not Dermot's only interest. Music was another of his enthusiasms. By the side of his bed, where anyone else would have had a bedside table, he had his own small upright piano; and on this he played with the skill of a lover. Seated before it, he would play for Michael the themes and motifs of the symphonies they would hear that evening, and instruct him in the developments and variations of those themes. Michael was his pupil in music as in politics, and never did master have a pupil keener or more responsive.

From Dermot Michael received the gift of ears: now he could really perceive the crystalline grace of Mozart, and the light ordered gaiety of Haydn (and be sorry for father and mother who'd never been to a concert in their lives). Now, when he was standing by Dermot's side, in the front row of the crowd, he really understood why Haydn and Mozart showed the classical spirit at its best; because, in their music, a vitality, spontaneous and eager, was disciplined into formal beauty. But if Old Uncle Haydn and the Young Mozart were honoured and loved by these two boys, their great hero was Beethoven. 'Beethoven is my man,' Dermot would say, and Michael echoed him, not slavishly but sincerely. In the symphonies of Beethoven there was a storming after something transcendent and glorious; a rush and upsurge of romantic dreams and exultant fantasies that almost broke the bands of formal beauty— crashing, crashing, crashing, and yet disciplined, just disciplined, and therefore lovely. And all this caught the heart of Michael till he too felt like bursting with delight. Standing by Dermot's side, in the van of the crowd, or seated with him on the floor, among the legs of the people, he would lose himself in dreams of greatness and fame. What manner of fame would be his? His open adhesion to a hated sect had probably injured his prospects in any career outside the little separated world of his Party. Very well. The Party must triumph, and, with it, Michael Townes—Michael Townes becoming perhaps one of its famous leaders, orators, writers, or statesmen. Listening with eyes at gaze upon the conductor, or upon the floor, he sometimes felt within him such a pressure of future achievement that it wafted him away into an ecstatic dream-state where Michael Townes was one of the great ones of the earth, his name inscribed among the immortals. Dreams such as these he was ashamed to speak of, even to Dermot.

It was not different at the ballet. Inevitable that these two zealots for music should be zealots for the ballet also, for were not the two arts sisters, children of the same god, the one aural, the other visual, and both entrancing? At the ballet Dermot and he would sit at the back of the stalls, where the price was within their means; and here Michael would find the solo dances entrancing enough, but, strangely, it was the perfection of simultaneous movement, in a quartet or octet of dancers, or in the whole corps de ballet, that filled him with a breath-taking delight and, at the same time troubled and disturbed him, charging him with a sadness at the imperfections of the world and the impermanence of beauty, and with a hunger to create something beautiful himself—Heaven knew what, but something which would approach perfection, and endure.

CHAPTER SIX

THE fascination which had drawn Harry to look at Michael's 'Leader' was considerably (and secretly) heightened by his sight of that dark handsome face. Those hundreds of black-shirted youths, too, some quite attractive, others repulsive, many rather frightening, had for him something of the fascination of alarm. And when, one morning at breakfast, as the family sat around the table in the living room, Michael began to talk about a huge meeting that his Movement was going to stage in the Great Exhibition Hall, 'the largest indoor meeting London had ever seen'; and when he said that there'd be banners and bands and trumpets, and that he himself would walk behind the Leader, being now one of the principal officers, and that the Leader would be the only speaker but, great orator that he was, he would probably 'speak for two hours without a note'; then Harry was quite eager to attend. And when Michael added that the Reds would certainly be there with their knuckle-dusters and razors and lead-loaded stockings, because for weeks past their papers had been publishing incitements to 'Smash the Fascist Rally' and half the walls in London had this slogan painted on them, and, furthermore, the Communist Party had scattered leaflets all over East London announcing a 'Mass Assembly' at Stepney Green on the night of the meeting and a 'March against Fascism'; and when, with eyes alight, he explained that, while there were no certain ways of keeping them out of the hall, there were plentiful ways of slinging them out, why then Harry's eagerness to attend was something much greater than he wanted Michael to see. He turned to Ida and asked, with a mouth not empty of bacon and bread. 'How would you like to go, Mother, eh? Just to see what these boys are up to?'

'Why on earth should we go?' asked Ida, pouring herself another cup of tea. 'We don't hold with them.'

'Heavens, no—but——' Harry played with the sugar spoon

in its basin, as if looking for an excuse there—'but one should hear all sides. I always say *that*.'

'Oh, yes, *do* come!' Michael pleaded. As a convert to Catholicism will long to take his family to a great Mass that they may see how splendid are the ceremonies, so Michael longed for father, mother and Beth to see his new religion now when it was going to present itself before the world arrayed in magnificence and tremendous in power. He longed also for them to hear the Leader whose eloquence seemed to him so wonderful. 'I'll get you fine tickets. *I* can get you the very best seats,' he added proudly. 'I'm now in a position to do so.'

'Well, what do you say, sweetheart?' asked Harry of Ida. 'I've never seen this Leader of his.' The lie spoke itself, in his great eagerness; and he was surprised at it and ashamed of it. Nevertheless he went on, 'I'd like to see him once in my life.'

'I don't want to go if there's going to be a lot of fighting,' said Ida—which left him pondering on the difference between women and men.

'And certainly *I* don't,' said Beth. 'You can wash Beth out, if there's going to be fighting.'

Extraordinary.

'I hate rowdy scenes,' the girl explained.

And to him the words 'rowdy scenes' were like a bell calling him!

'There won't be any severe fighting, I promise you,' said Michael. 'We'll see to that.'

His father's heart sank in disappointment. 'Why not?'

'Because at the first hint of organised interruption we shall sling 'em out by the scruff of the neck and the seat of their pants.' His father's heart recovered.

'Well, if they're Red hooligans, I don't mind in the least.' It was good to be agreeing with the boy. 'Kick 'em out with my compliments. Now then, Mum: what do you say? Will you come? I shall want to have someone with me. Shan't enjoy it alone.'

'Enjoy!'

'Well, you know what I mean. Enjoy this man's speech.'

'I shouldn't mind hearing him, if he's all that Mike says, but you know we can't both get away of an evening.'

'Oh, yes, we can. Walter and Old Agnes'll be there and I'll get Bensky in. Come along; we must have some fun together sometimes.'

'Well . . . yes . . . between you and me, I wouldn't mind going—"between you and I" I mean.' Ida had a strange belief that 'me' in most sentences was both ungrammatical and ungenteel. And though it came naturally to her to say correctly 'between you and me' or 'different from you and me', she always corrected it hastily into the abomination, 'between you and I' or 'from you and I', and felt properly ladylike again. 'It's nice to get away from them all once in a blue moon, I *must* say, between you and I.'

'Yes; and Thursday's a slack night. The lads have spent all their wages by Thursday and have to drink water out of their taps.'

'It's not natural to be cooped up here for ever,' Ida continued, musing aloud rather than speaking to the others.

'That's right, ducky.' And he quoted one of her favourite phrases. 'It's only natural to let oneself go, once in a way. Okay, Mike; that's settled. The old gentleman and the old lady'll come.' He turned to his daughter. 'And Beth?'

'No.' The girl looked at her plate. 'Beth'd like to see Michael in all his glory, but she'd better be here to help the others.' Which, though spoken merrily, was an exact expression of her secret heart. She *would* have liked to go with father and mother, now that Michael had assured them that there'd be no serious fighting, but she felt it her duty (if she was ever to overcome her beastliness and make herself better) to offer up her desires on the altar of other people's happiness. 'I shall quite enjoy being in charge.'

'Do you really mean that, Beth, ducks? Nobody ever knows what our Beth is really thinking.'

'Of course I mean it.'

'All right then. Get us two tickets, son.'

'What price tickets do you want? Half a dollar? Seven and six?'

'My God! Do we have to pay? Don't I get in free, as your old man?'

'Sorry, Dad; no. But I'll undertake to get you the finest seats for the money.'

'Well, I want to be somewhere where I can see everything.' He added quickly, 'And hear everything. Get us two seven-and-a-tanners.'

'Right-ho, Dad.'

70

'Fifteen bob! Hell, one could get twenty-three whiskies for that.'

§

If Ida went anywhere in public, she devoted two hours at least to the grooming and caparisoning and adorning of her fine massy shape, from head and breast to hips and heels. If it was an evening affair to which she was going, this necessity to look well in public threw a kind of blight backwards and laid waste much of the afternoon. For hours she walked about the private parts of the Lord of Wensley in dressing-gown and bedroom slippers, with her hair in pins. And, even so, the adornment was seldom complete when it was time to start.

Today, as Harry paced up and down an empty bar, waiting for her to appear, Beth, from behind the counter, said, 'Gosh, Mum doesn't half take a time about dressing.' But Harry, consulting his watch, reminded her, 'Well, you see, darling, she has a devil of a lot to cover, both upstairs and down. And today Mike has fairly put the breeze into her sails by talking about an audience of ten thousand. Dammit, she wants to give 'em a treat.'

All of which was kind and understanding, but when, after another ten minutes, another fifteen minutes, she still did not appear, Harry, glancing at his watch for the ninth time, sighed and whistled and said to Mrs. Benskin, who was now behind the counter with Beth, 'I hope you realise, Bensky, that every married man spends twenty five per cent of his life waiting for women. And, anyhow, you're smoking too much. That's one fag too many.'

'Oh, go along with you, Guv!'

'Yes, I quite understand that they've got to paint their lips and twist a curl here and there, and swing their backsides this way and that to see that everything's hanging properly—I quite see that it takes time—but I don't grasp why it takes hours. Ah, but here she is. At last. My God . . . but it was worth waiting for!'

Ida had come into the bar in a black coat and skirt with gold buttons, a white blouse whose frills foamed down the long declivity of her breast, an imitation fox fur, and—somewhat boldly for a woman of fifty—a white straw hat trimmed with spring flowers.

71

'Well, that's fine, Mrs. Townes,' he complimented her. 'And tell me, ducks—I never want flattery—but do I too look a howling gent?'

'I've seen worse,' she said. 'You'll pass in a crowd.'

'Good. Well, good-bye, all. Bensky, keep an eye on Walter and don't let him go standing any of his pals a pint of my beer. I'm but a poor man. And don't smoke too much, yourself. 'Bye, Agnes dear.'

All wished them good-bye and said 'Have a good time,' to which Harry replied, 'You bet we will!' and after extending an arm and saying 'Heil Hitler' and 'Sieg heil,' went out, joyously, with Ida to this fascist Jamboree. The awareness of particularly good clothes always affected Ida's posture, and she now sailed along the High Road with her bosom well forward, her back straight and her head high. And if Ida was feeling very much the lady, Harry too was conscious of his best bowler hat, best blue suit, and silver-topped cane. They were two persons well satisfied with their appearance, and the only difference in their carriage was that Ida's big bosom advanced handsomely before her, but it was Harry's stomach that went slightly in front of the rest of him, its prominence festooned with a heavy gold watch-chain.

'You don't really think there'll be any trouble, do you?' said Ida, as they neared the Underground station.

'If there is,' said Harry, and he lifted the silver-knobbed cane, 'this stick's as good as a cosh any day.'

'Oh, don't go getting involved in any rows, Harry. You know what you are.'

'I shan't go looking for trouble, you can be sure of that,' he promised. 'But if it comes to meet me . . . well, I mean to say! I take nothing lying down.'

'Oh, Harry, do be careful. . . . I suppose we were right to go?'

§

Directly they turned into the road that ran past the Exhibition Hall they saw in the distance a crowd of many thousands swaying and jamming and coagulating, as mounted policemen, some of whose horses were actually on the pavement, strove to push them backwards from the approaches to the hall.

They heard the uproar of voices—men and women hooting or shouting abuse at the police, or chanting 'Down with Fascism!' and 'We want that Leader, dead or alive!', or singing the Red Flag. Many times this din of voices was pierced by the screams of women who feared to be crushed by their neighbours or trampled or scuffled by the horses. Placards with Communist slogans waved like the sails of junks above that sea of heads, so turbulently ebbing.

Those who had tickets for the meeting were moving in a dense stream towards the doors, between two cordons of police. Harry and Ida joined the back of this stream, and soon were but units compressed in a mass. And never, surely, was a stream so sluggish as this. It moved so slowly that Harry at first complained, 'What the hell's holding us up?' and then fell to swearing intermittently. It took them twenty minutes to get to the doors, and then they saw what the obstruction was. Two cordons of Blackshirt boys, arms linked, were holding back the pressure of the crowd like policemen (no doubt very happy to play at policemen) and allowing only a few to pass at a time, so that their tickets or their faces could be scrutinised.

'What's the idiotic sense of that?' grumbled Harry. 'They can't stop the Reds getting in if their tickets were offered to the public. Perhaps they want to search some of us. Got a cosh down your bosom, love? My God, I'll knock anyone silly who lays a hand on you—or me.'

But Ida did not answer; she was perturbed lest the crushing should spoil her dress, and every now and then she murmured 'Oh dear!' and 'Oh, gracious,' or even, softly (because she didn't like vulgarity), 'Oh, damn.'

'Well, it's all fun,' he comforted her.

They got through at last and were handed from one extremely polite Blackshirt boy to another, till the last put them in their seats near the front of a high gallery, and left them with a smile.

'Not bad boys, really,' said Harry.

'I thought that last one was charming,' said Ida, arranging her dress. 'But why are they wearing gloves indoors?'

Gloves. Harry looked back upon the stewards. Yes, some of them were wearing kid gloves. He had an inspiration. 'I wonder if it's to hide iron rings on their fingers.'

'But why iron rings?'

'In lieu of knuckle-dusters,' he explained cheerfully.

'Oh, dear.' Ida looked again at those gloves. 'I rather wish I hadn't come.'

Harry's feeling was the opposite.

He glanced round the enormous hall. People were pouring in rivulets down the raked gangways to their seats, but not enough of them, it would seem, to crowd the hall completely. Michael had talked quite a deal of ballyhoo. In every gangway, except the central alley up the floor, Blackshirt stewards stood at the end of each alternative row. That central alley, unguarded and empty, streamed straight to the empty platform, carrying the eyes to it.

This platform was brilliantly lit under hanging 'billiard-table' lights. High above it the largest Union Jack Harry had ever seen was stretched taut, and from its base hung gold curtains like the dossal behind an altar. By now the audience was certainly crowding tier upon tier, to the very roof, so that Harry, looking above him, saw a great cloud of witnesses—pale faces in the dusk, beneath a ring of lamps that shone in the zenith like stars. Harry thought of the Colosseum under the Roman sky.

Somewhere, at some invisible console, an organist was playing a fantasia of old English airs, and suddenly stopped them—stopped them in the middle of a bar—and broke into another tune. This tune was unfamiliar to Harry and apparently to many others; but not to the devout: they immediately began to sing. Harry couldn't hear the words, but his neighbour, who wore a fascist badge, courteously passed him his song-sheet and pointed to a verse. Then Harry heard:

> Leader, Leader of thousands!
> Hope of our manhood, we proudly hail thee.
> Raise we the song of allegiance,
> For we are sworn and we shall not fail thee . . .
> Only through our Revolution
> Comes the revival of Britain at last . . .

'Good God!' whispered Harry. 'Did you ever hear such ——' The word he used was not 'muck.' It was a word for which Ida in her bar, disliking all vulgarity, would have demanded, not threepence for the blind box, but a dollar at least, and an apology.

As the chorus ended there came a silence, and then a great cheer as a drum-and-fife band entered from the back, bringing

74

a procession of stewards to that central alley. These dropped to their stations at the ends of the rows and so formed an avenue of young black figures. Now up this avenue, to much cheering, came the black flags, the Union Jacks, and the standards of the branches. They arrayed themselves on the platform in two masses, leaving an empty space between them. This space shone in the floodlights—and waited.

'That's the pitch, I suppose,' said Harry, thinking of days at the Oval with Michael. 'Looks a nice pitch. Well, the fieldsmen are in place; I suppose the batsmen come from the pavilion now.'

He had hardly said this when four trumpeters took up a position beneath the platform and, raising their silver instruments to their lips, sounded a fanfare. Instantly all eyes turned to the entry at the back; the whole audience rose as if to a king, and Harry was annoyed that he lacked the courage not to; spotlights from near the roof converged upon the entry; and, to the largest cheer of all, including a rah-rah college yell by the devout, the Leader entered. Stern, unsmiling, marching erect, in his black shirt, grey breeches and top boots, he walked up the centre to the platform, all the stewards giving him, as he passed them, the full Fascist salute. He was followed by some of his principal officials with whom, walking modestly behind all—even one pace behind that young Dermot with his scar—was Michael.

Pride inflated his mother's heart. 'Oh, he looks rather sweet, you *must* say. That black shirt does suit his fair hair so.'

'He looks damn silly to me.'

'Oh, no——'

'Yes, and so does that damned Dermot.'

'They must think a lot of him if they've made him one of their chief officers—our Mike.'

'They must be damned hard up.' Harry's nostrils suggested that this was a far more likely explanation. 'Him and that Dermot—officers!'

'I always said Mike was clever. They must think so too. Oh, but, Harry, it's rather wonderful at his age!' Ida, having no interest in current politics, had no great dislike for this manifestation of them. 'Don't you think it's rather wonderful?'

'No, rather shameful.'

The Leader had mounted the platform alone, leaving his officers to sit in the front seats before him. Michael was now

75

out of sight beneath the gallery. The Leader turned with military smartness and gave the Fascist salute to the whole hall.

'Good God, where are we?' muttered Harry. 'Nuremberg?'

The cheering and applause died. The whole arena waited. Waited some seconds. It was like waiting, thought Harry, for the opening batsman to take the first ball of the match. What was the man going to do with it?

Then, standing there in his floodlit isolation, without lectern or note, he began to speak.

The first words beat upon and bruised every ear-drum in the hall. Over-amplified by a battery of loud-speakers, they so shocked the ears of Ida that she loosed a little scream, then clapped her fingers over her mouth.

Hidden hands abated, gently, understandingly, the youthful fervour of the loud-speakers. The man, unworried, went on:

'Ladies and gentlemen, look around you at this vast amphitheatre. Never before, we believe, had so great an audience been assembled in a London hall to hear one single indifferent speaker. How is it that we of the Blackshirts alone can command such assemblies? Let me tell you. Look around now—not at this hall; no, close your eyes and look around you at the state of our country. Look fearlessly; and what do you see? Our people, our great and heroic people, crowded into slums or semi-slums; their children, if not starved, under-nourished; their menfolk, to the tune of millions, unemployed and wasting in despair; and everywhere the Usurers enforcing this state of things for the sake of their own profits. It is not the business of Big Business, ladies and gentlemen, nor of the Big Banks, to consider the interests of our country and its people—why should they?—they are international and work for their own interests only.'

Harry, listening, recognised the fount from which Michael drew his draughts of eloquence. Indifferent speaker indeed! This man was a platform orator, if ever there was one. Every modulation of his fine voice, every gesture of hands or shoulders, proved his genius for platform or stage. The very rhythm of his voice, the very grace of his movements, seemed to put to sleep all critical power in his followers and awake only Dionysiac enthusiasm. He had but to smile faintly for them to roar with laughter; but to raise his voice at a climax for them to cheer and clap and stamp their feet.

'Who shall liberate us from these hidden despots, these grey

76

eminences? Parliament? Ha!' A roar of contemptuous laughter endorsed his 'Ha!' 'Parliament can either dethrone them or truckle to them. Which does it do? Plainly it is content to be their instrument. Consider the Tories in the field, how they blow.' (Loud laughter.) 'I do not say that every Tory M.P. is corrupt. I suggest merely that they are ambitious men and know that the hopes of their Party depend entirely on the support of these great vested interests, and since they seek a career, they are careful to be good obedient boys. The Socialists? Is there any hope there? Which do the Labour members obey, you their constituents, or the great Trade Unions who pay them for their piping? The answer is obvious. Ladies and gentlemen, "M.P." today stands for Money Power.'

An uproar of cheers.

'The Press? Our so-called free Press? Let me ask you: what chance has an opponent of these, our real masters, to found a national newspaper in conditions where mass circulation has reached such a point that no newcomer can hope to succeed unless he has a million of money? I grant you that we are allowed to creep into the correspondence columns so long as we don't say anything they don't want.' (Laughter.)

'And who are these men with the millions? Are there any representatives of youth among them? Very few, I fancy. This power over us is in the hands of old men—old men who do not want change, first because the present system suits them well enough, and secondly because they are old—old—and no longer capable of new ideas. Our fates, our lives, are in the hands of grasping or stupid old men, all over fifty——'

Here Harry, who so far had been listening, not without some unwilling agreement, sat up as if a stray bullet had struck him. He was fifty-seven.

'I do not say that they are evil old men—not all of them. Some are just stupid, but most are greedy and——'

But now a satirical voice from the midst of one of the tiers called out, 'Excuse me, sir, but will you kindly——' This was the first hint of interruption, and a hint was all that it had time to be. A rush of young stewards bore down like a burst of waters upon the heckler, who in his unwisdom was standing up to put his question, and they seized him by the arms and the collar and bundled him out of his place and up the gangway to the doors, while all near him stood up to see. More extraordinary, the spotlights which had been resting on the speaker swept round their great fingers of light and laid them on this scuffle. Their splays of light followed in like a circlet of interested children as far as the door ; then bade good-bye to the ejectors and ejected and returned to look upon the speaker. So unexpected was this behaviour that Harry stood up to study it. Instantly a steward in his gangway called, 'Sit down, *you*!' and Harry was so enraged at a youth addressing him in this way that he hissed, 'Don't you talk to *me*.'

'You'll sit down if you don't want to be put out of the meeting,' said the boy.

Good saints above and twenty devils!—but the boy moved away so as not to give Harry the satisfaction of answering him. He never knew what he missed.

'My *God*!' muttered Harry, and slowly sat down.

The speaker on the platform had kept silence till his interrupter was convincingly expelled and the people were seated again. He must have maintained a silence of two minutes or more. To the chafing Harry this seemed unnecessarily dramatic because his battery of loud-speakers could easily have defeated any unamplified voice, or any number of voices, in this great vaulted space. When he did speak again it was to say, 'If there are any more Reds in the hall who are not sheltering behind their women, let them take good note how their interruptions will be handled.'

'Oh, to hell!' murmured Harry, and he longed to shout, 'Who said he was a Red?' and 'A man may speak,' but Ida laid a nervous and beseeching hand upon his knee.

'Now let us proceed in peace,' continued the speaker, to the laughter of the sycophants. 'We are quite clear, ladies and gentlemen, that the great instruments of Power arrayed against us can be overthrown only by a new instrument, an instrument of steel——'

'Ah,' thought Harry, 'I've heard that one before.'

'—and such an instrument, largely forged by our deprived, exploited, and frustrated youth, we have in our Party, where every man is sworn to a stern discipline and expected to sink his own desires in the service of others. In the service of you, ladies and gentlemen, who, whether you know it or not, are the mere driven herds of our financial overlords. In the service of our great country which we so love. In the service of Europe too, for the international Fascist struggle seeks——'

But Harry, anger still fuming and clouding his mind, was hardly listening any more. He was staring across the hall at the parapet of the gallery opposite, to which streamers were fixed with Blackshirt slogans: 'All for Britain,' 'We fight for Freedom and for Bread,' and 'Tomorrow We Live.' The voice of the speaker was but a wordless and undulating music far away. Until, suddenly, a voice from that gallery opposite yelled out 'You're telling *me*!' and Harry realised that this scoffing utterance was in retort to the words, 'Our great movement, with its army of disciplined and devoted young men, represents something new in the political life of our country——'

Proud of his retort the man shouted a variant of it. '*I'll* say it is!' Like the previous interrupter, he was standing in his place, a big-bodied, middle-aged, red-faced man, anxious to utter a good deal more. Unlike his predecessor, he looked anything but innocuous, and immediately all the stewards who could get to him stormed along the passages and down the stairs and closed upon him. They started to hustle him up the gangway and off the field of play. A searchlight swung to this new tussle and floodlit it, so that Harry, seated opposite saw all. He saw some of the young stewards, who hadn't the pleasure of gripping tight the offender's arms, strike him on his back and his shoulders with their fists. One of them was reaching forward with a gloved fist and bringing it down upon his head and his cheek.

'Here!' Harry was standing up in protest, while Ida was pulling at his jacket and saying, 'No! Don't speak. Don't speak. They'll set on you too. Oh, let's go—*go*.'

'Here!' Not listening to her, he pointed a finger of denunciation at the scene. 'That's not good enough!'

Two stewards came towards him, but they did not act—perhaps not liking the way he seized the base of his silver-knobbed stick, or the look in his eyes. They said only, 'Shut up, or you'll get some of the same treatment.'

'*Me?*'

'Yes, you.'

'Not from you. Not from little bastards like you.'

'Sit *down*,' begged Ida in anguished tones. 'Oh, why did we come?'

Meantime, to drown wide murmurings of disapproval, a phalanx of the devout were chanting repeatedly, 'We want the Leader. L.E.A.D.E.R.' and Harry bawled at them, 'You can

79

have him and keep him;' but fortunately for his safety the words were overlaid by the general din. He sat down slowly, deploring, 'My God! My God!'

The searchlight, having escorted the interrupter to the door, swung back to the speaker on the platform. Who continued, 'Let me tell this great and friendly audience that we expected these interruptions. We knew full well that numbers of Red firebrands were coming on purpose to spoil this meeting, and we are ready with the punishment which they assuredly deserve. It may interest them to know that we are quite grateful for these interruptions because they demonstrate to all you fair-minded people how necessary was the formation of our Defence Force. And now may I proceed? I ask this audience tonight, Do we go on being the shorn cattle of a few great financial farmers, or to-morrow do we live? Will you join us in offering everything you have within you in holy dedication to the service and salvation of Britain? Will you help us to build in this beloved Britain of ours a higher form of civilisation than the world has yet known——'

'Oh, come off it!' This was called out by a man seated only a few places from Harry and Ida. He added a word of contempt that certainly should not have been shouted in public, and prepared to leave in disgust. But he was not allowed to go unpunished. He was a roughly-dressed working man of thirty or so, and perhaps the stewards who had refrained from assaulting Harry thought him better meat and younger meat for their appetites. They rushed to him, and he struck out with a splendid right-hook at the first to arrive, almost sending him to the floor. Since he was of cruiser-weight size and, judging by this excellent blow, a boxer, another steward blew a police whistle, which brought a stampede of blackshirts from all parts to answer a call to justice. The spotlight came round to play upon the scrimmage, while the Leader stood still, one hand upon an elegant hip, saying nothing. The man was dragged by his captors up the gangway, receiving blows from all as he went. Several punched him on the face. He was gasping, blood trickled from his nose and lip, and one arm struggled to protect his head. To the exit they dragged him, the spot-light following dispassionately. They ran him out into the corridor, whose door did not immediately close so that Harry saw him thrown to the ground out there and kicked by all who could get a foot to him. He saw others run up; not to miss what their fellows were enjoying. 'Here! I can't stand this,' he cried, and grasping his stick furiously, struggled past the neighbouring knees to go to the man's rescue, but a young steward left in the gangway faced him. 'Sit down,' he commanded. 'Better for you if you sit down.'

'Mind your own business. If I see a man hurt I go to his help.'

'Perhaps you want some of it yourself?'

'Harry, Harry!'

'Seen you before at our meetings.'

'That's a lie.'

'You came to bust this meeting up.'

'I did not. Get out of my way, you little turd. Take your filthy hands off me.' Harry was now conscious that the spotlight was resting on him—on him and Ida!—and as if to justify this publicity he lifted his stick on high threatening the lad who presumed to manhandle him.

'Blackshirts, Blackshirts,' called the lad, 'here's another of them,' and stewards from the passage and gangway—and back from the corridor outside—came swarming down upon Harry. Remembering the excellent example of the bruiser who'd preceded him, he flung a straight-left at the chin of the nearest and saw, with joy—his last moment of joy—the young tough go crashing down on to his back.

'Let him have it. Punish him: he's asked for it. Twist his arm. Get that stick from him.' For Harry, shoulders to ears, back rounded, lips turned in towards his teeth, looking rather like a gorilla, was flailing around with his stick but whether or not he dented any sconces, they overpowered him, gripping his wrists and arms, while one got a clutch round his neck and forced his head backward. And so they dragged him out for punishment, while Ida screamed, her shrieks overlaid by the hundred-voiced roar: 'We . . . want . . . the Leader.' 'Let him go!' she screamed, and 'Oh, oh, oh!' and 'Brutes, brutes, *brutes*!'

One steward would not take this slander. He turned and said, 'Shut up, you old cow.'

'Oh!' She went towards them all—not knowing what for—to pummel them, to fight for Harry, to trounce the boy who'd called her a cow—but he, as she buffeted him, summoned help with his arm, and some women stewards, in black shirts, came tearing down, as willingly as the men, and set upon her. They treated her as their brothers were treating Harry, gripping her by arm-pit, elbow, collar, or wrist, and when she struggled, screaming to the high roof and even rejoicing to 'let herself go,' they fought like claw-bearing cats, so that her white-frilled blouse was ripped, the slip beneath it torn, and her great breast exposed.

'Oh, oh,' she screamed, panting, as they dragged her past up-risen and protesting people; but mingled with her terror and her pains was a pleasure that not all the rah-rah chanting in the hall could drown these screams she was 'letting them have.' In this she was a conqueror. The searchlight abruptly quitted her, probably thinking it wiser to concentrate all eyes on the platform. Harry, in the corridor, hearing her screams, fought and struggled with his belabouring captor, like an ink-spitting octopus in a net, till one of them gave him a blow under the heart that knocked all the breath out of his body. He sank to the floor, gasping, whereupon several kicked him. He was powerless now to go to Ida's help, and what would have happened next he did not know; but a senior Blackshirt steward ran up and said, 'Stop it, you boys. Are you mad? You go too far. Let that lady go at once. I'm sorry, sir, they've had real provocation and have completely lost their heads.' He stretched forth a hand to help him rise.

Harry could not speak, but gazed like a thrashed child at Ida.

§

Outside the hall great crowds had massed, and mounted police were slowly 'moving them on'. Harry, his head a furnace of anger, his mouth taut, forced an impatient way through them till he came into a quiet stretch and found a taxi. To the driver he said, 'There's a woman hurt in that damned hall. There's murder being done in there. It's a bloody slaughter-house. Can you drive us to Balham?' The driver, both interested and compassionate, said at once, 'Certainly, sir. Hop in,' and drove to a side door, as the kindly senior steward had advised. Re-entering the building, Harry walked along a corridor to a room which had been turned into a dressing station. There Ida sat, shivering with shock, a blanket about her shoulders.

'Come on, sweetheart,' he said, and gently took her by the hand.

'But I can't go out like this,' she objected, staring at him foolishly and dragging herself back. 'I can't. Look at me.

And here she saw an opportunity for another of those 'scenes' in which she rejoiced. 'Oh, my clothes, my clothes. They're ruined, ruined. Everything I've got on is ruined——'

He looked at her ripped blouse and uncovered bosom. 'Oh, well, I don't care what *I* look like,' he said, and furiously drew off his blue jacket and dressed her in it. 'There you are, sweetheart. I'll be better in shirt-sleeves if there's going to be any more fighting to do.'

'Oh, no, no,' she moaned. 'Don't take me into any more fighting. Oh, why did we come?'

'You'll be all right.' He put a supporting arm around her back. 'Come on, lovey.'

He helped her to the taxi, and all the way home held her by the hand, patting it sometimes. At home he gave her brandy in the bar and saw her into bed. Then went alone into the living room and waited for Michael.

§

Up and down the living-room he paced; up and down with hands gripped behind his back and at times crushing one another. Never such a damned-up storm within him. It must break out before he could even sit in a chair. *He* to have been submitted to that! He, not some little Red hooligan boy. He, fifty-seven years old, and a man of substance and position. To have been 'punished,' as they said, by youths whom he wouldn't have employed as potboys. He who'd been a sergeant-major before whom such whipsters had trembled; who, commanding the battalion once, had taken 'Orders,' when little twenty-year-olds like them had been marched up before him for punishment, with their caps off. The more he thought of it, the more he ached to go back and find those boys . . . but this could never be. No receptacle for his wrath anywhere but Michael.

And his wife, *his* wife, to have been dragged like some street harridan, and her clothes torn off her back—oh, my God, my God! Certainly his indignation at this thought was coming second to his fury at the violences done to his own dignity, but it was an enormous indignation, none the less. And it swelled till it was an actual pain in his head. For he believed to a high degree that a man must be chivalrous and fight anyone

83

who insulted his woman. That Ida, his Ida, should have been—oh, why didn't Michael come?

But Michael did not come. An hour passed, and two, and three, without sound of a key at the door or a step on the stair. He looked often from the window, but never a sign of the boy. He went sometimes without hope to the street door and stepped out on to the pavement—but no: the Balham High Road, which in the day-time rattled and trembled under the traffic, crooning its endless song of wheels and horns and engines—this long broad road which was no parochial link but a wide canal for the streaming traffic of the world lay for an hour or two quiet and almost empty under its marching lamps. A late lorry went by; and some late hurrying cars. Far away along the pavement a policeman walked languidly from shop door to shop door trying their locks, and flashing his light on shuttered windows. His were the only footsteps in the road.

Was Michael not coming at all?

Two o'clock. Three o'clock. He took his balked pain up to his bed and lay by Ida's side, but could not sleep. The violent scenes of the evening played themselves between his closed eyes and sleep. Beneath his windows the traffic of the world began again, purring and sighing and rocking the house, but still he lay awake, recreating those scenes, and tossing with a fury unreleased.

CHAPTER SEVEN

AFTER the excitements of the meeting, Michael and many of the stewards had gone to the Black House that they might talk and talk for half the night about the various fights and fracas in which the Red toughs had got all they asked for and possibly a little bit more. Stewards from all over England were being lodged in the Black House for that night, and when at last they should go to their beds, it would be to palliasses laid side by side on the floor. For they were young men and ready to lie hard. Meanwhile they talked and talked. Michael, since his seat had been under his parents' gallery, had not seen the spotlight playing on them, nor, thanks to the *fortissimo* chanting behind him, had he recognised any screams as his mother's. And everything that he was hearing now justified (because he wanted it to) the measures of punishment which his friends had applied to the Reds. They showed him the weapons they had reft from the Reds: rubber coshes, spiked knuckle-dusters, mounted razor blades, and old cut-throat razors. He looked at these trophies and was justified. Proof here that they'd come to make violent trouble—and had got it. Overpowered and out-numbered they had been defeated at every point and shot out into the night. He longed to go home and brag to his parents of the victory. He longed to hear what they thought of the Leader's magnificent speech and his mighty peroration, after the Reds had been swatted like wasps. Surely his father had been impressed.

In the morning he had to go to the Black Bookshop and help his editor-in-chief prepare his account of the meeting, but all the time he was aching to get home and hear all, and justify all. He made a point of getting back soon after three, because then the bars would be closed to the public and he could have some quiet minutes with his parents before they went to their bedroom for their afternoon sleep.

Yes, the house was closed when he arrived, and the bars empty, so evidently the cleaning and restocking was done, and his parents upstairs. He hurried up to the living-room and there saw his father finishing his late meal and his mother and Beth clearing away the plates and cutlery.

'Hallo,' he began.

No one answered a word.

'Hallo, folks.' He spoke louder and with an exaggerated jollity, because he was not without fear that they might have disapproved of some of the violence last night.

His father laid down his cheese knife and rose.

'Well . . .?' It was the tone of a man who says, 'What have you to say for yourself.'

'You don't seem very cheerful. Isn't everyone happy?'

'It's no good riling the boy,' suggested Ida sadly, as she went to the sideboard and pulled open a drawer.

'What? Didn't you enjoy our little gathering last night?'

'Do you know,' demanded his father, 'that your mother had the clothes torn off her back by a mob of your viragos? Your mother?'

'Yes, actually torn off,' said Beth, who had ministered in a passion of pity to Ida on her return. 'I've never seen anything like it. It's too terrible.'

'Mother? Good gracious! Why?'

Harry, glad that he'd mentioned Ida first, now came to the matter of himself. 'And that I was dragged out by a dozen ruffians and thrown to the floor and kicked?'

'No! Good lord, no! Oh lord, I'm sorry.'

Sorry! Evidently the boy didn't realise the fullness of the outrage. 'Your mother was in a state of collapse.'

'But why? I don't understand. Did you interrupt?'

'I rose to protest against the foul treatment your thugs were meeting out to anyone who dared even ask a question. I don't stand by and watch bullying. I never have.'

'It wasn't foul. It was absolutely necessary. They'd have wrecked the meeting if we hadn't cleared out every Red——'

'Was I a Red?'

'I'm sorry if they made a mistake.'

But Harry didn't want to hear an apology; he wanted to speak the words that would hurt Michael most, just as in the old days he would yield to a craving to strike him for his rudeness, or for what in the army they used to call 'dumb insolence.' 'If you want to know what I think of your Leader, it's this: he's a maniac.'

Michael blanched. A wrath like his father's stood in his eyes. The eyes stayed very still.

'He ought to be put away as a danger to the community.' Harry, past wisdom, continued to strike. 'He's stirring up treason. "Laying down their lives for the Fascist Cause"— what can that mean but civil war? He ought to be locked up.'

Still staring into his father's eyes with a look steady and cold as the muzzle of a gun, Michael said, 'I will not stay and listen to words like that about the greatest Englishman this century has produced. I'll go out of the house if you dare speak of him like that again.'

'Michael!' Ida stood quite still with a pile of plates in her hands. 'Michael, what are you saying?'

Beth also stood quite still to watch and hear.

'If I dare! Hark at the boy. I'm to be dared to say what I think in my own house. Thank you, *no*! I repeat, the man's a political monster. Why, it's plain he's only out for power for himself——'

'And you can believe that of him?' said the staring Michael, softly.

'Of course I do. What are all you silly schoolboys but tools to get him what he wants——'

'Mother, will it be convenient if I pack what I can and go today? You could send the rest after me.'

'Michael, don't be absurd,' cried his mother. 'You know your father gets hot and doesn't mean half he says.'

'Me hot? I mean every word.'

'You must remember that he was kicked and knocked about, and no man likes that.'

'It's not only that he gets hot, Mother. It's that he's such an intolerable fool.'

'Gosh!' Beth clapped a hand over her mouth and looked at her father.

'Michael! *Please.* You mustn't. *No*, Harry, *NO!*'

For Harry had stepped towards the boy with fists hanging ready. Michael flinched, as he used to do when a child, but recovered, and then, without moving, looked coldly into his father's eyes. And his father could not lift a fist. 'A fool? I'm to be called a fool, am I, by an infant like this?'

'Well, what am I to say? Only a fool thinks that anyone who differs from him is mad or bad and ought to be put away. It's infantile.'

87

'My God, the boy can go if he wants. And I don't care a damn how soon.'

'Good.' Michael laughed. If his father chose to hurt him with hot words, he preferred to madden the man with his calmness. 'Then there's one point at least on which the excitable little man and I are agreed.'

'*Little?*'

'Michael, how dare you? And Harry, *will* you not say such things to the boy?' Ida stamped her foot at him. 'Michael, don't listen to him. Oh, why are men such fools? What does that silly man with his silly meeting matter? I'm sure that, with his top boots and his ridiculous salute, he reminded me more than anything else of a peacock strutting about. But if Michael likes to think him a god, let him. Don't let a ridiculous man posturing about in a ridiculous uniform come between us all.'

'I quite agree,' said Beth who, though suffering an agony of doubt lest Michael really meant to go, must always, in public, hide her love beneath words of satire. 'Why doesn't this man, whoever he is, grow up?'

Michael moved dramatically towards the door. 'I am going. I really am. I've long had it in mind to go. It's clear I'm alone in this house——'

'*No*, Michael,' cried Beth, the agony and love bursting through.

'You all join in slandering a man just because you're incapable of understanding him. Ah, well. . . . Luckily I know where I can go.'

'Michael, come back!' cried his mother.

'Oh, no, I'm not staying. I'll go today. Just between you and me, I can't stand any more of that man. 'Bye, folks.'

'Michael!' This was almost a scream. Ida was on the edge of one of her 'scenes'. 'You can't mean what you say. *No!* You're not alone in this house. I love you. So does your father.' She sank as if sick on to a chair. 'He always has. And you shouldn't call him "that man". Oh, why did we go to that awful meeting?'

'I'll get on with the washing up,' said Beth, who had quickly mended the rent in her cloak of satire, 'and then I'll go and write some letters. Let me know when you've all come to your senses.' She picked up the loaded tray and went out.

'Tell that girl to shut up,' said Harry—but too late. She was beyond the door.

Unable to shoot at her, a lost target, he fired sideways at Michael. 'And as for the boy, he can go where he likes. He's hurt me more cruelly than anyone else in my life.'

'Michael, you hurt your father. Calling him names.'

'Perhaps; but why does it never occur to old people that they can hurt young people? He's often called *me* a fool, and now he calls a man whom I happen to revere a maniac. I don't stay to listen to such things.' He moved nearer the door.

'Where are you going, Michael? Oh, oh!' Ida rose.

'Just as far from that man as I can get. Good lord, he talks of bullying, and what's he but a bellowing bully. I suppose it'll never penetrate his thick skull that he's no longer a sergeant-major, and that some of us feel no particular compulsion to tremble and obey, just because he yells. Personally I find him a comic figure——'

'Michael, take *care*!' Ida threw a frightened glance at Harry. 'Take care what you're *saying*.'

'I'm saying that he thinks he's necessarily right on every subject under the sun when really he's just about as ignorant and ill-informed——'

'Get *out*!' In Harry's eyes there was something very like a maddened child's tears.

'Oh, don't worry. I'm getting out. And for good and all, thank God.' It was true that Michael had long had a dream of getting away from home and living alone, somewhere near Dermot, but a desire to teach his father a lesson had bidden him wait till some such opportunity as this, when he could make an heroic exit, after giving full utterance to the resentments festering within him. But now that he'd chosen, like his mother so often, to 'let himself go', the anger, unbridled, was forcing him to say violent things which he must later live up to, if he was not to seem weak; and to seem weak, *vis-à-vis* his father, was something no longer possible to him. 'I'm sorry, Mother. I hope you and I will see each other sometimes—and Podge too—but as for Daddy, I've done with him. I'm through.'

And even as Francesco Bernadone (later to be known as St. Francis) cast off his clothes at his father's feet, and with them his patrimony, and walked out of the palace, so Michael walked calmly through that living-room door.

Ida flung herself back upon her chair and her head on to her arm. 'Oh, no, no, no.' Harry, his face very pale, walked towards her, put an arm along her shoulders, and patted them. 'Never mind, sweetheart. He'll come back.'

'He won't come back. You've driven him out. It's your fault. Your fault entirely.'

'Oh, my fault, is it? Be damned to that.' He moved away. 'Christ, I wish someone was on my side sometimes.'

'He'll never come back. He's as stubborn as you are.'

'Me stubborn? I'm not stubborn. I deny it.'

'Oh, yes, you are. The most stubborn person I know. . . . Michael . . . Michael, my boy . . . He'll never come back unless you apologise.'

'Unless I *what*? I'll see him in hell first.'

§

As Michael went out of the room into the passage, Beth, who'd been hiding there in the darkness, her tray of plates in her hands, scuttled away into a bedroom, out of everyone's sight. Here, as so often before, she waited, trembling, and listening to Michael. She heard him moving about in his room and knew that he was packing a bag. She heard Ida go into him and, after much impassioned talk, come rushing out, possibly to throw herself on her bed in despair. For thirty minutes Beth stood in that room, alone and wondering, the tray laid on a washstand beside her. When at length she heard him descending the stair, obviously with a heavy bag, she ran after him very softly, coming near to him in the hall.

'Hallo, Podge.' He had heard her, and he turned his head. There was little but sadness in his eyes.

'Michael, you're not really going, are you?'

'I certainly am.'

'No, Michael, *please*.'

'I don't want to leave you and Mum, but I'm not staying another day in this house with Father.'

'Oh, but he didn't mean anything he said. Forgive him, can't you? Yes. Forgive him. We're none of us perfect. *You* get hot too and say horrible things.'

'I can forgive him all right, but that doesn't mean I've got to stay and put up with him. I can forgive him because I understand him, but if ever there was a man who justified all we say about democracy, it's him. He's the type that any hired press can influence any way it likes. Did you ever see a better argument for some leadership and discipline in a nation?'

'Oh, never mind that.' That he should want to talk his wretched politics when she was longing to take him in her arms and press a kiss on his sad face—and on his lips! When her heart, palpitating, and her throat, athirst, and her body, quickened if shamefully, were all craving him! 'Michael, don't go. Think of Mother. . . . Think of . . . me. Please don't go.'

'I must, Podge. I'm glad things have come to a head at last. I feel ever so much happier now that I've broken with him.'

'Oh, don't say such things. Where will you go to?'

'I shall stay with Dermot at first——'

'Damn that Dermot.'

'Now, Podge, don't *you* start abusing my friends. Dermot's a good bloke.'

'I'm sure he is. I'm sure he's everything you say. But . . . we shall see you sometimes?'

'Podge darling, I shall love to see you and Mum—and even the old man one day, if he comes with a white flag.'

'*That'll* never happen.'

'No, I can't quite see it happening. Okay then; this is the final rupture. But not with Mum, and not with you.' He stooped to kiss her. 'God bless, Podge.'

She flung her arms around him because that word 'Podge darling,' which he'd never used before, and the faint sadness in his eyes, seemed to warrant her in doing so; and indeed he submitted to her willingly. Now at last she had him tight against her. She felt his body trembling in her arms and knew that her love, in such a moment, had shaken him to tears. That justified her in pressing him even tighter, and her pleasure in his body shamed her.

They broke apart at last; and—oh, so strangely—she was happy as he went out through the door. She walked to the step and watched him threading through the hurrying people in the Balham High Road, till she could see him and wave to him no more. Then she returned into the house with her heart buoyant and floating on air, like a girl who'd been kissed for the first time by the man she loved.

CHAPTER EIGHT

In West Kensington, just where the stucco houses end and the red-brick roads begin, there is a terrace of tall red mansions, somewhat over-dressed with white stone. The windows of their four stories look down the long stucco streets, and the dormer windows of their attics gaze over the world from among the red tiles. Ornate and lofty, they were designed for the last of the big Victorian families who, though no more than middle-class, had incomes ample enough to sustain substantial homes. Not forty years of life as 'family residences' did they enjoy; even before the first of the German wars, even in the beginning of this wild century, every floor had become the flat of some indigent and struggling household. 'Brittany Place' the terrace is called, and its face is as sad as that of any other creature who has failed in the world.

The cheapest of these flats, of course, were the dormered garrets under the tiles or the rooms in the deep basements. Dermot O'Néill had long had a room in the basement of No. 13, and now Michael made himself a home in the garret of No. 7. It pleased his dramatic sense to think that four miles of London now separated him from the Lord of Wensley and his youth, and that the broad waters of Thames rolled between him and his days of dependence. He furnished the bare boards with a few cheap pieces: an iron bed, a bit of rug, a washstand, cupboard, table and chairs. This bareness was no distress to him; it was swallowed up in his pride in 'having his own place'. He was proud of the view from his high window over an inland sea of chimneys and spires, and often at sundown, or perhaps in the night silence, he would stand and look southward over London towards that part where the Balham High Road must run like a canyon below the roofs, and his family were serving about the bars, or lying asleep. He was proud, too, of being able to say to his Blackshirt friends, 'Come round to my place. That's best. We can talk quietly there.' And then these disciples of his—'disciples' they might well be called, for he stood high in the Movement now—would come and sit on his bed and table and chairs, and plot and scheme with him, till their dull restricted London lives were turned into adventure and lit with the stage-light of conspiracy. In that low-roofed garret they were not ill-paid clerks or drab out-of-works, imprisoned by the bricks of an endless city, but soldiers in a bivouac on a battle's eve. One might liken them, these youths in a bare upper room, to Catholic Britons in Tudor or Caroline times. Save that they wanted, as patriots, to bring Britain into the European Fascist fold instead of into the fold of the Universal Church, their emotions were little different. Their politics were to them an all-possessing religion whose service was their love, their joy, and their game.

§

That room may have been small and bare, but Michael's ambitions were large and ever more and more agreeably furnished. Since both Dermot and he were now chief lieutenants of the Leader they were sometimes invited to the fine homes of his wealthy or aristocratic supporters. Michael now knew what it was to be served by butlers and lackeyed by valets, and he wished very much that his father knew that he knew. And since he was a fair-haired and well-favoured youth with a voice of much charm, and since he spoke on the party's platforms with apparent brilliance (after laboriously learning by heart every word and gesture) there were fine ladies in stately rooms who flattered and made much of him. One foolish woman, the ageing daughter of a baron, was clearly in love with him. He had enough taste—and enough self-distrust—not to be completely spoiled by this coddling and flattery, but he did begin to have dreams of a very high place (under the Leader, of course) in the Fascist State which was bound to come. No question that the Leader was the Napoleon of the Movement, but when, like that conqueror in 1804, he was chosen emperor by the will of the people, there should be a seat for Michael somewhere in his court. The present social system, let it say what it liked, offered few climbing ladders to boys who were heirs neither to money nor to power. Where was a ladder for him except in the Fascist Movement?— and this offered him, less a ladder than an automatic lift. His speeches, because he gave such pains to them, because he modelled them so carefully on his Leader's, and because he

93

possessed for their instrument so appealing a voice, had drawn from many an audience all the applause and cheering that his weakness hungered for—oh, if only his father could have heard it sometimes!—and surely this new reputation as one of the party's best young speakers justified his dreams.

Then, to increase his self-esteem, there was his travelling in Germany (paid for out of Party funds) and, above all, his visit one September to the Nuremberg Rally. These wonderful and unforeseen visits swelled his love of 'Germany' as a romantic idea, which had been begun by Bach and Beethoven and Haydn (for Austria was included in 'Germany'), and by Mozart and Schubert and Hugo Wolf; and yet further nourished and exalted by the philosophers and writers to whom Dermot had given him a fervent, and even fulsome, introduction: Kant, Hegel, Schopenhauer—Goethe, Lessing, Schiller. Michael studied translations of these, often with knitting brows, and sometimes with sighs of defeat—but what you study earnestly you grow to love.

As potent as any of these in swelling his sentimental love of 'Germany' was the kindly face and gentle breast of the land itself. He loved its rolling uplands so tidily cultivated, its dense forests and sweet aromatic pine woods, its Gothic cities and mediæval villages so like the coloured illustrations to a fairy tale. He loved to meet the happy, singing wanderers of the Wander-vögel, those tall blond lads who had escaped from factory bench or office stool, and in shorts and open shirts, with rucksacks slung, tramped along in loose procession, over the moors and through the pine woods, singing the songs of old Germany.

But greatest of all experiences for Michael and Dermot was the Nuremberg Rally, the Great Annual Convention of the Nazis. First they saw and loved the old city with its moat and bas-tioned walls, its crooked streets of half-timbered houses, with red roofs and steep gables, its churches of rich Gothic, and its old castle of the Margraves on a sandstone hill. From every window and turret on this day hung the flags and banners, red-white-and-black, of the Nazi Party. Then they stood in the vast arena where how many hundred thousand, packed between earth and sky, greeted their Fuehrer or sang to the music, or cheered the parades of Storm Troops and Hitler Youth —why, it made their great meeting in the Exhibition Hall seem like a Vestry! Who could doubt that here, as in other parts of Europe, was the Great Modern Faith that would leap the frontiers and possess the world?

But the atrocities—all this talk of atrocities by the present masters of Germany? What said Michael to them? His answer to such talk was hot—because insecure. These tales were lies, he said—propaganda put out by terrified Capitalist lords who must defeat a party that proposed their overthrow. Here and there some brutalities might have occurred, because Nazism and Fascism were Revolution, and revolutions always brought some fury and bloodshed. How about the atrocities of the Reds in Russia? And in Spain? Or to look nearer home—did not the British invent concentration camps, when they were crushing the humble Boers; did they not, when applying the iron hand to India, fire mutinous Sepoys from the mouths of their guns?

And so his love was only increased by all the attacks on the Beloved.

§

Michael lived in that garret two years and more—and then the bell rang over Europe. The warning bell, telling the nations to prepare for war. It was the fifteenth of March, and the world heard that at six in the morning of that day the armies of the German Fuehrer had crossed the frontiers of Czechoslovakia and a few hours later marched into Prague. Czechoslovakia, yesterday a free Slav nation, was now under a new master. But it was more than one frontier the Fuehrer had crossed that morning. He had crossed from Pan-Germanism, which many had been able to understand, and some to support, into regions of haughty imperial conquest. One more step on such a road, and the world was at war.

Michael, at six in the evening stood at his window looking over London while he justified to himself this tremendous step by a man who, as one of the three great leaders of Fascism, was (and must remain) one of his heroes. It was not too difficult to justify. Nationalism, he told himself, was an unworkable creed in the modern world, and the new Revolution must have done with it. A revolution must employ force sometimes, and this capture by it of Czechoslovakia, Europe's bastion, was the New Order on the march. Bloodlessly marching.

Bloodless—so far. . . .

He was compelled to justify the German Leader like this because he would not, could not, admit an error before his father. He'd lauded this man before his father.

He was thinking thus, as he gazed over the housetops towards Balham and wondered what this field of roofs and chimneys would look like if war came to London—when he heard a step on the stairs. He turned an ear to listen.

All the treads of the staircase in that lofty house were bare so that footsteps were heard in every room on every floor. But these steps, by some precognition, Michael knew were coming up and up to his door. They came up the last narrow flight which led only to his door. This outer door, making his 'flat' self-contained, was a poor, narrow, improvised thing, placed unnaturally on the top-most tread, but he was proud of it because it was his own private door. On it was an aluminium name-plate saying 'Mr. M. Cawdor Townes.'

His bell rang loudly in that bare-walled garret: a little echo of the bell over Europe. It was followed by an imperious knocking, possibly humorous, but heavy enough to startle his heart on this day of strange things. He ran to the exciting summons and opened the door.

'Dermot!'

There stood Dermot, his short broad body in a Hitler trench coat with a black high-necked sweater beneath it, such as no new law could stop him from wearing. The scar from lip to ear seemed to be dragging down his mouth more than usual, but perhaps this was only a quizzical grimace, for the eyes above the mouth were merry. They were gazing into Michael's with a deliberate mystery in them. He clapped his right heel against his left and stretched forward his short arm. 'Heil Hitler,' he said.

'Certainly,' Michael agreed. 'But why?'

'The Ides of March have come.' Dermot, as eloquent an orator as Michael (and a far less nervous one) had a fund of picturesque allusions such as this; and Michael, whom Dermot had really taught to read fine literature, was well able to recognise this one, and to cap it.

'Yes,' he said. 'And gone.'

'Leaving what legacy behind?' demanded the graceful speaker.

'Well, what legacy, you ass?'

'Merely the certainty of war.'

'No, no, there won't be war.'

'Michael, my son, one day I shall teach you not to assert things just because you want to believe them. One day I shall teach you to look facts in the face without mercy to yourself and really to *think*.'

'I *do* think,' said Michael, a little sullenly because he didn't like being chided for a weakness, though he saw at once that Dermot's reading of his answer was exactly right. 'But I don't feel at all certain there'll be war.'

'There'll be war within a few months.'

'Well, for the lord's sake come in, and don't just stand there saying War. We must discuss this.' As he said that, the sullenness departed, ousted by the delight of the conspirator. 'Come we must talk it over. Gosh! All I know is that I'm not fighting against the things I believe in.' He said this grandly as they crossed the narrow lobby to his room. 'No one's going to make me do that. I'll go to prison first.'

'It may be there'll be no need to do that, Mike.' Dermot took a chair by the table, and Michael sat on the bed. 'Why do that? Have you forgotten what I suggested to you?'

Michael had not forgotten it, but he had thrust it below memory because it seemed so extreme and frightening. 'No, of course I haven't,' he said emphatically, because his diffidences must never be seen; he must hide the fact that he'd been frightened by the plan. 'Of course not, but . . .'

'I suggest the hour has come for decision.' Dermot liked dramatic utterances; the orator took command of him, even on a garret chair. 'There's no more time for dallying.'

'Why? When do you imagine the war will come?'

'Just as soon as the harvests are in, and while the earth of Europe is still dry. August, let us say. So you'd best choose one way or the other. If we are to do anything we must do it soon, while the road is still open. For my part, I have chosen.'

'You are really going?'

'Like hell I am.'

'At once?'

'Aye.'

'My hat! . . . but it's a hell of a decision to make.'

There should have been no need for decision, had Dermot and Michael been the same now as they were a year ago, for then they gave unquestioning obedience to their Leader. But some time since, he had issued his decree that every young

Blackshirt, in the event of a war, must fight for his country, no matter who the enemy might be. 'Britain First.' 'All for Britain.' And on this count Dermot, ever ruthless in his thinking, and in the actions which his thinking demanded, seceded from the first Blackshirt Party and started a Movement of his own which he called 'The New World Fascists.' But ruthless though his thinking might be, he did not choose to perceive that he'd done this largely because he enjoyed political intrigue and loved the dignity of schism. Michael went into the new venture with him, partly because his views were the same as Dermot's, partly because he loved his friend, and not a little because he too suffered always from a predisposition to schism. Both still revered their late Leader and would defend him hotly against all detractors, but they held that the great and good man was wrong in one very vital point. By his papal pronouncement he had declared patriotism to be the over-riding duty of all his followers, but they, Dermot and Michael held that patriotism existed only to be over-ridden. It must be transcended by something larger and nobler. Their loyalty—and never were there two more ardent loyalists—was to the New World Order which, by very definition, must be international.

'Patriotism, in its present feverish form, oh Michael me boy, is merely provincial.'

Thus Dermot, sitting on Michael's bed.

So he had argued for years past, and now, seated at Michael's table, he said, 'The Great Clash is upon us, Mike, and the smash for one system or the other. Either the old rotten system will be smashed in pieces, or our New Deal for Mankind, and can you doubt which it'll be?'

'But do you mean, Dermot, that . . . well, that, if it comes to it, you'll fight against England?'

'My answer is that I'd be fighting *for* England, but against her present masters. I have no damned loyalty to them. Like Ivan Karamazov I returned my ticket to them long ago.'

'And you're really, *really* going?'

'Of course. And damned quickly.' It was the tone of a man proud to be of stronger will than his hearer. 'And what about you?'

Michael's heart was shaking. He was frightened by this sudden need of a decision: frightened of turning the stuff of talk into the stuff of action. But since Dermot must not see the timidity in his blood, he answered flippantly, 'It's a walloping

98

big step. Are you really satisfied that everything will be all right?'

'Absolutely. Stan Laker and Paddy Boyne are over there, doing fine. Stan is teaching English in a large school on the Tauentzienstrasse; Paddy is actually working in their Foreign Office, as an "adviser" if you please, advising on their propaganda. He's quite one of the Boys there now—so my friend tells me.'

'This darned "friend"—who the devil is he? Surely you can tell *me*.'

'Not on your life. Or, at any rate, not yet. Enough that he—or "she", if you like—has summoned me to come. I have been warned to be ready.'

'So likely it should be a she!'

'And that,' said Dermot, 'is all you know.'

'I think it's just nonsense, all this mystery between you and me.'

'It is not. Besides, apart from a name, which isn't leaving my lips—I'm not going to be the first to break faith—I could tell you precious little. No one tells anyone much in this game, lest someone should squeal.'

'Well, tell me what you can, Mr. Scrupulous.'

'They give you plenty of money. Enough for your fare by air from London to Berlin and for your expenses for some time—though you'll be housed in a slap-up hotel at first. Quite likely it'll be the Bristol on the Linden, only a little way from the Tiergarten—the very best part of Berlin.'

Linden . . . Tiergarten . . . Berlin . . . Michael's heart thrilled as he sat on the bed, unmoving, but staring into the quizzing eyes of his Tempter on the chair.

'Even so,' said Dermot, nodding.

'But, Dermot, what beats me is why they should think you and I are worth all this.'

Dermot grinned. 'Because German Intelligence is usually rotten, and it thinks we are bigger pots than we are. Good! Let us take what the German gods offer.'

'Yes, but wait. They put me into a posh hotel. What then?'

'Then they put you into a decent job. Probably the same sort of job as Stan's—teaching English. Seems there are hundreds of these commercial schools, all crying out for teachers of English. My—er—my "friend"—says you could get private pupils as well. No one like the Germans for earnest study. I don't suppose you'd make a fortune, but your income would be a sight better than it is now.'

Michael kept silence. Strange, but the most tempting morsel in this dish laid before him was not the prospect of living in some comfort; it was the prospect of flying in an aeroplane to Berlin. He had never flown yet. But—to wrench out the last of one's roots from one's native soil! One thing to advocate such a conquest over natural instinct, but to *do* it! And now. So suddenly.

'Well?' asked Dermot, bored by the silence. 'What's stopping you?'

'Nothing,' said Michael, but in that merely formal tone which means, 'Something. Something that I find it difficult to say.'

Dermot, perceiving that 'Nothing' didn't mean nothing, burst out into a statement of *his* view—which was a view that made short work of hesitations. Always words came easily to him; often too easily so that fine dramatic sentences rushed from him like sparkling cascades before he was quite sure what they meant or whether he fully agreed with them. History, he said, was marching at the double towards an epoch's end. And a good thing too! All the old political faiths and loyalties, and all the little limited patriotisms—were being eroded into pieces. Their day was done and the refuse pits waited for them. Why? Because they fitted no more the nature of man. And if this was so, then the old blind tyrannies would exert all their powers (which were enormous) to stem the advance of a larger creed. It would be the great final test, and could one hesitate on which side to range oneself? *He* was in no doubt.

Michael assented with his brain to most of this outburst—had he not said similar things time after time to audiences or to his family?—but his blood, and the trembling heart which he must not uncover—still resisted the conclusion which Dermot had drawn. So much so that he could not speak. Or nod and say, 'I too.'

And Dermot, getting a little annoyed at this failure to respond to his eloquence—he had convinced himself by it and was feeling proud of it—said somewhat sneeringly, 'All right. All right, old boy. Stay here and fight for everything you detest and against everything you believe in.'

The words were something of a tonic in Michael's halting

blood. He honestly did not want to fight against the things he believed in; and he could not live without Dermot's approval and love. So he said, 'I shall certainly not do that.'

'Do what?'

'Fight against my whole religion.'

'Oh, yes, you will.'

'I just *won't*. I won't be a traitor.'

'You'll have to, unless you quit. If you stay, you'll either be conscripted or you'll be put in prison as a conchy or a Fascist. M.I.5 has probably got its eye on you already. It's probably got a large and most damning dossier about you.'

'Good lord! Do you think so?'

'Naturally I do.'

'Damned if I'll be put in prison. . . .'

But what then? Why was he not really the hero he wanted to be? Why did a weakness of nerves so often drag at him so that he had to tear the nerves before he could act boldly? He would *not* be less than a hero—*not* less than Dermot. So, answering, not only the Tempter sitting on that chair, but also the weaker Michael sitting within himself, he said, 'If that's the idea, Dermy, I shall certainly go.'

And as he said this, he saw with excitement and fascination the adventures before him: the flight in an aeroplane, the voyaging in new countries, the conquest of a new language and literature, and the chances of advancement and fame, which in Britain must all be wiped out by the War. 'By God, I'll go,' he said.

§

Nineteen days later, not quite sure what he was doing, his heart trembling both with excitement, since in a few hours he would be aloft in a plane, and with misgiving, because then he would have destroyed the last bridges behind him, he came rather slowly down the four flights of stairs from his garret to the handsome doorway of that once proud house. He came slowly because he had a heavy bag, but did not want anyone to help him with it, or to ask him where he was going, or to see him go. His footsteps on those bare treads must have been heard in every flat where women were working at sinks or with brooms, but no one in the house, and not he himself, understood the full meaning of those echoing steps. Michael, the dreamer, must always hope all things, and if in this moment he was sad at leaving London, perhaps for ever, yet he was also full of hope and excitement—and of pride too. Pride because he was being bold and escaping quietly from the barricades of a city in which there could be no full life for him. 'Tomorrow, perhaps, we live.' No one, hearing the steps, knew that the person on the stair, because he had reacted violently from the discipline of childhood, was now the perfect schismatic. Never mind what party he joined and enthusiastically served, he walked among them after a time with a suppressed schism in his heart. There was that in him which *needed* to be in opposition; that which must drive him always into the separateness of a minority, and even perhaps into a martyrdom wilful and perverse.

PART II

CHAPTER ONE

THE third of September, 1939, at half past ten in the morning; and Captain Townes, Walter his barman, and Beth, his daughter, were all in the cellar of the Lord of Wensley, moving about among the beer pipes hanging from the ceiling, the casks on their stillage, and the piled crates of bottles. Harry and Walter were both in their moleskin cellar aprons but they were not tapping the casks or cleaning the pipes; Harry was forcing stout upright posts under the ceiling by hammering wedges beneath them, and Walter was fixing an old grey army blanket to the door by nailing laths over it. Beth, standing on crates was sealing chinks in the high shallow window with strips of adhesive paper. The three of them were working in the dusty, beer-tinctured air by the light of two naked electric bulbs.

'Damned if there's a better Refuge Room in the whole of Balham and Tooting,' said Harry, as he came erect from hitting the wedge with his mallet. He pressed against the stout post, his eyes on the new crosswise beam above. 'I'm all for this war, but it mustn't spoil my beer. We've always prided ourselves on the way we've conditioned our beer, haven't we, Walter?'

'Indeed we have,' said Walter.

'Yes, and I'm not having mustard gas in it now. Just you seal up that window properly, Miss Beth.' He looked at the thermometer on the wall. 'Lucky we've got the cellar-heater to keep us and the beer at a nice even temperature.'

'Never mind the beer,' said Beth. 'It's the Towneses I'm worrying about. And especially Beth Townes.'

'We and the beer'll be perfectly safe down here from everything but a direct hit. And if it's direct hit we shan't know anything about it. We shall perish among the beer which is a thoroughly proper way for a good publican and his family to die. Beth, when you've done that—but look: put putty in that hole there—death could come sneaking in through there—take pencil and paper and jot down all the things we'll need. Ready, are you? Good. Well . . . a table and some chairs. An air-raid may last hours. Mattresses, in case we have to sleep alongside the beer. What else? Oh, the portable wireless so that we'll know what's going on in the world above us, and who's winning. Some tinned grub, I suppose (there's plenty to drink), and I say, Walter!——'

'Sir?' replied Walter, to show that he was listening, even if his face was towards his blanket.

'You'll have to hang another blanket across one of these corners so as to give us some privacy when we want to— well, you know what I mean.'

Walter, not without an abashed glance at Beth, since he could hardly approve of cloacal jokes before a lady, answered quietly, 'That I will do, sir,' and kept his face to the blanket.

But Harry was delighting both in his joke and in his barman's doubt about it, and he dug in it further in search of fun. 'Perhaps you'd better screen off two corners, one for the Gents and one for the Ladies. That's what any decent pub has.'

'Don't be disgusting, Daddy,' said Beth. 'What else do I write down?'

'Well, a couple of *them* . . . and . . .' Now he staged a joke which he'd prepared an hour ago upstairs. He hammered a nail into the wall, produced a shaving mirror from his pocket and hung it up. 'That's for your mother to do her hair in and paint her lips and wag her behind at while the bombs are falling. She'll want to meet Death like a lady.' Tilting the mirror a little, he saw his waist. 'Lord, I'm getting too fat. Beth, I've a brand-new shop-front down here. It sticks out a mile. Well, it at least means that your old man's advancing ahead somewhere.'

'Would you kindly tell me what I've to write down?'

But Harry was now studying his face. 'Hell, what a face! Beauty's sure passed me by. Tell you what else, young Beth: two pickaxes.'

'Pickaxes? What for?'

'To dig ourselves out with, when the Lord of Wensley's on top of us.'

'I should suggest a prayer-book instead,' said Beth.

'A prayer-book's an idea, certainly. Yes, but we'll have to teach some prayers to old Walter. These intellectuals don't pray, do they? By the way, put down a Shakespeare for old Walter, and some books on philosophy. Ah well, I don't see why we shouldn't live very happily down here.' He felt his stout post again. 'Or die nice and quickly.' He stooped to kick at a wedge under the post and, straightening his back, hit his head against the new cross-beam above. 'Damn to hell!' he said. 'What I endure for my country. . . .'

'Is our Family Funk-hole complete?' asked Beth in her most satirical voice.

'Just about complete, lady.'

'And you really think it's necessary?'

'Of course I do. By heavens, yes. This is as dangerous a spot as any in London,' he announced proudly. 'That's so, isn't it, Walter?'

'I shouldn't care to say, sir. It's hardly a question on which I feel competent to pronounce.'

'Nonsense, Wally. Hark at him and his "questions on which he feels competent to pronounce"! Some of these intellectuals, Bethy, get so intellectual that they've hardly any mere horse-sense left. If there's one place in London which the Nazis will bomb to jumping blazes, it's Clapham Junction. Smash that to pulp, and you cut all the routes to the invasion coast.'

'But we're a mile from Clapham, Daddy.'

'My dear child, from twenty thousand feet in the air, that's to be next door to it. Then there are the Thames bridges. We're not so far from them. And all the factories of South London. And all the millions of streets. He can kill more to the acre in South and East London than anywhere else.'

'Well, don't be so jolly about it.'

Beth, in truth, was terrified at this prospect of war over London but, as usual, she hid her real feelings by words that said almost the opposite of them. When Harry had offered her the chance of leaving London, after asserting that for his part he'd die with his beer, she had only said, 'I'm not going. Is it likely? Let them do their worst'; because, with Michael gone, it seemed clearly her duty to stay with her father and mother. So she pretended she had no fear. Sometimes she even felt glad that war had come, because it gave her a chance of sacrificing herself. But secret fears, yes, for never was anyone more capable of private fears than Beth. How could she who, waking in her dark bedroom at night, must put on the light to make sure she hadn't gone blind, or, waking to a quiet at three in the morning, must listen to her watch to make sure she hadn't gone deaf—how would she fail to hear many aeroplanes approaching at night, or to smell the creeping gas, or to feel a trembling of the house as if bombs were falling?

As for Ida, she had said, 'I've lived in London all my life and I'd be miserable in the country.' To Ida the silences of the country seemed worse than bombs. But then, wholly uninterested in politics or war, and naturally sanguine, she could hardly believe that war would come to the Balham High Road. If she thought about the War at all, it was to feel sure that we'd 'beat them in the end, as we did last time,' and that they'd never be able to cross all that water in the English Channel—in both of which ideas she was right, of course, though Heaven knows why, for they were against all logic, in the mad British way.

None the less, at this very moment, she burst with her big body through Walter's blanket, causing even him to utter a gentlemanlike oath; and she was pale and breathless. 'Listen,' she panted. 'I've just met old Bossy Jehoram. He says the Ten o'clock News said "Stand by for an important announcement." He says the Prime Minister's going to speak to the Nation at a quarter past eleven.'

'That's War,' said Harry.

The whiteness of Beth's face could not mask her fear, but her words did. She just said, 'What'll happen?'

Harry said, 'Maybe we'll know in five minutes.' And he looked at his watch and at Beth and Walter who had suspended work and were staring at him. 'Yes, our ultimatum to Germany expires at eleven. It's five to eleven now. Walter, we'd better hurry up and finish this job.'

'War!' breathed Ida.

'Yes. And I'm glad. It's time we came to terms with these ruddy Germans. This time they've invaded one country too many, and we'll have 'em out. Yes it's "Time now, gentlemen, please. You've had your Last Drinks."'

'But Harry . . .?' began Ida. 'What . . .?'

'Well what?'

'Michael? What about Michael?'

Harry bent down and hammered at his wedges again. This was unnecessary, for they could be driven no further, but it saved him from speaking. Of Michael nowadays he never spoke.

But in an hour as momentous as this Ida persisted. 'Have you forgotten Michael?'

'I have not. I only wish I could. Beth, dash up and get the wireless set.'

'But what'll happen to him?' cried Ida. 'He's over there. In Berlin.'

'What do I care what happens to him?'

'Oh, don't say that! Oh, where is he? Perhaps he's no longer in Germany. Perhaps——'

Michael had sent to Ida some picture post-cards of Berlin and other places, doubtless hoping that his father, when he saw them, would be impressed by his travels. To Beth he had written not a word, and she had borne this bitterness in silence, knowing that Life was like that, and that brothers didn't write to sisters, any more than they kissed them properly. And, anyhow, it was sinful of her to love him in the way she did.

'He's in Germany all right,' sneered his father, 'and he ought to be here, ready to fight for his country. I only wish they'd take *me* to fight.'

'Oh, will I ever see Michael again?' wailed Ida, sitting on the chair which Beth had vacated.

'You may see him when they invade us. See him in field-grey and spiked helmet. If he comes in that kit, I hope I may be the one to kill him with my own hand.'

'Harry!' protested Ida; and Beth, who'd returned with the wireless set, muttered to herself, as one who despised melodrama.

'Maybe he'll come in an aeroplane. Maybe he'll lead a few hundred Boche aeroplanes to London. St. Michael and all his angels.'

'Be quiet, Harry! He is your son.'

'He is not. No more. Michael von Townes!'

'Well, he is still mine. What are all the wars in the world compared with one's son? Do you mean your country means more to you than your son?'

'Yes.' But, ashamed of this, he changed it to, 'I'll never forgive him for what he's done.'

'How you can talk like that, I don't know—you who kneel down and say your prayers every night.'

'It's simple, Mother,' said Beth. 'Most Christians are the last to learn anything about Christianity.'

'You shut your trap,' recommended Harry.

But this was not a recommendation that Beth was likely to accept. 'You didn't call those people dishonourable who came to England from Russia or Germany because they hated their governments; you said they were brave. Michael may have been idiotic, but he's not been dishonourable.'

Harry heard nothing in this world that he didn't wish to hear. 'Switch on the wireless,' he said.

Beth turned the knob. They heard only a noise like the sea—the wide sea that sighed and murmured between them and the enemy—until, abruptly, a voice began to speak. The Prime Minister was speaking to Harry and Ida, Walter and Beth; he was with them among their beer pipes and barrels and kilderkins. 'We and France,' he said wearily, 'are today, in fulfilment of our obligations, going to the aid of Poland, who is so bravely resisting this wicked and unprovoked attack on her people. The situation in which no word given by Germany's ruler could be trusted, and no people or country feel themselves safe has become intolerable. And now we have resolved to finish it——'

'Hear, *hear*,' endorsed Harry.

'Hush,' whispered Ida, and Beth said '*Tsh*' too.

'Now may God bless you all. May He defend the right. It is the evil things we shall be fighting against—brute force, bad faith, injustice, oppression, and persecution——'

'And all traitors and treachery,' added Harry.

'Oh, *quiet*, Harry. . . . Do, please!'

'Against them,' concluded the tired voice, 'I am certain that the right will prevail.'

He had barely ended his words and faded from their midst like some disembodied spirit, when something penetrated that cellar which no window-parapets of sand and ashes could keep out. They might keep out bomb-splinters; the gum-strips might keep out drifting gas; but neither could keep out the long, undulating, anguished wail of the air-raid siren.

The voice of the new-born war had entered the Lord of Wensley.

'Do you hear that?' asked Harry, swinging round to three pairs of staring eyes. 'Aha! The pavilion bell! They've come out to play. God—already!'

'What do we do?' asked both Ida and Beth. Were great metallic birds approaching London with death?

'You two girls stay here. That much is clear. What's the time? Just on half-past eleven. Well, I'm going up to clean my bars. No German aeroplanes are going to stop me opening my doors at exactly the right time. Nor are my bars going to be any less clean today than any other day. Nor is the landlord not going to be in his place. Coming, Walter?'

'Yes, indeed,' said Walter.

'That's the spirit that made England great! Sound lad, Walter, even if he does lap up philosophy all day. London's only intellectual barman. Come along then, me lord. First things first.'

'No, Harry,' pleaded Ida. 'Don't go up yet.'

'I thought we were making this hole precisely for this purpose,' said Beth; and sighed again at the heroics of men.

'Not for me. It's all right for you girls, but my place is on my bridge. Either he misses the old Lord of Wensley or he hits it. If he misses it, I shall be all right; and if it goes down, I'll go down with the old ship. Besides, I shan't see anything down here, and I want to see the fun.'

CHAPTER TWO

In the years of peace the Lord of Wensley had always been a popular house. It had been so before Captain Townes took over its tenancy, though Harry, like any vicar or rector, always implied that his predecessor in the living had been less than effective, and it was he himself who had built up his present congregation. Harry would often liken himself to a parson and never failed to point out that the standards of character which the brewers demanded of their tenants was every bit as high as anything a bishop demanded of a vicar. 'God help us,' he would say, 'but before the brewers'll accept a chap, he has to bare his soul, and all his past, to them, and his missus's too, in a way that I'll be bound few padres have to do. You'd think they wanted an archbishop, not a publican.'

The comparative smallness of the house had helped its popularity. The customers felt that their thirst was being attended to, and their troubles or joys listened to, not by a landlord's hirelings, but by the members of one family. 'The Guv'nor' was nearly always there between his counter and his glittering bar-back, or Ida, his lady, was there to listen (and a champion listener Ida was) or Beth, his lass, who was plump and round, and a pleasure to tease. And Old Agnes and Mrs. Benskin had been with the Captain so long that they seemed part of the family too. By now the company had grown to prefer these comfortable old ladies to any golden barmaids, just because they were not young and 'fresh' but old and mature—or 'old and mild,' as the wits said.

Because of his house's popularity there'd never been a year in which Harry had not been able to show a good profit; but equally there'd never been a year in which Harry, for all his outwardly jovial nature, had not feared in his heart that next year he might fail to make enough to meet his needs. And now that war had broken over the world this secret fear was great indeed. It became deathly despair when the Government, promptly producing a War Budget, imposed new taxation on a scale hitherto unknown, raising the rate of income tax, levying an excess profits duty, and, worst of all, adding to the already monstrous taxation on wine, spirits, beer, and tobacco.

But most unexpectedly, the War, after a week or two of alarming quietude in the bars, revealed itself, not as a depressant of trade but as a stimulant. Common danger and a common purpose had raised up a new fellowship all over London; fraternity and mateyness had blossomed in the black-out; and more people rather than less were coming into the bars, some of them people who'd never been in pubs before. There was a new public for the public house. The partitioned bars behind their black-out curtains were a place of light in the great dark. And out in the great dark were comrades on duty who liked to drink together when their turn of duty was done: air-raid wardens, both men and women—and some of the women real ladies; men from the Auxiliary Fire Service and the Demolition and Rescue squads; and even young girls from the London Ambulance Service or the First Aid Posts. Then there were soldiers and sailors on leave with their sweethearts or wives, and the Local Defence Volunteers, or Home Guard, in great force—but that was later.

Even in the daytime when the black-out was lifted like an extinguisher from the streets, and the sun shone or the rain fell on the Balham High Road there was often an enlarged company in the bars at noon. Women of all classes, obliged to take their places in the long shopping queues, became sisters while they waited (some of them) and gradually they learned the men's habit of taking one another into a saloon bar for comfort and rehabilitation.

§

The Captain's bars were dressed for war. On that first day of the War, in the evening, the King had broadcast to his people, calling upon them to stand firm and united. 'We can only do the right as we see the right,' he had said, 'and reverently commit the rest to God.' Harry, hearing this, had taken the picture of the King from its corner in the Saloon and put it in the most prominent place of all, the place of honour, on the chimney-breast above the marble fireplace.

In peace time there had been genial announcements on wall or counter, wherewith he discouraged those optimists who had notions of paying for their drinks with a cheque, or of getting their debt chalked up on a slate. One of these said, 'The Bank Manager has agreed with the Landlord of this House not to sell beer, and the Landlord has agreed with the Bank Manager not to cash cheques.' And another: 'In this House, Gentlemen, the only slate is on the roof.' Now these discouraging notices were partnered by those which Authority had asked him to display for the encouragement of his customers in the business of war. All of them went straight on to his walls. There they were: 'Freedom is in peril. Defend it with all your might;' '*Your* courage, *Your* cheerfulness, *Your* resolution will bring us victory;' and 'There is no despondency in this House. We are not interested in the possibilities of defeat. They do not exist.' In addition to these there was one which he'd printed himself and pinned up between one on Betting and another on Young Persons. It said: 'This House will be opened at all permitted hours during the War or until such time as it is destroyed by enemy action.'

§

The Captain was happy, in the first months of the War, serving from within the long central U of his bar-counters. He enjoyed 'being on his bridge,' as he put it; enjoyed listening to the talk nearest to him and joining in it while he polished his tumblers or wine glasses. 'If you want to hear the Voice of Old England at war,' he would say afterwards proudly, 'it's in the pubs that you'll hear it'; and this was probably nearer the truth than many another of his sentimental utterances. And the Voice of England, beating up against him in his bars, was more often derisive or facetious than rabid or alarmed. The people had ceased to worry about enemy aeroplanes overhead because, after the air-raid alarm in the first few minutes of the war they did not hear the sirens again. Not for many months did they hear them again.

That alarm which, in Harry's phrase, 'rang the curtain up,' being a false alarm, was a fruitful ground for the comedians. 'Tell you what,' said Piggy Weyman one evening in October. 'Someone in the Town Hall got so excited at the old Prime Minister's speech that he sat on the handle of the siren, and it went down. And all England went underground. Just like that.' A flip of Piggy's fingers.

'No. Oh no,' announced Bossy Jehoram, the huge fat Jew, firmly. 'It was nothing like that. They were just celebrating the opening of the War, and some bright lad thought that a go on the siren would be a good "hear, hear" to the P.M.'s speech. That was all it was.'

'Yes, that's about it,' said Harry, wiping a goblet. 'And it was quite a good idea. Stirred the people up, and let 'em know there was a war on.'

'Yes, but why didn't they really come?' asked Jehoram. 'Everyone knows they've got thousands of aeroplanes with their noses pointed towards England. What stopped them? They can't be afraid of us. They know we've no aeroplanes worth speaking of. And no army worth calling an army. We've a navy, of course, but that can't fly. We shan't be ready for another three years yet, so why the hell didn't they come? And why don't they come now? They've wiped Poland off the map, and France has gone to sleep; they ought to be free to call on us. Beats me. Beats your Uncle Oram.'

'Yes, it's disappointing, isn't it?' said Harry. 'Night after night and no fun.'

'Oh Harry, you are the limit!' protested Ida who was standing beside him, fingering a gold pendant on her bosom. 'You shouldn't say such things.'

'Well, one gets tired of waiting.'

''Course one does,' agreed Jehoram, 'and while we're waiting, Walter, give this gentleman here—' meaning Harry—'a drink. Don't give him too much. He's still young.'

'That's very gentlemanlike of you, Jehoram,' said Harry.

'And give one to Ida too. Something strong to weaken her resistance. Think I've a chance with her, Harry?'

'Maybe. I don't know what she gets up to in her spare time.'

'Oh, Harry, give over all that nonsense, do.'

'Lord alive!' exclaimed Harry. 'Where's Piggy?' Piggy Weyman had been there a minute before but, as often happens in a bar, he had suddenly disappeared.

'Gone to look for the War,' suggested Jehoram.

Piggy Weyman was the landlord of the Balham Star on the crown of Balham Hill, and, after the fashion of publicans, he was often in Harry's saloon paying a courtesy call on a brother of the Trade. He would come and lean on Harry's bar, just as Harry would go and lean on his, for both were proud of being good Brothers Bung. 'Courtesy calling' might some-times explain his elbows on Harry's bar, but Harry, winking at his customers, would say, 'Piggy's here because he prefers my beer to his.' P. G. Weyman was called Piggy, not only because of his initials but also because his nose was small and upturned (a snout if ever human had one), his face was double-chinned, and his little body had been well fattened up by his beer (whether or not it was inferior to Harry's).

'I've got a lovely Refuge Room down there,' Harry was saying in Piggy's enforced absence, 'and it's just wasting. Not that I'm going down to it. This is going to be my corner if the bombs fall.' He pointed to his little office at the head of the U. 'That's what I call the heart of the Lord of Wensley, and that's where I'll sit down, and if necessary die. But I expect to be all right in there. The bomb splinters'll have to tear through all you fellows before they reach me. Ah, here's Piggy. Any signs of the enemy, Mr. Weyman?'

'No, and it's a full moon. The Lord God's provided wonderful weather for the War.'

'I know,' Jehoram agreed. 'Couldn't be pleasanter. It must be disappointing to the good Lord when He's done His best for us all.'

This led to an argument about God, as to what He was doing, or would do, in the War. Its closure was moved by Piggy Weyman who said, 'Either He's up there, in which case He's neutral, like Scandinavia, or He's not up there, and in that case what are we talking about?'

'He's no business to be neutral,' declared Bossy Jehoram, who was ready to boss even Heaven.

'Oh, I don't know,' argued Piggy. 'It must be very difficult for him. After all, the Germans are His boys too.'

'Well, He should drown 'em,' asserted Jehoram. And that led to a discussion on the Germans.

One Jim Stacey, a red-headed builder, suggested that there was nothing for it but to 'kill 'em all off.' As a kind of surgical operation, he said, since they were a diseased part of Europe.

'What? All eighty million of 'em?' asked Jehoram. Not that he, as a Jew, hated the persecutors of his race any less than Jim, but that as a man of ostentation he wanted to appear more intelligent than these unsophisticated chatterers. 'Eighty million men, women, and kids?'

'Yes, exterminate the lot,' Jim declared. 'And then we'll

have some peace. *You* ought to agree with me,' he said, looking straight at Jehoram's heavy, drooping nose. 'Hasn't old Hitler said the time has come for the final solution of the Jewish problem? Well, what I say is, Let's have a final solution of the German problem.'

'And be every bit as bad as they are?' asked Jehoram. 'Is that what you want, my blossom?'

'I don't see that . . .' objected Jim slowly.

So Jehoram explained it to him. 'Mass killing is never justice. It's the opposite. Can't you grasp *that*? Work it out in your spare time. And when you're in my company, please talk sense. I find you a little exasperating.'

'But *he* does it,' cried Jim, heating up. 'Isn't he sinking our ships with everyone on board, men, women and children? Isn't he letting loose his murder mines all over the seas?' Jim, the typical saloon-bar wiseacre, had recently read this phrase 'murder mines' and was proud to use it.

'And what are our mines doing?' demanded Jehoram. 'Giving their ships a new coat of paint? Or a rise in wages for everyone on board?'

'That's different. . . .'

'Oh, why don't you drop dead?' said Jehoram, simply.

Since relations between Jehoram and Jim were now less than happy, Piggy Weyman, a publican and so a peacemaker of sorts, came in with a pleasanter point for discussion. 'I'll tell you what the real trouble is,' he said. 'This little old Hitler's a bachelor, and so he's got nothing to occupy his mind but all this nonsense of war. If he could find a nice girl——'

'I still think that we——' began Jim, who, slightly wounded, wished to resume the fight.

But Piggy wasn't going to let him. 'And I've an idea, just a hunch and no more,' he said, 'that he's had all the war he wants at the moment. Now that he's polished off Poland he says he's ready to talk peace, and I'm not at all sure that we shouldn't be wise to do a deal with him.'

'*No!*' cried Harry, and brought his hand down upon the counter with such emphasis that the wine glass he was wiping snapped its stem. 'He started the bloody war, and now it's we who'll end it.'

Ida pushed the 'blind box' along the counter towards him. 'Threepence, please,' she commanded, more interested in the adjective he'd used than the patriotism he'd expressed.

'God, what a woman!' said Harry, and put in his pence.

'I don't like vulgarity and never did,' Ida reminded him.

She drew back the box, and Piggy, impatient of the interruption, continued, 'He never really wanted war with us . . . never. If he did, why hasn't he bombed us? Why isn't he overhead now?' He pointed upward at the Lincrusta ceiling, tawny with the smoke of their pipes and the pipes of a thousand predecessors. 'I can't hear him up there.'

'He'll come,' Harry promised. 'Give the poor lad time.'

'Oh no,' Ida pleaded. 'Do you really think so?'

'Of course I do. His bombs are waiting in piles over there, and some of 'em have got Balham and Tooting written on them. Maybe there's one labelled Lord o' Wensley.'

'Yes. Exactly. Quite,' Piggy agreed enthusiastically. 'And that's why I say, let's do a deal with him while he's rattled.'

'Not on your life, Piggy, old horse,' declared Harry. 'Never. Never. So far as I'm concerned, he can shove his peace offensive in his pocket.' This was not quite the way he phrased it: but Ida was now chatting with a Mrs. Stephens and he could speak his mind as he liked.

'You haven't a—' To justify himself Piggy was about to say, 'You haven't a boy in France waiting to be killed', but he remembered the understanding among them all never to say anything in front of the Captain that would remind him of his son. Covering up his dangerous start, he turned quickly to the wounded Jim Stacey and asked after his children who'd been 'evacuated' to Sussex.

And then they were all talking about the evacuees, and how unwelcoming some of the high-and-mighty ladies were on whom they'd been billeted, and how 'with people like that it's always someone else who's got to be patriotic and sacrifice theirselves.'

'That's so,' said Harry at last, 'and time, gentlemen, please.' He glanced up at the clock. 'Drink up now, ladies and gentlemen, *if* you please.'

Obediently they drank up and, saying 'Good night, Harry . . . Ida . . . Walter,' filed out into the night. Into the great dark around. Harry followed them to his threshold and looked out at the night before shutting his door. In the thick sapphire darkness he saw nothing but the masked lights of vehicles whispering along the High Road slowly; the cat's-eye glimmer of a cigarette attached to some unseen man; and the searchlights uneasily sweeping the eastern sky whence the raiders might come.

He heard nothing but this whispering or battering of invisible wheels and the footsteps and laughter of invisible people—probably of men and women who, like his own guests, had just left the pub doors for their homes.

He waited a few seconds, then shut and bolted his door on the night and on anything that might be coming to birth from its dark womb.

§

P. G. Weyman, from the 'Star' up the hill, being the nearest fellow-craftsman to Captain Townes, was one of his familiar friends; but Harry had no such admiration for him as for Dick Templer; he had a laughing affection for him, and no more, for Piggy was a fearful liar. His richest field for gathering lies—and he pulled some fine blooms—was the old war, in which, like Harry and Dick, he'd played his part—if nothing like so large and dangerous a part as his lies portrayed. The number of shells and bombs which had 'only just missed him' because they'd exploded six inches too far or failed to explode, was prodigious. Remarkable, too, the number of times he'd have 'blown to blazes if he hadn't, ten seconds before, gone to the latrine', or 'been sent down the Line to the Q.M.'s dump.' And the number of good chaps, both officers and non-commissioned, who'd been 'killed at his side.' Certainly his horse would have been 'killed under him' if he'd been a mounted trooper, but this distinction he did not claim.

He was immensely proud of having been wounded behind Ypres and innoculated against tetanus at a Field Dressing Station, after which, refusing to go to hospital, he'd returned to the boys in the Line with his head bound round like a turbanned Sikh. As a matter of fact (so Harry learned with delight from a fellow who'd been in Piggy's regiment) this wound was not from a shell-splinter, as he gave out, but from a nail in the roof of a van on to which he'd been hurled as the wheels went over a shell-hole. But the anti-tetanus injection was true, and his return to the Line with a bandage round his head. For this heroism, said Piggy, he'd been recommended for the Military Medal, but 'as you know, Harry, by 1917 recommendations were ten a penny, and unless your name came first out of the hat, you never heard any more of it.' He'd been twice recommended, but without the luck, either time.

Twice, not thrice, nor five times; Piggy always gave verisimilitude to his lies by a certain modesty. He'd played for his battalion at Soccer, but he'd hardly say he was the best in the team. He'd played chess for them, but only at fourth table: he was not quite in the same class as the top-table boys. He'd *nearly* shot for them at Bisley, being on the reserve list for the team, but he'd hardly call himself a crack shot; in the second rank, really. He'd spoken to the King in France, but only, of course, when he was Duke of York. 'Yes, he wasn't King then.'

Few of these tales did Harry or his guests believe, but they never hurt Piggy by uncovering their disbelief; they listened and winked at one another and joked about them afterwards. 'As far as I can see,' they would say, 'it was Corporal Piggy Weyman who won the last war for us. Why they're not using him in this war, I can't imagine. He's wasted up there at the "Star," pulling up beer to commonplace chaps like us.'

'They probably *are* using him,' said Harry. 'In some very secret and important work. But he hasn't told us about that yet.'

§

'What'll you have, Jehoram?' asked Harry one day as Jehoram's figure, big and dark, stepped into the bar and without smiling lifted its hat to the assembled company, bowing this way and that, and with an especial reverence towards the landlord. 'It's on the house.'

'Mind your own business, Harry. This is going to be your uncle's treat. What may I have the honour of standing you— just to keep you sweet?'

'Oh, well—ta, Jehoram—a small whisky.'

'Jumping Jehoshophat! I hoped you'd say something cheaper than that. Okay, milk that bottle for yourself and for me too, and give a drink to old Walter—but only a half of wallop. Can't afford two whiskies. There now: that's enough. He can't drink more than that. . . . Cheers, Walter.'

'Prosit, Mr. Oram, sir.'

'To hell with "Prosit"! That's damned German, isn't it?'

'Indeed it is not, sir.'

'Well, what is it? Damned Latin, is it?'

'It is indeed.'

'All right then. Let it stand. We're no longer at war with the Romans. I've no doubt they were as bestial as the Huns, but I can't bear any malice against them after fifteen hundred years. Throw me one of those biscuits. My mouth waters every time you pass them.'

'Like the dogs of Pavlov, sir?'

'Like what? Is he being rude, Harry?'

'Lord knows what he's talking about. I never know, half the time.'

'I was referring to Pavlov, sir, the great Russian——'

'Oh, I know all about Pavlov,' interrupted Jehoram, steam-rolling Walter's explanation flat before it was properly upon its legs. 'You can't teach me anything about Pavlov. Even I can keep pace with you there. She was a great Russian dancer.'

Walter released a slender smile. 'You are thinking of Pavlova, sir. Anna Pavlova, the ballerina. I was speaking of Ivan Pavlov, the scientist, who died a year or two ago. He did wonderful experiments with dogs when he was pursuing his researches into the secretion of the gastric juices and the physiology of digestion generally. Among other things he found that, after a time, his dogs would salivate whenever he came near them, whether he was bringing them food or not.'

'Did he now?' Jehoram feigned an enormous interest. 'Really! Great Heavens!'

'Yes, and his work has proved very influential among philosophers and psychologists. Especially the Behaviourists.'

Jehoram listened; gaped; then bowed towards the lecturer. 'Harry, what a man! Where did you find him? What's he doing behind your bar? He ought to be at Oxford or Cambridge, dishing out Latin and Greek instead of pulling up milds and bitters. It must be an education to live with him, though, personally, I find him rather a strain. Push him back into the Public, and let's get on with the War.'

CHAPTER THREE

Thus throughout that winter, while the war remained in hibernation, waiting for the sun, Captain Townes was a happy man. Trade and talk were brisk in his bars; the number of his pals was larger than ever; and when his bar doors were closed he had a new interest in his allotment on Tooting Bec Common. Here he'd been allotted five rods of London soil, from which he intended to get potatoes, peas, radishes, lettuces, marrows and scarlet runners. 'Dig for Victory'—the notice hung in his bar. He would come home from this digging with an appetite like a raging lion seeking what it might devour, and he would shout to Ida, 'Gimme food, sweetheart. Been working like a navvy for you all. Jump to it, everybody. Food for the old gentleman. And plenty of it. Thank you, girls, that's fine.' And he sat down to a heaped and hot plate of meat and vegetables brought to him by Ida and Beth. 'Gosh, I'm having a good war so far. Enjoying every moment of it.'

And, 'Oh, Harry!' Ida would chide—she who spent so much of her life discouraging his flippancies and vulgarities. 'You didn't ought to talk like that.'

Which, of course, meant that he didn't ought to say the truth but only what people thought decent. The truth was that Captain Townes, so far, *was* having a good war. There was only one focus of dumb unhappiness in his heart and this was the question, which neither his family nor his friends must ever speak aloud in his presence: 'Where is Michael?' But he asked it of himself again and again, and again and again, as he dug on his allotment or cleaned the beer-pipes in his cellar. 'Where is the boy? Where . . . but only God knows.' Sometimes down in that privacy he would even ask himself, 'Was it partly my own fault that he went? Why am I such a vain, conceited, hot-tempered beast?' And coming up the cellar steps with such thoughts, rather slowly, he would stop, stand still, and think with a sigh, 'I am so damned proud. If only he'd said something—one word of sorrow and affection—I could have made it up to him. I'd have made it up to him in some big way. But I shall never be able to now.'

§

Every day, and all day, up in the living-room, the voice of the wireless went on. Singing, talking, praying, preaching, blaring music—its voice was as unceasing as that of a ship's engine in a journey round the world. It accompanied Ida's steps plodding about the living-room, crossing from living-room to kitchen or bedroom, and returning again. Ida, having no 'daily help' in wartime, had to do most of the housework up there, for Beth, as an air-raid warden, was often on earnest duties at her A.R.P. headquarters. And Ida, alone up there, weary of the sink, the beds, the crumbs under the table, and the holes in Harry's socks, and having no one at hand to chat to, made of the little wireless set on the living-room sideboard, her companion and comforter, and in a new but real sense, her daily help. Never mind what it played, sang, or said—dance music, records, theatre organ, prayers, geography for junior schools—never mind, it sweetened labour, it stretched forth a hand and lifted one up from the trough of gloom, it gathered one's thoughts by the arm and drew them away from Michael—Michael, where are you? . . . shall I ever see you again? . . . are you even alive? . . . why did you have to go like that? . . . Oh, Michael, come back one day.

Her other friend and ministrant in the living-room was the window. She moved between wireless and window. Often she came with her broom, her duster, or her polishing cream, and looked down on the Balham High Road. She liked to see the red buses going by, and the motor-cars uninterested in Balham, speeding into the haze towards the Surrey Hills or the sea. She liked to hear the low diapason of the traffic, down there in a valley beneath her. A wind-music with percussion it was, *crescendo, diminuendo, rallentando, crescendo*; blasted often by the impatience of klaxon horns, but never halted to a silence; because it was no more capable of intermission than the surging murmurs of the sea. She liked to hear the steps, steps, steps, of pedestrians going past her doors, the laughs of some of them as they travelled into the distance, and the shrill gabble of children at play.

Of battles beyond the Channel, and of the falling of thrones and kingdoms, she thought only seldom, for her interests had never ranged beyond a small world of family and friends, and she could not adapt them now to the giant shapes which were moving with huge shadows around her. Of these she thought hardly more often than she thought of the little round planet whereon they were astir, whirling in its garment of vapours round the sun.

§

Incredible, but it was New Year's Eve again—'How time flies! Sweetheart, we're getting old'—and once again all his regulars were in his bars to bury the old year with gaiety and to welcome the new year with songs. They sang all the old songs and, since 'there was a war on' included some patriotic ones, but, being British and therefore embarrassed by patriotism, they sang, 'We'll hang out our washing on the Siegfried Line' with rather less ease than 'Mother Machrae.' Most of them suffered some discomfort when Jehoram, who, as a Jew, was less subject to their reticences, favoured them with 'When Britain first at Heaven's command Arose from out the azure main,' but rather than that he should suffer with them they sang the chorus. Strange, but they found it easier to sing similar stuff about Ireland; and they roared from the summits of their voices, 'Sure a little bit of Heaven fell from out the sky one day'—Ireland always doing the opposite from Britain—'And it dropped upon the ocean on a spot not far away. . . .'

But nothing could give this vigil and watch-night service quite the gaiety of other years, and the songs were often inclined to sag down into talk.

'It's all very fine,' said Piggy Weyman, as a chorus died, but here's 1940, and what's it going to bring us? By New Year's Day, 1915, everything had happened. I'd had my first wound. Granted it was nothing much, a mere shell-splinter in the leg, but at least I knew the war had started. I was lucky, of course, it was no higher——'

'1940'll bring us something,' said Bert Muncer, a grizzled and red-faced old-age pensioner. Perhaps it was symptomatic of the dissolving of all class-barriers that Bert was in the Saloon and not in the Public. 'Yes, make no mistake, it'll bring us something.'

'That we may safely grant,' sneered Bossy Jehoram. 'But Mr. Weyman's question was "*what?*" If you ask me, I should say the Little Corporal's just holding his hand for a few wet months, and in the spring he'll attack everyone everywhere with everything he's got. All hell'll be let loose then. That's what we believe in Fleet Street. It's what I might say we *know*.' As a journalist and 'newspaper man,' Jehoram always liked to hint that he, and Fleet Street, knew a hundred secret things which they were too law-abiding to publish. 'I could tell you a thing or two if I liked.'

'Well, tell us, mate,' urged Bert Muncer.

'No.' Jehoram cast up an eye at a new notice in the bar: 'Careless Talk Costs Lives.' He directed his tankard towards it, and went on, 'I'll tell you this: ever since November there've been enormous concentrations of German troops on both the Dutch and Belgian frontiers. The Belgians expect something soon—if not today, why then tomorrow. And how right they are! When he comes, he'll come with one terrific rush through Belgium; he'll attack France and tear the heart out of it so as to get to the Channel Ports; and then, Captain Harry Townes, sir, it'll be our turn.'

'Well, we're ready for it,' said Harry, but with no warrant behind the words; only the pressure of a great love.

'Mark my words,' continued Jehoram, more interested in pouring out his own views than in turning an ear to Harry's, 'this 1940's going to be his year of decision, if he can make it so. You watch and see if I'm right.' Proud of his phrase, he repeated it. 'The year of decision.'

'Well, that's all right by me,' said Harry. 'He can have his decision just as soon as he asks for it. On his knees.'

Once again, at midnight, he said 'Time, ladies and gentlemen, please,' and went with them all to his doors to speed them into the dark. And he stood awhile looking out at the blue-black night. He was looking at 1940.

§

1940, and still quiet. The same quiet endured for three months—and then the great events began, the great flaming sixty-nine days which burned out the Europe of yesterday. April was hardly established in the sky when the Germans invaded Denmark and Norway; Denmark died in a day, Norway was conquered by the month's end. On the tenth of May the Germans struck at Holland and Belgium; the Dutch resistance collapsed in four days, the Belgian army surrendered in eight. Southward to France. On June 5th the Germans flung themselves at France along a front from the sea to Laon; they occupied Paris on the 14th; on the 16th the French surrendered. Britain was without an ally in the world, and the Germans were at the Channel ports, only twenty miles away. 'What has happened to France,' said the Prime Minister in a broadcast that night, 'makes no difference to British faith and purpose. We have become the sole champions now in arms to defend the world cause. We shall do our best to be worthy of that high honour.'

'My God, yes!' said Harry.

§

So awful and heart-sinking were these daily and nightly news that Harry, even before the fall of France, could hardly bear to open his paper and look at them. And after one black evening—the blackest so far—when that little wireless set in his living-room told him that the Prime Minister of France, addressing the Senate, had announced the fall of Amiens (which, with its women, Harry remembered so well) and stated that France was in 'grave danger,' he did not for some days switch on the wireless again. 'It's all too painful,' he said. 'No one wants to suffer if he can dodge it.'

Perhaps that address of the French Premier had hurt him so deeply for a reason that he could not disclose. Pacing his carpet miserably, he had heard the announcer's voice, so impassive and gentlemanlike, give the Premier's words about 'traitors, saboteurs, and cowards'. But then, suddenly, that serene and imperturbable voice, after reporting a speech which offered nothing but pain, said something which pierced him with an exquisite joy. 'At the conclusion of his address M. Reynaud offered his thanks to the Royal Air Force for the total and heroic help which it was giving to France, and as he said this all the senators in the Chamber rose as a man and cheered.'

Harry, walking the carpet, turned his face away from wife

and daughter that they might not see his lips or his eyes. 'God, I'm the darnedest fool,' he said, 'but if anyone praises England in these days my bloody eyes fill.'

For three days he did not listen to the wireless nor glance more than perfunctorily at the headlines in the papers; and so it was that he did not see a piece of news, rightly called sensational, two evenings later. Ida saw it, Beth saw it, Walter, Old Agnes, and Mrs. Benskin saw it, but none of them spoke of it to him.

There was no avoiding it in the bar, however. He was leaning on his counter and talking to Dick Templer, who had come in for a whisky before his dinner, when a voice said, 'I don't see what else we can do. You can't take any risks in war. Not now when the Huns are just about to spring at our throats. He and his Blackshirt lads might have helped them.'

Harry straightened himself abruptly and looked at the speaker: a lank Scot called Jock MacIntyre. He suspected that Jock had deliberately raised his voice that the 'Guv'nor' might hear. Not all were as anxious to spare him as his family were, and his friends. Loudly the voice pursued, 'It makes sense to me. He was always pro-Hitler and pro-Mussolini, and who's to say he and his boys wouldn't give them a helping hand if they came over here? Well, we aren't having that. We've seen enough of what fifth-column traitors can do in Norway and Holland.'

'What are you talking about, Jock?' asked Harry.

'About that precious Blackshirt Leader, our pocket Hitler, and his boys.'

'What about them?'

'Haven't you seen your paper, Guv? They're all safely in quod. All stowed nicely away in prison.'

'In *prison*?'

'Aye.'

'But why? Why?'

'Because, Guv, the Home Secretary wanted them where he could find them. And there he's going to keep 'em just as long as the war goes on. Which'll be for a year or two yet.'

'But. . . .' To his surprise Harry felt both shock and displeasure. He turned towards Dick. 'But can he do this, Dick? You're a lawyer and know all about these things. You can't imprison people for years without trial, can you?'

'You can since last night,' said Dick, quietly as usual, but grimly. The pale blue, humorous eyes beneath the thatchy grey eyebrows smiled grimly. Standing at the counter, he sipped his whisky and said no more.

'Why since last night? What happened then?'

All eyes were turned towards Dick, as towards an expert.

'Come on, you old Trappist monk; it's time you said something,' urged Harry. 'What happened last night?'

'The Emergency Powers Bill.' Dick put down his glass. 'It's here in the paper, Harry. It gives the Government complete control over all persons and property, yours, mine, everyone's. As far as I can see, all our liberties are in pawn and can't be redeemed till the War's won. It was passed without a division; with nothing but cheers to speed it on its way.'

'And quite right too,' said Harry.

The others murmured the same.

But that man in prison! That impressive figure whom he had watched with a fascinated mixture of hatred and admiration. In prison. In a cell with barred window, bare walls, and steel door. Say what he would, Harry could not at first get used to the idea. The man's politics might have been repellent and the methods of his worst followers insufferable, but surely he had been no traitor to Britain. Harry remembered words from that speech; high-falutin' words, bombastic and therefore embarrassing words, but hardly the words of a traitor. The man loved Britain almost as much as he loved himself, Harry felt sure. He loved it as Harry loved it.

But far stronger than his interest in that figure was his desire to believe that England did not really do wrong. So aloud he said, 'I suppose we had to do it. Yes. I reckon we had to do it. I reckon it was right.'

'All his Principal Boys went in with him, so that puts an end to his Pantomime,' said Jock, and it was clear that he said it with a purpose.

Harry stared at him. He began to see what he was hinting at. And he turned again to Dick. 'Would they have put Michael in prison, Dick?'

Dick shrugged. 'I suppose so, Harry. He was very active in the Movement, wasn't he, and, indeed, had his own little Fascist party later. They'd have been bound to take him, I imagine.'

At which Ida, who had joined the listeners, said, '*No!* They'd never! Not Michael!'

'Yes, Ida dear,' Dick corrected. 'As it has turned out, he was playing with a very explosive mixture.'

'Well, then, all I can say is, I'm glad he's gone. I want no boy of mine in prison. I never heard the like!'

'Have you any notion where he is now?' asked Dick. Since Michael had at last been mentioned in public, he was free to speak of him further. 'When did you last hear from him?'

'Not for nearly a year. Not once since the War started. But how can he write, if he's over there in Germany?' She was finding excuses for him, because many were now listening to her. 'He got properly caught over there, you see. For all I know, he's been interned. Or maybe he's escaped out of Germany. He may be anywhere on the Continent. He may appear at the door one day; others have got out. Or—' her lips began to tremble—'we may never hear from him again——' and she gave herself to her handkerchief and to a few public but controlled sobs.

Harry, wiping his counter savagely and then tossing the swab aside, said, 'I didn't agree with a word the young fool said—good night, madam; good night, sir—' this to a strange couple departing—'but you don't put boys in prison for being fools.'

'No,' agreed Dick. 'Or we should have all of us gone inside, once upon a time.'

'He's no criminal to be put in prison,' said Ida, touching each nostril with the handkerchief, which she then replaced in her belt. 'He was a good boy, a perfectly good boy, until that awful Dermot got hold of him.'

'That's right, dearie,' said a woman, to comfort her, 'I can't see as how it'd have been fair to put him in prison. It was not as if he was one of these violent young devils, of whom we've a sight too many around here, if you ask me. He was not a young beast like them.'

And Harry said, 'No, I agree with that,' as if that were about the most that could be said for the boy.

CHAPTER FOUR

In the days that followed the fall of France, Harry would leave his bars and hurry upstairs to the living-room, not only for his supper, but also for a piece of nightly entertainment. He liked to tune in to a German station and hear the news and the 'Views on the News' as broadcast in English by the gentleman whom all Britain, rejoicing in his sneers at Britain, had nick-named, for some reason never properly explained, 'Lord Haw-Haw.'

'He goes well with my supper,' Harry would say, rubbing his hands with happy anticipation, as he left the bar. But it was not desire for amusement alone that drew him so promptly up his stairs; there was a yielding to fascination too—the fascination of anger and danger and deep interest like that which had been exercised upon him by that handsome and sinister figure, Michael's Leader, now in prison.

It was easy to leave the bars in these sunny July evenings. Never in memory had there been a lovelier summer; day by day the sun had the sky to itself; the grass on the common was burnt brown, and the edges of the leaves on the tall elms too; the soil was dry; and everywhere the men were out in their back gardens or on their allotments, till the splendid sun went down behind the chimneys, and it was time to deal with a splendid thirst. A few persons would be in the bars—husbands on the way home from the City, perhaps, and a lonely woman or two—but Ida or Beth would be there to serve them. Ida and Beth were always content to release Harry and Walter for their supper and their news because, like most women, they were not serious listeners to politics and war. 'I can't waste my time with that silly Hitler,' Ida would say. She much preferred listening to women friends on the other side of the bar.

On a July day which had been beautiful with sun and warm air, after a night with the moon riding high, Harry filled himself a quart tankard of beer and left the bar for his supper—this time with Beth instead of Walter, because it was a Friday night and she was going to a special church service.

'Come on, Beth,' he said, leading her up the stairs. 'Give the old man his grub. Who knows: this may be the last decent meal we have before the Huns arrive. It's ideal weather for an invasion. Seems to me the Lord God's been on their side from the beginning—but Lord knows why. Perhaps you can tell me, being a good religious girl. It's weeks since they polished off France and I thought that air raid on London, a few days ago, was their first real knock at our door.'

It had not, in fact, been an air raid on London, but had come close enough to cause the sirens of the capital to sound for the first time since that morning when they proclaimed the opening of the War.

'Perhaps the old Hun likes to keep us waiting,' continued Harry as he entered the living-room and tuned the wireless set in to the Hamburg wavelength. 'Come on, Beth. Fetch the food for the troops. Probably he thinks of us as prisoners in a condemned cell suffering suitable torments because we don't know when the executioner's coming. It *is* a bit like that, I must say. Thinking every night in bed, To-morrow I may have to shoot Beth to save her from a fate worse than death. What's that you're bringing in to eat? Ah, nice lamb chops. Good. Where's your Mum got those from? A wonderful woman, isn't she?'

Ida, a completely honest tradeswoman who would never dream of cheating a customer or, indeed, any single individual, had no such scruples where a large corporation was concerned. The Railways, the Bus Companies, His Majesty's Customs, the State with its new ration books were all fields for her gentle, unobtrusive fraudulence. If a bus conductor forgot to take her fare, she got off at her destination without troubling him about his omission but rather with a sense of achievement in her heart. The only time she returned from the Continent, it was with a most beautiful and most dutiable silk shawl wrapped round her waist under her corsets. This was well beyond the vision of any customs officer, and she ascended the train at Folkestone well content. So now she paid as little heed as possible to 'this rationing nonsense', and by bribery and cajolery, bought all the meat, butter, bacon and eggs she felt necessary for Harry. 'A man needs his strength kept up,' she would say. Or 'He likes a little something nice, once in a way.' Or when the whole family sat down to a patently illegitimate meal, 'Well, it did cost a pretty penny, I admit, but it's nice to let oneself go, once in a way. And have a little something nice, once in a way.'

So Harry sat down now before a plate well covered with meat, gravy and vegetables. He smacked and rubbed his hands with approval over it. He heaped salt and mustard and sprinkled pepper. Then, with his mouth full, for he was an inelegant eater, he said 'Come on, Haw-Haw. Let's know when the party starts. Come on, old boy, it's fifteen minutes past.' And he imitated the nasal tones, so rasping, derisive and assured, of that celebrated comedian. 'Jairmany calling, Jairmany calling. . . .'

Beth, little interested in what the man might say, had drawn a book to the side of her plate and was reading it as she ate.

The music ceased in the little mahogany box on the side-board, and for a second nothing came from it but a low breathing, a sound that might have been the darkness on which it drew, and whose mouthpiece it was, made audible.

§

Harry looked again at the clock and at the radio. 'Come on, chappie,' he encouraged. 'I want to hear you. You're the sauce to my meal.'

Instantly, almost as if it had heard him, the radio gave forth a station recognition signal: four opening notes of 'Deutschland über Alles', followed by two 'pips'. The same signal again, and then the voice spoke, smug, sardonic, rasping as an iron file. 'Jairmany calling. Jairmany calling. Jairmany calling. Here are the Reichsender Hamburg, Station Bremen, and Station D.J.I. on the forty-one metre band. You are about to hear the news in English.'

'Good,' said Harry.

It spoke the news—derisively. 'The Fuehrer made a great speech to the Reichstag tonight in which he demonstrated clearly, or clearly enough for all unbrutalised intelligences, that, just as Britain and France were responsible for the commencement of this war, so now Britain alone is responsible for its continuation. For his part, he said, he had no desire for the war to continue. The question of Poland was fully settled ten months ago, and now France had seen the futility of carrying on with a wholly unnecessary war. The Fuehrer reminded his audience that as far back as October, 1939, he appealed to the heads of the enemy states to stop the war, but achieved no result save that he was abused and spat upon. And from that day to this the English leaders had declined even to mention peace——'

'I should say so!' endorsed Harry, from a mouth still full. 'Lucky we've got no lunch trade, so all your Mum's got to do is to cook for the old guv.'

'The Fuehrer concluded his great speech with these words: "In this hour I feel it my duty before my own conscience to appeal once more to reason and common sense in Britain and elsewhere. I consider myself in a position to make this appeal because I am not the vanquished seeking favours but the victor speaking in the name of reason."'

'And the answer to your appeal is a lemon,' said Harry.

Next the voice spoke with apparent frankness, but more apparent irony, of the latest British air raid. 'During the night enemy aircraft flew over nearly all the districts of Bremen, and the indiscriminate bombing of non-military objectives with high-explosive and incendiary bombs was continued. During these raids one civilian was killed, one river tug and two houses damaged, and one shed destroyed.'

'Sez *you*! An amusing lad, isn't he?'

After the news the speaker came to his regular 'Views on the News.' And he began, 'We do not envy our colleagues of the B.B.C. their task of having to break the news of defeat and failure to the British public day by day. However, during the Polish campaign, the fighting in Norway, the occupation of Holland, and the battle for France, the B.B.C. has had plenty of practice in limping after events and perverting the truth, and they now do it with a skill which I, for one, can but admire. For our part we desire to tell you the truth only and to discuss it with you. Usually that is my function, but this evening I am happy to delegate the task to another. Here in our studio is a young Englishman to speak the simple truth to you. He comes from London. He was born in South London, educated in a London school, and for some years was a working journalist on a well-known London newspaper. But after a time he gave up a promising career in journalism to devote himself to working for friendship and co-operation between the great sister nations, his own and Germany.'

Harry had laid down knife and fork and was staring at the set.

Beth had looked up from her book. He turned to look at her. She turned upon him her startled eyes.

'Our speaker tonight must be typical, we feel, of thousands of young Englishmen in London and other of your big cities. With great courage he completely refused to take part in a fratricidal war against Germany and, rather than do so, and in pursuit of his policy of friendship between our two nations, he came over here before the war to teach English in German schools and colleges. I will ask him now to speak to you.'

A new voice began; and sharp was the contrast between the announcer's voice, nasal, rough-edged, self-assured, and this new voice, young, fresh, even beautiful in quality, but nervous. It began and stumbled and had to clear its path before it could go on. And sometimes as it went on it was caught back by breathlessness. 'As you have heard, I am a Londoner. And I love London, and do not want to see it destroyed. I love my country too, as much as any of you, and it is because I long to do something, however small, to save it from terrible disaster and humiliation, that I speak to you now. Perhaps I may tell you that, holding the views I do, I have been invited many times to broadcast in the English service, but until recently I have steadily, for reasons of sentiment, declined to take any part in Germany's war against England, just as, for conscientious reasons, I had refused to fight for England against Germany. It was not until I heard, with a great shock, that all those who before the war advocated friendship and co-operation with Germany instead of hate and hostility had been flung into prison without trial, there to languish perhaps for years, that I consented to speak. These men were my friends; some were men whom I revered'— now a gathering anger began to inflame the young voice and give it courage—'and I can keep silence no more. If the voices of my friends, who have committed no fault except to hold a different view from that of the financial and big-business tyrants who now wield control over Britain, are to be silenced in gaol, then I will speak for them.'

'Dad!' cried the startled Beth, and could say no more.

They listened longer.

'Dad . . . can it be?'

'Fetch your mother.'

Beth ran to the stairs and down them a little way. 'Mum . . . Mum . . . come quick . . . *quick*.'

'What is it, darling?'

'Oh, *come . . . please.*'

Ida hurried up the stairs.

'Listen,' commanded her husband, as she appeared in the door.

She listened and turned pale.

'I still urge a reconciliation between our countries. You have heard how the Fuehrer has offered peace to Britain and invited her to come to friendly terms with him. To this generous offer the only response has been the obstinate and, as it seems to me, ridiculous statement that Britain will continue this fight until either she or Germany is destroyed.'

Harry spoke. 'That is Michael's voice, or I'll die.'

'Mum, can it be?'

Ida stood near the door with one hand grasping the other. 'Michael . . . Michael,' she breathed excitedly, and it was an outrush of love, not of anger.

'It isn't Michael,' Beth insisted, but with no confidence.

'I know my own son's voice.' Her voice was now level and low, as she began to wonder whether Michael was doing a dreadful thing.

All were silent. Now that Beth was certain she was hearing her brother's voice, all her love poured out to him, whatever he was doing; and it was a love like the sweet, precious agony of a girl-lover. 'Oh Michael, Michael, then you are alive. You are alive and well. I was getting used to the idea that you might be dead. I was letting my love become hardly more than a memory. I may see you again one day. Oh Michael, my love . . . my love. . . .' Here he was in the living room, speaking to them. The family was together again; Ida near the door, Harry sitting with bent head, Beth herself standing and turning her eyes from one parent to the other, and Michael arguing as he used to do.

'So far the Fuehrer has held his hand. The German aeroplanes have done little more than keep an eye on Britain's war measures. But it needs only the Fuehrer's word for them to change their load from cameras to bombs. The German Luftwaffe is now the most terrible instrument of its kind in the world, and I can assure you that if it has to make an attack on England, and on London especially, it will be such an attack as the world has never seen.'

'God,' muttered Harry without lifting his head. 'Does he think he can frighten us?'

Walter stood in the doorway. 'Mr. Templer is in the bar, sir.'

'Oh, go to hell! To hell.'

Walter stared. 'Has something happened? Is something the matter?' He looked from him to Ida and to Beth.

'Oh, go away . . . go away. . . . No, is Dick in the bar, did you say? For God's sake ask him to come. And quickly.'

But at that point Walter heard the voice—and stood awhile, listening, astounded. Harry, head still bowed, pleaded gently, 'Bring Dick up, Walter, old man.' And Walter, making no comment, went down.

'Shall I switch it off, Daddy?'

'Shut up! Let him speak.'

'Since the Luftwaffe and the German army are the strongest military instruments in history, and since no power is now allied to Britain, and no support is coming to her side from any part of the world, there can be but one outcome to this war. Britain will fall.'

These three words, in Michael's voice, were what Dick heard as he came in. Walter came behind him, wanting to hear more. Dick had not known why he was summoned, since Walter had only said, very quietly, 'You'll hear, Mr. Templer, sir.'

'You wanted me, Harry?' he began.

'Quiet! Quiet, Dick! Hell—be quiet!'

'Britain will fall.'

Glancing around in bewilderment, Dick saw Harry seated with his eyes on the plate before him and one arm resting on the table; Beth sitting near him with her hand outstretched to rest over his; and Ida standing immovable near the door.

Harry raised his eyes. 'Dick, listen. Just listen.'

'The Fuehrer's idea has always been the creation of a powerful Reich, comprising all Germans everywhere, with Britain, not as a broken enemy, but as a mighty ally and friend. Surely that is an idea worth consideration and discussion. Germany, with all its overwhelming power is now on your doorstep; and I ask you, which is the better way: to open the door to her in friendliness or to force her to batter it down?'

Harry's sad eyes stayed on Dick's. 'Recognise that voice?'

'It sounds like Michael's.' Dick's words, sharp, crisp, military, hid all feeling.

The mother spoke, but very low. 'That is his voice.'

Dick did not deny this; and just then Harry saw Walter in

the passage behind the silent Dick. 'Walter, old man,' he said wearily, 'see to the people in the bar. Someone must see to them. For tonight at any rate. Whether I'll ever open my doors again, I don't know. No, Walter, stop! *Stop!* The wireless isn't going in the bar, is it?'

'No. Indeed no. It has not been on all the evening.'

'Okay, old man. Good.'

Walter went, and Harry turned again to Dick. 'Dick, what are we to do?'

'Could it be another voice, Harry?'

Ida shook her head, but did not speak. And since Dick said no more, Harry bent his head again and sighed, 'God . . . God. . . .'

The young, modest, charming voice went on. 'Naturally I know nothing of the plans of the German High Command for the invasion of England. But it does not need much sagacity to foresee that the capital will be attacked from all directions simultaneously. It is to be expected that a terrific drive will be made against London from the directions of Harwich, Dover, Hastings, Newhaven, Portsmouth and Southampton. Beneath such a drive, mounting every known and unknown weapon, France was crushed to pieces. And what is the plain, simple truth for you? Just this. That your strategic position is hopeless. That you are on a sinking ship. We none of us doubt your bravery and fortitude, but is it not possible to be sane and sensible as well? What sanity is there in the braggatry of your leaders who breathe dire threats against Germany with no means of executing them; and what sense in their vaunts about freedom, and about fighting for freedom, when they cast into prison those men of Britain who, because they loved their country, preached sanity, reconciliation and peace? Englishmen, be done with this wretched war. Save the country you love, and I love, and the London you love, and I love, from such destruction as one trembles to think of. There is no hope of victory for you against the might of German arms; only the certainty of defeat——'

Harry rose and shouted like a child, 'Turn it off! Turn it off! I can't stand it.'

Beth rushed to the set and silenced it. Silence till Harry said, 'Shame . . . shame . . . oh, shame. . . .'

Suddenly Dick leapt upon the set and switched it on again. He said softly, 'No, Harry, you must hear a little more.'

'Why?'

'Because everything may turn on whether they announce his name.'

'What do you mean by "everything"?'

But Dick raised a hand for silence. The first voice, the nasal, rasping, file-like voice, was now speaking. And again it seemed as if, over there in Germany, this mordant speaker had heard what Dick had said, and was providing with grim enjoyment, the answer. '. . . will be broadcasting weekly, from now onward, in the English and European services. It may interest you to know that Mr. Cawdor Townes—' a rasping emphasis on the name *Cawdor*—'though a Londoner born and bred, is descended through his mother from the great Campbell of Cawdor Clan whose founder, Sir John Campbell, was the son of an Earl of Argyll and of a lady who could trace her descent from that most famous Thane of Cawdor, Macbeth, King of Scotland. Thus the blood of a Scotch King must run in his veins. No doubt he is not unique in this. Who can say that the same blood is not in the veins of many other Campbells and Cawdors? Well, all I can say is, let them hearken to one of their very famous clan.'

'Did you ever hear such blithering, blithering nonsense?' asked Harry of the tablecloth, at which he was staring.

'That is the hand of Dr. Goebbels, I think,' said Dick. 'Most of his propaganda is ludicrous.'

'Macbeth, King of Scotland! We shall not only be hissed in the streets, but the laughing-stock of all England. The whole world is listening.' Saying this he saw, as from a train window, twenty thousand aerials among the chimneys of London. 'And what does it matter if they gave his name or not? Our Intelligence would have identified him in half an hour.'

'It is possible,' Dick assented unwillingly.

'Well, anyhow, they've got his name now.' Harry drummed his fingers on the table.

'Oh, Michael . . . why did he do it?' Ida bewailed, falling into a chair.

'It is parricide.' Proud of the word, Harry said it again. 'Parricide.'

And Dick, walking forward to a chair, found himself thinking. 'Parricide perhaps, but not quite as you mean it, Harry.'

'Dick, what has he done? You are a lawyer. Is this treason?'

'Yes.'

'I see . . . I see . . . Yes . . . And, Dick . . . what is the punishment for it? Eh, what is the punishment? This is your godson.'

From under his bristling grey eyebrows Dick's eyes said. 'Don't ask me that before his mother.'

But Harry insisted, 'Come on! Out with it. The only punishment is death. That's right, I know.'

'*Death!*' cried Ida.

Dick said, 'The law knows no other punishment.'

'And quite right too,' interrupted Harry.

'*Right?*' Ida almost shouted at him. 'Don't talk such nonsense. I never heard such rubbish. *Death?*'

'Treason is the highest crime known to the law,' Dick reminded her. 'Greater even than murder or rape.'

'Then the law is mad and wicked. Greater than murder? Who ever heard such stuff?'

'I can understand it,' said Harry. 'What's the point of broadcasts like those except to prise open the door for those who want to murder England?'

'I don't care. I don't care about that. What's one's country compared with one's son?'

'Or one's brother?' came from Beth in her chair.

'No, dammit,' objected Harry, 'where the hell should we be in this ghastly moment if every mother in England said that?'

'Yes, but . . .' but Ida couldn't find an answer.

Beth could. 'There seems to me,' she offered sarcastically, 'a very slight difference when one's country's fighting at one's brother's side, and when it's out to kill him. Of course I may be mistaken.'

'He's a traitor. A traitor.'

'And if it's a question of fighting against England for Michael,' she proceeded, not heeding him, 'I'll do it any day.'

Nor did Harry heed her. He turned to Dick. 'Then the boy's put his head straight into the noose?'

Ida flung her face into her hands. 'No . . . no. . . .'

'If we win the war, yes,' said Dick.

'And if we lose it?' asked Harry.

'If we lose it, I suppose everything'll be all right for him.'

'May we lose the war then!' cried Ida. 'May we lose it!'

'Hear, hear,' said Beth emphatically.

Harry could only shake his head and answer feebly, 'We've got to win this war. Haven't we, Dick? Got to.'

'Yes . . . yes . . . but, Ida dear, Michael need never come back to England.' He said this only to comfort her, because he knew that if Britain won the war she would rake the world for all her traitors.

'Then I shall never see him again? Never? Never?'

'Perhaps in ten years, when passions have died down, he could come back and take a smaller punishment.'

'You may see him sooner than that,' suggested Harry. 'He may come in the wake of an invading German army. If so, I only hope that his father'll be there to deal with him.'

'Oh, how can you say such wicked things?'

'Your boy did better than mine, Dick. He was killed. Killed fighting for his country. Christ, I envy you.'

'Harry!' cried Ida. 'Oh, you're wickeder than he is—you, his father! Wish him killed like poor Dick's lovely boy! What has he done? Is it all that important? He's just on the wrong side, that's all. He believes he's right. And, anyhow, what harm can a mere child like that do? He said he loved his country.'

'He is a traitor to his country. Dick said so.'

'He only said the Law said so. And the Law can be *too* stupid—it often sounds like a bad-tempered child to me. It's possible to have two views about the War.'

'No,' declared Harry in a loud voice. 'Not when an enemy is at the gates of your country. I may be a fool, I may have no great brains, I may not have *his* brains, but, by God, with all my heart I know this: I fight by the side of those whose homes are next to mine. Those who've talked with me all my life in my own language. Those who've come in and drunk my beer, and are my people—oh, God, that's right, isn't it, Dick? Those who fought by our sides in the last war. And if we all have to die, I'll die with them.'

'There's no talk of dying,' sighed Beth.

Harry rose. 'I don't know about that. Didn't he promise that London would be bombed till it was smashed to pieces? Aren't *we* London? Take this damned food away; I can't eat it. Put it in the pig bin. I'll go down and help poor old Walter. The bars must be filling up now, and, oh lord, oh lord, I've had enough of this.'

He walked angrily past them all and down the stairs to serve his customers.

Ida watched him go. 'I didn't agree with what the boy said, Dick; naturally, I didn't,' she explained, 'and I suppose he never ought to have done a thing like that, but I can't see that it was *quite* as bad as Harry makes out. Do *you* think so, Dick? Harry always takes things too much to heart, and I simply don't believe people are going to take it as seriously as all that.'

'Let us hope you're right, Ida dear,' said Dick, because he knew that for Ida, to hope so was to believe so, and to rest. Let her have peace while she may.

'It was rather clever, you *must* say, Dick. He was always terribly clever; he always wrote articles beautifully; and they must think the world of him, mustn't they, if they're going to use him like that, at his age.'

§

For the rest of 'permitted hours' that night Harry served his customers, very quietly, for him, and without saying a word about the weight on his heart. Some people noticed his quiet-ness and asked Walter, 'What's up with the Guv'nor?' but Walter, far too much the gentleman to betray a confidence, said only that the Captain was a bit tired—conditions in war time, what with shortages of beer and spirits and tobacco, imposed no small strain upon a landlord who wished to be fair to all.

But when at last the doors were closed, and it was everyone to his job—the men to sweeping up and re-stocking, the women to polishing glasses and washing out the swabs—Harry, sweeping vehemently, said, 'I'm putting up my shutters. I'm closing the house. I am disgraced. I don't know how I'm going to face my friends or anyone else when they all know. And most people probably know by now. I shall feel them whispering about me, and gaping at me as the father of Michael Cawdor Townes, and bringing in other leathernecks to look at me. It may be quite good for business, but I'm not making money out of my son's dishonour.'

'You take it too much to heart,' said Ida, from the other side of the counter, where she was cleaning an ash-tray.

'How can one take it too much to heart? My son a criminal. Wanted by the police that they may hang him. And all Eng-land knowing it. No, my God!' He came upright above his broom. 'I close my house. I go and hide my head somewhere in shame.'

Beth left her place at her mother's side, lifted the counter flap and, coming up to him, put one hand on his arm and then both about his neck. 'No, Daddy. Daddy darling, you don't go; you don't close your house and run away; you've done nothing to be ashamed of, and everybody loves you. You stay here and face everybody. And so does Mum. And so does Beth.'

He smiled down at her sadly, but it was his first smile since he'd heard his son's voice. He turned to Walter, who was bringing the loaded refuse-bin from behind the bar. 'Walter, old son, what do we do? Would you, in my place, put up the shutters and go?'

'Indeed I would not, sir. So far as my counsel's worth anything, it is similar to your daughter's.'

'But what about you? Aren't you ashamed to be one of us?'

'I am not. No, sir.'

'And you're not quitting us first thing tomorrow?'

'No, sir. Nor on the next day. Why should I? I have no desire to be anywhere but in the Lord of Wensley.'

'But, Walter, the old Lord of Wensley is now a notorious place. I should say, one of the most notorious places in London.'

'Hardly that, if you'll pardon me. Nobody of intelligence is going to visit any blame on Madam or you.'

'Yes, but so few people have intelligence, Walter. And, in any case, they'll pity us. And I've no use for being pitied. They'll stare at us and point at us.' Suddenly he straightened up again, over the broom. 'Well, to hell! *Let* them. Let them shoot their goggle eyes out of their heads. I don't run.' Vigorously he resumed his sweeping. 'You're right, Beth darling. I stay. I'm no deserter. The show must go on. And I'll damned well be on my bridge in the morning.'

Picturesque and heroic metaphors like these always inspired him, and next morning, almost cheerfully, he called out, 'Come on, Family. Come on, Walter. Back stage, please. Curtain up in a hour. Captain's Rounds.' And down he went into his cellar for his daily inspection, to gage his casks, adjust the pipes, and make sure that the room's temperature was round about 55° F, else would his beer be sour and clouded. Then upstairs to join Ida and Beth in polishing mirrors, counter, glasses, glass shelves and cabinets, till he'd given them never such a shine—'few pubs in London have our standards, eh, Walter?'

He polished the glass fronts of the pictures, and especially that of the King. The war-time cards he dusted, and one he now placed in a more conspicious position. Words were echoing in his head, 'There is no hope of victory against the might of German arms; only the certainty of defeat——' and the card which he now moved to the bar-counter itself, beside the place where he usually stood to talk with his friends, was the one which said, 'There is no despondency in this house. We are not interested in the possibilities of defeat. They do not exist.'

The clock struck eleven, and immediately he flung wide his doors to the warm July air. 'All Balham must know by now, Walter. We shall have proper crowds today. Well, let 'em come.'

But, in the main, they behaved handsomely, his customers. They said not a word about the new voice from Germany, though their eyes told him that they all knew; not a word unless it was, 'It's a long time since you've had a drink on me, Harry. Have one now;' which said all they wanted to say. Later on Harry opened the subject with a few of his best friends among them, like Piggy Weyman of the Star, and then they merely said comfortable things like, 'Well, it won't make any difference between us and you, Harry; you can be sure of that;' or 'We know it must be hell for you and Ida, but nobody's got nothing against you;' or, perhaps, 'I'm damned if I blame the boy as much as some do. He's got a bit above himself; that's all; the young ass.'

And in gratitude for this faithfulness Harry would sometimes say to his friends—no, more often than sometimes; so often that they came to know the speech by heart: 'I believe in saying prayers, as you know, and I like young Beth to go to her church, but I shall always maintain that there's more Christianity in a London pub than in most churches, if by Christianity you mean brotherliness and goodwill and standing by pals in trouble, and not being too damned hard on someone who's gone off the rails. I've often said to our padre here—he's a decent bloke—"Crikey," I've said, "I've had a look at some of the old women in your congregation and, my hat, padre, if a poor girl went wrong, I'd lay she'd get a damned-sight gentler deal from the fellows in my pub than from some of your old cats." Beer puts some Christianity into chaps—it does, really, and better, I dare say, than a good many sermons; though whether it's the hops or the barley or the yeast, I'm hanged if I know.'

His big Club Room he had long given to the Local Defence Volunteers, or Home Guard, as a headquarters, but, having 'turned sixty,' he had not supposed it was his duty to join them; now, after Michael's broadcast, learning that they willingly accepted 'old codgers of his girth,' he joined up and did his parades and guard duties as regularly as the youngest, often employing at his own charges someone to help in the bars while he was away.

Fascinated to hear that voice again, seeking the shock and pain of it, he would make an excuse for going down into the cellar, where deliberately he'd left the portable wireless, soon after seven each night, for that was the time when Lord Haw-Haw and others of his troupe broadcast to England. Always, after very quietly locking the door on himself, he made noises with his casks or his pipes or his stock, and perhaps sang gaily, because he didn't want the family to know that he was waiting, half in bitter fear, half in excited hope, of hearing a young fresh voice begin, 'Germany calling. Germany calling. . . .'

But if he listened to his son, and his son's friends, secretly and underground, the loyal English voices, telling the news or their Views on the News, spoke from the loud-speaker in his bar, with his customers standing around. And, three days after Michael had spoken, the Foreign Secretary answered him, and the customers listened with their glasses in their hands and their eyes on the loud-speaker, Harry with his elbows on the counter and his head drooping.

'Many of us,' said the Foreign Secretary's voice, 'will have read two days ago the speech in which Herr Hitler summoned Great Britain to capitulate to his will. He says he has no desire to destroy the British Empire, but there was no suggestion in his speech that peace must be based on justice; no word of recognition that the other nations of Europe had any right of self-determination, the principle which he has so often evoked for Germans. His only appeal was to the base instincts of fear, and his only arguments were threats——'

'Absolutely!' said Harry aloud, still looking down upon his counter. And within himself, 'Are you listening, sonny? Over there?'

'That is why, in every part of Britain, in great towns and remote villages alike, there is only one spirit, a spirit of indomitable resolution. We realise that the struggle may cost us everything, but we shall not stop fighting till freedom for ourselves and others is secure.'

'Fair enough. That goes for Mr. Weyman all right,' said

Piggy Weyman, landlord of the Balham Star, who was leaning on Harry's bar at the time.

§

They came. They came across the Channel in the clean, dry weather and, spreading all round the coasts of Britain, bombed the ships and harbours. Then, crossing the coasts, they began to bomb inland. They came nearer and nearer to London. One day in August they attacked from morning till evening; just after mid-day they were in large formations over the Thames Estuary and bombing Tilbury and Northfleet; by the evening they were above the south-west suburbs and near to Balham. As near as Croydon aerodrome, and Mitcham and Merton and Wimbledon.

The assembly in the bar was large that evening because these gregarious Londoners liked to be in the company of others when they could hear bombs dropping. And this evening they heard the thuds of many bombs, and felt the tremor of the Balham earth beneath them. 'Hey! Please don't shake the beer,' Harry cried, as his house vibrated. He went to the door to see if there was anything to be seen. As he stood by his door he heard, behind the thrumming of the traffic on the High Road, the general hum and pulse of London, and he felt proud that this vast and mighty engine couldn't be stopped or even slowed down by a German bomb or two in its works. 'Business as usual,' he thought as he watched the traffic and the workers hurrying by; and he returned to his counter that business might be as usual in the Lord of Wensley. Soon another bomb—or was it a dropped 'land mine'?—detonated with loudest roar yet, and Harry said, 'Hey, someone laid an egg then! Anyone want to go below instead of going aloft?' No one did; not even after an excitable fellow had come in and told of several people being killed only two miles away from where they stood with their glasses in their hands. 'Well, if it's coming to us, it's coming,' they said, and continued drinking. And when at last it was ten-thirty and time to go to their homes beneath the uneasy London sky, they said, 'Well, good night, all. Good luck.'

§

Harry awoke. The siren was wailing in the night; the whistles of the air-raid wardens were shrilling along the High Road; the guns were already firing far away. He sat up in bed. Now the gun-fire was nearer—and listen!—yes, he could hear the bumble-bee hum of an enemy aeroplane—and of another, and another. A 'crump' as the first bomb fell, at no great distance. Enraged, the guns, from sites yet nearer, sent their shells shrieking up into the zenith. One of the bumble-bees stopped. 'Got him!' cried Harry, and ran from his bed to the window.

'What is it? What is it?' asked Ida.

'They're really here now.'

'Here?'

'Yes, here at last.'

'Oh . . . Harry . . . what do we do?'

'Wait a moment: maybe they're farther away than they sound.'

The guns were flashing on a clear sky. Flashes of colourless light; but far to the south there was a coruscation of red, smoky gold. A fire? Searchlights were playing on the indigo sky. Sometimes they converged together, and he delighted to see the bursting of London's shells at the very point where the beams met. 'Hi! Come and see,' he said. 'This is fine shooting. That's the stuff to give 'em, lads. Come and look. Quick!'

But Ida said only, 'Oh, Harry . . .' and stayed huddled up in bed.

The sky was now bespattered with shell-bursts, but the enemy continued to hum and beat, seemingly at a great height, and one of his new whistling bombs came screaming down. Ida screamed too, 'Oh, oh . . .'

Now a huge 'crump' rocked the house and jumped his heart from its seat, and Ida said, 'Oh, let's go down to the cellar. *Please.*'

He replied only, 'That was the nearest yet. It was on the Common, I think;' and at the same moment Beth knocked at their door and asked if they hadn't better take shelter.

'No, to hell,' he said. 'You and your mother go, if you like. I don't leave my bed for any ruddy German. And, anyhow, I've quite decided that I'd rather go down with the old house than have it come down on top of me.'

'Well, can I come in?' said Beth.

'Yes, of course. Get into bed with your Mum and comfort her. No, look. Come and look.'

Searchlights, from every coner of the sky were approaching one another in mutual recognition; they had agreed on an aeroplane's whereabouts, and they met and shook hands there. Yes, and in the hub of their twenty spokes, the enemy aeroplane glistened like a luminous fly. Shells burst in constellations around it, but it came on, speedily, relentlessly.

'It's coming our way,' said Harry.

'Oh, God, it sounds to be almost overhead,' murmured Beth.

A flash like lightning startled their hearts out of their breasts and threw them back from the window, as a bomb assaulted the earth, apparently at some place northward along the High Road. A London gun, near at hand, replied to the insolent bomb by blowing a brilliant hole in the night with a splintering crack, as if the night were made of wood.

'Oh God!' escaped from Beth.

'Close. Damned close, that bomb,' said Harry. 'Well, this is what the boy promised us. Here it is. Greetings from my son overseas.'

The reverberations died, and they heard voices. 'Where the devil are the Rescue blokes?' 'The Deputy Post Warden's arrived, and the District Warden.' 'Mr. Castle's down in the Battle Post.' 'Ah, here they are.' An orange and crimson glow, arching across the sky, from Herne Hill and Brixton to Wandsworth and Putney, had suspended the black-out, and by its light they saw a Demolition and Rescue lorry race along the High Road below them, followed by a Stretcher Party car, with four stretchers on its roof.

'Here! Battle of Britain be damned,' said Harry. 'This is the Battle of Balham. I'm going out to see.'

'No, you won't be allowed to get near.' Beth had quickly put a hand on his elbow to stop him.

'Oh, yes, I will. If I put on my L.D.V. armlet.'

'No, no, don't go out; stay with me; stay with me,' cried Ida. 'You're not to go. I won't let you go.'

'Tracer bullets! Gee, I haven't seen tracer since '16 in France. At least come and see, Ida ducks. It may be your last chance.'

'Oh, what a thing to say to Mum when she's scared to death!' Beth protested.

'Well, you know what I mean: they may not come so close

146

again. Wonder where that last bomb fell. On Balham Hill, I thought. A devil of a lot seems to have happened up there. Seems a pity not to go and see.'

Almost abruptly the night quietened. The guns stopped speaking; the enemy's hum went out of hearing; the searchlights switched off; and the road below them resumed its midnight silence.

They went back to bed. Harry slept heavily, because the disturbed night had tired him; slept so heavily that it was a little while before he realised that someone was shaking him awake. 'Daddy . . . Daddy!' he heard.

'Oh, hallo, Beth. What's the time?'

'Nine, but that doesn't matter. Daddy, it was the Balham Star they hit last night.'

'God, no! Is anyone hurt?'

'Yes . . . Mr. Weyman . . . he's . . . he's dead.'

'Piggy? *Dead?* Oh, Beth, no. And Angela?'

Angela was the widowed Piggy's daughter and home-maker.

'No, Angela's safe. Mum rushed round and brought her here.'

For the first time he noticed that Ida was not in the bed at his side. 'Is Angela all right?'

'Yes, except for shock; terrible shock. She was buried alive for hours and nearly mad when they got to her. They wanted to send her to hospital, but she wouldn't come away till they found her father. They got to him but . . . he was dead.'

'Oh, poor Angela. I'll come. I'll come.'

Angela Weyman was remarkable for being completely unlike her father, and certainly no model at all for a pictured angel. Whereas Piggy had been round-bellied, with a snout for a nose, she was long and narrow and stringy-necked, with a nose sharpened to a point. Perhaps because feminine graces were impossible to her, she walked always with a masculine tread and a springing gait, her skirt above thick stockings and shoes. Since her mother's death she had been her father's main support in his bars, so that his customers called her 'the star-turn at the Star,' or rather more aptly, 'the pillar of the Star.'

Harry got himself into a dressing-gown. Piggy. Piggy Weyman killed. Killed by a bomb's direct hit. No romantic Piggy lie, this, but the truth. Oh, how proud he'd have been if he could have bragged about it in after years, over his own bar or Harry's! But Piggy's lies were quenched for evermore.

Harry went down to the living-room. It was empty. Angela was not there. No one was there. He heard voices down in the Saloon Bar: Ida's, Beth's. He went down rather slowly.

Piggy . . . Piggy Weyman. Piggy Weyman. The first instalment of what the boy promised us.

With Michael's compliments to his dad. . . .

He opened the Saloon door.

Angela was sitting on a bench near the wall, trembling. Nothing mannish about her now, unless she was like a young soldier blasted by shell-shock. On the little table before her stood a glass of brandy which Ida had mixed for her. Her head was sunk into her shoulders, and her shoulders were rounded over the table. Her shivering body was wrapped in a working-man's overcoat.

Ida sat at the girl's side with one fat hand gripping Angela's hand where it lay trembling by the glass. Beth stood near them both. The street door, which should be locked, was a few inches ajar.

'Angela, my dear!' he said. 'Come upstairs; come up and be comfortable.'

Ida said, 'No, she wants to stop here. She won't come upstairs.'

'Okay, Angela dear.' And he went to shut the street door.

Angela screamed, '*No. No*, Captain Townes, *please*,' and sunk her face in her palms.

'She can't stand being shut in,' said Ida, putting an arm around her.

'I'll get over it.' Angela lifted her face from her hands. 'I'm sorry to be so silly.'

'I understand,' he said. 'Drink up, dear; it'll do you good.' He pulled a saloon chair to the little table and sat before her. 'Tell me all about it.'

'Yes, tell Mr. Townes,' urged Ida gently. 'It always helps to tell things.'

Angela looked up at him with enlarged and frightened eyes. 'There was only Dad and me sleeping in the house. I heard all that firing and was wondering whether to run down to the shelter, when I heard that awful bomb which seemed to have dropped on the Common. Then I rushed in to Dad and begged him to come down, but he said, "No, not on your life," so I

148

ran down alone, and I was hardly in the cellar before the thing fell and all the front of the house came roaring down, and all the front half of the cellar with it, so that, when the cloud of dust settled I saw that I was completely shut in with only about a yard or two to stand up in. This back part of the cellar stood up because Dad had propped up the ceiling with heavy beams, like you did yours, Captain Townes; but I didn't know how soon it would all fall in on top of me. And I imagined I must suffocate and I gasped and choked, thinking I *was* suffocating. I screamed to Daddy, but there didn't seem any hope of being heard if the whole house was just a mountain on top of me. Then I felt mad with horror and wanted to die because the horror was unbearable; I held my breath, trying to die; but one can't. I shut my eyes, trying to imagine it was a nightmare, but I opened them, and I was still there. I feel now that I can never, never, be in a shut room again, but I shall get better. I'm sure I shall get better. I don't know how long I was there; it seemed hours and hours, but they had guessed where I was, because Mrs. Milsom next door told them how I was rather a coward and always ran down to the shelter——'

'Not a coward, dearie,' said Ida, patting her hand. 'Just sensible. If only, only, your Dad had gone too!'

'I gave up hope of them finding me and, feeling certain that the ceiling and all must crash down soon, I lay on my face so that it would fall on my back—and then, all of a sudden, I heard voices, far away, like, men's voices, and I screamed to them to come. I called and called, and a voice said, "All right, my duck; stick it out. It'll be all over soon." And from then on they kept shouting out jolly things to cheer me up, like "Here we are. Here's the old firm. Nothing to worry about now." They were making a tunnel just big enough to squeeze along on their stomachs, and all the time it must have seemed to them that it would fall in and crush them to death, but they kept on talking jollily to me. They even sang as they came. They sang "Here we are again"—you know that old song—oh they're wonderful these Rescue men.'

Harry nodded with tight lips.

'They had to keep talking and singing for a long time because they could only come very carefully for fear of bringing every-thing down and killing me instead of saving me. They were chancing their own lives too, of course, but they came on singing and laughing. I shall never forget when a hand came through a crack, and I knew that the horror might be over soon, and I might be going to live, after all. They passed a long rubber tube through to me, and shouted to me to drink from it. It was tea: glucose tea. They enlarged the crack and one man struggled through; he told me to crawl back with him, but when I saw that tiny low tunnel I was such a fool that I didn't dare go along it. I neither wanted to stay where I was nor go along there. So he turned round and hung my arms about his neck, and said, "Hold me tight, ducks; it's all right if you hold someone tight. Now shut your eyes and come. Come for a ride." And he crawled along somehow, me holding him tight, and then—then at last—we were out in the air and the daylight, and a great crowd was cheering.'

Harry had risen and walked for one moment to the bar window, because his eyes must not be seen. He returned to her, and she said, 'I kissed him and all of them, while the crowd cheered and cheered again——' so in that moment had her real femininity shattered her half-masculine disguises. 'They kissed me back, and wrapped me in blankets and wanted me to go to hospital or rest centre, but I couldn't go till they had found Dad——' here she collapsed in tears. Ida laid her lips on her brow and kept them there till the girl could speak again. Then she said, 'I have nothing left in the world now; I have neither Dad nor home nor work.'

Harry said, 'There's a home here for you for always, if it's any use to you.'

And Ida said, 'Of course,' and Beth said, 'Of course.'

'I counted Piggy one of my best pals,' he explained. 'So you can be sure we'd try to make up to you for everything.'

'No,' she said, 'it's sweet of you, Captain Townes, but I know my auntie will have me. She lives in Oxford and wanted me to come at the beginning of the War, but I wouldn't leave Dad.'

'Like our Beth.'

'Yes, Captain Townes.'

'I'll take you there to-day, if you like. In my little van.'

'No, not yet. I don't want to leave Dad till . . .'

'Then you'll stay here. Beth will sleep with you. You and she will have our bed——'

'But I'm such a fool. I feel I want to be near the street so that I can run out into the air——'

'Then I know—I know what we'll do. You shall have . . . another room; it will suit you perfectly'—it was Michael's old room but this he did not wish to say—'because it has the flat roof of the outhouse just under the window and you can sleep with the window wide open. And Beth will be there with you. Ida, take her up there and show her it, and let her rest there with Beth a little. Beth'll lay there with you and hold you, dear, if that'll be of help.'

§

They went, and Harry stood alone in his bar. He went out into the street through that open door and walked as far as the ruins of the Balham Star. The dust of its fall, and of the Demolition Party's work, still fogged the street. He looked through the travelling dust at the mass of scree and detritus which had once been the Saloon, Public Bar, and Private of the bright Balham Star, and he could not rid himself of the memory that it was Michael who had heralded this invasion, this punishment, this death of his neighbour and friend. He squared his mouth as he thought of this. When he walked back through the open door of his Saloon, he looked around and imagined it as piles of rubble under a smoke of dust. The next instalment? Immediately he took down from the wall and placed in the most prominent position he could find, which was on the mantelpiece under the King, the printed card which said, 'This house will be opened at all permitted hours during the War or until such time as it is destroyed by enemy action.'

PART III

CHAPTER ONE

'GERMANY falling . . . Germany falling. . . .' Michael stood at the window of his high hotel bedroom and, looking towards Unter den Linden and the Wilhelmstrasse, saw the copper glow shaped like a dome of light over the city. One would have said that the whole administrative and fashionable centre of Berlin was burning in the night. He heard the shattering fire of the ack-ack guns, and especially the deep roar of the great gun in the Tiergarten; he saw the searchlights fingering the fiery sky, and the tracer bullets shooting like dotted lines of light up their white beams; he heard the scatter of shrapnel and the splinters on roof and roadway; but neither shells nor searchlights nor bullets stopped the throbbing of the British aeroplanes overhead. Their bombs, whining or whistling on to buildings struck with a crash, and an avalanche roar; but if they fell in the Tiergarten or any other of the parks, they hit the earth with a dull thud that made his window quiver like a palsied thing.

He stood in the dark, because his black-out curtains were pulled open, but the copper light from the sky was so strong that, had he wished to, he could have read by it. Far beneath him the whole length of his street was visible, as in a sunset glow. It stretched before his eyes, empty; empty of all but menace. An air-raid warden, in his tin helmet, emerged from one of the basement shelters, whose entrance was indicated by a phosphorescent light, and walked down the street like a dog scavenging at midnight. Once this official saw a man turn into the street, and instantly he rushed towards him, glad to exercise authority, and ordered him forthwith into a shelter, as one orders a dog into a kennel.

'Germany falling . . . Germany falling. . . .' The words beat in Michael's head in the place of those he had spoken into the microphone almost weekly now for three years: 'Germany calling . . .'

Germany falling. Was it so? Could it really be so? Three years ago, three interminable years ago, he had announced to all Britain that the Battle of London was about to begin; and he had fully believed that it must end the war before that year was out; but now, three years later, three years of black-out and scarcity and siege law, here was the Battle of Berlin. It had begun in November, and never a night but it had filled the hours of dark. Field-Marshal Goering had promised that his Luftwaffe would never suffer a single enemy plane to approach Berlin—but listen! Listen to the loud unbroken humming of them. Hundreds of them.

'The British are always slow and late, but they arrive in the end,' he thought; and an old pride stirred, for it was native, and not to be killed.

He was feeling no fear. His excitement and interest—and this unsuitable pride—quite overlaid any physical fear. For this reason he preferred to stand at his sixth-storey window and watch the spectacle rather than to obey the strict regulation that all must take shelter with their gas masks. 'I'd rather go down with the place than have it come down on me,' he had said—so like his father he was.

Almost certainly he was the only person on this high floor; and this was a symbol perhaps of his loneliness in the world: a man without a homeland, and outside the Law.

Had his father stood watching the Battle of London? And Mother and Beth? But wait: all that was three years ago. And as long ago as October, 1940, Goering had announced that his Luftwaffe had laid more than a third of London in ruins. Father, Mother, Beth—dead? Three years dead? And the Lord of Wensley? He saw again its signboard above the pavement: a lordly figure on his battlements brooding over a green patch of England. Was it down like a fallen flag: three years down?

'God! That one was close!' The tall hotel had seemed to sway.

He opened the window lest the glass should blow in, and immediately his eyes began to smart and grow moist. An overhang of black smoke was travelling towards him, its under-side lit red by some building aflame. Across the city it travelled, apocalyptic, like a message of doom.

Was the incredible going to happen and Germany be beaten? Were his own countrymen going to win, after all? And, if so, where would he hide from them? He could not run east-ward, for there the incredible was already happening and the

Russians were driving the Germans back and coming slowly towards Berlin. Nor run south, for there again the incredible was afoot, and the British and Americans were advancing up the spine of Italy. Even as he stood here, disaster was advancing from the east and the south. To the west? But one could no longer feel certain that it would not come, in its own time, from the west. 'No army in the world,' the Fuehrer had proclaimed, 'will get past our Western Wall.' But so also had Marshal Goering boasted, 'No enemy aeroplanes will ever get near Berlin,' and listen. Listen to their droning overhead. And to that bomb . . . and that.

§

He closed the window, drew the black-out curtains, and shut himself in from this war of the nations. Flinging himself on to the divan bed, he left the raid to do its worst. And he lay thinking, as the bombs thumped and clamped around him, and the room trembled.

Had he been completely wrong about Germany's might? Wrong about the hopeless weakness of all democracies? He did not want to be proved wrong. Not before the Family. To be proved a fool before his father—oh no! But what would it really matter since the proof of his folly would bring death to him?

And yet it *would* matter. At death, and beyond.

Death? And he still in his twenties?

But the chief thought that kept him tossing was this, that his marriage to Germany was indissoluble, and it was failing.

§

One sleeps at last when one is young, and Michael slept, well accustomed now to the nightly noise of battle. When he awoke, the city was quiet. Going to the window and looking towards the Wilhelmstrasse, he saw that the glow in the sky was out but that smoke was drifting over the whole area. Many buildings must be smouldering still. Snatching a quick breakfast, he went out into the streets, and the first thing that struck him was a smell of gunpowder, as of a firework sizzling on grass, and instantly he thought of his father and himself on Tooting Bec Common, celebrating the Fifth of November.

A brief walk brought him to a corner of the Wilhelmstrasse, and here he saw that all its northern stretch, with its ministries and embassies and Chancellery, was cordoned off and smoking. In the fog of dust and smoke the fire-fighters were standing in the roadway by their hose, content, apparently, to stand and stare. Michael stood and stared too, but a warden, perceiving him, promptly and imperiously waved him away. He obeyed, as all did in Berlin.

He went slowly on, working his way round the Potsdamer Bahnhof, parts of which were a ruin, so that its posters, 'Do not Travel,' looked out of date. He crossed the Potsdamer Brücke and walked along the south side of the canal till he came to those broad avenues, the Kurfürstendamm and the Tauentzien-strasse, where the shops and cafés and restaurants were. Here, two miles from Berlin's real heart, the damage was much less. Many of the shop windows, however, were blown in or out, and again and again he trod on glass splinters as he walked.

After the night's battle the people in the streets were quiet. The dowdy German women, with their taut blonde hair and round unpainted faces, walked wearily and in silence to the shops so sparsely dressed with food. Doubtless they'd been in their cellars most of the night. Many people were streaming eastwards with rolls of blankets or other bedding under their arms. They were some of the million and a half Berliners who left the city at night to sleep on friends' suburban floors or even, if the nights were warm and dry, beneath the pines of the Grunewald. Dark Jewish women were among them, and they held their bundles against their breasts to hide the yellow star of Judah which they'd been ordered to wear over their hearts, so that Aryans might sneer at them or spit at them, and Aryan children throw stones at them. Michael, whenever he saw that large black-edged yellow star sewn on the frock of some black-eyed child, felt glad of the bombs last night and the night before and the nights to come.

Most of the men on sidewalk or roadway were in uniform, for this was a nation in ferment: he had to make his way through soldiers in grey, S.S. men in black, or Nazi officers in brown, with wide breeches and shining jackboots. Down the road came trucks in column loaded with troops, and caterpillar tractors hauling big guns. An S.S. battalion in steel helmets, and with their flag in front of them, followed behind. All the men on the pavement saluted the flag, while Michael carefully turned his eyes away. So a man keeps his eyes from a woman with whom his love-marriage is a failure, and to whom he is tied.

He had not gone much further when he saw one of the Nazi officers, a fat, shaven brute with a bulging neck and the strap of his breeches constricting his stomach, walk quickly towards a Jewish woman who was holding her handbag against her breast to hide her yellow star. He pulled the bag down and pushed her off the pavement into the gutter. The handbag, which flew on to the road, was run over by a big black Mercedes in which sat some staff officers of high rank. She was a woman of over fifty, small, with short legs, and as she fell on to one knee her eyes filled and her mouth squared like a child's. Pity leapt up in Michael and he hurried towards her, helped her to her feet, and recovered her bag for her. She looked at him with her drowned eyes, not daring to speak. And he comforted her in his excellent German, of which he was now very proud. 'Seien Sie doch nicht traurig, nichts dauert ewig. Never mind, my dear. Nothing goes on for ever. It always seems as if it will, but it doesn't.'

She shook her head, denying this comfort. So he put his hand on her back tenderly and said the equivalent of 'Keep up a good heart. Things will get better one fine day.'

And she, staring, said, 'But you are not German. Who are you?'

'Das macht nichts. That doesn't matter. I am nothing.' He lifted a hand. 'Leben Sie Wohl.'

'God bless you,' she said.

'Und Sie auch . . .'

The Nazi officer came towards him threateningly, and at the same time two S.S. officers, splendid in black and silver, rushed out of a shop to punish him because he'd helped a Jew. But a tall young German, with a gentle face, nodded approvingly at him and stopped, as if he would defend him from attack. Michael grinned back at him, flung up his head, and walked straight on, pretending a fearlessness which he did not feel. In fact, alarm was throbbing at his heart, but pleasure at what he had done sat there too.

They let him pass on, unmolested.

Turning out of the Tauentzienstrasse into a narrower street he came to the restaurant where he was to meet Dermot. This was an expensive restaurant, but since the Propaganda Department had selected him as a good card to play in the broadcasting game, they had lifted him out of his simple lodging in Charlottenburg, set him down in a luxurious hotel, and kept him warm with an ample expenses allowance. He came often to this restaurant because it was a good place to break his journey to the radio station off the East-West Axis. The proprietor was a huge heavyweight of sixty, with hair *en brosse* and a paunch so large and protuberant that it tilted him backward as he walked. This backward-leaning seemed the only way he could hold the business up. A Party member since the first days, he wore his badge conspicuously and greeted his familiar guests with an outstretched arm, a click of the heels, and 'Heil Hitler.'

Michael was a familiar guest, and in the beginning he had been ready to return this salute, but for some time, and for reasons he did not care to uproot and examine, he had tried to slip into the restaurant quietly so as to avoid doing so. Today, soured by the memory of that Jewess, and of those S.S. men in their cocky black and silver, he was resolved, come mobbing or lynching, not to say 'Heil Hitler'. If only he could slip in unobserved—but no: the hefty proprietor, standing between his tables, saw him at once and with pleasure. Out came the arm, fat fingers extended; click went the heels. 'Heil Hitler.'

'Guten Morgen,' replied Michael.

The proprietor frowned and smiled in a way half friendly, half hostile. 'Unser Gruss ist "Heil Hitler",' he reminded Michael.

'Ja, ja,' agreed Michael, with no less friendly a smile, but his heart was hammering as he passed on.

'*Heil Hitler!*' called the proprietor, and came a little way after him, seeming almost as ready as the Nazis in the street, to teach him his duty.

Michael was now at a table, and he bowed and grinned and waved a hand, and compromised with 'Grüss Gott.'

Undetermined what to do, for Michael was not the first since the British bombing began, to refuse him a Hitler salute, he waited too long, and his moment for action was lost. He walked slowly back to his door.

'Auf Wiedersehen,' Michael called to his back, and waved in amicable farewell.

A fine display of independence, but his heart was still thumping at his defiance. All eyes were on him; some were angry eyes.

What punishment would come to him now?

Fortunately, at this early hour, the eyes were mostly women's eyes. Apart from the waiters, the only men in the place were two middle-aged men reading papers at the next table and a young lieutenant with a Hitler cross. One of the two readers had looked up from his paper, and as it was the *Völkischer Beobachter*, Hitler's own paper, Michael feared the worst from him, but, strangely enough, he only smiled. The other man returned his eyes to his *Berliner Morgenpost*. The lieutenant had a sword-scar on his cheek, probably won in his student days, and might be assumed, therefore, to enjoy contention, but apparently he did not wish to act alone. The waiters, old men, did not suppose it was their business to beat up their master's guests. So the ripples round the pebble which Michael had tossed, died away; and the unseen palpitations of his heart died too.

§

Ah, here was Dermot; and Dermot got the greeting; got it all the more emphatically because the proprietor knew him for Michael's friend. 'Heil Hitler!' Dermot did not hesitate to return it. He returned it elaborately, almost mockingly; flinging out his arm as if he would shoot it from its socket, clicking his heels with a smack, and remaining in this posture, stationary and statuesque, while the people watched. He looked extraordinarily small, stocky and cheeky before his mountainous host. His performance over, he bowed deep, smiled, saw Michael, came to his table, and gave him the same salute all over again.

'Oh, shut up,' muttered Michael.

'Be not disloyal, dummer Kerl. At least not in a public place.' Sitting down, he dropped his voice lower. 'Not before the sausage-necks, *if* you please. How are you? I trust you slept well in the stilly night.'

'Perfectly, thank you,' answered Michael. 'What are we having? The usual?'

'What else?'

An extremely old waiter, with a fallen-in mouth that never stopped moving, stood between them, and Michael, putting down his ration card, ordered coffee and cake. The waiter accompanied his 'Dankeschön' with an extremely low bow, his mouth working all the time, and departed.

'Then you didn't notice any noise in the night?' pursued Dermot.

'Nothing unusual.'

'I see.' Dermot nodded several times.

'Nothing different from the last twenty nights.'

'Not a little livelier, wouldn't you say? Well, it may interest you to know that our beloved Propaganda Ministry is largely a ruin, and so is the Little Gentleman's Chancellery and the Air Ministry, and most of the stations. Such fun.' Ever the orator, and ever ready for the harshest thought, he added, with a relish for both his language and his statement, 'The apples of wrath are ripe, old boy, and are falling, falling. . . .'

What was the echo—the echo in time just past? Ah yes: 'Germany falling . . . Germany. . . .' Michael answered nothing.

'So do you think you're wise, Mike, dear boy, to live in the very centre of the orchard, as you do? It's quite a lot safer where I am.'

The young man with the sword-scar looked admonishingly at Dermot but when he saw Dermot's scar, from lip to ear, he concluded, presumably, that he must be trustworthy. He resumed his drinking.

Michael had noticed his look and, whispering 'Ssh!' to Dermot, tossed his eyes up, warningly, at the notice on the wall: 'Beware of Careless Talk.'

But Dermot, as the senior, and in his own view the stronger and more fearless, of the two, didn't care for correction, and deliberately continued, 'Of course, I'm not saying that my apartment is out of the apple orchard. It's only about three miles from the Chancellery, and a bomb aimed at the Little Gentleman might easily hit Little Dermot.'

They had been speaking in English, and one of the Germans at the next table, the student of Hitler's own paper, proud perhaps of his perfect English, and knowing that these two were broadcasters in the English service, joined cheerfully in their talk. 'You need not worry, gentlemen. It is all right. There is nothing to fear. They only sent over a couple of hundred planes, and you will be able to announce tonight that we shot down two hundred and forty.'

The other German laughed. 'Ja, ja. "Denn wir fahren gegen England." I hope you noticed us sailing against England last night.'

'No, I cannot say that I noticed it,' said the first German, his face completely serious. 'I should have said, on the contrary, that they were hanging out their washing on the Siegfried Line.'

'Nein. You must not get them wrong. These English meant nothing hostile by their little visit. They meant it all very nicely. In fact, I'm not sure that they did not come over to surrender. I cannot really see what else it could have been, in view of what our estimable Reichsmarschall Hermann Goering has said. It could not be that he tells lies.'

'It could not.' The first German sipped his drink. 'Filthy stuff: apple tea. Ah, well; what I say is: Enjoy the war if you can, because it'll be sweet compared with the peace.'

Dermot turned and looked at Michael. 'What have we to do with peace?' he said.

'What do you mean?' demanded Michael, fear touching his heart with icy finger.

'I see you don't know the allusion. I had a pious mother who made me read the Bible. "Had Zimri peace who slew his Master?"'

'No, I don't know it,' Michael agreed, as one who didn't wish to.

'Ja, it's a good war,' said the second German. 'First there's nothing worth eating, and now we're not allowed to sleep any more. I spent six hours in a freezing cellar last night, sitting on a wicker chair which let all the cold air through, and singing "Heute gehört uns Deutschland", when really I didn't feel at all confident that even Deutschland would belong to us to-morrow.'

In the first days of the War an orchestra had played on the dais at the far end of the room, but this had long since gone. Now only a loud-speaker on the wall played to the guests. It was half way through an old and gentle folk-song, redolent of the sweet German countryside, when it stopped—sharply cut off. A second or two of silence, and then a voice announced that a communiqué would be heard in a few minutes.

Instantly the proprietor, who had disappeared into his office, reappeared, as if summoned to duty. The folk-tune, so abruptly slain, did not rise again; a loud martial air sang in its place; this too stopped abruptly, cut down in its youth; and the Nazi Anthem, the Horst Wessel Lied, succeeded it.

'Have we won the war?' asked Dermot.

'Who is we?'

'Precisely,' agreed Dermot, savouring the grim question. 'Who is we?'

Michael, hearing the Horst Wessel song, saw the London Embankment, and the Blackshirt boys marching eastward behind their Leader.

This memory, sad and yet dear, was interrupted by a fanfare and a roll of drums. The proprietor, standing before his customers like a schoolmaster before a class assembled for 'Preparation', at once raised a pedagogic hand for silence. It was his function to see that none of his guests spoke or moved, or even munched, while the News was being announced. The people obeyed him. They became seated statues, unmoving. Not a sound troubled the restaurant; not the clink of a cup or spoon; hardly the creak of a chair.

Through the window, on the far side of the road, Michael could see a cluster of people standing in silence, as they were ordered to do, before a loud-speaker on a lamp-standard. Sad people, apathetic people, he thought. Three years before, when war was announced, he had seen a crowd of not more than four hundred assembled before the Chancellery—as a London crowd would assemble before Buckingham Palace—and incredibly silent, apathetic, and indifferent to the war, they had seemed. Now, after nights of bombing, their indifference seemed more like despair.

'From the Fuehrer's Headquarters the High Command announces . . .'

'What now?' muttered Dermot from the side of unmoving lips, like a mischievous schoolboy at Preparation.

The communiqué stated that in the Chernyakov area the German army had taken the offensive and forced the Russians to retreat on a wide front. Many important strong points had been captured. Further, all attacks on Znamenka, the railway junction on the Dnieper, had been repulsed with great loss to the enemy. Great heroism had been shown by the air force in defending this vital stronghold in the German defences.

'So!' murmured the second German approvingly.

Michael, listening to this talk of success, knew that he was feeling relief. His love of Germany and the Germans might be sick unto death, but life was sweet to a young man, and it was the German armies alone which could save him now. It might be wicked to wish their triumph, but one wanted to live. Not to hang.

Now the announcer was stating that the Japanese were advancing successfully and had captured the city of Changteh.

'Good,' mumbled Dermot. 'Perhaps the Japs'll save us, but they've quite a way to come. About five thousand miles, while the Russians have only about five hundred. And what the hell's five hundred miles to an army in these days?'

God! thought Michael. Might they be here so soon? Any day now? To conceal this fearful thought, he whispered on to his plate, 'Wonder if they'll say anything about the raid last night.'

'Oh no. That was not worth mentioning. Only about twelve hundred people killed.'

The proprietor, having heard a whispering in class, looked sternly their way. He shook his head reprovingly, just as the announcer answered their question for them.

'The British made another senseless and ineffectual raid on Berlin last night. Some damage was caused, and a few casualties; but most of their bombs fell in parks and open spaces. Bombs falling in the Tiergarten area severely damaged the Brandenburger Tor and many of the monuments in the Siegesallee.'

'That won't do,' muttered Dermot. 'I've just come back along the East-West Axis, and the old Brandenburger was looking just as solid and hideous as ever. And all the old bounders were safely on their pedestals in the Siegesallee. That was your Dr. Goebbels. He put it in to stir up an hate. What a mutt the boy is, because it will be completely discredited in twenty-four hours.'

The proprietor made a step to come and speak very seriously to these disobedient pupils but was halted by the band playing 'Deutschland über Alles', which must be honoured with stillness, and a salute.

§

When all the people were seated and chattering again, Michael began, uneasily, 'Dermot?'

'Yes, my son?'

'Is the War lost?'

'By whom?'

'By Germany.'

'Yes, my son.'

'But, Dermot—what are you saying?'

'The truth.' Dermot smiled as he gave this brutal answer.

'But——' Michael didn't know what to ask next. He had wanted to extract some hope, however small, from Dermot, but should have known that he'd get only the cynical truth. 'Then—when will the end come?'

'The end? I don't know. But *They* will come next spring. This bombing of Berlin is the obvious preliminary to invasion.'

'No.' Michael would not hear this. '*We* couldn't get across the Channel, and they won't.'

'Who's "we"?'

'Oh, you know what I mean: if Germany couldn't get across, Britain can't.'

'Britain and America can. And will. Everyone knows it.'

'Well, then . . . how long before . . . the end?'

Dermot shrugged. 'Remembering that Unser Fuehrer has announced that he'll never surrender, I should say, in one year —two years——'

'Two years? He can't hold out as long as that. Won't it be France over again? France was downed in a month.'

'Germany will be downed, but not Mein Fuehrer and his boys. They're going to betake themselves to a secret redoubt in the Bavarian hills. They're storing it already with colossal dumps of arms and ammunition and food. Gangs of men are at work there night and day. I understand that the funny little man has some idea of issuing from this Alpine citadel and reconquering the Fatherland. He must be thinking of Elba.'

Michael sat musing on this; and at last inquired, 'Yes, but what about us?'

'Meaning Dermot and Michael?'

'Of course.'

'I should like to think there'd be a corner for us somewhere in the mountains, but no; not a hope; you can get shut of that pretty notion.'

'Then what?'

'Well, we were God-damned fools not to get ourselves naturalised before September, 1939, when the war started. They couldn't have touched us then. We missed that boat badly, Mike—I suppose because we never imagined Germany could lose. Such an idea certainly never entered my head, and its absence will probably cost me my head.'

Michael stared into his face. He heard not a sound from

the restaurant. For all he heard, the long room around him might have been empty and quite still.

Dermot rolled a crumb of cake into a ball and with his thumb nail shot it into the air. 'From the minute the War started it became high treason to get naturalised.'

'Are you sure?'

'Of course I am. Didn't I look into the matter directly I suspected we might lose?'

'But, Dermot—don't just be merry about it—what do we do, you and I?'

'I imagine we cease to be Dermot and Michael and become Heinrich and Joachim. With false papers in our pockets. That's been arranged, I'm told.'

'But will false papers be any good?'

'No. Our late countrymen will go through Germany with a tooth-comb to find us.' He touched his scar twice. 'They'll find *me* very easily.'

Fond as he was of Dermot, Michael's instant feeling was relief that *he* had no such scar. 'And me?' he asked.

'They'll find you all right, but less quickly.'

'What—among eighty million people?'

'Certainly. Haven't you ever noticed that no escaped convict in England goes many days without being picked up—among fifty million people? Oh, they'll get you; don't worry.'

How much of all this was true and how much harsh sayings? Michael knew his Dermot well. He knew that Dermot's thinking was invariably more fearless than his own, and he had always admired its hard, unyielding, steel-like edge. But he knew also that Dermot prided himself on this ruthless thinking and on the show of fearlessness with which he matched words and actions to his sternest conclusions. And he tried now to believe that Dermot was exaggerating the danger in which they sat, for the sake of this self-display. But it might not be so. Michael always suspected that Dermot's mocking words might be covering dismays that he must surely feel but cared not to show. Within the flamboyance did not fear sit trembling, sometimes?

'If you don't believe in the chance of escape,' he resumed, after fiddling with cake-crumbs too, 'what do you propose to do?'

'Oh, I'm clear what I'm going to do. I shall do all I can to save the ship, not because I love the Fatherland any longer, but because I happen to be on it. The Germany of our dreams,

Mike, is dust and vapour—if it ever existed. This present brutal Germany is indecent in the extreme. I'm just bored with it. My only comfort is that Britain's no better. If you think the British are any better than the Germans——'

'I do.'

'Well then, take a look round as you walk home. They start later, that's all; but once they start, they're as ruthless as any people in the world. The only difference between all peoples, nations, and languages is this, that if our side massacres, it's a necessary duty, but if the other side does it, it's a barbarous atrocity. Everything shows that the human race, whether they call themselves German or English, is an institution stupid and brutish beyond redemption, and I, for one, am quite ready to contract out of it, when the time comes. So, if there's no saving the ship—and there isn't—I'll go down with it. And I've no intention of being picked up, just to be let down again at a rope's end.'

Michael fell into silence. Death? At so early an age? And soon? One year . . . two years . . .?

§

During that silence the restaurant was annihilated and Michael was back in his first year in Germany, the year of Germany's triumphs and his own high hopes. Dermot was even then in the English editorial department of the German broadcasting stations for Europe. He had not hesitated to become first a reader of news in English and, after he'd proved his worth, a commentator at a salary of a thousand marks a month, with a bonus at Christmas. After a time he had persuaded Michael to come into the service of the Rundfunk—not without difficulty, for Michael had a fear of the word 'traitor' and of the consequences which were tied to it like a kite's tail; not without assuring him that the danger was *nil*, because Germany was sure to win. At first Michael consented only to write scripts in English; less bold and less whole-hearted than Dermot, he balked at the overt step of speaking aloud to the whole of England. It was not till he heard of his late Leader's imprisonment that in a passion of loyalty to that most brilliant and attractive Captain, who'd always been 'so frightfully decent' to him, he announced that he cared nothing any more whether England heard his voice or knew his name.

Dermot, delighted, reported this at once to the head of the Concordia Bureau (by which somewhat inappropriate name the Germans called their company of British broadcasters) and, like most men when introducing a possession of their own, whether horse or dog or china vase or candidate for service, exaggerated his value above anything he really believed. He declared that Michael had great experience as a writer and speaker in England; that he was known to thousands as a young leader of the British Fascists; that he had a voice of quite exceptional quality; that he was a charming youth, and youth should appeal to youth; and that he was related on his mother's side to the Kings of Scotland.

These interesting facts the Head of the Bureau, a certain Dr. Hetzler, submitted to his immediate superior, and thereupon with the wind of German thoroughness behind them, they cruised rapidly about the Propaganda Department and the Foreign Office till they came to their final dock, on the desk of no less a person than Dr. Goebbels himself, Minister of Propaganda and Public Enlightenment.

The dossier arrived on the little doctor's desk at a bright moment, and he leapt at it like a fish at a gaudy fly. His policy at this time was to speak peace and brotherly love to the English, and to employ only Englishmen in this task, since they alone understood their crazy and unaccountable race. They alone would make the right kind of jokes that this incurably frivolous people required. It seemed that the German broadcasters had been making the wrong ones. So he gave instant orders that Michael Cawdor Townes should be 'put over the air in a big way,' and heavy mention be made of his connection with King Macbeth.

And straightway Michael, from being but a scribbler in the Rundfunk, rose high above all on the wings of Dr. Goebbels' favouritism. He soared high above Dermot who had introduced him. They housed him in a lavish hotel in the fashionable centre of Berlin while Dermot had only a small apartment in a minor street, nearly three miles away. They gave him a lavish allowance for his expenses there. Once again Michael sat in a high place and could live with fine dreams. It was 1940; there was no question but that Germany would win the war, and quickly; soon all Europe would be enjoying the New Order and a Pax Germanica; it was the Hour of Change in history, and he, Michael sat with the future in safety and comfort. The British broadcasters had been promised good positions in Britain's New Order, and one of Michael's dreams, as he sat in his hotel room or at the radio station, was of himself as a man of power in England, with an office and a car, who would drive out to Balham to help—perhaps even to save—his family and his friends. He could not be happy at the thought of a London pulverised by bombs, or of an England overrun by German armour, so he eased the hurt of these thoughts by this dream of himself arriving in the Balham High Road for the rescue of family and friends.

Thinking this, he would remember happy summer days at Kennington Oval, watching cricket at his father's side, when 'the old man' would be quite as excited as he was, and happy birthdays when the whole family, and Uncle Dick and old Walter, would be assembled in the Lord of Wensley; and he would feel that it would be a good thing, a comfortable thing, to be friends again with the old man. This dream of helping family and friends served to sweeten his palate sometimes when he felt on it the sour taste of treachery. He would further dispel this taste by drinking again and again from that cup which told him he was a young man whose wisdom had lifted him above the childish xenophobias of simple herd-minds.

In no great time the little Doctor Goebbels learned to his astonishment that these English, whose responses were beyond the understanding of any sane man, and whose levity did not lessen even as total disaster approached them, were greeting his new discovery, the descendant of King Macbeth, with gales of laughter and calling him 'Young Macbeth', just as they called his best broadcaster 'Lord Haw-Haw.' But at the moment the little lame man was too busy hurrying after his own war, and too interested in new horses he'd found for his stable, to countermand the order that Michael Cawdor Townes was to be kept in luxury, and nobody in Germany was ready to rescind it without higher authority, so it was still in force three years later, and likely to be in force till the War's end.

§

If, as 1940 passed, with England uninvaded and unbeaten, and London much smashed about but still lively and unafraid, Michael in his hotel room, on winter evenings when all was quiet, began to doubt both the victory and the Creed of his new Masters, he would struggle to resist this failure of faith; and if he fell to brooding upon all these rushing rumours of angry deeds and terrible, dark preparations against the Jews in the prison camps; if, with fingers pulling at his lips, he considered frightful whisperings about gas wagons and gas chambers and crematoria, he met them with a refusal to believe; he shut his brain and his ears to such stories—because his faith must not fail, and his father be right. And happily for him, in 1941, Germany attacked Russia, and he could turn his thoughts to something in which he really believed. He could preach a crusade of Western Man against the menace of Communism. This was a war of the European Spirit against the savage Asiatics, and, for sure, Germany must win. He must do all he could to help Germany win. And as Michael was one who must ever hope, he could not doubt that Germany would win.

Hitler attacked Russia just in time to save Michael's soul.

But it was short-lived, his new ease. Almost directly, in September, 1941, he saw the devilish thing in the streets before him, and he could blind his eyes and gag his thoughts no more. In September, 1941, all the Jews in Germany, of six years old and over, were ordered to wear the yellow star with its black J as the badge of their degradation. They were now a branded people, and Michael could not bear the sight of them coming towards him in the streets. The stitches with which the stars had been sewn on hurt him—especially those stitches with which some mother had sewn the badge to on a tiny girl's frock or a little boy's coat. She must have sewn it there with the strings of her heart, this invitation to contempt and mockery and cruelty. 'Unclean. Unclean, this little child.' These sad outlaws were no longer allowed to travel by bus or tram, unless they had a special permit because their slave-labour was far away; they must not board a train till all the Aryans had entered and chosen their places; in the hospitals, no matter how urgent their pain, they must wait against the wall till the last Aryan had passed by. 'Unclean.' Every Jewish shop had to carry on its window 'Juden Geschäft', and if Michael deliberately went into one he often found, when he came out, a group of men, or even of men and women, waiting to abuse him. But soon such Jewish shops were few and far apart, because the most of them had been smashed and looted by jeering toughs, and now stood boarded up, possibly with the words 'Juden Geschäft' still visible, and explaining why. Sometimes Michael passed a gang of Jews on hands and knees scrubbing the roadway while a ring of delighted spectators mocked them.

In England he had accepted the anti-Semitic clauses of his party's Creed, but he was not tough enough for this.

Where now could he find the strength to plod on in the path he had chosen? He found it (because he had to) in the fact that the better Germans expressed—in private—a disgust at this vileness as deep as his own, and were capable, many of them, of doing hidden acts of kindness to Jews who had been their friends—and sometimes to those whom they'd never seen before. For his comfort he collected in his heart every such kindly incident and reminded himself of British racialism in India, of their Herrenvolk attitude there, and of Amritsar. He told himself that if the rumours were true about the gas chambers and the crematoria, it was no less true that the British were submitting thousands of helpless women, children, and babies to agonising death by their obliteration bombing.

Poor comfort, because it did not make the Germans better worth serving than others, but merely no worse.

And in the deeps of his heart, he knew that Germany under its present masters, *was* worse. This then was the real hour of his sin, because he shut this knowledge down in a dungeon, out of his hearing. He muffled the voice of his own spirit and sinned against the light. He continued his daily work for Germany, speaking to Britain, to America, to Africa, with the lie in his heart. In his long hours of freedom he found what pleasure he could in strolling alone down the glades of the Grunewald, or swimming alone in the Havel, or rowing, a solitary oarsman, on one of the lakes round the city, or listening, perhaps with Dermot, to Mozart and Hadyn and Hugo Wolf in one of the restaurants in the woods. What else could he do but spend the passing days in some such fashion? He could not rise and go back to his own people. There were no longer any exit doors in the House of Rimmon.

CHAPTER TWO

So, as a wrecked man lives on the empty seas only by favour of a small, unstable raft, Michael clung to the only thing he could still believe in, the Defence of Europe against Russian Communism. It was of this, whenever possible that he spoke in his broadcasts to Britain; of this, and of reconciliation, and of an end to fratricidal war. He tried to believe that in doing so he was doing some good, but he knew well enough, and sadly enough, that one of his motives was a desire to save Germany from defeat since so alone could he save himself.

Almost daily he went to his duties in the Radio Station off the East-West Axis. Usually, a lonely figure, he walked there along the Axis, that magnificent straight avenue which led for miles through the Tiergarten to Charlottenburg and the West. Arrived at the Rundfunk, he might work on scripts for future use or take one already prepared to the censors, with whom he would wrangle for half an hour, in the effort to retain his own words. Often they let him keep most of them when the necessary half-hour battle was over, for they were not bad fellows, and he and they were good friends. Then he went out into the evening darkness, and down through a terraced garden, to a long, low wooden building that seemed hardly more than a cowhouse. It was divided up by insulating boarding into tiny box-like studios, in each of which there stood only two chairs and a table with a microphone. Michael went to the chair before his microphone, and read his script to England clearly and carefully, while a monitor sat in the other chair with a copy of the script in his hand, following it most vigilantly, to see that Michael didn't add any dubious words to it or play any monkey tricks on it by mysterious tones and stresses in his voice.

And far away in England his father sat in his cellar listening. On any evening when he suspected that Michael might be speaking Harry would sneak down to the little radio in the cellar, hoping that neither Ida nor Beth would know where he was, or perhaps he would offer some excuse for work down there and then he would make suitable noises with crates or bottles or casks in the hope that the family wouldn't guess that he'd gone fascinated towards his pain. But of course Ida knew, and Beth, and Walter, and Old Agnes and Bensky; they knew and kept their knowledge to themselves.

And there they were, father and son, one night in 1943; Michael in his narrow and boarded shed with script and microphone before him, and Harry in his cellar among his kils and barrels; there they sat with hundreds of miles of hills and plains, towns and seas, stretching between them.

Harry was sitting on the only chair, with a mallet in his hand and hammering the chair-leg every now and again that the people upstairs might imagine he was putting a vent peg into a cask or a tilt underneath it, or perhaps tapping a new barrel. But whatever the mallet was doing, his eyes were on the little wireless set which faced him from a shelf among some soft-drink bottles. Once he whistled an irrelevant air so that Ida—or Beth—or Walter—might suppose him happy.

The set was emitting its low breath before speaking. But now—stop hammering!—the station gave forth its signal, loud and clear. He jumped up and turned the set down a little and sang rather loudly, 'There's an old mill by the stream, Nellie Dean.' Then sat again on the chair.

'Germany calling. . . .'

It was not Michael's voice, and for a moment he thought, 'Is he dead? This bombing. This bombing.' It was no voice that he recognised. And since the news had no interest for him, he choosing to believe it all lies, and since there was only one voice he wanted to hear, he got up and rattled about and hummed and, opening the door, carried up to the bar as ostentatiously—and innocently—as possible a crate of light ales. He stowed them noisily—then doubled back to the cellar, lest he should be late for 'Views on the News.' Quietly he closed the door on himself.

He sat on the chair, hit a cask with the mallet, scraped his feet up and down, as one active and mobile, and waited for the news to end. And as he sat there waiting, he heard the buses and lorries drumming along the High Road just above him and wondered how many of the passengers or drivers were pointing to the Lord of Wensley as the home of Michael Cawdor Townes. It had come to his ears, through Ida and her gossiping friends, that the current joke, all over England, was that the Lord of Wensley was soon to be renamed 'The Traitor of Tooting.'

The news had stopped, thank God; and his heart beat violently in apprehension. Would it be Michael giving the 'Views on the News'?

It was. It was his voice, that young, clear, boyish voice that he'd heard so often calling to him at stump-cricket on the Common, or speaking excitedly at his side when Surrey was saving a match at the Oval. It did not seem excited tonight. It sounded tired and sad.

But at least he was still alive, and, relieved by this knowledge, Harry said almost merrily to the set, as if it were a mask over the boy's face, 'Ah! Not quite so cocksure, Mike? Getting the breeze up a bit, eh?'

Beautiful and clear, the boy's voice answered, 'Make no mistake about it, you people of Britain, Germany in these days is fighting for you. She is fighting to save Europe from the unspeakable tyrannies of Bolshevism, and Europe nowadays includes Britain. The Channel today is no more than a river——'

'A jolly little river, none the less, Mike. It kept your boys out in 1940.'

'It can be forced by modern craft as easily as the Dvina or the Dnieper——'

'Yes, crossed both ways, sonny. Just you wait and see.'

'So, should Soviet Russia ever overcome Germany, nothing on this earth could save Britain from Communism. In that day England's great story would end, and her great heritage be destroyed. I love England and its people. They are my people——'

'So, Michael?' For a moment these words had lifted Harry's head and softened his pain, but he could only shake the head sadly and spread hopeless hands. 'But go on, lad. The boy can *write*. He knows how to write a speech. He could always do that.'

Across a continent, and between the thunderings of London lorries, he could hear the pages of the boy's script rustle. 'And I wonder how in the name of sense you English can help the Russian barbarians in their effort to destroy the German people who are your kin in blood and in spirit. It is fratricide. And not only fratricide but, should it succeed, suicide. National suicide.'

'Rats!' scoffed Harry. But not too confidently. Not quite happily. And unaware that he was speaking aloud.

He gave the chair-leg another hit with the mallet, feeling he had been quiet too long. 'Damned nonsense,' he affirmed, but at the same time sighed.

'If there were any sense in the world, the English and the Germans, blood-relatives, would unite. They would be fighting shoulder to shoulder to repel the most terrible threat to civilisation since the barbarians swept down upon the decadent empire of Rome. And then the War would be quickly won. We should have peace tomorrow. But have no doubt that Germany, even if Britain continues in her treachery to western culture, is in a position, not only to defend itself, but with the aid of time, to win this war——'

'Ah, you sound a wee bit doubtful, laddie. I know that tone. You begin to doubt.'

'I can assure you the German people have never been so active in their resolve to bring this war to a successful issue. If you in Britain think anything else, if you imagine that your Asiatic allies are going to get into Berlin and pull your chestnuts out of the fire for you, well, all too soon, ladies and gentlemen, your hopes will be transmuted into the disappointment, and your jubilation into despair.'

'Sez *you*!' he scoffed again; and all the louder because in truth the words had rather frightened him.

'Were Britain with the aid of Russia capable of gaining a military triumph over the Germans she would in that event be confronted with a situation far more dangerous and complicated than that which existed in September, 1939, when she made the crass mistake of declaring war on Germany. The Bolshevik tyranny would be at her door.'

'Perhaps she prefers that to your Nazi tyranny.'

'It is because I have believed this from the beginning that I have regarded it as my duty to my country, to you all, to take the unpopular side and speak as I do to you against a war which can only end in misery for you all. I ask you to believe that there are times when loyalty to a truth can transcend even one's loyalty to a flag that one loves. It can be another form of that loyalty.'

'Won't do, sonny; won't do.'

'I remember people used to say to me in England, "What's the difference between Fascism and Communism?"'

'Yes, that was your old father. That was the old man. At last we're going to hear, are we?'

At that time there was another listening—a short dumpy little figure outside the cellar door, with an ear turned towards its chink, and eyes strained and stilled in the effort to hear. Beth, knowing full well why her father had gone down to the cellar, and why he was staying down there, and why he was banging with his mallet, had seized upon a minute when business in the bars was slack and crept down the stairs to the shut cellar door, that she might learn that Michael was alive. And now, to her astonishment, she was hearing two voices: her father's and Michael's. Quite natural these two voices sounded, there in the cellar; quite as they used to sound in the old days; her father and Michael in argument. And yet they were arguing across countries and seas.

Michael's voice: 'There is all the difference in the world. Communism was the invention of an embittered Jew who did not perceive that the historic struggle of this age is not the conflict between class and class but the struggle of all men everywhere against the few International Masters of the Money Machine——'

'Beth, Beth,' called Ida from above, and Beth rushed upstairs guiltily, her heart pummelling her for her sin, and her lips framing some such words as, 'I just ran down to see if Daddy wanted any help. He's been there so long.'

But it was not necessary to lie. Ida was happily involved with two strange customers, a man and woman, and Bossy Jehoram who had just come in, was waiting to be served. Beth sped to him. Michael was alive. She'd been hearing his voice. And one day, perhaps—oh, surely one day—she could see him again; they would all be together again.

Meantime, down in the cellar, occasionally hammering his chair-leg or a cask nearby or the cement floor, like a member of a dance-band who must supply varieties of percussion, Harry was hearing an answer to his oft-repeated question.

'. . . Communists promise that the propertied classes—and that probably means *you*—you sitting listening to me—shall be liquidated——'

'God!'

'Communism, you see, denies the right of property to all men, and this is to do violence to human nature. And what has been the outcome of this impossible attempt? A ghastly despotism that can only achieve its aims by means of the whip, the prison, the torture-chamber, and the firing squad. And that is what they purpose to bestow upon Europe. Is that what you wish to come to you?'

Harry could only stay silent now, because he would not gratify the boy with 'Lord, no.'

'Moreover, Marxism, being openly atheist, has no religion of any kind and therefore no stable morality. Its only morality——'

'Yes, but come off religion, Mike, old son. Maybe we're not so sweet on your Hitler's religion. Maybe we like his morality no more than the Bolshies'. Eh? What-say to that?'

'Would you wish to know the fruits of this new cynical morality? Well, we have proof that in the last months thousands of German women, from twelve years old to eighty, have been raped, some of them twenty times over——'

'Oh dear . . . oh dear. . . .'

'Is this what you want in England, in London? I beg you to take these questions to heart and to ponder them. My final word is this: if you in Britain thwart the effort of Germany to defeat the Russian tyrants, then in ten years' time, if not sooner, you will know that I have spoken truth to you this night. That is all. Good night, England.'

The set went into silence.

Harry got up and switched it off. 'Lord God, I hope the boy isn't right,' he said. 'Those bloody Russians. . . .'

And he went slowly and thoughtfully up the stairs. Damn! 'Ought we really to help them to win? Is he converting people? It's dreadful what he's doing—shameful—but he's right in some things. Those God-damned Russians. . . .'

He stopped on the stairs, a man halted by Doubt. 'But was he right that those bloody Germans could yet win?' *No*! But then—if the bloody Russians won, would Britain be doomed, anyway? No, no; he would not hear of it, and he walked quickly up the stairs, his indecision at an end (or so he wanted to think). 'Not a bit of it. We'll defeat the German swine first and then, if necessary, the Russian swine. One thing at a time, boys. Crikey, yes. Meantime, let them help us all they can to finish off this job first. They're doing very nicely, thank you. Maybe we shall have to deal with them afterwards. . . .'

But this didn't quite appeal to his sense of sportsmanship, to his memory of actions and gestures in which he and the boy Michael had gloried, when they sat together on the terraces of the Kennington Oval. It was all very unhappy and confusing, and he sighed as he went back behind his bar.

CHAPTER THREE

'This is the End.' Michael in his high hotel room sat sideways by the window, his arm along the back of a settee. One leg was drawn up under the other, and his spare hand played with its ankle. A lonely brooding figure he seemed; and well might he brood, for he was looking out at Berlin in the bright April daylight, as the city reeled to its fall. 'The End.'

Its enemies had been coming closer and closer for weeks now; from the east, from the south, from the west. And what could one do but sit at a window and stare out hopelessly? Stare at the constant flashing of enemy guns or at the flickering of distant flames on the sky. And listen hopelessly. Listen, not to bombs brought from British airfields, but to shells whistling from guns in the suburbs. Today the roar of a collapsing house meant the visit of a shell, not of a bomb. Listen to machine-gun fire, but not from guns served by Britons in the Berlin sky, but to sub-machine-guns held by Russians in the Berlin streets. They had come fast in these last days, the Russians; terrifyingly fast. Nine days ago, on the Fuehrer's birthday, they had still been miles away; now they were in the suburbs, east and south and west. Rumours, rushing in front of them, told that they had taken Spandau in the west and Tempelhof in the south, and were even now at the Jannowitz Bridge, not a thousand yards from the eastern entrance of Unter den Linden. With their tommy-guns and grenades they were fighting along the streets, through the houses, over the roofs and down in the Tubes.

Not two miles from where he sat. Like the Foreign Office near by, his huge hotel had been bombed and one part of it put out of use, but most of its rooms were undamaged, so he could still sit here and watch. But not for long. Two miles away. One should go. Should get out. Quickly. But where to—where to, if the Russians were on three sides of the city, and the British (so rumour said) were already in Lüneburg, and must soon meet the Russians storming towards them from

Stettin? That would close the gates of escape in the north. And in the south—why, the Americans had already met and shaken hands with the Russians in the south, somewhere near Leipzig.

Should he go towards the Americans? Would they perhaps be kinder to him than the British and the Russians? To the Americans was he a 'traitor'? Where were the nearest Americans? He had last heard of them north-east of Brunswick. Perhaps they had already linked hands with the British on Lüneburg Heath. He picked up again the only Berlin newspaper he'd been able to get today, a single sheet of only quarto size, to see if it said anything about the Americans. No; it contained little but the propaganda handed out to it by Dr. Goebbels' department: 'The hour for Berlin has come:' 'General Guderian is defending the city:' 'Berlin will be true to herself;' 'The Fuehrer is among us.'

Where to go? Nowhere to go. Or no knowledge of where to go.

Dermot? Ask Dermot? Learn what Dermot was doing. He had not seen Dermot for days. Dermot had been in Hamburg, broadcasting his last talks from there, but Michael had learned, when he gave his last broadcast from the radio station off the Axis, that Dermot had come 'skipping back' to Berlin when he heard that the British Seventh Division was only a mile from Hamburg.

Was Dermot then in his Berlin apartment? Useless to telephone. Most of the telephone lines were out of action, and those still working were reserved for the soldiers defending the city.

But if the Russians were still only at Spandau he could get to Dermot in Charlottenburg. Yes. Go quickly. Nothing else to do. He went down the hotel stairs hurriedly, like a man with an alarming ache who must seek a doctor's verdict even if it confirms the alarm, even if it prophesies death. He found that the great arched vestibule of the hotel had been turned overnight into a hospital. Civilians lay on stretchers all over the vast cold floor of pale green tiles, and doctors, nurses and wardens moved among them. Other patients on stretchers, with other nurses and orderlies tending them, lay under the arcades that ringed the vestibule. Some of the stretchers, he observed, were merely improvised things—doors snatched from ruined houses, sacking nailed between poles. The whole area smelt of blood and antiseptics and dried earth. At one place he slid on a spatter of blood. He picked his way through the casualties, while they watched him from the floor with waxen or bloody faces and suffering eyes. As he got near the door he saw some soldiers on hotel chairs, wounded, but only now being bandaged. Soldiers here? Was the fighting so close? Or were they some who had run from it?

'The End.'

§

Out in the streets he walked quickly, keeping as far as possible to the side streets—why, he could hardly say; possibly because every now and then a shell whistled over, to crash sickeningly into some hitherto unwounded building, and he felt safer, more under cover, in small narrow streets.

But whether he sped along narrow streets or wide, he could not doubt that he was looking at a city which was lying down to die. Many of the smaller houses had either collapsed into hillocks of scree or were gutted walls likely to fall outwards when the next shell shook them. Many of the great buildings were just high cages of tormented and writhen girders with their concrete floors fallen, or tilting to a fall. One street came to an abrupt close where the whole front of a warehouse had cascaded right across it and met the jumbled ruins of the house opposite. It had half buried a lamp-post in its fall.

Hardly a house in the residential streets seemed occupied. Almost every window was smashed, and few of them showed any attempt at patching the grimy shards and jagged cavities. They just gazed, in their broken fashion, at the desolation before them, and Michael trod ever and again on their splintered glass. In the rooms behind them dwelt only the wind.

Yet there were people about—people with eyes as hopeless as these windows. A pale suspense was on their faces as they turned to watch him hurrying by; their own steps were slow and sad. Some went through the doors of these broken houses; others came out of them; so presumably they were living in their cellars, crowded together. He passed some who were drunk and singing; a sight sufficiently unfamiliar in these sober streets to seem a symptom of the end. Two men, walking behind him and celebrating the End of the World, sang sentimentally 'Lily Marlene' and then roared satirically, 'Deutschland, Deutschland über alles.' A still more striking symptom, he thought, was this, that on no man anywhere did he see a Nazi badge.

In the Charlottenburg streets the ruin was less. Whole roads were intact, including the one where Dermot's apartment house stood. Nearby was the Masurenallee where stood the short-wave station of the Rundfunk, in one of whose studios he had so often spoken to Britain about the assured triumph of Germany. He went to take a last look at it before going up to Dermot. It was little damaged but apparently deserted. It looked like a vacant red-brick mansion, not very large, but too large to find a tenant.

He gazed at it for a few seconds, certain he would never see it again, and remembering his last broadcast to Britain two days ago.

He was proud of that broadcast, even as a man on his death-bed, or a prisoner in a death cell, might be proud of a last testament he had penned for his friends. He liked to think that in his script he had written the truth with courage and in fine words; actually he had written it with the suicidal courage of despair. The three censors, no less despairing, had read it before his eyes and passed it back to him without wanting, as always in the past, authority for every word in it from an official spokesman, a German newspaper, or a press-conference hand-out. Friendly fellows, one a hearty naval officer, they had read it and shrugged their shoulders and shot it back across the table to him with tired and defeated grins which said, 'Okay. Let it go. Nothing matters any more.'

'I have said always that if Britain were to defeat Germany, the price of victory would be at least as great as the price of defeat. And I say the same now, in these my last words to you. Britain's conquest will be barren; it will leave her poor and hungry and powerless, and with a far greater problem, and a far greater enemy, in front of her than she had six years ago. An alien enemy. An alien enemy of enormous size and over-whelming power whose resolve to master the rest of the world will be curbed at no point by old contemptible bourgeois notions of mercy and honour and tolerance and understanding. At this tragic hour we are ending one long epoch of Europe's history in a storm of fire and fury; in the new epoch which will lie before us when the guns cease, Europe, if she is to survive, will have to unite against the alien enemy, with England and Germany as friends and partners. I have said this from the beginning, and I say it now at the end. Good night, Britain. I bid you good night.'

So he had closed his broadcast, not without dignity, he felt, and not without an emotional power in his voice, however, tired and sad it had been; and he had wondered whether his parents and Beth, if still alive, had heard him. He hoped, greatly hoped, they had. And that, somewhat impressed, they were nearer to understanding him and forgiving him.

§

With these words, in which he took this melancholy pride, echoing in his mind, he turned into Dermot's street and, crossing the entrance hall of his apartment house, climbed three flights of sham marble stairs to his door. The door was unlatched; it was blowing against the latch in a draught; and, wondering, anxious, he pushed it open.

'Dermot,' he called. 'Dermot.'

There was no answer, and his anxiety became alarm. Had Dermot, ever quicker to act than he, gone already from Berlin—gone for ever and left him alone?

'Dermot! Dermot, old man?'

Quickly he crossed the little coat-hall and opened the sitting-room door. Dermot was there, standing by one of the two double windows, and looking out, with his fingers locked behind his back. The windows were lofty, and he looked very small there.

'Come in, Michael, old son. Come in, pray, and sit down.' Always Dermot liked to show no surprise, to keep calm and undemonstrative, no matter how sudden a visit, how unexpected a voice. It was a favourite 'stage business' with this performer. 'Make yourself at home, buddy.'

Michael looked around the room. Oddly different, this Herrenzimmer from an Englishman's study. Perhaps it was the white-tiled stove in the corner, the double windows looking out into the street, and the large bookcase filled with the German poets and philosophers whom Dermot loved, that stressed the difference. He went and sat on the edge of a brown-plush chair, like one whose call could only be brief.

'This is the end of everything, I suppose, Dermot?'

'Of course.'

'Well, what are we to do? What do you think you're doing now?'

'Doing? I'm watching to see them come. At any moment

I expect to see some gross potato-faced Russian officers driving along the street in a staff car. Billeting officers, let us say. They may even choose this for a billet.'

'They won't be here yet.'

'Are you sure? They're in the north part of Grunewald and in the Reichssportsfeld. And, by the way, they have taken the Anhalter Station, which is delightfully close to you.'

'They've *not*!'

'So I'm told.'

'God! But—Dermot—what're we to do?'

'Do? Why, obviously get out. Quit.'

'Yes, but how? How, if they're all round us?'

'Well, if you can't get out north, south, east or west, there's only one other way!'

'What way?'

'Upwards, old boy.'

'Upwards? How do you mean?'

'I mean the same way as the Fuehrer. Isn't he our Leader? Where the Fuehrer leads, I follow. Heil Hitler.'

'Please explain what you're talking about.'

Dermot came from the window and sat carelessly on the arm of one of the brown plush chairs. 'The Fuehrer will make his ascent to Heaven very shortly. And most of his loyal pals will follow up after him, like a flight of angels. Chaps have been coming this way from the Chancellery all day. They've been dodging through the Tiergarten trying to get to the C.-in-C. with messages from the Fuehrer and Dr. Goebbels. Some of them, in their natural excitement, have not been as discreet as they ought to be, and it's wonderful the stories that have come along to us, over the bush telegraph. True stories, I'm pretty certain. The Fuehrer who, as we've heard more than once, "will never capitulate" is going to commit suicide instead —though what's the difference I'm not clear. He was always rather woolly in his thinking, that little man.'

'Good . . . God . . . God!' Michael breathed in a whisper.

'Yes, and the loyal Dr. Goebbels says he'll hobble after him. And many of the others in the Bunker are going to do the same. Those who are not there—Reichsfuehrer Heinrich Himmler and his staff and Reichsmarschall Goering, and all the rest of the hierarchy, will ascend to Heaven from different parts of Germany. The Reichsmarschall, of course, will put on his finest uniform first——'

'But when—when will they do this?'

'Tonight? Tomorrow? Plainly Berlin can resist for only a day or so more. If that. And when they've done it, they're going to set the Fuehrerbunker on fire. We live in the heroic age, my boy.'

Michael stared, speechless.

'The Little Gentleman has handed poison phials to them all as his parting gift. They've thanked him for this great courtesy, and they're going to do it all in the high Viking fashion. So'm I.' Grinning, Dermot drew from his waistcoat pocket a small brass cylinder, some two inches long. He tossed it up and caught it playfully; then extracted from it a tiny phial, apparently made of glass, and held it up. 'As I said, I'm getting out. And this is my little exeat. In Hamburg they offered me false papers or this, or both. Actually I took both, but this is my real choice. It's been sitting in my pocket, waiting for today—or tomorrow.'

'But what is it, what is it?' asked Michael, though he knew well enough.

'Keep calm; it's nothing to get excited about. Just the old classic remedy for life. Cyanide. A bit hackneyed, I'm afraid —something of a cliché—but what matter, since it's swift and sure and merciful.' He made a pretence of cracking something between his teeth. 'Click—and that's all. I'm told that Reichsmarschall Goering has some of these little fellows in the pocket of each of his forty uniforms. Would you like one? To be frank, I've more than one about me. There you are. Take it if you like. Its great merit is that it'll do its work before they can wash you out like one of your old man's beer-pipes and bring you back to life.'

Michael stared at the capsule which Dermot was offering him. Did that tiny case hold death and escape and perhaps a future in another world? Were the answers to all questions, and Heaven and Hell, and forgiveness or stern punishment, shut up in it?

Do you want it?' asked the tempter, smiling, as it were indulgently.

'No . . . no . . .' he said at first, hesitating. Younger than Dermot, of softer intelligence and less forceful will, he must still hope . . . hope. . . .

'All right then: hang.' Dermot tossed up the capsule and deftly caught it. 'Hang by the neck. Swing round and round.'

'Nobody's offered me false papers, or anything.'

'No.   In Hamburg they've still got their wits about them, if not much else.   In Berlin they've gone mad.   Hamburg's got no more use for Berlin.'

'But, Dermot, surely there is still some hope.   Can't we make a run for it?   Come and have a shot at it with me.'

'Mike, if I saw the least hope of escaping I might attempt it. But there isn't any; there just isn't.   Face it, don't funk it: that we've got to die, either by hanging or by this.   If I don't take this in time there's a risk I may lose my choice, and I don't intend to lose it.   Many of the ideas we started out with, Mike, were good and right, but as usual, as always, they got into the hands of knaves and fools, with the result that they're all gone bad on us. The human race is hopeless, old fellow; in eight thousand years there's been no helping it or raising its head except for a little while; it sinks back always into roguery and loutishness.   A dull-witted and murderous crowd, except for a tiny few who can do nothing about it.   Take a look at Hamburg where I don't know how many thousands of men, women and children have been roasted alive—by us—by our British boys.   We arrange our own crematoria.   And without benefit of gas.   I'm tired of it, utterly tired of it, and so—directly I see the first Russian coming towards me—' he held up the capsule again—'I'll drink this little glass to him—to him as the last of the humans I ever want to see.'

Michael bent his head; then raised it and looked from under his eyebrows at Dermot sitting there on the arm of a plush chair. And he remembered how, six years ago, Dermot had sat on a garret chair in London and prompted him to leave his native country.   Now there he was—playing the same part ˙on a grander scale and urging him, not without grim, flamboyant jests, to leave the ranks of humanity.

But this time Michael was even less eager to obey.   'No, no, Dermot; let's make a bid for it.   Come with me.   Yes, do.' He began to crave Dermot as a companion.   'We can change our names—we can say we escaped from an internment camp— we—we could say we were refugees from the East——'

Dermot, grinning, pointed to the scar on his face.   'Can I change my mug?   I guess every soldier in the British and American armies is looking for my ugly face.   Yes, and listening for this voice.   "Germany calling.   Germany calling."   You and I have done our little job too long and too well.   They don't love us at all.   In Hamburg a monitor showed me a broadcast from London in which we were honoured by a mention——'

'*We* were?'

'Not by name, but the gentleman said, "As for the radio quislings"—that's you and me, laddie—"we shall pursue them to the ends of the earth till we find them." Some such sweet words.'

Michael's invisible heart and veins seemed to quake and shiver, as if Death, like a cold ghost, had come close behind him. He began to think, Should he jettison pride and say 'I think I'll have that capsule, Dermot, after all,' but he said only with a revealing stutter, 'The British and Americans are nowhere near us yet.'

'No, but, hell, I find the proximity of the British less disturbing than that of the Russians. The Russians have sure got us on their list, Mike. Haven't we abused them steadily to the whole world for four years? And they're very bloody men.'

'Not all, Dermot.' *Oh, let me hope a little.*

'Those that give the orders are. Those that have the say-so. And they may have a fancy to put us to the torment. Not nice. And there's another point, Michael: we could be caught by the German police, or the S.S. men, and hung as deserters or renegades. I'm told there are deserters hanging on trees and lamp-posts everywhere. So I'm sorry you won't take my advice and drink this little lot to the Ivans. Ah, well, let's drink something else as a parting ceremony. One for the road. I've something quite good here. From generous Hamburg again.' Opening a side-door of the bureau, he produced liqueur glasses and a bottle of Danzig Goldwasser. 'Auf Ihr Wohl. Pity to waste the rest of this, but I mustn't get too drunk to take my other liqueur when the time comes.'

Michael, who'd accepted his glass with a shaking hand, asked, 'Are you really going to do that?'

'Most certainly. Why stare so?'

'No. Dermot . . . no.'

'I most surely am. You can take that as settled. Now let's discuss something else.'

Michael began to believe him. And he looked at his face thinking, 'Tomorrow that face, bright-eyed now, will be wax-white, with jaw fallen and eyes fixed and staring.' And as he looked in silence he knew that, for his part, he could not do this final thing. Not yet. Oh no, not quite so quickly. One must hope a little longer. Dermot had always worshipped the ruthlessness of his own thinking, and now was he going to sacrifice himself in honour of this idol? Or was it that he, Michael, would end by offering himself as a victim to the exactly opposite quality in his character—the ever-springing, sentimental hope in him?

'Dermot, where would you . . .?'

'Where will I do it? If the Russians give me half a chance, I think of strolling out into the Tiergarten and choosing a nice tree by one of the lakes and sitting down under it. I was out in the Tiergarten yesterday and all the trees had sprinkled themselves with green; they were taking no notice of the shells. There were flowers everywhere and the scent of spring and of the good old earth. I tell you the smell of the lilac seemed the very smell of the opposite of death, and yet . . . yet I thought this would be a good place to end up in—a bit too disciplined, perhaps, like everything else in Germany—but beautiful . . . beautiful. I don't know why one should have this fancy to die in a beautiful place, under the sky. But one has . . . one has . . . Why look at me like that? . . . Besides, I don't want to give any trouble to the good people here. They've been very decent to me, the caretaker and his wife, and they've troubles enough of their own just now. They're scared to death, Mike, and they don't want any extra trouble on their third floor. In the Tiergarten I shall probably be only one of several other lads lying around, and they can sweep me up with the rest.'

Michael sipped the brandy to clear a brown-sick taste from his mouth. He did not speak.

'And you?' asked Dermot.

Michael laid his glass on a table and sat with elbows on knees and hands clasped, thinking.

'I shall at least have a shot at something else first,' he said.

'All right. As you wish, old boy.'

He had hardly said this when a shell crashed into a neighbouring street and a house-wall slid away with a roar.

Dermot walked to the window; on principle he never rushed anywhere. 'That was quite near. The nearest yet,' he said calmly.

Michael had leapt up. He was now at the window too. 'I thought it was in this street.'

'No, it was not anywhere in sight. But look. What in Beauty's name are this lot?'

German soldiers in their scuttle helmets were running down the street—running this way, eastward, as if from the Russians in the west. Stubble-bearded, hollow-eyed and caked with mud, some of them were so young and slender that their big helmets sat on them like candle-extinguishers. Perhaps they had been ordered to proceed at the double to some threatened position among those covering the centre of the city, but they looked like the fragments of an army in rout. Civilians stood at doors and windows, watching them in bewilderment.

'They look busy,' said Dermot.

'I'd better go.' Michael's heart and limbs were now trembling. 'I'd better get back. Quickly.'

'Yes. Guess you're right there. Things are happening somewhere.'

'Well. . . .' He wanted to go in haste, but . . . how did one say goodbye?

Dermot helped him. 'Then this is where we part, old son. Good luck. Fare you well. Leben Sie wohl.'

Another loud detonation—and another—they were shelling Charlottenburg. Shells streaked over with long screams before they detonated. 'Well . . . yes . . . I'd better, I suppose. . . . Yes . . . well . . . goodbye, Dermot.'

'Bye, bye, Mike. Auf—but no, there's no sense in Auf Wiedersehen. Glückliche Reise.'

That was all. After all their years together, and with death assured to one of them tonight or tomorrow, fear did not permit them a worthier farewell. Michael smiled back, raised a hand, and hurried out into the street. It was not of the shells that he was afraid—no more than his father could he feel much fear of them—it was of the Russians behind the shells. And only later that evening he remembered, with some sickness, that in his haste he had forgotten all about that capsule and his desire at least to have it about him, in case of need. He had not asked Dermot for it, after all. But he did not think of that now. Running, walking, running again, he hastened homeward to the heart of the city and his hotel room. What other place of refuge had he? None in all Berlin; and as an animal, hearing a shot, scurries into its lair, so Michael ran to the room which for five years had been his home. As he ran he remembered a hay-field years ago, and the hay-mower going round and round it, and the rabbits racing from the farmer's loud gun to the still standing crop, there to cower till the mower reached them. He thought of rats on a ship climbing higher and higher, even on to the Captain's bridge, as the hull sank and the waters poured in.

CHAPTER FOUR

ALL that evening, most of the night, trapped by doubts and treading his room, Michael worried the question, 'What can I do?' as a dog might worry a bone that will not split open. To go out into the streets towards the Russians seemed as bad as to stay here and wait for them to come. Or—a new alarm— to wait till an S.S. press-gang came into the hotel, nursing their sub-machine guns like babies at the breast, and forced every idle male into the guerrilla bands assembling for the Last Stand S.S. Blackshirts . . . Blackshirts on the Embankment in London. . . . The Leader in his black shirt at their head. . . . The proud black flags and the quietly confident drums. . . .

If the Russians suddenly appeared in the street below—or if they rose before him in a street through which he ran—how could he escape from them into death? Could he perhaps snatch a gun from some dead soldier in the street?

So he stood or strolled or sat, thinking; and the last hours of Berlin darkened about him.

Some time after dark a great silence fell upon Berlin. No reverberation of the surrounding guns; no machine-gun chatter; no whip-cracks of rifle fire; no shells crashing or splinters spattering. And in this silence the ever-springing hope lifted its head again. Was it so certain the Russians would do anything to him when they came? Might they not just pass him by and leave him where he was? They couldn't arrest everyone. But this hope was a poor wilting plant: they would know him for English; he had no false papers—oh God, why had he not asked Dermot for his, since Dermot would have no use for them? But he'd never have had the indecency to do that, and, anyhow, it was too late now. No, they would intern him first, then find out who he was, and then—oh, why had he not taken that parting gift from Dermot?

Because all Berlin was now quiet he lay down on the bed in his clothes; lay with his eyes often open, and thinking, 'This is the last time I shall see this room.' How silent the night.

'Silent night, holy night'—he lay repeating these words as one does who cannot sleep, and remembering Christmas Eves at the Lord of Wensley with boisterous company singing in the bar. He saw his father behind his counter, conducting the gentle carol with his tankard or his festival cigar.

Happy days. If only they could somehow come again. If only he could sleep and, waking, find that all this battle and terror around him had been nothing but a nightmare. Wake and find himself in his childhood's bedroom in the Lord of Wensley.

He drowsed and woke—to daylight, and a room in Berlin. It was morning, and the guns were awake too, and speaking.

He rose and went to the window. But there was no change in the street. From the hotel passages came the usual sounds of chambermaids sweeping and gossiping.

He bathed his face; cleaned out his mouth which was dry and acid; and, for want of anything better to do, went down to the Restaurant. The hotel was still functioning automatically, since no one had told it to stop. He was still known to the staff as one of Dr. Goebbels' favoured guests. The little doctor might have long ago forgotten him; he might even, if a strong rumour was true, be dead; but before going he had not countermanded any orders about der Englaender Townes, and so the hotel continued in its first obedience.

Michael went to his customary table. He could not eat, but only drink, and he sat there, sipping his malt coffee and listening to the shell-bursts. His heart bounded and thumped and quivered at each close explosion.

A big heavy old gentleman with rounded back and arthritic limbs, leaning heavily on his rubber-ferruled stick, came limping towards him. One step at a time he came, with occasional support from a chair. First the stick, then the foot: tap—tread—tap—tread—tap. Catching Michael's eye, he gave him an extraordinarily pleasant smile, despite this incapacity and slow advance. At length he lowered himself on to a chair at the next table, with some panting and a final heavy sigh. This achieved, he laid his thick stick on the floor beside him and looked again at Michael. His old eyes were mischievous. And not only mischievous, but sparkling with intelligence. 'Well, young man,' he asked breathlessly, 'what do you make of it all?'

'God knows what to think, sir.'

'Hey, but you're not German! Um Gottes Willen, you're not a Russian, are you? You haven't arrived yet, have you?'

Michael said that he was of Scotch extraction (which sounded safer than 'English') but that he'd long been a naturalised German; a lie that he always told.

'Scotch? Well, on the whole I'd glad you're not a Russian. I gather from the learned Dr. Goebbels that the Russians have not evolved far from the anthropoid apes. You don't look like an ape-man. Ah. . . .' He sighed again heavily. 'I've been helping the other doctors in the hotel here. The place is a damned Casualty Clearing Station, and I thought——'

'You're a doctor then, sir?'

'I was, hundreds of years ago. But, ach, I've forgotten all the medicine I ever knew. I can still apply a pretty bandage, however, or turn a tourniquet. And, praise be to God, I can still give a lad a shot of morphia. Or better still, a child. I put three little children out of their pain yesterday, and I thank Heaven I was able to do it. Ach, but I'm tired, tired. . . . At it for sixteen hours. . . . Far more patients than a lame old dog could deal with.' He laughed suddenly. '*Ha!* My mother was a Jew, and they tried to stop me practising ten years ago, but they were glad of me yesterday. Doch, I think so.'

'I'm sure they were, sir.'

'I got some sleep when things quietened down . . . four hours perhaps . . . but then, dear God, when you spoke, I thought for a moment the Ivans had come while I slept.'

'They'll be here soon, I suppose?'

'Here to dinner, I should think. This is probably your last breakfast without their company. But I don't know; I'm no strategist. Maybe that as the ring round the city contracts it's easier to hold.'

'Maybe,' Michael agreed, and the hope sprang again.

'And there's sure to be a Grand Last Stand round the Chancellery. The Little Gentleman there will certainly have ordered it. He likes things done in the grand manner. So a few more hundred Germans will die.'

'But there's no real sense in going on fighting, is there?'

'None whatever, I should say. It's just a last courtesy to the enemy. We must kill a few more hundred of them; that's only polite.' He cast a sidelong glance up at the notice 'Beware of Careless Talk' and almost winked. 'We can all talk the truth now. A pleasant change. A nice feeling. None whatever in continuing the war either, mein junger Freund. And the sooner it ends, the better. But with this little man in command, *we* can't end it; we can only wait for your late countrymen to come and do it for us. And may they come quickly.'

Such treason this sounded that Michael stared in astonishment; so the old doctor, sipping his ersatz coffee and breaking his bread, explained wearily, 'If the Master of the House goes mad and sets it on fire, there's nothing to do but call the neighbours in, however little you may have loved them in the past. I only wish your countrymen could have arrived before the Russians.'

'Where are the Russians now?'

'I can give you the latest, if the highly informative porter in the vestibule is right. On the north they've reached the Weidendammer Brücke and they're burrowing towards us underground and should pop up at the Friedrichstrasse Station. On the west they've reached the Leipzigerplatz and overrun most of the Tiergarten——'

'The Tiergarten? Then the whole of Charlottenburg is in their hands?'

'I imagine so.'

And Dermot now?

Lying dead beneath his chosen tree, face a waxen pallor, eyes glassed and staring up at the tree's branches.

And he, Michael, absolutely alone.

Alone in a city awaiting sack.

'Ah well,' the doctor was saying, 'I've not been able to do very much. Just staggered about and stitched up a score or so of lads. Mere cobbler's work, most of it. "Cobble and cobble as best I may"—your British soldiers used to sing that in the last war. Know the song? The last war—I had a real part in that story—*quorum pars magna fui*.' He sighed sadly. 'In command of a field hospital at one time. They weren't so worried about your Jewish grandparents then. I suppose your father did his share too, nicht?'

Michael nodded and said Yes, that was so.

'Ah well, I'll drink this to his health and yours and go out and do some more of my cobbling. It serves a purpose, of course, but don't imagine it has anything to do with the war. That's past the best cobbler's art now, and certainly beyond any repairs the little cobbler's apprentice in the Chancellery can do. Why, the Almighty Cobbler Himself, supposing He was not bored beyond exhaustion by it all, as undoubtedly He is, could hardly stitch it up to last three more days. It's for the rubbish dump, mein junger Freund, and I imagine His Excellency the Little Gentleman will follow it there, if indeed he doesn't precede it. So . . . so . . . ' The doctor, having drunk his coffee, was pressing himself out of his chair with the help of his stick and the table. The stick forced up his heavy right shoulder like a hunchback's, but his face, turning towards Michael, was as merry as his body was enfeebled. 'Young man, it mounts up, the time I spend each day, pushing myself out of chairs. Ah . . . Ugh . . . ah . . . See you at mid-day, perhaps, if the ape-men haven't come.'

'And if they have, sir, what then?'

'Well, I don't suppose they'll worry about an old hunk of decrepitude like me. In any case, I'm not worrying. If things turn out too bad a doctor always has the means to die quickly. I prepare my own little pills, you see. Kellner, die Rechnung.'

Michael's mind had jumped at the idea of asking him for one of those pills. He tried to frame the words, but his vanity would not allow him to—even though the price of such vanity was death . . . or worse. He said nothing.

But as the doctor paid the waiter and limped away, Michael came to his decision. One could not just sit and wait while the ring closed around one. If only the enemy were held till dark, he would make his bid tonight. He would try to get through the Russian patrols. There could be no continuous line in the net-work of streets and among these great house-blocks, even if many were ruins. One could slink from door to door, from ruin to ruin, from cellar to cellar.

§

Throughout the morning the Russian bombardment was somewhat formal and desultory, and, according to rumour, the situation was stationary. There was even talk of a slight improvement: German troops had advanced a little way in the east and retaken the Schlesiche railway station. A comforting word, this, to run about the halls and stairways of the hotel, because the Schlesiche station was the best part of two miles away.

Most of the afternoon Michael spent in his bedroom or in the corridors, waiting for the night. But about four o'clock a rumour met him everywhere; an excited rumour that ' something very strange was happening at the Chancellery.' The bombardment was continuing intermittently and as it were indifferently, so Michael thought it safe to walk out of the hotel as far as the Wilhelmplatz and take a peep at the Chancellery.

He did so; and more than ever was it plain to him that this was a world metropolis in its dying hour. One of the roads he must take was but an alley between hills of rubble and rock that had once been masonry. Not a street but had its disembowelled houses with their entrails in the road. From houses recently hit—he passed two such—the people were bringing out furniture, bedding, china ware, silver ware and other chattels or treasures and piling them sadly on sidewalk or camber. Here and there were cars which had been killed and smashed out of shape as they stood—or as they ran—just like human beings. On the air came a smell of burning tar from roads where falling flames or sparks had melted the tarmac and set it alight. The Chancellery, bombed, blinded, and empty, looked the same as yesterday, but behind it a tall straight pillar of smoke was rising—just such a smoke as rises skyward above some oil dump evacuated and burning.

Was it—could it be—the smoke of a Viking's funeral pyre?

Suddenly the Russian bombardment quickened, as if they had seen the pillar of smoke and were angry lest some ceremony had tricked them of a prey. Shell after shell burst around the Chancellery. Michael hurried between shells, dodging from porch to porch, back to his only home.

If—if it was as he thought, then that smoke was surely a signal to the world that Germany's hope was at an end, and the war could end with it. That smoke made final his decision. And with resolution came something like peace. If any German barricades were still left, he had his pass from the Ministry of Police enabling him to get to his radio stations and studios, and Germans would obey such a document, though the heavens were falling. If he ran into Russian control posts, well, he'd be one of those refugees from the east who'd been wandering about western Germany for months now. Let him but get through the Russians, and he would work his way northwards—towards his own people. If he had to be taken, better be taken by them than by the Russians. They were not quite merciless like the Russians. Notoriously capable of magnanimity, they might even, if he frankly admitted it all, treat him with leniency. Or perhaps he would tell them a naturalisation lie: that he'd become a naturalised German before the war started. How could they ever prove that he had not applied for and received naturalisation, when most of Berlin was rubble and ashes?

Yes, he would go back in some hope. At twenty-nine how can one do other than hope?

§

For some reason, fanciful, superstitious, he waited till such clocks as were still alive struck midnight. Wearing all the clothes he could, since this seemed the best way of carrying them, he stood in his room, waiting. The clocks struck, and as if this were his marching order, he lifted the rucksack which he'd filled with other clothes—it was the rucksack which he'd often taken on picnics in the Grunewald or by the lovely Havel lake—and, carrying it like a bag, went softly down the stairs and out of the hotel.

He did not think of it at the time, but this was the beginning of his walk home. Here were the very opposite steps from those which he'd taken, almost exactly six years before, down many flights of stairs and out of a tall red house in London.

§

The streets were not as dark as he could wish, because the black-out was flushed by a glow from some buildings ablaze, apparently in the Wilhelmstrasse. Did this mean that all had flown from the bunkers behind the government buildings, after setting them on fire? In the Wilhelmplatz by the light of these blazes he saw a straggling group of people—ten men and two women who had all the air of fugitives—hurrying towards the underground station. They went into it, and he followed them—at a distance. They went quickly down into the shallow tunnels, and he kept pace with them, feeling a relief and a slowing of his heart as he got well below the ground.

All was dark here, for the railways had been dead for days, but two of this party had electric torches. The leaders were now standing still and talking together; they took no notice of him—nor indeed of two others who had come trailing behind him. Perhaps he was not the only straggler who'd attached himself to those who knew a way to safety. Could these people, he wondered, be fugitives from the various government bunkers

—even from the Fuehrerbunker itself? The leaders, following their torch beams, now led the way along a tunnel between track and walls with Michael in his shyness following last of all. Whenever the torches went out and they stumbled on in ultimate darkness, a terror seized him lest he should lose touch with them in this blackness and, having no light, find no way out. The sweat jumped on to his brow and his temples beat with this imagined horror, which was only slightly eased when the torches flashed on again, or a shaft admitted the blue of midnight from above. Then the sweat chilled in the mildew-cold of the tunnel, while his heart faltered back with sickly beats. They stumbled on through the close, dry, sulphurous smell till they came to a station. Here, after a discussion, they crept up some stairs and arrived at the booking-hall and street entrance. Michael could not see where it was, and he never knew, because he dared not speak and draw notice to himself. The street into which they stepped was quite dark, and they could see their way only by the white-painted kerbstones. The whines and 'pings' of sniper's bullets, and the distant explosions of thrown grenades, whether by the Russians or the guerrillas, were the only sounds of war. Michael followed the grey shapes and low voices in front of him.

These shapes were going forward very slowly, very stealthily; if they spoke, it was in whispers. And suddenly the leaders stopped, so that the straggling file contracted into a cluster, and then it was that he learned that they were close to the river and were debating how to get across it. How was it possible, since the Russians must surely have their strongposts and road-blocks at every bridge? One man whispered of taking it in turns to swim the river between the bridges.

As he heard this—that he, Michael, now stood but a few yards from an enemy who would be merciless, his heart battered at his side. The sweat stood upon his palms and chilled there in the night. His knees and elbows shook, as he heard a voice gasp, 'Oh . . . oh. . . .' It was his own. He smelt the river.

Still not knowing where he was, he could only keep feebly abreast of this drifting group of runaways. But would they—dared they—attempt a passage of the river and, if so, dared he follow? Was a bullet coming to him any minute now?

'Nein! I know a better way. That is certain death.'

'Ja, richtig. You're right. That way is suicide.'

'Ja, selbstmord. Come this way.'

Abruptly they turned and walked back along the street. Immense the relief. They came through other streets to another station and went down the stairs again. Yet greater relief. Taking to the tunnels, they went for mile upon mile in the opposite direction, as it seemed, from the way they had taken before. When at last, after three hours at least of stepping and climbing and stumbling, they arrived at a station and came above ground again, it was the first rose-flushed grey of dawn. And, as always, in this hour before sunrise, the guns were silent. Michael, looking up and down a broad and empty highway saw that they were far to the west of Adolf Hitler Platz and in the Heerstrasse. All here was as quiet as in any other dawn, and the party walked on, softly but quickly, till they reached the Pichelsdorf bridge over the Havel Lake.

Here at the boat station they seized upon two pleasure-skiffs and crowded into them, but Michael had not the courage to beg a place with them. The craft were overloaded already. He stood on the bridge and watched them row away southward towards—what? He did not know their plan, and never knew. He watched them sliding out of sight and remembered how often he and Dermot had rowed happily together on this lovely sheet of water.

He was now alone in the broad street, and day was brightening. But he felt easier. Since he was now to the west of Charlottenburg, which the Russians had overrun yesterday, he must be well behind their main lines. Before him stretched a wide highroad. In the hotel he had carefully studied maps to learn which roads would lead him towards Lüneburg and he knew that this one at least bore north-west towards Nauen, and would take him the first twenty-five miles of his journey. He started forth upon it, a hundred and forty mile journey, walking quickly—very quickly—wishing to put all possible miles between him and Berlin before it was full day. Quickly onward. Vaguely towards Lüneburg Heath where, so he had heard, the British were waiting in their camps for the Peace which at last was coming towards them.

It was the first of May. Presently the distant guns opened upon Berlin, but all around him, as he walked on, were the peace and charm, the burgeoning trees and the ripening warmth, of a May morning.

CHAPTER FIVE

SEVEN mornings later he opened his eyes from a torment of dreams and saw the pine trunks beside him. He was lying prone upon the earth, and impatiently he flung himself upon his back as a man does on a bed of fever. Then he saw pine branches above him. Why pine branches? His hot, fevered fingers picked at pine needles among which he lay. The first sunlight of morning had driven, or partly driven, the stormy clouds from his consciousness and, staring up into the trees, he tried to remember who he was, and what he was. He was Michael Townes. He was in Germany. He had come out of Berlin—when? Days ago . . . days. He had reached—what had he reached?—where was he lying now? Look at that figure walking through the night. It was his own, and yet it was another's. You could watch it. It was hiding in an empty building—or no, was it not in the forest?—because of a Russian patrol. It was hurrying along the roads from village to village and seemed to have left the Russians behind for ever and to be in the only parts of Germany which neither Russians, British, nor Americans had yet overrun. No enemy anywhere. No sound of shelling anywhere. The Russians were now lords of Berlin, as once the Greeks of Troy. Not in these tranquil fields could be heard the shouts of celebration, the wails of mourning, or the screams of rape and slaughter. That farmhouse to which the figure ran when the rain tore down. The farmwife at the door, shaking her head and turning him away. Not unkindly, but saying that she does not know who he is, and the punishment for sheltering deserters or escaped prisoners is death. The Fuehrer has said so.

'But the Fuehrer is dead.'

'Ja, ja, the Fuehrer is dead. Or so the radio said. But do you believe it? We believe nothing the Nazis say; they've lied to us so often. Maybe he's dead, but the Reichsfuehrer isn't.' She grimaces. 'Not the faithful Himmler. Not the gentle Heinrich.'

'Oh, but please . . .' No, she shakes her head apologetically, presses money from her pocket into his hand, and repeating 'Nein, nein,' pushes the door shut against him; and the figure goes back into the deluging rain.

It wanders wretchedly on, that dream-figure, till at last, desperate because the wet of its clothes is now touching its skin, it sees another farmhouse and runs to the narrow shelter of its doorway. But is this the same night or a later night? A fat man in braces opens the door, looks him up and down no less suspiciously than the farmwife and shakes his head. 'Nein, nein. They come in their jackboots early in the morning and take you away. They took Herr Wasserman away, and when he came back to us you could not recognise him. He was *old*.'

'But all that is over now. The Nazis are finished. Don't you notice the silence? The Fuehrer is dead.'

'Yes, and the refugees have stopped now, Gott sei Dank. It is so. You are the first for days. And you—you are not German? You are English or American?—but don't tell me any more. No, don't say anything. I know nothing. But ach, you are wet through. Poor fellow. See over there.' He jerks his big head towards his barns and winks. 'I do not know what happens over there, and it rains too hard to go out and see. I do not go out again till tomorrow.'

'Dankeschön,' says the figure, and that night sleeps in a shed and naked under sweet-scented hay and straw, for he has cast off the sodden clothes. It is cold in the night, and, remembering it, Michael shivers, shivers convulsively, on the pine needles.

On and on, in the still wet garments, through village after village, each in its coronal of trees. A friendly carter, looking at him suspiciously but asking no questions, takes him up into his wagon and brings him into a town, whose name he has forgotten. Try as he will, he cannot remember it, here under the trees—but he gets a lodging in the town, and no one cares who he is.

Deep forests of pine and larch. The fringes of the great Lüneburg Heath; and now fear in its fullness, for somewhere on these high uplands are the British—his own people.

The clouded pictures are fading from his mind, to become wild and horror-touched dreams again; but what had actually happened was this. It was the fifth day since his flight from Berlin, and he had walked through the cool, shadowed forests till he found himself climbing out of them on to heaving wastes of heath and scrub where the spinneys were but few, and there seemed no movement anywhere except the trees bending and ruffled in a westerly wind and some lonely sheep grazing on the harsh, ungenerous soil. Knowing nothing else to do, he walked steadily northward over these rolling highlands, while the wind, half a gale and sighing loud or keening, smote him on cheek and shoulder. A wind from the west, and coming perhaps from Britain, it was sweeping across the Great North Plain of Europe towards the Russians and Moscow and the boundless steppes—and what was he but a speck in its path?

Twenty miles or more he walked that day, and suddenly, in the evening, breasting a ridge, he saw tents in the distance. They looked very small because they were far away in a wooded coombe. The British tents? He walked closer and looked down upon them—but from a sufficient distance still. His heart panted and pumped. Yes, before one of them, large as a marquee, was a white mast at which a Union Jack tore fretfully.

He stood looking down upon them and dared not go further. Who could he pretend to be? How could he deny his name? Were there not some who, at the first sound of his voice, would suspect? Yes, he had woven the net for himself with threads from his voice; and, thinking this, he turned back. For a while the wind dropped, to leave a warm and gracious May evening, and he wandered about, thinking how lovely life might be if only this fear were taken from him.

The woods were many in these parts, and that night he lay under trees, listening to the stridulation of the crickets or to the melancholy call of a tawny owl, which bird he likened to himself, since it hid and huddled in trees and feared anyone who approached. In the morning he went and looked at those tents again. But he could not approach them; on the contrary he ran when he thought he heard someone approaching him. At the sound he went quickly down a slope, like a man who has climbed stairs and comes down again, his purpose abandoned. And all day he wandered on the heath, now this way, now that, but ever at about the same distance from his own people. He did not know how to go forward or how to go back. Was there ever a loneliness like that of a man wandering between two states, to neither of which he belonged? There was no fellowship, no kin, behind him or ahead. These wastes of moorland were a No-Man's-Land in which alone he had a place of standing.

§

That evening the rain came again, with a yet more unpitying wind, and despair sickened his heart as he huddled in the only possible shelter, under trees, and watched the rain travel eastward over the tops like veils of thin muslin. And suddenly he began to shiver; an ache crowded into his head; his skin registered every touch of the wind; it prickled with the cold; his back ached as never before; and now came a tremor that racked him almost pleasantly—but it forced him to sit down—to lie down—and the lying down was sweet and pleasant—but scarcely had he taken its relief before he felt driven to get up and walk—and the getting up was sweet and pleasant too—even though, as he walked, a rigor doubled him up like a saint bowing to the earth, and he had to lie down again. But he could not stay in any position and desperately he walked out into the rain—he ran—he rested against trees, huddled in his coat and craving warmth—he walked on again—he came to a sandy road between pines and hoped it might lead him to a village; but the pain in his back and a new and more violent rigor drove him under the wayside trees and flung him down on to the pine needles.

All night he lay there, while his mind went tossing away on a tide of dreadful, hurrying dreams.

§

Two young officers came along the sandy road between the pines, one strolling by the right-hand gutter, the other by the left; two slim lads in British battle-khaki, one with two stars on his shoulder, the other, who looked no more than nineteen, with only one. They carried no arms, but the younger one swung a greengrocer's basket at his side, a most unmilitary accoutrement, which at least suggested that Peace had come.

The senior, Lieutenant William Prescott, said, "'Fraid it's a washout, Stewey. It's too early. Much too early. You seldom find Fairy Rings till June. Pity! They're lovely eating. No good looking under the trees, Stew; they don't like shade.

Late summer and autumn's the time. Still—with luck we may find something.'

'Aye, it's tu airly for Fairy Rings,' agreed the junior, Second Lieutenant Stewart Craig, who was walking in front. 'They call 'em Scotch bonnets where I come from.'

'They would.'

Prescott, glancing at the glengarry which Craig was wearing, thought he ought to be able to make some joke about it, but before he could think of anything the least satisfactory Craig stooped and picked a fungus. 'This laddie any guid, Bill?'

'No. No good at all. Shouldn't go for anything that's directly under the trees without asking me.'

Craig chucked his find into the ditch. He looked into his basket. 'It's an awfu' puir lot we've got here, Bill. No' a verra guid show for an afternoon's wairk.'

'Yes, they're mostly morels, but morels are quite nice eating. We'll get the corporal to stuff 'em with something tasty. My old man was a dab at that. Okay then, Stew, I guess we'll ease off for home. We were saps to come out as early as this. Late May's the earliest, really. But you never know what's going to happen in Germany. Germany leads the world. Deutschland über alles.'

They strolled on through the peaceful day, making their way slowly back to camp. The sandy road went undulating ahead of them, over the open heath, and the pines and larches accompanied it all the way in a narrow strip, three or four abreast. Beyond the trees they could see the tumbled moorland stretching to the feet of the brilliant sky and bearing little on its swells but heath and brushwood and outcrops of quartzy sand. Sometimes the sand blinked in the sun.

'No, it's a wash-out,' sighed Prescott. 'I half hoped that, with a spot of luck, we might find a few chanterelles, but they're not showing up. Hi!—but Christ!' He had stopped and was peering across the ditch into the shadows beneath a company of pines. 'Stew! Stewey! Here.'

Craig turned at his voice, startled.

'God!' Prescott leapt the ditch and walked into the pines. Craig ran back and joined him.

Prescott was looking down upon a man lying prone on the earth, his face resting upon one arm, and the other arm flung out to its full length beside him, with its fingers bent among the pine needles. The man's clothes were soaked and deranged, and a few feet away from him lay a rucksack so sodden that it might have been dipped into one of the heath ponds.

'Lord presairve us!' said the young Craig. 'Guid Gud! He's no dead, is he?'

Prescott put his finger gently on the man's shoulder. It shivered away like a snail's horn at a touch. 'No, he's alive all right. But he's absolutely soaked to the skin. His clothes are like pulp.'

'Then he's been there aw' night. There's no' been any rain since last night.'

Prescott spoke to the prone figure. 'Say, old boy? Are you all right? No, no answer. Line disconnected or gone dead. Hell, Stewey, d'you know any German?'

'Not a word. "Guten Morgen", and "Gute Nacht, gnaediges Fraeulein",—but neither o' them's verra appropriate to this occasion.'

At the sound of their voices the man threw himself over on to his back, and they saw that his face was dirty with six days' growth of beard. It was dirty also with earth and rain—or earth and tears. His eyes looked into their eyes; then closed, while his fingers picked at his coat.

'He doesn't look like an ordinary tramp,' said Prescott. 'He hasn't shaved for a week, but those are damned good clothes, or were once.'

'Aye; he's no working man. Luke at his hah'nds.'

'He looks a gentleman to me.' Prescottt touched him again. 'Say, old son . . . mein Herr?'

The eyes did not open, and Prescott laid his fingers on his brow. 'He's in one hell of a fever. I should say his temperature's about a hundred and ten. We must get him to a doctor.'

'Get him to a padre, if he's a hundred and ten. Has he no' got any papers on him?'

Prescott felt in the man's breast pocket, but did not like to trespass further. 'I don't know. What do we do now, Stewey? Where do we go from here?'

'He's out again, is he?'

'Looks like it. Yes. Passed right out, I think. Say, mein Herr . . . can you hear me? Perhaps he's a Russian refugee. Say, Tovarish?'

The eyes opened; they tried to look round on the heath, but the sunlight troubled them. The man blinked and shook his head hopelessly. His lips trembled and his voice gasped, 'Who are you? Where've you come from?'

'Christ, is he English, Stewey?'

'Sounds like it.'

'He could be. He doesn't look the typical brutal, ghastly Hun.'

'But those clothes of his are Jairman. No British tailor ever tairned out a suit like that.'

'That's true. Could he be an English prisoner escaped? Sloshed a Bosche and pinched his clothes—stout fellow!'

'Who are you?' The man's strained eyes swung from one to the other. 'Where do you come from?'

'That's rather what we want to know about you, old boy. Are you a p.o.w.—what? A British p.o.w.?'

'Get me something to stop this—to *stop* it. This pain. Oh . . . my . . . God . . . oh. . . . Morphia—the old doctor talked about morphia.'

'Yes, you're not feeling too good, are you? Never mind, never worry; we'll get you something, but we haven't got it here. What do you say to a fag? Eine zigarette, what—eh?' Prescott's hand dived into his tunic pocket for his cigarette case. 'Expect you could do with a fag.'

The man did not seem to understand. 'Is it time?' he said.

'Time? Time for what? What do you mean?'

'What time is it in Balham?'

'Chrimes, he's nuts, Stewey. Did he say Balham?'

'Sounded verra like it. Mebbe he meant Bairlin.'

'It's somewhere about three, chum. Fifteen hundred hours. He's British all right by his accent. And a gentleman, I should say. Say, squire, you're British, aren't you?'

The man stared as if he didn't understand the question. Or, even, as if he didn't know the answer. '*You* are British?' he said after a time.

'Not a doubt about that. But what about you, chum? Oh, hell, Stewey, he's out again. He's not here any more. . . . Wait. . . . Wait! He's coming back again. He's with us again. Good. Listen, brother: we want to help you, so can you tell us who the hell you are? Your name, see? Yes? What did you say?'

'Is it over?'

'Is what over?'

'Der Krieg.'

'Der what, Stew?'

'Krieg. Krieg's the War. *I* know that. He wants to know if it's over.'

'Oh, ah, the War? The jolly old War? Yes, that's all over. Yes, rather! Fini. Kaput. Old Jerry finally surrendered at two o'clock this morning.'

'What day is it?'

'It's the seventh of May, and tomorrow'll be V-day, we think, when everybody's going to celebrate like it's the Resurrection or Judgment Day or something. Now be a gent and tell us who you are.'

'Who am I?' The man lifted up the small of his back, restlessly, groaned, and turned to one side. His mouth dropped open and his eyes closed.

'Gone again. Stewey, nip back like billy-oh and get an ambulance. He's dying, I think. Tell 'em he's on the edge of eternity and if they don't hurry he'll tumble right in. I'll stay with him, poor blighter.'

'Okay, Bill.'

Craig hurried between walking and running towards Lüneberg.

Prescott sat on the pine needles and lit himself a cigarette. The sick man lay on his side, facing Prescott, but with eyes closed. And they stayed together thus, unmoving, except when Prescott lit himself a cigarette. After a while Prescott realised that his fevered patient was muttering. He bent an ear to him.

'I speak to you as one Englishman to all Englishmen. Is it worth it?'

Strange words. Prescott leaned lower.

'Consider. The most important harbours in Europe, spread over a nine-hundred kilometre front, are in German hands. Nothing has happened so far—true—but the British . . . let me tell you . . . are becoming more and more apprehensive of this ominous quiet. . . . Nerves are stretched to breaking point as the people of that unhappy isle scan the air every night before they go to bed and thank God that they are alive as yet. . . . Is Dad alive and Mum and Beth? . . . Oh, God . . . God. . . .' Suffering, he swung over on to his back and stared up into the pine branches. The sunlight trembled in bars across his face. 'Is all South London flat? Is the old Lord of Wensley still standing?'

'Wensley!' exclaimed Prescott, remembering something. But

the voice had mumbled into nothing, and he leaned closer, saying, 'Yes? Yes?' to start it again.

The man opened drowsy eyes, stared bemused at Prescott, and asked, 'Am I going to die?'

'No, no; we'll get you all right; don't you worry.'

'Are you getting me loud and clear?'

'What? Come again.'

'Are they getting me loud and clear in Balham?'

'Yes, yes.'

'A few days ago I was in Dunkirk, ladies and gentlemen, and never was there a more striking example of the efficiency of German air attack. . . .'

'Yes? Go on. Go on.'

'The whole town was one ruin; the ships were sunk in the harbours and the quays blown up so that loading, unloading and storage were all alike impossible. . . . And yet only a small part of the German air force was employed. Now . . . now the whole might of the Luftwaffe faces Britain. . . .'

In amazement and excitement Prescott had risen to his feet. 'God alive!' he exclaimed. 'Good lord! . . . I believe it's . . .' That to him, of all the world, should have come this luck—the luck of stumbling on Michael Townes and taking him back as a prize. The fame that would be his. The story that would be his—to tell for evermore. He felt pity for this poor helpless castaway at his feet, but his pleased excitement was uppermost, and he knelt down by the man's side. 'Old man, listen; try to tell me. Is your name Townes, by any chance?' In a friendly, bantering attempt to stir a memory, he added, 'Germany calling—what? Eh? Germany calling.'

'Germany calling. Station Calais, five one four.'

'Yes. That's right.'

'You are about to hear the news in English.'

'Yes, yes?'

'The 2015 English news bulletin for the Africa zone. . . . Oh, God!' The sufferer turned on to his other side. 'The Midnight Postscript in the 0015 Calais bulletin. . . .'

'Yes; and is—is your name Michael Townes, by any chance?'

The sufferer turned again, looked with straining, fever-puzzled eyes into his questioner's face above him, and said at last—still staring—'By courtesy of the Berlin shortwave station . . . which has placed its facilities at the disposal of Michael Townes——'

'And are *you* Michael Townes?'

'—that he may speak the truth to his listeners . . . Britishers the world over. . . .' But his eyes closed as he drowsed away again.

'It is! I'm sure it is. All right; rest, old boy. The lad came from the Lord of Wensley, or the Traitor of Tooting, as they call it now. Of course it's him. Good God! The poor, poor bloke.' Prescott walked on to the road and looked the way Craig had gone, aching for him to return.

§

'Who are you?' Was it himself who had asked that? No. An English voice. And how long ago? Surely he had dreamed he was broadcasting. And now: 'My friend's gone for an ambulance. We'll soon have you comfy and get you well again.'

So. The riddle had solved itself. That marquee with the flag in front, down by the trees. The British. He could not get to them, but they had come to him. And, on the whole, he was glad that something had happened, because he felt too ill, too awful, to be afraid. Only take him somewhere where they would stop this pain in the back, this ache in the head, these nightmare dreams. And this shivering. Pile the blankets on me, *please*. Have you comfy and get you well again—but what for? Because you can't hang a sick man; it wouldn't be decent. You need him in good condition——

'It won't be long now. The camp's only two kilometres away, and the ambulance'll come waffling along like stink. You wouldn't like to tell me your name, would you? No? I quite understand. Please yourself.'

Michael shut his eyes again. He was too tired, too drowsy, to wrestle with the problem whether to tell his name or a lie.

They had him now. They would take him back to England. He would see old London again—or no: he would be shut in a blue prison van. Brixton Prison? How well he knew it. Or Wandsworth Prison perhaps—both in his own South London. Could you climb on a stool and see South London from a cell window through the bars? It was at Wandsworth that they——

'Ah, here it comes. Smart work. Now we shall be all right. Two hoots, and we'll have you in hospital. It's coming at a hell of a lick.'

Michael opened his eyes. The English officer was standing in the road and waving in exaggerated greeting to someone or something. A grey van with a red cross above its driving seat slithered to a halt right in front of him. Three men sprang from the driving seat like firemen from their engine, and two of them ran to the back of the van and flung wide its doors. The third was a very young officer whom Michael half remembered seeing before. This officer stood watching.

The first officer spoke rather low. 'Chaps, do you know who this is?'

'No, sir,' said the men, fixing open the doors.

'Stewey, old cock, do you realise who we've got here?'

'No. Haven't a clue. Do *you* know?'

'He's——' and he dropped his voice to mention a name.

'My . . . *God*!' said the young officer.

'It's never!' said the men, leaving their van at once and coming to look down on him. 'Him, is it? Gawd's Christ!'

Michael turned over on to his face and closed his eyes that he might not see theirs gazing down.

'It is. I'm certain of it.'

'Gawd! And he doesn't look a bad chap.'

'But how do you know, Bill?'

'Did he say so, sir?'

'He's been blethering about his home in South London, The Lord of Wensley, and broadcasting to Britishers the world over. I knew his voice then—directly. We've often turned it on in the Mess for ten minutes' light entertainment.'

'So that's '*im*, is it?' repeated one of the men, looking down upon his prostrate figure and musing. 'Well, he's properly crashed and bought it, hasn't he? And right in our lines, as you might say.'

'It's my guess he was coming to give himself up,' said Prescott.

'Was he, and all? Well, it'll be "finish" for 'im.'

'Yes. Bring the stretcher . . . poor devil.'

Very gently they were lifting him on to a stretcher. Gently they spread blankets over him, with encouraging words. One of them placed Michael's left arm, which was hanging helplessly down, comfortably within the blankets. 'There. That's better, mate.' They slid the stretcher into the van and two of the men sat beside him, smiling down with the friendly grins one gives to a sick man. A voice on the road said 'All serene? Good. Right away, guard,' and the van moved off smoothly, past the pine trees, and gathered speed.

So they carried him home to his own people.

CHAPTER SIX

FAR away from the pines and sand of Lüneburg Heath, far away among the crowded buildings of South London, the Lord of Wensley was loud with voices—voices talking, shouting, laughing, singing. Its bars, Saloon and Public, were as crowded as on any New Year's Eve, and indeed this was the Eve of a New Time, a New Beginning. The Eve of Peace. All knew that at any moment the Prime Minister would announce the end of the German War and proclaim tomorrow as Victory-in-Europe Day and a national holiday. This was the eve of London's Great Party; and already the Captain's bars were adorned with little flags— flags which he'd rushed out and bought that morning from street-sellers who'd sprung up on the pavements of the High Road like so many flowering shrubs. These toy flags stood on counters, tables and bar-back, while two large Union Jacks framed the portrait of the King.

They were all there behind the bar, Captain Townes, Ida, Beth, Walter, Old Agnes and Bensky, because the customers were many; all the 'regulars' and many others were there, and most were drinking deep in honour of Victory.

The free space beneath the browned Lincrusta ceiling and above the mahogany partitions of the bars seemed as thick with voices as with smoke. Music came from the little wireless set on its wall-bracket, but no one gave *that* any attention; all preferred the music of their own voices in community song. Some of the songs were sung in sequence; others, like some sentences in the High Court, ran concurrently; some were appropriate to the great hour; most were not. A ring of men and women near the doors were singing

> The elephant on the back of the flea,
> Vive la compagnie

and tripping to the measure forward and back. Five young soldiers on leave preferred a private gathering and sang 'Here's to good old beer—drink it down,' rather more appropriately since they were waving their cans and tumblers to the music. A school of older men, two of whom, grey and wrinkled, were lately disembodied Home Guards, were remembering their old forgotten war of thirty years before and singing with some appropriateness but little decorum

> Après la guerre fini,
> Anglais soldats parti.
> Mademoiselle in the family way,
> Après la guerre fini,

though they did, in consideration of the ladies present, drop their voices into a whispered unison for the last lines, 'Mademoiselle can go to hell Après la guerre fini.'

Yes, the second German war was dead. They waited but to hear the solemn announcement of its passing and the call to its lively obsequies tomorrow.

Captain Townes, rapidly wiping cans and wine glasses, talked across the bar to Bossy Jehoram. A long cigar fidgeted between his lips as he wiped and talked, for this was a festival, certainly. Near them stood Dick Templer, who, shy and quiet as ever, took little part in the talk, and none in the boisterous singing, though he watched this with his pale blue eyes smiling from beneath the untidy grey eyebrows. Grey?—no, these heavy eyebrows were almost white now, for he had touched seventy this year. And his friend, Harry, was sixty-five! 'We grow old, brother,' Harry would say, 'we grow old.' Beth, further along the counter, would have liked to talk with her Uncle Dick, but she hadn't the heart to shake off a lively young soldier who, rather drunk and 'perfectly sweet' (as she said) was serenading her with uplifted glass and eyes bright with inspiration and impudence, 'If you've never been the lover of the landlady's daughter, Then you cannot have a second piece of pie.'

Harry, hearing these old songs of 1914–18, even as he wiped and talked, said sadly to Dick, 'We've been hardly more than base wallahs in this war, Dick;' and when Dick suggested that they'd tried to do a bit in the Home Guard, Harry, recalling rather than hearing, asked him, 'Remember the 11th of November, 1918, Dick, and your speech in the Mess? No, of course you don't; you were too tight. He was as tight as your stays, Ida ducks, but, being a lawyer, he thought he ought to make a speech to the Colonel. I expect he was so blind that he thought the C.O. was a beak. He got up and said, "The old Bosche is beaten, shentlemen, and, in my sub-mission, this is a very great moment; we shall never see any-thing like it again in our lifetimes." That's what he said, honest he did, and look at us now! D'you remember, Dick? No, you were too tight.'

'I don't believe a word of it,' said Ida; and to look at Dick now with his close-trimmed white moustache and the stiff white eyebrows, it did seem an unlikely story. 'I don't believe Dick ever got tight.'

'Good lummy!' Harry was appalled at the simplicity of women. 'My dear girl, you've no idea what a lad he was thirty years ago. Why, someone told him to shut up, and Dick leaned over the mess table and tried to slosh him a five-penny one on the bonce. He'd tell you it's all true if he were the least bit talkative. Eh, Dick, deny it if you can, you big stiff.'

Dick only smiled gently and said nothing.

'You see? He no longer tells lies, now that he's a quiet lad and a changed character, so he can't deny it. What you none of you realise is that it was Dick who taught me to drink.'

'Ho, ho; that's a good one,' scoffed Bossy Jehoram. 'I should think you turned to beer from your mother's milk. Give me another half, anyway, Harry, if you've got it. How's the beer holding out?'

'Plenty for all. Why, my dear chap, the brewers' drays have been dashing all over London with extra beer for the boys. All pubs are open till midnight tomorrow—unless the licensee's failed to notify the cops—and if there's one such licensee in London I'll lay down and die.'

'Yes,' Here Dick came in with a story. 'I saw some of their drays trying to get down Whitehall this evening, but—well, you should have seen Trafalgar Square and Whitehall. The omnibuses and cars could hardly move along for the crowds streaming up and down——'

'Don't care a damn about the omnibuses and cars,' inter-rupted Harry, 'but they mustn't stop the brewers' drays.'

'And the strangest thing of all was that the police were being treated everywhere as the heroes of the hour. Everyone seemed to think he'd got to pat at least one policeman on the back or shake his hand. They were queuing up to shake the hand of a police sergeant in Parliament Square.'

'Good old London cops!' said Harry.

The old apologetic twinkle was in Dick's pale eyes and the never quite completed smile at his lips, as he proceeded, 'And in Strutton Ground there was an old lady of ninety with a comic hat on her head lifting up her skirts and dancing a very pretty minuet with her old man, to the accompaniment of a mouth organ. I stopped to look and she greeted me with "What cheer, me ole china!"'

'Good old London!' Harry was delighted, and the festival cigar in his lips danced up and down as he spoke. 'Still alive and kicking. They never got London down.'

'Stop, Harry! Listen! Look!' Ida had touched his arm. 'Old Mr. Mallalieu's going to do his stuff.'

'No!' Harry objected. 'No, don't let him. Silly old man.'

'Oh, yes, let him do it, if he wants to. You must let him do it once in a way. It makes him so happy.'

'Well, it makes me feel awful,' grumbled Harry. 'This isn't a theatre; it's a drinkshop.'

'Never mind you. Everybody's entitled to enjoy themselves once in a way. And to-day of all days. . . .'

Old Andrew Mallalieu (his real name was Andrew Hinds) was a patriarchal actor in a wide-brimmed black hat and a long black overcoat, with a dirty brown cardigan underneath it. An old barnstormer, his grey locks hung à la Irving, his putty-coloured face seemed made of dry rubber, and his eyes rolled this way and that as he spoke, whether on a stage or on a bar floor. He came often to the Lord of Wensley from his lodging in Brixton (where the old actors and artistes lived) not, as he said, because he cared for the company there, but because he enjoyed the walk by Tooting Bec Common. He would come towards the Saloon doors with his black sombrero on one side and his malacca cane swinging between two elegant figures, its silver knob as wrinkled, as tarnished, as himself.

Jehoram, self-appointed M.C. as usual, yelled out, 'Silence, everyone! Switch off, do! Andy's got some good words for us. Good words. *Shut* up, will you? Go on, Andy. Kick off.'

And Andy, loosening up his shoulders for some fine gestures with arm and hand, as might a busker before entertaining a pit-door queue, cleared his throat richly and moistily, threw forward his chest, moved his old lips up and down several times to prepare them for action; then raised a commanding finger and began:

> Why ring not out the bells aloud throughout the town?
> Dauphin, command the citizens make bonfires,
> And feast and banquet in the open streets
> To celebrate the joy that God hath given us.
> All England will be replete with mirth and joy
> When they shall hear how we have played the men . . .
> Come in, and let us banquet royally,
> After this golden day of victory.

Whereat old Andy brought his hand to the front of his cardigan and bowed low, rather in advance of the applause.

'Hurray,' shouted all, and 'Encore,' though Harry muttered, 'He's a silly old man,' and Beth, amused, contradicted him, maintaining he was 'adorable.'

Mr. Mallalieu, more than ready to give an encore, loosened up his shoulders again, opened wide his long black overcoat which he'd been absent-mindedly buttoning, said, 'Well . . . certainly . . . if you really wish it, dear boys,' and advanced a listing shoe forward and an uncleanly hand outward, to command a silence meet for his voice.

> Oh, let us pay the time but needful woe,
> Since it hath been beforehand with our griefs.
> This England never did, nor never shall,
> Lie at the proud foot of a conqueror,
> But when it first did help to wound itself.
> Now these her princes are come home again——

he swept a graceful hand towards the young soldiers—

> Come the three corners of the world in arms
> And we shall shock them——

here he stamped the forward foot as if to shock with this weapon the corners of the world—

> Nought shall make us rue,
> If England to itself do rest but true.

He bowed again, and the people cried 'Bravo' and 'Hurray' and some clapped, though it was obvious (to all but Andy) that most of them had been embarrassed by this too explicit patriotism. But like all English audiences they were merciful and anxious to put at ease an actor of whose performance they had, in fact, been rather ashamed. They clapped, and Andy, bowing yet again, said, 'I have a kind soul that would give you thanks, And knows not how to do it but with tears.'

'Don't mention it, Andy,' begged Jehoram. 'You're very welcome, I'm sure.'

Others whom Andy couldn't hear jeered among themselves but not so Harry, for at the words, 'Come the three corners of the world in arms, And we shall shock them,' he had been forced to turn round to his bar-back and fiddle with bottles.

And, turning, he heard for the first time his little wireless set.

'Stand by for the News,' he roared, glad of the chance to be a full man again, and swinging round to his company, 'Silence all. Big Ben. Now for the greatest news ever.'

And Bossy Jehoram, who didn't easily yield command of a crowd, bellowed in echo, 'Silence! Silence all, and damn you.'

They obeyed, and in all the bars beneath the Lincrusta there was silence, as for a curtain's rise. Harry murmured to Dick, 'My God, Dick, I'm glad you were here for this.'

§

The last note of nine o'clock died, and the announcer spoke.

'The Allies today officially announced that Germany had surrendered unconditionally. The surrender took place at 2.41 a.m., French time, at the little schoolroom which is General Eisenhower's Headquarters. Colonel-General Jodl, after signing for Germany, said, "With this signature the German armed forces are delivered into the victors' hands."'

Silence at first in the bars. The news was too big for noise. Silence till one of the young soldiers said, 'Well, that's that, chaps.'

The job of him and his mates was done.

Jehoram who must show off his attainments, even in this hour, said, 'Fine. Napoo,' and transposed ' Napoo' into his, as he supposed, admirable French, 'Il n'y en a plus. Voila tout.'

The announcer, not pausing for such comments, was pursuing his story, so Jehoram, having said all he wanted to say, roared, 'Silence! Let the gen'l'man continue.'

'The end of the War,' the gentleman was saying, 'will be officially announced in a broadcast by the Prime Minister at three o'clock tomorrow afternoon. In view of this fact, to-morrow will be treated as Victory-in-Europe Day and regarded as a holiday. His Majesty the King will broadcast to the people of the British Empire and Commonwealth at 9.0 p.m. Parliament will meet at the usual time——'

Not interested in Parliament's meeting, many in the bars began to talk again, and the talk would have become general if Jehoram and Harry, nearer the radio, hadn't heard words of such interest that Jehoram felt moved to yell, 'Listen again, boys. *Shut* up! What a lot of gasbags you are. They've found Goebbels.'

'What? Alive?'

'No. Only what's left of him. Listen, can't you?'

'Reports reaching Moscow today stated that the bodies of Dr. Goebbels and his wife and children had been found in an air-raid shelter in Berlin. The children appeared to have been put to death by poison. Some reports add that the charred bodies of Goebbels and his wife were found in the garden of the Chancellery where abortive attempts had been made to burn them. The Russians also report having finally identified a body as that of Dermot O'Neill, the British broadcaster in the German radio service.'

A great silence in the bars now.

'His body was found in a wooded part of the Tiergarten, the great park of Berlin, on the bank of one of its many lakes. By his side was a book of Heine's songs, opened—whether by accident or design no one knows—at the song, "Ich grolle nicht, und wenn das Herz auch bricht"—"I do not murmur, even though my heart is breaking." There were no wounds on the body, and it is believed that he committed suicide by taking poison as the Russians entered the city.'

Harry had been nodding with satisfaction. 'And good riddance to *him*,' he said softly.

'Hush, Harry,' muttered Ida at his side. 'The boy is dead.'

'For which may God be praised.'

'You shouldn't say such things.'

'I shall certainly say them. It was that little wretch who did everything. He was always a tempter. He lured my son from me, and now he has probably lost him to me for ever. He can rot.'

Only those who heard nothing of this, and knew nothing of Captain Townes's son, dared to speak, and their voices rang loud in a silence. 'Well, he's done the hangman out of a tenner.' 'Yes, he didn't mean to fall into that little tradesman's trap.' 'Wish to God they'd got him alive,' said one of the young soldiers, 'and handed him over to us'—but a hand quietened him, and a whisper 'Keep your great mouth shut, you bloody young fool.'

'Why?' demanded the speaker, but he was never answered, for now the announcer was saying, 'There is news also of another British broadcaster in the German service. It is reported from British 2nd Army Headquarters that Michael Townes was captured this afternoon——'

'Hurray!' shouted a stranger, as he might have done, in previous months, at the sinking of a German battleship—but very quickly, and by all near by, he was silenced.

'—on Lüneburg Heath, not far from the place where all the enemy forces in North West Germany surrendered three days ago to the 21st Army Group——'

All eyes had turned to Harry, Ida, and Beth. The company stood like statues. Ida was staring—gaping—at the wireless set. So were Harry and Beth.

'Two officers walking on the heath found him lying under some roadside trees in a state of high fever. Some reports say that he spoke first in German and then in English and that the officers at once recognised his voice; others that in his delirium he admitted his identity. He was taken in an ambulance to the 74th General Hospital, Lüneburg, where his condition is said to be grave.'

'Oh, oh!' A cry from Ida, who was shaking her head in her usual abandonment to despair. Beth led her to a stool behind the bar and tried to comfort her as she sat, moaning.

Harry only stared at the set which, with its wooden indifference, was telling him this news.

'There is no suggestion that Townes had attempted suicide. On the contrary, he is reported to have said in hospital, "I know that others have committed suicide, but I didn't want to do that." The assumption is that he had been wandering near the outskirts of the British camps with a view to surrendering. The B.B.C. understands that his case has been considered in the Attorney-General's office and, if he recovers, he will be brought back to England to face a charge of treason.'

Harry turned to a stranger at the bar. 'What's for you, sir? Sorry to keep you waiting. Same again? And you, Dick? What's yours?'

But neither answered. There was only a silence of compassion in the bars.

Harry looked straight at all his customers. 'Go on, boys,' he urged. 'Enjoy yourselves. It's nothing to do with you.'

'What'll they do to him, what'll they do to him?' Ida was moaning.

'But he's alive, Mum,' Beth was comforting her. 'He's alive, and the war's over.'

'He's ill. He's ill. They said so. He may be dying. They must let me go to him. Oh, oh!' And the uncontrolled head-shaking began again.

'Take her upstairs, Beth,' said Harry in a low voice, 'and look after her. George, what about another little one? Same again? Good. And you, madam?'

Dick said, 'You go with her, Harry. We can manage down here. Or why not close the bars for tonight? Everyone'll understand.'

'Not on your life! Close this night of all nights? No, thank you, Dick. Beth'll look after her, and I'll stay here. One of the family should be on the bridge tonight. Yes, sir, what's yours? Brown ale? Right, sir; we've plenty of that.'

But, from now on, there was little more than whispering in the bars. The memory of that news, and the sight of the Captain there, damped down to less than a smoulder the gaiety of the company hitherto. Harry, perceiving this, said, 'You're right, Dick, I'd better keep away. I'm spoiling their fun. Let 'em be happy. Walter, take over command. Perhaps one of these lads'll help you. See that Dick's happy.'

'No,' said Dick. 'Let me come with you.'

'Oh, yes, do, do,' said Harry. 'Come, Dick, old man, do.'

§

In the living-room above the bar Ida sat in an armchair gazing in front of her without speaking, a hand gripping each arm. Her abandonment to misery had resulted almost in a trance. Beth knelt on her heels at the side of the chair and kept one hand resting on one of her mother's and often pressing it. Dick sat on the sofa, his fingers playing a silent tune on its arm. Harry walked back and forth, back and forth, talking, protesting, despairing.

'They say he'll be tried for treason. What the hell is treason? Simply that your opinion as where your duty lay was different from the vast majority of your countrymen's. Granted, if you like, that your opinion was foolish—idiotic. Grant that it sprang from obstinacy and bumptiousness. Well, you don't execute a lad for being idotic and bumptious.'

At the word 'execute' Ida started in her chair as if stung by a whip. 'No, no. No, no, no,' she murmured, and '*NO!*' And she fell to rocking herself in the chair and sighing 'Oh . . . oh, dear . . . oh . . . oh, Beth . . .' Beth's fingers closed upon her hand and clasped it tight.

'Seems to me,' pursued Harry, after looking Ida's way, 'that if you do that you're as idiotic as the lad himself.'

'I agree—in part, I think,' said Dick, beating his song of bewilderment on the sofa. 'But this is war, you see. And since war is idiotic, so, inevitably, are most of its fruits. It's a regression from a decent civilisation to crude tribal law.'

'Damn tribal law. Nobody loves his country more than me, but, by heaven, if our government had been Fascist or Bolshevist, *I'd* have been a traitor. Were the French maquis traitors because they helped us invade their country and kick out their pro-German government?'

'Yes, and likewise no,' said Dick. 'Treason, like beauty, lives in the eye of the beholder.'

'Or were the Free Germans under Paulus—or whatever his name was—traitors because they helped the Russians overthrow their filthy Nazi government? No; heroes. What it amounts to is that you're a hero if you back the winning side and a traitor if you back the other.'

'Just so.' Dick nodded, and beat his tattoo.

Execute: Harry was really looking now at that awful word. His hands behind his back grasped and squeezed each other like those of a man who fights his pain, and for a little he trod the carpet in silence, as he saw the boy Michael playing cricket with him on the Common or Follow-my-leader all over the house, or sitting beside him at Kennington Oval and nudging him in the ribs when the umpires came from the pavilion to begin the game. He stopped in his walk and faced Dick.

'Every penny I've got is his for his defence, Dick. I don't care what it costs. I've got a few thousands tucked away, because we've always lived carefully, Mother and I. It's his, isn't it, Mother? Don't you worry, girl; if money can do it, we'll save him.'

From the bar below came loud singing. The crowding company down there, at ease again, had renewed their celebration.

They were roaring in chorus and stamping or marching so that the house shook. Harry distinguished the words because he knew them well.

> At the halt on the left form platoon!
> If the odd numbers don't mark time two paces,
> How the hell can the rest form platoon?

'I'm glad they're happy,' he said. 'That's what the old Lord of Wensley's for. Mike was only a lad when he made an idiot of himself and went over there. Twenty-four—and we're all cocky young fools then. *I* was. So were you, Dick, I'm sure. But we were all right, because we agreed with the majority. Personally, I hadn't the brains to do anything else. I don't quite know when Dick came to his senses, Beth—oh, yes, I do, though.' He waited, and then said softly, 'You lost your boy in that war, Dick; I in . . . but yours went with honour . . .'

'Michael did what he thought right, Harry.'

'I suppose so . . . Dick—my God, Mother, I'd forgotten it!—Dick's used to defending lads in trouble. He'll be able to do everything for him. Thank God, we've got Dick, Mother. If anyone can get him off, Dick will. Eh, Dick?'

Dick did not answer at once, because he could not say Yes. He did not believe the answer was Yes. He said only, with bent head, 'I'll do everything on God's earth. . . .'

'Oh, yes, *please*, Uncle Dick,' murmured Beth, from her place at her mother's side. 'You will save him.'

Harry resumed his troubled walk. 'At least he was not a coward. Even if it was muck he believed in, he risked his neck for it.'

'True enough,' said Dick.

'He was always fearless in fighting for his nonsense even before the War. And if he was coming to give himself up when they found him, well, that was brave. He didn't take the easy way out like the other fellow. He came to face his accusers. Yes, I'm glad he did that. Dick . . . Dick, was it my fault that he turned traitor like that? I remember you used to say——'

Here Ida spoke, out of her trance. 'If ever a boy had a good father, it was you.'

And Beth, trying to comfort all, said, 'Yes, Dad. We've had a wonderful father, Mike and I.'

'But I used to shout my head off at him, and he was only little. And then he used to look frightened. The tears jumped into his eyes, so that I hated myself for hours afterwards and wanted to make it up to him with presents and things.' Overwhelming him, flooding him as he walked up and down, came the old motive, 'I was harsh and cruel with him, and I must make it up to him.' Oh, *yes*. With all I've got. But how? *How?* Maybe there's only a little time. And he'll be in prison, and I shan't be able to get to him. They won't let me make it up to him—ever now. Oh, God, Michael boy——

From below, louder than ever, as if the crowd in the bar had multiplied and a hundred voices were singing together, came the chorus:

Then away, love, away, Way down Rio!
For we're bound for the Rio Grande.

'They must have crowded in, Dick, since they heard that news. They've come to look at us. Well, it's all good for trade. I guess that for the next day or two we shall be the most popular house in South London.'

'He's ill.' Ida was speaking again. 'He's gravely ill. The man said so. Won't they let me go to him? I should be with him.'

'Will they let her go, Dick?'

'I don't know. You see, he's not only a patient, he's a prisoner.'

'But he's ill!' Ida almost shrieked. 'He's *ill*. He may be dying.'

'They'll get him better, Ida dear,' Dick consoled her. 'I was in two General Hospitals in the old war, and they do everything for you. They'll make him well.'

'Yes, and what then?' demanded Harry. 'You know all about these things, Dick: what then?'

'They'll bring him home and there'll be a preliminary hearing before the magistrate at Bow Street.'

'And then?'

'The trial at the Old Bailey.'

Harry paused, stared at the carpet, and walked again. 'Yes. The trial. Rex *v.* Michael Townes. My son. Perhaps it'd be better if he didn't get well.'

'Harry, Harry,' hissed Ida. 'Don't say such things.'

But Harry, ever a violent man, and a sentimental, was determined to say it. 'Perhaps it would be better if he died. My

God, if I were in that hospital I'm not sure that I wouldn't help him to die.'

No one spoke.

Below they were singing, 'For to-night we'll merry, merry be, Tomorrow we'll be sober.'

'They're happy,' said Harry, halting to listen. 'Look, they sound like a big crowd down there. I must go down and help old Walter. It isn't fair to leave him like this. I don't fancy I shall spoil their fun any more. Half an hour's passed since that news, and it's forgotten.'

'Shall I come and help you, Dad?' asked Beth.

'No, you stay with your mother. And, Dick, say all you can to comfort her. She's always trusted you much more than me.'

Having said this, and sighed, he went alone and somewhat heavy-footed back to his bars.

§

'Walter, old man, isn't it time you left this old ship with your captain's blessing?'

'I fail to see why, sir.'

'Well, hasn't this last bit of news really holed her beneath the water-line?'

'No, sir. No, indeed. I don't see why.'

'Don't you? I should say it's a proper torpedo.' He and Walter, both behind the counter, were cleaning and re-stocking the bars after the last of the customers had gone. 'It'd have been better if they'd never found him—if he'd been lost somewhere among the millions in Germany. Then with the war over, his name and his doings would gradually have been forgotten. But now. . . now, as Dick Templer says, they'll bring him to England, and there'll be a tremendous trial, which will fill the front pages of all the papers, as a change from battles and victories.'

'A cause célèbre,' said Walter, stocking the shelves under the counter with light ales and stouts.

'A what?'

'A sensational case, you think it will be?'

'Of course. Of course. A god-send to all the editors in the dull days of peace. Every paper in England and America will seize on it. Every disgraceful thing he's done and said will be raked up and blazoned to the world; everyone will turn their hatred on to him, as a nice change from the Germans; and the old Lord of Wensley will be—more than ever—a place of shame. We shall be lucky if we don't have stones through our windows, and the bars broken up. I quite think we may. Oh yes. Don't you?'

'Indeed I do not, sir.'

'*I* do. I certainly do. I know our Balham hooligans.'

'No sir. The human animal is not remarkable for rationality, but it's not so senseless as that. Not even its young. It has no quarrel with *you*.'

'I wish I thought you were right, Walter, old boy. But I don't feel so sure. No, I don't. And it's only fair to say that you can go over the side, whenever you like, and take the last boat home. Personally I shall stay on the bridge to the end. Chuck us that counter swab; I may as well keep my bridge clean and shining till the end. You don't feel that this is the moment for you to cast around for a happier job?'

'No, indeed, sir. No, to be sure.'

'I'd give you a testimonial in a thousand. "The best bar-cellarman bar none", I'd say. And that's no lie, either. We'd be sorry as hell to lose you, because you've been like one of the family so long—but, devil take it, it's no longer a family to be proud of.'

'I disagree profoundly, sir. Most profoundly. If I may venture the opinion, I should say the Lord of Wensley is one of the best-run pubs in London, or in the world.'

'Oh yes, I agree with you there. Yes, I'm pretty sure of that. The pub's all right, but——'

'And hundreds of others know it, and in my view it'll more than counterbalance any discredit that may accrue from—but if this were not so and you were right in your assumption that the trial will hit the Lord of Wensley a mortal blow, well, then I can hardly conceive a moment less suitable for leaving you and Madam . . . and Miss Beth.'

'By God, Walter, old son, thank you for that, and throw me another swab, you old scoundrel, before I weep.'

§

Next morning, the morning of VE Day, Harry and Beth wandered out together to see the flags and the crowds and hear the victory peals. 'I should like to share a little in the Jollification,' Harry had said. 'We shall never see another day like this. And there'll be nobody much in our bars today, if there's anybody left in Balham at all.' And when Beth said, 'I'll come too,' he had answered, 'Yes, come on: we can't worry too much about anything today.'

Besides, they had drawn some comfort from their morning paper. Under the headlines, 'Michael Townes Captured' the paper had described in picturesque detail the 'dramatic discovery in a desolate part of the great Lüneburg Heath of Michael Townes, for whom everyone had been searching' and his arrival at British Second Army Headquarters, where the excited soldiers, gathering round, had welcomed him back with sardonic Fascist salutes and mocking cries of 'Germany calling. Germany calling,' to which, though conscious, he made no reply. High officers of the Intelligence Corps and of Scotland Yard were hurrying from London to his bedside, said the paper; but it somewhat spoiled the drama of this by adding, 'His condition, however, is not now thought to be as serious as was earlier imagined. He is receiving the best possible care and treatment, and there is every confidence that he will make a complete recovery.'

So there it was . . . and, relieved of immediate anxiety about him, they wandered out to see the Prince of Days. There was no getting on any bus whose nose turned westwards, for all were crowded to bursting point. So, to be sure, were the Tube trains, but they managed to squeeze into one of these and at Leicester Square alighted with the outflowing stream.

'The proper thing to do on these occasions,' said Harry, 'is to pay a dutiful visit to His Majesty with our compliments, and then go and stand and stare at Eros.'

So they went first to the Mall where thirty thousand people stood staring at the windows of Buckingham Palace while they cheered and chanted and called for the King. 'Stood'—well, not all; hundreds sat all over the Victoria Memorial and the piers of the Australian and Canadian Gates. They cheered everything and anything that passed—a bus-load of beefeaters going to the VE Day investiture, a hansom cab which seemed to have come out of another century, and a policeman escorting a rude but now good-humoured man to some place of temporary admonition.

After the prescriptive visit to the Eros statue, they walked, Harry and Beth, down the Strand and Fleet Street to the steps and wide terraces of St. Paul's. St. Paul's bells were crashing their chimes down upon the thronging crowds below; and behind the chimes, against the London sky, stood the huge dome, noble and tranquil, and yet somehow homely, kindly, and, as it were, smiling, like some old matriarch who'd seen many generations rise and pass and remembered them with charity and hope.

Around dome and steeples the pigeons were swirling in dismay —frightened by the bells which for years had been dumb. So they had scattered and wheeled, no doubt, when the same bells rang Trafalgar and Waterloo and Armistice 1918.

Streams of people were pressing through the cathedral's doors in response to the loud invitation of the bells, and Harry said suddenly, 'Come, Beth darling. Shall we go too?' She said, 'Oh, yes, Daddy dear,' and so they joined a slow-moving stream, exchanging at last the noise of voices and footsteps for the vast quiet within; an echoing silence which was hardly changed from silence by the organ's low music. Sudden and strange this contrast: the happy noisy crowds without, and this sober congregation here, tranced by noble arches into silence.

So massed were the people in nave and aisles that Harry and Beth had to insinuate themselves very slowly into a place where they could stand and see. It was whispered that the Lord Mayor, Aldermen, Sheriffs and Liverymen of the City were somewhere up in front and far away, but so far as Harry and Beth could see this was a dense gathering of London's unknown and ordinary people, those who had no high seats in her councils but who maintained the state of the city. And he and she found a place at last where they too could stand among the anonymous.

Harry found it hard to sing, but he was so moved by the first hymn, sung by all these thousands, that he did join faintly in it: 'Now thank we all our God.' Sometimes he stopped singing to listen to the echo of the hymn's words in the high spaces of vault and dome: far away and dying, it sounded like the murmur of a great cloud of unseen witnesses. The long-drawn echo of the Amen might have been their last Amen for those who had served. He bowed his head with the rest for the Prayers and raised it for the Lesson. With what a charged quiet those thousands listened to the Lesson. He could feel, by sympathy, the beat of their hearts. He felt Beth, pressed against him by the crush, trembling in response to the tremendous words—

'The enemy said, I will pursue, I will overtake, I will divide the spoil; my lust shall be satisfied upon them; I will draw my sword, my hand shall destroy them. Thou didst blow with thy wind, the sea covered them; they sank as lead in the mighty waters.'

Harry would have liked to kneel and plunge his face in his hands, but he was jammed far too tightly against unknown neighbours for this, so in a period when all who could do so were kneeling, he just closed his eyes and, after thanking God with the rest of them (since one should not speak of one's own needs first) prayed the prayer that he alone of all that multitude must pray. 'Oh God, in thy mercy save my boy from the terrible threat which hangs over him. Comfort him in his great unhappiness now, and give him courage and strength to face all that is coming to him. Forgive him all that was very wrong in what he has done, and if in any way it was my fault, send thy punishment to me and let me bear it for him.'

He felt a little easier after this and was joining in the next hymn, when he knew from the shaking of Beth's shoulder that she was sobbing. He felt for her hand and held it, pressing it, for the rest of the service. He dropped it only to stand to attention when this great concourse of Londoners was singing, as perhaps never so sincerely before, the National Hymn. 'Send him victorious, Happy and glorious, Long to reign o'er us . . .'

But 'The King against Michael Townes.' That was yet to come.

Nevertheless he stood at attention in honour of the King.

PART IV

CHAPTER ONE

CAPTAIN TOWNES parked his little blue Huntingdon van in Garrick Street—why not? the road held two lines of carts, drays, lorries and vans in attendance on Covent Garden Market. Then he and Ida walked along Floral Street, that narrow gorge that winds between high fruit warehouses and printing works to Bow Street. Beth was not with them, for though her heart was aching to see Michael again, she had consented to take her parents' place behind the bars that *they* might see him, after the police court hearing and before he was returned to prison.

As the father and mother came into Bow Street they saw before them the heavy grey-fronted police court with the high white-pillared cliff of the Opera facing it. Between these two palaces, staring inharmoniously at each other, rang the din and clatter of the morning's market: carters, lorrymen, pitchers, and porters loading and unloading crates and boxes, or trundling trolleys and handcarts, and discharging either function with shouts and laughs and oaths. The street between the two palaces smelt of stored apples, green produce, horse manure, and dry, powdering earth.

Thus the market of the world went on, never halting, loud, rude, and vulgar, with Pleasure on one side of the cluttered roadway and Judgment on the other.

A long queue of sightseers waited outside the doors of the police court, and the men of the market shouted jokes at them while labouring on van or lorry or strewn pavement. 'Get me a couple of stalls.' 'Hope they swing him like this 'ere sack—crash!' 'Ask 'em to wait till I've tidied meself up.' 'Won't they let you in? Love locked out, eh? Well, *he*'ll get a seat all right.' 'Gi' my love to the beak.'

Harry took Ida's hand and, gripping it tightly, led her through these voices to the police court doors. She was trembling because she was going to see Michael for the first time in six years; and she kept touching her eyes because it was in a prisoner's dock that she would see him. She was dressed in her best; three

227

hours had been barely enough to array her for this appearance in a public place. She desired all in court to see that Michael's parents were 'good-class people,' and somewhere deep among her griefs was a small pleasure in this excuse for wearing her best.

At the doorway Harry spoke to the hatless police sergeant in a clear voice, refusing shame. 'I am Michael Townes's father, and this is his mother,' he said; and immediately the sergeant, his voice kind and understanding, answered, 'Oh yes, sir. Come this way. This way, Madam'; and Harry's heart went out to him because he had shown no dislike of them but only a gentle courtesy.

The door of the courtroom was open, and the sergeant ushered them through it. And there, talking to other men in their dark lawyers' weeds, was Dick.

'Dick,' called Harry.

'Ah!' Dick had turned and seen them. 'Come,' and he led them to a bench behind the dock. The back of this bench was the partition to the narrow, bare, seatless area where a few of the public, as a necessary evil, were allowed to stand and stare. At least Harry and Ida were privileged to be this side of that partition, and to sit.

Ida was trembling more now, as she saw the courtroom, so Harry secured her hand again and kept it in a tight grip.

He sat and gazed around at this oak-panelled chamber as it waited for the day's drama. Everywhere, on different levels, were little brown enclosures or pews, not unlike the pens in a sheep-market: one for counsel, one for the usher, one for the solicitors in the well of the court, and behind them all thrust away at the back, this bare pen for the public whom no one loved. A pity he was in no mood for joking, and might never joke again, or he'd have liked to say, 'This is clearly the Saloon Bar, Dick, and that the Public.'

The two most striking things in the room, being both upraised, were the dais for the magistrate's desk and the dock for the prisoner. The magistrate's dais was spacious and made splendid by the royal arms above his high-backed chair; the dock was narrow as a coffin, and since its railing was of ornamental iron-work it looked like a cage—say a cage in which a calf was being carried to market.

They sat and waited. And while they waited there was much lively and often laughing chatter among the lawyers, the police, the Intelligence officers, and the Clerk, who had just come to his desk. One tall handsome man, most perfectly tailored and groomed, stood with his hands on his hips talking to a smaller and older man whose heavy black eyebrows were even thicker and more protruding than Dick's white ones; and since he was the most impressive person in the room, Harry touched the usher's gown as he passed and asked who the tall gentleman was.

The usher, a long bald man, seemed pleased to be an expert instructor. 'That's Mr. Hesketh Raynes, Counsel for the prosecution,' he said, and, lowering his voice in an access of reverence, added, 'And that's Sir Hugh Clinton, the Director of Public Prosecutions, that he's talking to.'

'I see,' said Harry, and he felt Ida's hand tremble in his. 'Thank you. Thank you very much.'

At about half-past ten an elderly constable, grey-haired and smooth-skinned, who looked more like one of the higher clergy than a junior policeman, admitted the sightseers to the public space. They streamed in with a noise of many feet, and those fortunate enough to be first leaned on the oak partition. Not more than forty or fifty were able to crowd into that confined area, and the policeman with the face of a bishop beamed apologetically on all the rest and shut them out.

Harry considered the public who'd come to gaze on his son. Loafers, drifters, many of them seemed; a crowd from the dusty street who'd come out of the wind. Those leaning on the partition let their mouths fall open as they gaped at the room. Others leaned like street-loungers against the back wall. Not all, however, were idle loafers; some were plainly respectable burghers whose curiosity was wholly legitimate; and of a sudden Harry saw, standing all together against the back wall, a squad of lads in belted trench-coats such as the Nazi Fuehrer used to wear. One was a broken-nosed prize-fighting type, with a dull, sad, jaw-dropped face. No doubt who they were: a few sad disciples of the Cause now slain; Michael's followers and friends of the old brave days. Three of them, including the careworn prize-fighter, wore high-necked black sweaters, which was the nearest they could get to the forbidden black uniform of that fine heroic time.

Harry, looking at them, side by side there, loved them, not for their creed, which he hated, but because he knew that they were on Michael's side, and their hearts his. And because they seemed such a pitiable remnant of that army of youths which

229

had marched behind their black flags and black drums singing
the Horst Wessel song, or had massed their shining standards
and Union Jacks on a stage in 'the greatest indoor meeting in
the world.' He saw them looking round a cramped police
court with a narrow dock.

'Stand up, please! Silence!'

The bald usher had called this from the dais, and all stood
as the magistrate entered from his private door. He was a
small, plump, peak-faced man, rather like a white-headed and
bespectacled budgerigar, and he bowed and smiled at his pals
in the counsel's pen, bowed and smiled at the solicitors on their
lower level, and bowed and smiled vaguely again, in a kind of
general benediction, at the usher, the press, and the police.
The only persons he didn't bow to were the public in their place
at the back. Then he pushed home his rimless glasses and sat
down.

All sat as he sat, and only then did Harry see that Michael
was standing with his back to them in the uplifted dock. He
had been ushered through the prisoners' door by the gaoler.

There was Michael standing within the dock's iron rails.

§

Harry's heart, unprepared, shook first with shock; then with
an ache of pity. The boy was so plainly trying to make a good
impression: to appear at ease and confident. His fair hair he
had damped and brushed most carefully; his suit, arranged
for this first appearance before his countrymen, showed a clean
white handkerchief peeping above his breast-pocket; he was
holding his body erect, with head up, one hand resting on the
iron rail, and his eyes looking straight at the magistrate—but
it was all no good: his blood did not obey his will; it had
drained his face; the arm, stretched towards the dock rail,
was disobedient too and trembling; his mouth, a law unto itself,
twitched.

'Oh, Michael boy, I am with you . . . we are with you . . .'
and Harry bent his head. Ida had murmured 'Oh!' aloud,
but fortunately no one heard her, because all were settling
down in their places and rustling their papers or whispering
together. He clasped her hand tight as if to check all speech
with a tourniquet.

The Clerk spoke from his desk beneath the magistrate. He

was a young man of little more than Michael's age, a junior acting in the absence of the Chief Clerk. His little brown moustache looked very fresh and new, and his hair was brushed up from his brow in a quiff like a breaking wave. ' Michael Cawdor Townes is charged for that he committed high treason in that between September 3rd, 1939, and April 26th, 1945, being a person owing allegiance to our Lord the King, he did traitorously adhere to the King's enemies, elsewhere than in the King's Realm, contrary to the Treason Act of 1351.'

He read the beautiful and terrible words in an exceedingly bored way. Either he was like a reviewer who has read so many thriller-tales that nothing in that kind can excite him any more, or, being young and insecure, he wanted to appear not only worldly-wise but world-weary—even as the other young man, in his dock, was acting confidence, fearlessness, and ease. The words read, he tossed the document carelessly back on to his desk and, sitting there, joined his hands before him as in prayer. He gazed dreamily over the linked fingers at nothing at all— unless it was at the wall above the usher—with his brow sadly wrinkled, as one who is patient only because he is paid to be. One felt that he was tolerant of humanity because there was nothing else to be done about it.

Counsel for the Prosecution, tall, handsome, splendid, began to speak from his uplifted pen, and the little magistrate leaned back on his throne to listen—with an encouraging smile.

'Sir, in this case I appear with my learned friend, Mr. Eliot, on behalf of the Director of Public Prosecutions, and the accused is defended by my friend, Mr. Templer. The charge is one of high treason. Now, sir, you will know well the Act of King Edward the Third which states that if a man do levy war against the King in his realm, or be adherent to the King's enemies in his realm, giving them aid and comfort, he is guilty of treason. Such has been our law for six hundred years. You will furthermore, I have no doubt, be familiar with the words of Sir James FitzJames Stephen, namely, that "everyone commits treason who"'—he paused to give emphasis to the next words—'"either within the realm or without it, actively assists an enemy at war with His Majesty the King."

'Now, sir, I do not think I shall need to detain you very long because, in my humble submission, the few witnesses I shall call will show you that there is ample evidence for the consideration by a jury of this most serious charge.

'Now, sir, let me deal first with the nationality of the accused. He was born in London in the year 1915, his father then being a sergeant in the armed forces of the Crown, fighting for his country—so effectively, I understand, that he later received a commission and rose to the rank of Captain. . . .'

Quiet, level, unexcited, the Voice of the Offended Nation flowed on.

§

Dick, in his pen, sat watching this elegant counsel, a man whom, since he was a member of his own club, he knew well. There he stood, Hesketh (or 'Trilby') Raynes, in a graceful attitude, one fist resting on a hip so that his well-tailored jacket was pushed back, and speaking with a voice that was beautiful in quality and beautifully controlled. Every word and clause showed that his mind was as well ordered as his garments. He seemed a perfect flower of manhood, with all the bloom of early success upon him; and, thinking this, Dick turned suddenly to look at the prisoner in the dock behind him. Alone of all there, except the counsel speaking, he was still standing, palpably uncertain whether an accused man was suffered to sit down; and standing there, he seemed in some ways the opposite of Raynes: a lad with a mind that was *not* well ordered; a graceful but imperfect flower of manhood, whose bloom had now been dashed from it so that it could do nothing but wilt and fall.

At that very moment the gaoler, a policeman so corpulent that his tunic was cut to the shape of a cathedral bell, returned from the prisoners' door and, shocked to see his charge still standing, touched him on the arm and bade him sit. Michael smiled at him gratefully, if sadly, and sat in his cramped cage.

The loneliness of him uplifted there in that iron cage! What could one do to save him? Listen to Raynes—how answer Raynes, how answer?

'Our law regards treason as the most serious of crimes because in its essence it is murder at its worst. A true instinct, I submit, assures us all most forcefully that, just as a man may not lay murderous hands on his father who begat him, or on his blood brother, like Cain, or on his companions of the table, like Judas, so he cannot be suffered to do the like upon the people of his tribe or his nation. And to comfort and aid, as this young man did, an enemy who was slaughtering his countrymen,

232

and raining death upon our cities, was manifestly to do no less than this. It was to sharpen a sword for use against Britain and to load her enemies' guns for them.

'Now let me briefly rehearse the actions of the accused. In April of 1939, when war appeared inevitable between Britain and Germany, he left London for Berlin, travelling with his British passport which, be it noted, covered him all the way with the King's protection. He left—and I can only assume that his idea was to get as quickly as possible from a sinking ship.'

Dick felt a stir in the dock behind him. It was as if the prisoner had wanted to cry out, 'No, *no*!'

'If that was his opinion I make bold to say he differed from all his compatriots who, even in the darkest hours, never for one moment entertained the thought of defeat. Arrived in Germany, he was given employment as a teacher of his English language and on the outbreak of war taken into the service of the Reichs-Rundfunk-Gesellschaft—that is, the Broadcasting Company for the German realm. His tasks at first seem to have been to write, or edit, English scripts, but later he was allowed to address to us his own comments on the day's news. The prosecution will produce for you, sir, a receipt signed by him and discovered in the rubble and ruins of a German radio station, which shows that he would receive from the German pay office fifty marks for each broadcast.'

He paused, looked down upon the foolscap pages in his hand, and, apparently addressing them rather than the magistrate, remarked as he idly turned a page, 'One can hardly fail to think of those thirty pieces of silver for which another man sold his Lord——'

Instantly Dick was on his feet—and most politely Mr. Raynes stopped. And bowed to Dick. And waited to hear what on earth he could want to say.

'Sir.'

The little white-haired magistrate, hearing this word from the solicitors' box, shifted round in his seat to hear also, after giving Dick his encouraging smile, and his nod. 'Yes, Mr. Templer?'

For a few seconds Dick turned his white barbed eyebrows towards the papers on his desk; then directed them at the magistrate. Seventy this year, and grown leaner rather than fuller with age, he looked more than old enough to be the father of the handsome counsel whose ears he must now box.

'Sir, I protest in the strongest possible terms against that most improper comment from my learned friend. His function in this court is merely to lay before you such evidence as he has in support of his case, and not to speak of it before any of us as proven.' His anger getting the better of him, he snapped, 'And even were it proved, it would not, I submit, deserve *that* comment.'

The magistrate, having heard this view of Dick's, swung his eyes back to Mr. Raynes, who, tall and splendid, bowed with courtesy, and with some show of humility, to Dick; whereat the magistrate shifted to the other corner of his large chair, to hear from Mr. Raynes what such courtesy portended.

'I am grateful to my friend, Mr. Templer, for this very proper rebuke.' Mr. Raynes, his bow completed, grasped his hips with both hands in such a way as to push back his jacket, and addressed this gratitude to the air immediately in front of him. 'And I apologise unreservedly, if through a moment of carelessness I have used words which at this stage my friend feels to be misplaced.'

'I most certainly feel them to be misplaced—if "misplaced" is not far too weak a word. Let me assure my learned friend now, lest in some later moment of carelessness, he should misplace his words, that my client has an answer to all these allegations, and that those defending him will not tolerate any prejudging of the issue in this highly improper way.'

Again Mr. Raynes bowed. You would have supposed his gratitude was enhanced by this generous addition of three more blows with the whip. And Dick bowed in gratitude for Mr. Raynes's gratitude. And, catching the infection, the learned magistrate as near as possible bowed too. But he said nothing. Apparently he thought that everything which need be said had been admirably said already. If he was a little like a be-spectacled budgerigar, he was not like one who chattered on his perch. His habit was obviously to do little more than issue encouraging nods and smiles to whosoever might be in need of them.

An answer to all these allegations! The words had astounded Harry. What possible answer was there? What had Dick in mind? What forlorn rearguard action was he fighting in a battle lost as soon as begun?

Meanwhile, all differences between learned friends adjusted, the prosecutor was continuing his speech. Not once did he look at the prisoner. As he spoke he looked into the vacancy between him and the opposite wall, as if seeing there the events he described; or he looked up at the skylight as if seeing them somewhere beneath the blue of heaven. Sometimes he looked at the gold ring on his finger, and sometimes at the four trim finger-nails of one hand; but never once at the protagonist of his long story.

Impossible not to believe, thought Dick, that Raynes was enjoying the exercise of an art which he practised so well; that he drew pleasure from the richness of his vocabulary, the clarity of his phrasing, the management of his voice, and his courtesy to the magistrate and to all whom he must address. How could it be otherwise? His every attitude and movement suggested that he was conscious—again how otherwise?—of his fine presence and excellent clothes. Now he was throwing forth an arm to release a gold-linked shirt-cuff; now both arms hung from the lapels of his jacket; now they were folded across his breast as he continued the story.

From Raynes Dick dropped his eyes to that bored young clerk seated with hands joined (as in prayer) because so far there was nothing he need write down. Dick could not love him: he looked too content to be a dull wheel of the Law's machine, uninterested in his part, and unmindful that the wheels of this great engine, having caught with their cogs that other young man, seated in the dock, must mangle him to death before they cast him out.

Then Dick's eyes swung up to the magistrate, enthroned above the clerk, and he thought of him as the Ears of the Offended People. Under the royal arms the little white-haired man sat there listening on behalf of the King in this matter of 'The King against Townes,' but Dick couldn't help wondering whether, in such a tribal matter, a magistrate could listen also on behalf of that Abstract Justice which sits above the tribes.

§

Ida, listening to a speech which to her seemed utterly and finally damning, sat with teeth biting her lips and her large fat fists clenching and unclenching in despair. After a while, as the musical voice sang on, she who had never taken any interest in political talk transferred her interest to the room and its furnishings. Its oak panelling, its cream walls, its wooden stall from which that gentleman was speaking, its—its iron-railed dock—seeing that dock again, she gripped a thumb tight to save herself from crying out.

Thenceforward she kept her eyes fixed on Michael—*her* Michael—uplifted there above the heads of others for his shame and their gaze. How had this come about? How could this have happened to a boy who'd always been good and kind and loving to her? Now Michael too, either wearying of the speech or desiring not to hear it because it hurt too much, was letting his eyes rove about the room. He was looking at the hanging lamps shining in their globes like yellow moons—at the pressmen scribbling away in their box—and so, bringing his eyes right round behind him saw for the first time his father and mother. Till now, though he knew them to be in court, he had not dared in his shame to turn and look for them and meet their eyes. Even now this meet of the eyes after six years was accidental. But Ida, who had been waiting and waiting for this moment, seized it like a thrown line and sent from her fixed and longing eyes all her love and, by means of a little sad smile, all her encouragement. He smiled back at her, and at his father, who had lifted a hand in friendly greeting.

A sharp-eyed reporter saw these exchanges and, immediately guessing who Harry and Ida were, drew the attention of his colleagues to them. They all looked Ida's way, and then began to write rapidly. A 'mother story' for Britain. The mother of the notorious prisoner sitting near the dock and sending messages of love, whenever possible, to him. Ida, unseen of them, shook her head again and again, as if this could stay their pens. Oh, why must they do this; why couldn't they let her alone? Leave me alone. Leave me be. She had never wanted to be other than a simple woman living as comfortable and gossipy a life as possible among her neighbours and friends, and here she was, caught up in a mad world of men who must ever be fighting and killing one another. Her thoughts were confused and inarticulate, but somewhere among them was the question, How came it that she who had never been interested in history, or desired any part of it, had been snatched by invisible hands and hurried into the middle of its greatest storm?

§

Counsel was now concluding. Still elaborately courteous, he said with a glance at the clock, 'I must apologise, sir, for taking so long over my opening, but fortunately the witnesses I shall now call will not be many nor take up very much of your time. In the main their business will be to produce certain documents. When these documents have been read I submit that you will be more than satisfied that they support this charge against the accused. I shall begin at the beginning of the story.' Holding his brief before him and leaning gracefully against the wall of his pen, he said, 'I shall call . . . let me see . . . yes, Captain Arthur Cyril Gates of the Intelligence Corps.'

The grey-headed constable with the episcopal face went forth into the passage and called, 'Arthur Cyril Gates'; then returned in advance of a spruce and assured little man in neat battle dress. He directed this spry little man towards the witness box, but the little man, resenting instruction, insisted, '*I* know, *I* know,' as one who was well used to courts and their ways.

He stepped into the box and when the usher handed him the card on which the oath was printed, waved it aside as much as to say, 'I'm an old hand at this game, usher, and need no book.' Then he held up the testament, spoke the oath, and got it wrong.

'I swear that the evidence I shall give to the court shall be the truth, the whole truth, and nothing but the truth.'

Mr. Raynes smiled in a completely tolerant and unreproving way. 'Those are not quite the words, Captain Gates. Perhaps, after all, you'd better take advantage of the usher's card.'

The witness said, 'I'm sorry, sir,' and blushed at this initial slip; and Mr. Raynes demurred, 'Not at all, Captain Gates;' and Captain Gates now recited in a loud voice, 'I swear by Almighty God——' laying emphasis on these words so unfortunately omitted, and concluding with the other words he had left out, '. . . so help me God.'

He smacked the testament on to his shelf, bowed to the usher in gratitude for his aid and turned and faced Mr. Raynes, who smiled in gratitude for this prompt reparation.

'I'm sure your evidence, Captain Gates, would have been just as truthful whatever oath you swore, but you will agree it's best to have everything absolutely right. Now will you help me? . . . I want you to tell the learned magistrate all about . . . let me see . . .'

The magistrate swung from the north corner, so to say, of his handsome chair to the south and leaned back in it to face the witness—after giving him the encouraging nod and smile.

'On the tenth of May in the course of your duties,' began Mr. Raynes, 'were you sent on an important mission to a hospital in Lüneburg?'

The bored young clerk unlinked his fingers and, lifting his pen from his blotting pad, gazed at the witness with a face as devoid of interest as a picture-frame standing empty on a desk. He was ready to write with the insensitiveness of a dictaphone the captain's replies.

'I was.'

The clerk wrote—but perhaps not quite like a dictaphone or any other machine, thought Dick, because a machine does not register boredom.

'And in the discharge of your mission did you visit the accused, Michael Townes?'

'I did.'

'Did you say anything to him?'

Nobody seemed to think this an absurd question, and the witness affirmed that he had said something.

'And what was that?'

'I said I was charged with the duty of investigating the activities of those British subjects who broadcast for the Germans during the war. I then cautioned him in the usual form of words before putting any questions to him. I then——'

The clerk raised a sad little voice. 'Please, *please*, would you speak slower? I am trying to write down your evidence in the form of a continuous narrative . . .' and straightway the magistrate, that most gentle president, smiled disarmingly at the witness, said 'You're a *little* fast, I think. Just watch the learned clerk's pen,' and nodded encouragingly.

'I see, sir.' The captain bowed.

'Yes?' inquired the clerk, intimating that he had now written all and was ready for more boring words.

'I then spoke of certain documents——'

Raynes interrupted. 'Did you produce those documents to him?'

'I did.'

'And they were?'

'One was a certified copy of an entry of birth——'

'Yes—well, let's take that first. Is this it?'

'It is.'

'And he admitted that it referred to him?'

'He did.'

'And what does it say?'

'It says, "Date Twelfth of February, 1915——"'

Ah, those birthday parties in February, thought Ida, in happy days before the war.

'"Name, Michael Cawdor. Boy. Father, Henry Edwin——"'

And was it for this, thought Ida, that I suffered those agonies that night long ago? And that I was so proud when the agonies stopped and they told me it was a boy. That night long ago when I cried to Heaven for mercy or for death . . . and Harry wasn't there . . . and then the pains stopped, and they told me it was a boy. Was it for this? And I said, Oh, can you let his dad know? He'll be that proud. If I know him, there'll be drinks all round in France tonight.

'Did he tell you anything of his employment in Germany?'

'Yes. Some things.'

'Captain Gates, you are an expert interrogator: what was your opinion of his answers?'

But Dick was on his feet again in the well of the room—not more abruptly rises a grouse from the heather, at sound of a shot. 'No!—really, sir!—I object. Captain Gates is here as a witness to facts, not as a judge on those facts——'

Why's he objecting, thought Ida. Seemed to me a most sensible question, and I should like to have heard his answer.

Mr. Raynes had bowed to his reprover. 'I am very much obliged,' he said; and by his friendly smile you could almost believe him. 'I desire to be nothing but fair to the accused. Thank you. Thank you very much. Now, Captain Gates, if we may proceed: did he consent to make a statement?'

'Not at once, sir. He said he would like time to think.'

Oh, Michael, my poor darling. Time to think. Poor child. And all these men here to down him—all happy and prosperous, and he alone there. Where's that Dermot? Why isn't he there at Michael's side?

'And what did you do then?'

'I said that I would return next day, so that he would have time to think.'

'And the next day?'

'He said he would like to make a statement. He had in fact

239

written one in pencil and at his own request he dictated it to me and then signed it.'

'Is this the statement?'

'Yes, sir.   That is it.'

'You produce it?'

'I do.'

Counsel read, 'I was born in London in 1915 while my father was on active service in France.   I would wish to say that, like my father, I have always loved my country and have always conceived myself as fighting for her best interests.   There has been no sincerer desire than this in my life.   My father was a strong Conservative but, if I took a different view, it was not that I was less patriotic than he——'

Of course you weren't, my darling.   I know you weren't. I have always told your father so.

'I could not believe that war with Germany could bring anything but disaster and accordingly I left England rather than take any share in courses that I was sure must injure her. I may have been wrong, and even foolish, but I fully believed that the New Order which had already established itself on many parts of the Continent, substituting a wholly new economic system, would be best for Britain too.   I held then—and hold still—that the present political and economic system in Britain contrived to enslave the people, despite all its shows of political freedom.   This is a view from which, even now, I cannot and will not recant——'

Oh, why say things to put their backs up, darling?   You were always so argumentative and obstinate.   But he's clever; they must think he's clever.   I'm sure I could never write anything like that.

'I felt it my duty to be loyal to my beliefs and to propagate them wherever I could.   But directly Britain was at war I could not bring myself to speak on the German radio, until I heard that the man who had been my Leader, and whom I revered, and many of my friends too, had been unjustly, as it seemed to me, thrown into prison, without trial, without sentence, and without even that assurance of discharge after a time which the worst criminal enjoys.   I consented to broadcast then, but, even so, I devoted most of my scripts to appealing for reconciliation between Britain and Germany.   I felt more than ever justified in this course when Russia became Britain's ally against Germany, because I was certain that in the end this alliance would cost

Britain far more than any negotiated peace with Germany. I feel bound to add that this opinion, however unpopular, is one that I still hold——'

Oh, *darling*, don't—*don't* keep weighting the scales against yourself. It's your life—your *life*.

And Dick, his eyes on the floor of his box, was thinking no less. With much compassion he was picturing this boy, alone in his distant hospital and quite ignorant of the law, composing almost proudly this rather pompous and surely suicidal apologia. He saw him sitting down with his pencil and writing most carefully, for hour after hour, his own death-warrant.

'Many of my ideas were submitted to the highest officials, in the Foreign Office, the Propaganda Ministry and the Rundfunk, and largely adopted by them——'

Oh, darling, that is you all over: just a little bit conceited and self-important. It puts their backs up—any appearance of bragging or bumptiousness: they don't like it in young men. Your father never did.

'For instance, when I pointed out the unwisdom of allowing other British broadcasters to snarl at my countrymen as fools or knaves instead of appealing to them as friends, they understood what I meant and instructed the censors to allow me, as far as possible, to speak in my own way. And perhaps I may add here that I have spoken in the same tone to the German people, urging friendship between our two countries—in, of course, their own laguage, which I now speak fluently.'

He speaks German? Fluently?

'I still believe that when Britain knows, as I know, the full story of the brutal massacres, the unrestrained lootings and the bestial rapes in which the Russian barbarians have indulged throughout Germany, then an understanding between Britain and Germany will be demanded by all sensible people, so that their lives, their freedoms, and the honour of their womenfolk may be preserved. In this connexion I would respectfully suggest that as one who has now many useful contacts in Berlin, and a long experience of broadcasting technique, and can speak in colloquial German, I could still be of some service to my country as I have always desired to be.'

Hope sprang in Ida's heart at these nice words. Surely that's an offer which should appeal to them, she thought. And they were words to touch any heart—poor boy. Sensible words too. I never did like the Russians.

Counsel laid the statement down. Now, Captain Gates, here are other documents. You recognise them?'

'Certainly. They are those which I produced to him in hospital.'

'And he admitted that they were his or referred to him?'

'Certainly.'

'And you produce them now as Exhibits Two, Three and Four?'

'I do.'

'Very good. We will hear them translated later.'

Oh, what documents? Ida's hope rose higher, because she must always hope that something yet to be explained would prove to be good news.

Mr. Raynes had sat down and was readjusting sleeve and cuff after their slight disturbance by his gestures with his brief.

Dick had risen from his lower level—on the room's floor. 'Captain Gates, you showed the birth certificate to the accused, and he accepted it as his own. There is no dispute about that. But would you tell us now, did you ask him any further questions about his nationality?'

'No, sir.'

'You did not probe the matter further, nor encourage him to speak more upon the subject?'

'No, sir.'

'So there was no reason why he should say more?'

'No, sir.'

Ida turned towards Harry, who had whispered, looking at her with surprised eyes, 'What's he getting at?' She shrugged, because she couldn't answer this, but she hoped with a big hope that he is getting at something which would be of help to Michael.

Dick looked down at the floor of his box, as if ideas for subsequent questions lay there on its bottom. 'Tell me, Captain Gates, in what condition was he when you saw him? Sick and recovering from severe fever, was he not?'

'I believe so, sir. But the M.O. assured me that he was well enough to be interviewed.'

'Quite . . . quite . . . I'm not suggesting for one moment that there was anything improper in the interview. Not for one moment. . . . I just want to hear from you how far he was disturbed or confused or at a loss what to say.'

'I don't think he was confused, sir.'

'Come, Captain Gates! Here is a lad who has wandered in the pelting rain for night after night and is at last picked up off the ground, drenched to the skin and in a state of high fever. The doctors and orderlies in the hospital give him every attention, I'm sure, but he is under close arrest with a terrible charge hanging over his head—a charge carrying death, Captain Gates! He is quite alone—more alone than many men have ever been, because he has no hope of welcome or chance of rest in any country. Nowhere is there a friend to advise him—and are you seriously suggesting that he was not a little confused, a little bewildered, as to what to say to you, and what not to say?'

'He need not have spoken at all. I cautioned him to that effect.'

'I know you did. I'm sure you did everything with perfect propriety. But can you not imagine that you must have seemed very formidable to him?'

Perhaps this suggestion did not displease the little man. 'It is possible,' he concluded.

'Very possible. And, in spite of that, he consented to help you all he could?'

'Yes, sir. He had his statement all prepared for me.'

'But there was questioning by you about points in the statement?'

'A few.'

'And you maintain to the court that he seemed perfectly at ease in his manner and his answers?'

'I do.'

'Oh, Captain Gates! I do not challenge your veracity in the least, but I must question your imagination. Let me ask you: did he say anything about being greeted at British Army Headquarters with jeers and jibes and shouts of "Germany calling"?'

'No, sir.'

'Strange. Well, never mind; we'll get that in evidence later. So this is the position: he lies there, ill, terribly alone, and among young men of his own age who have scorned and derided him. Can you not conceive how he must have thought that on his answers to you depended his life or his death?'

To this the witness gave no answer beyond a lift of his shoulders.

Dick waited, leaving, as it seemed, this reluctance in answering to make its effect on the court. 'On the contrary then, Captain Gates: would you say that he seemed hard and cold and indifferent?'

'Oh, no, I wouldn't say that.'

'Well, shall we put it like this: would you say that he seemed anxious to please you in every way because he could but feel that, in a sense, his life was in your hands?'

'It may have been so, sir.'

'Thank you, Captain Gates.' Promptly Dick sat down.

The clerk, with the utmost weariness, sat back, lifted his foolscap sheets, and rapidly, tonelessly, automatically, read over the long continuous narrative that he had made of this witness's answers. In the same level and lifeless voice, having reached his last full-stop, he asked, 'Is that correct?' and on Captain Gates replying 'Yes. Correct,' passed the deposition towards him, as if glad to be quit of it. 'Will you sign that and understand that you are bound over to attend the Court of Trial,' he mumbled; then linked his fingers before him on his desk, as one who could rest from labour and meditate for a blessed interval on matters far away.

§

'Lieutenant William Prescott,' called Mr. Raynes, who had risen.

The policeman, with cries, gathered this witness from the passage and directed him to the witness box.

'Mr. Prescott, will you tell the learned magistrate what you were doing on the afternoon of the 7th of May this year?'

'Yes, sir. I was walking on Lüneburg Heath, looking for mushrooms.'

A titter in court, so unexpected this detail.

'And what happened? Perhaps you will tell the court in your own words.'

Lieutenant Prescott described the finding of a young man lying under the trees by the roadside—and Ida, listening, trembled in her place and bent her head and touched her eyes with her handkerchief.

'Can you see this young man here?'

'Yes, sir.'

'Will you point him out?'

'He's the gentleman over there.'

Ida felt grateful! to him for the word 'gentleman,' and raised her head.

'The gentleman in the dock?' For the first time Mr. Raynes looked towards the prisoner and gave him a quite friendly smile, 'Did he speak at all?'

'Yes. He asked where I came from. And what the time was in Balham.'

This curious answer produced a taut silence in the room, an absolute silence, as might a line in a play. Even Mr. Raynes seemed moved to leave it for a little in its lake of silence. 'In what state was he?'

'Oh, semi-delirious, sir.'

'Did he say anything in his delirium?'

'Yes, sir. He seemed to imagine he was delivering a broadcast, not, I think, to Britain, but to some other country.'

'Why do you think that?'

'Because he said something about the British being more and more apprehensive of the unnatural quiet. He called us "the people of that unhappy isle."'

'Anything else did he say?'

'Yes, he said "Is the old Lord Wensley still standing?" and "Is Dad alive, and Mum, and Beth?"'

Here Ida's sobs were heard all over the court, and Counsel paused in sympathy, and the reporters wrote.

'Mum and *who*?'

'And Beth.'

'You knew that the Lord of Wensley had been the home of Michael Townes?'

'Yes sir, the whole army knew that.'

'Did you ask him anything?'

'I asked him if he was Michael Townes.'

'And he replied?'

'Something about the Berlin short-wave station having given Michael Townes an opportunity to speak the truth to Britishers the whole world over.'

'I thank you.' Mr. Raynes sank to his seat.

The field was open to Dick. 'Mr. Prescott,' he rose and asked, 'did he at this time know clearly what was happening or what he was saying?'

'Oh, no, sir. Not at all clearly.' It was evident that the witness was glad to be able at last to speak some words in favour of the prisoner—and for this Ida loved him.

'He was in a miserable state, was he?'

'Very miserable.'

'Did you search him in any way?'

'As well as I could without hurting him.'

'You found no false papers on him?'

'No, sir. Nothing.'

'And no arms?'

'Oh, no, sir.'

'And he offered no resistance whatever to his capture?'

'No, sir. He was in no condition to do so—but I don't think he wanted to, either. No, I'm sure he didn't.'

'Thank you. Did he, perhaps, later, when his brain was clearer, say anything to you on this point?'

'Yes, sir. He said he was coming to give himself up, but didn't like to at first.'

'Why not?'

'Because he was afraid.'

'On arrival at Army Headquarters what sort of reception did he get?'

'Very mixed, I'm afraid. Some fellows were decent to him, but most were booing and jeering and imitating his voice.'

'When he was lying on the stretcher, sick?'

'Yes, sir.'

'How did he take this?'

'He shut his eyes.'

'Shut his eyes, you say?'

'Yes; as if that would help him not to hear.'

Dick nodded in understanding. 'Did you say anything to him then?'

'No, I only kind of patted him on the shoulder to comfort him.'

The tears burst from Ida, and Oh, you are good, she thought.

'Did he make any remark?'

'Yes.'

'What was it?'

'He said, "Oh, will anyone ever understand?"'

Dick made a little bow to the witness, and sat down. 'Thank you, Mr. Prescott.'

Again Ida's hopes rose. Resting in trust on Dick, she thought, He is winning pity for the boy, and they will let him off. Let him off with a large fine, perhaps, which Dad will pay. Oh, yes, let him off; let him off. She knew no more of the Law than of politics, and when Death is at the door one must barricade it with any and every hope to hand.

The next witness was a beautiful old man with far-spreading silver hair, a pale brown Southern skin on fine Hebraic bones, and a shapely figure. Here was a famous visitant in the London Courts, Mr. Toledo, the interpreter, who could deal with all the languages along the Mediterranean, and those, no less, of the Gothic north. His business now was to interpret the documents found in the radio stations of Germany, or elsewhere, and assembled by agents such as Captain Gates to weave the death-robe for Michael.

Mr. Raynes read his translations, and Mr. Toledo confirmed them. And more and more damning they sounded, till all those hopes of Ida's which had been rising fairly high—and those of Harry which had risen a little way too—were dust. And these were the documents from which she had dared to hope good news! One was a Payment Order. 'To Mr. Michael Townes. For broadcasts, Views on the News, English propaganda. At fifty marks. Remuneration, three hundred marks.' Another was the official appointment of Michael as 'a commentator for the group of countries, "England."' 'You are hereby instructed to prepare political comments in the English language, and I am to inform you that your stipend will be increased to a gross monthly salary of one thousand five hundred Reichsmarks payable on the first of each month.'

Mr. Toledo endorsed or corrected these interpretations with an exquisite control of phrasing, enunciation, and voice. He was the practised and perfect witness, whom all watched with fascination. His fine features seemed cut in wood because of their coffee-brown skin beneath the glory of white hair; and his manner was as courteous as that of an old Castilian grandee while he spoke the words most damning of all. In his courtesy he spoke them slowly, clearly, for the clerk's sake; and that bored young man was able, for once, to undo the wrinkles on his brow and write his story without those distresses that approached despair.

The only despair was Ida's and Harry's. How could any future evidence, or any subsequent argument, heal the mortal mischief done by 'fifty marks' and 'one thousand five hundred marks'? They looked at their son in his dock. His hands were fingering one another, and his lower lip had fallen as he sighed. They were near enough to hear his sighs and see his cheek twitching. From outside, in quiet moments, came the noises of the market: shouts of porters, stamping of horses' hooves, whistling of happy pitchers, hammering of crates, and the hum and sigh of London's traffic behind. Was Michael, the prisoner, hearing all these market sounds and thinking that he would never stand in the friendly huckstering world, a free man, again?

Oh, darling, they will look at your youth and have pity and forgive. They *must*. It will be all right; I'm sure it will; yes, oh, yes—it will be all right in the end.

The magnificent old interpreter had finished his lethal work, and Mr. Raynes was sitting down.

'No questions,' said Dick, without rising. Oh then—was Dick now hopeless too?

§

Counsel for the Prosecution rose again. 'Daphne Queensbury Fowler,' he called.

'Daphne Queensbury Fowler,' repeated the policeman to the passage. 'Miss—or is it Mrs.?—Fowler. Come along, please.'

And into the court, like a breath from the spring day outside —indeed, bringing a breath of perfume as from a massed flower-bed—carrying her golden head like a cresset alight and radiant, came a witness to lift the eyes of all men from their dreary documents, and to waft them away from the drab routines of the law, and into—what?—perhaps into thoughts about the mystery of beauty in this our universe, or about femininity and its arch adaptations to masculine company, or about illusions that had been theirs in their youth, and were now departed.

Miss—or Mrs.—Fowler, in a two-piece suit of turquoise blue, tight about her hips and about her rose-pink blouse, walked to the witness box with the elegance of a mannequin displaying to this mainly masculine audience a dress well suited to the month of May. The scent of a thousand flowers went with her—and trailed behind her. The close, staling air in the room was slightly the fresher for it. This heavy atmosphere had for some time been visiting Ida with fears of headache, sickness or fainting, so that she yawned often on her hard seat; and now this sudden entry and passing of a spring-like fragrance was moment-arily a restorative—but Ida was not grateful to the ministrant for it. The golden hair—so luminous that one felt that some of the day's capricious sunlight had walked in—had most obviously been waved and burnished for this important public appearance. The bloom on her skin was more perfect than God would give to any of His creatures because He is an artist and knows that absolute perfection is always displeasing because too good to be true. Today was her day. This was a case all the world was watching, and she had a part in it. A part in history, and she went tapping on her high heels towards it.

A man in the public area behind Harry exclaimed almost aloud, 'Crimes, we're in luck today.'

'Yepp. Hell of a treat,' said a voice beside him.

'A nice little piece for a Crown witness,' observed another. 'Where did they get her from?'

'From the Crown jewels,' suggested a distant wit, who'd probably never spoken to the questioner before—but such a vision in a room of weary men will launch a thousand quips.

Even Harry in his dejection, which was complete, could almost smile at this one: it sat so well on the too-radiant figure now standing in the box. Her dress-ornament of glittering paste flashed in the lamp above her; and what appeared to be golden guineas swung from her ears as she turned to take the oath-card from the usher, giving him a smile, since, though bald, he was a man. The reporters, certainly not less human than the lawyers, gaped for quite a space at her as she spoke her lines. Nor did the clerk, being also a man, watch her with quite the dull despair that most witnesses caused him. He had the best view of all, for he sat at his desk immediately in front of, and below, the witness box. She smiled down on him.

The bitch, thought Ida.

The magistrate had swung round in his chair to hear this new witness, and he gave her a small chivalrous smile to help her on her way.

In short, this was a masculine court, and universal tenderness flooded all.

She patted her hair into place above her ears and above her neck, and was now ready to do her part.

Mr. Raynes spoke. 'Is your name Daphne Queensbury Fowler?'

'Oh, yes.' She put her head to one side, as at a flattery.

'And before your marriage were you Miss Cummins?'

'Before I married Mr. Fowler, yes.'

'And when you were Miss Cummins did you work in the monitoring service of the British Broadcasting Corporation?'

'Yes. That's right. For five years.'

'Lucky B.B.C.,' said the voice behind Harry.

'You were a very highly paid stenographer?' Mr. Raynes smiled, indulging in a little male flattery.

'Oh, I don't know about *that*.'

'Because of your skill and accuracy?'

'I shouldn't like to say that, either. I was quite *good*.'

'I understand that you have since left the B.B.C. to get married.'

'Oh, yes.' Apparently she did not wish this to be in doubt.

'Lucky Mr. Fowler,' muttered the voice.

'Yes, directly the war was over and Mr. Fowler could manage it. We always promised to do that, you see.'

Mr. Raynes gazed at her as if not certain that he saw, or why he should see.

'What did you say?' demanded the clerk. And he sighed, '*Would* you speak a little louder?'

'Yes, keep your voice up,' advised the magistrate, and you felt he'd only just stopped himself adding 'my dear.'

'Pardon?' she queried, not expecting words from that direction.

'I have to render your evidence into a continuous deposition,' explained the clerk. 'Would you therefore—very kindly—let me hear it.'

'Oh, yes. I'm *so* sorry. I *beg* your pardon.'

'You were saying?'

She repeated the mutual promises of herself and Mr. Fowler. The weary clerk shrugged, and, knowing nothing else to do, and no precedent for doing anything else, wrote them down as evidence.

These obstacles overcome, Mr. Raynes proceeded, 'Now, Miss Fowler—I beg your pardon—*Mrs.* Fowler.'

She smiled her willing, even pleased, forgiveness.

'If you will be good enough to look at this—is this the book in which you made shorthand notes of broadcasts from Germany in June, 1940?'

She looked at it, her golden head turning this way and that. 'Yes. That's right. . . . At least, it was in June *and* July, to tell the truth,' and she emphasised the words '*and* July' with an uplifted forefinger like a teacher before a class of infants.

'And this is the one you used in April of this year before you left the B.B.C. to marry Mr. Fowler?'

But Dick was standing now. 'With respect, sir: I must suggest that, though I'm sure we all want to help Mrs. Fowler, it would be better, and indeed only proper, for learned counsel to let her speak for herself instead of putting words into her mouth.'

'Yes . . . yes . . .' agreed Mr. Raynes with a bow and a smile to Dick. 'I rather thought I heard my friend making some fully justified mutterings. I am much obliged. Very much obliged. But I take it there is no dispute about these broadcasts?'

'None whatever,' said Dick.

'Well, then!' Mr. Raynes chose to change from disarming conciliation to righteous irritation: you felt that anywhere but in a court of law he would have added, 'What the hell?' 'Perhaps I can satisfy and appease my friend by some such re-phrasing of my question as this: I shall be obliged, Mrs. Fowler, if you will assist me all you can by telling the court this: what is this book?'

'Pardon?' she said, her thoughts disarrayed by this controversy between Mr. Raynes and Dick.

Mr. Raynes, wishing to help her, as who with any gallantry would not, pronounced very slowly, 'Look at that book. . . . Now what is it?'

She performed her usual 'business' over the book, moving her head to left and right, very prettily, as she scanned it. Then said that it was what Mr. Raynes had said it was, all along.

'Thank you. I am much obliged. And you have seen these transcriptions made of your notes. Do you accept them as correct?'

'Oh, yes. Definitely. Absolutely. Oh, yes.'

'Right.' Mr. Raynes turned to the magistrate. 'You would wish these transcriptions read, sir?'

The little magistrate smiled most helpfully at counsel. 'Well, just so much of them as you consider desirable for our present purpose. Always supposing Mr. Templer has no objection to this.'

Dick rose. 'There is no dispute about these broadcasts, sir.'

'Thank you.' Mr. Raynes bowed—very sarcastically this time and palpably recalling his friend's unnecessary interposition of a few moments ago. 'Well, let us take only a few parts from the last of them, delivered a day or two before the end of the War. A copy for the learned magistrate . . . one for the clerk. . . . Thank you . . . Mrs. Fowler, it begins, does it not: "This may be my last broadcast to you, and I shall take this opportunity of explaining those motives——" oh, well, we've had all that in his statement—"I held that the economic system of Britain was out of correspondence"—had all that too—"economic system . . . enslavement . . . yes . . . yes. . . ."' He turned a page. '". . . in Italy and Germany where they were fashioning political and industrial institutions much better adapted to the needs of the time and more likely to bring life, opportunity, and security to the people. I was convinced that this was the beginning of a new age for Europe and that it was my duty to help it march onward and into my own land." That is correct, Mrs. Fowler?'

She nodded—with smiles.

The clerk shut his eyes, in a new onset of despair.

The magistrate, in his gentlest tones, explained. 'The learned clerk has to take down in longhand everything to which you testify—and, you see, he cannot take down a nod.'

'Oh, I see. No, of course not. Yes, that's a transcription of my notes. Definitely.'

And I listened to him broadcasting those words, thought Ida. I listened secretly out of Harry's sight, who was listening to them down in the cellar, thinking I didn't know. And I was so happy to hear them, because I said to myself, 'The War's over, and nothing can harm him now;' and all the time that creature was sitting in the B.B.C. taking them down. . . .

'"It was only when I learned that your government had imprisoned without trial——" no: we've had that . . . h'mm . . . yes . . . turn to the end. Do you see this closing passage: "We in Germany have drained the cup of suffering which the Russians have filled for us, and it would seem that now we pass it from our lips to yours."'

Mr. Raynes looked up from his reading. 'You accept all this as a correct transcription, Mrs. Fowler?'

The golden head swung through a small arc to the right, so as to put some feminine charm into the answer, 'Oh, yes. Yes, indeed.'

'Thank you, Mrs. Fowler.' And Mr. Raynes sank into his pen.

She gave him a charming farewell smile as he sank, and,

perceiving that another gentleman was stirring on a lower level, turned to be of service to him. But Dick rose only ten inches to say, 'No questions.'

'Oh, pardon. I'm sorry,' she murmured.

The clerk, careless of her sorrow, read his manuscript story in his dead voice, rapidly. He asked, Was it correct? got the answer, 'Oh, yes. Absolutely;' and passed it to her to sign.

'Yes. Thank you. I understand.' And she comforted him with a reassuring smile, of which his now death-mask face registered no reception at all.

The magistrate, however, in his chivalry, felt a compulsion to help and guide her to the end, just as a man of gallantry will desire to guide a woman across a road, though she could get across quite well, and possibly better, without his help. 'That is all,' he said to her, and you could almost hear the suppressed 'my dear.' 'That is all, Mrs. Fowler. Thank you very much;' to which she replied, 'Not at all,' and, carrying her head slightly to the left for a change, and drenching with her fragrance her path through the air, clicked prettily on her high heels to a seat immediately beside Ida.

Ida moved six inches away. Then three inches more. She looked through the side of her eye, at the turquoise suit, the flesh-coloured stockings, the patent shoes, and pressed up her lips with distaste. And there they sat side by side, she who had listened to Michael's broadcasts with love and relief, and this creature who had taken them down for his damnation.

§

'That is my case, sir,' said Mr. Raynes. 'On that evidence I ask for a committal.'

The magistrate looked questioningly at Dick, to learn if he had any submission to make; but Dick only shook his head. So the magistrate leaned forward and faced Michael.

The gaoler touching Michael's arm, bade him stand. Michael stood up promptly. Deliberately he stood with head erect, spine straight, and arms smartly at his side, like a soldier at attention—or like a condemned man who would face the firing squad fearlessly.

'Michael Cawdor Townes,' said the magistrate. So far he'd had little to do but nod and smile benignantly and offer encouraging words and smile again. Now it was his time to speak and he leaned back comfortably in his big chair to do so. But he spoke no louder than a guest in a drawing-room to another guest standing before him; no louder than a teacher on his dais to a boy in a front desk. Harry had to turn his head sideways to catch what the little man was saying. 'Michael Cawdor Townes, I trust that you are appreciating the terribly serious nature of this charge against you. There is no graver charge known to our Law—if indeed there is one as grave. It is the charge of high treason, in that—' he looked down on his desk, then over his spectacles again at Michael—'"you did traitorously adhere to the King's enemies, elsewhere than in the King's realm . . ." I have to inform you of your right to call witnesses and, if you so desire, to give evidence on your own behalf. I give you clearly to understand—' he was reading again—'that you have nothing to hope from any promised favour and nothing to fear from any threat, that may have been held out to you to induce you to make admission or confession of your guilt, but that whatsoever you say may be given in evidence at your trial, notwithstanding the promise or threat. . . . Do you wish to say anything in answer to the charge? You are not obliged to say anything unless you desire to do so.'

Michael turned helpless eyes towards Dick.

Dick rose. 'My client does not wish to give evidence at this court or to call any witnesses. He says he is not guilty and reserves his defence. He has a complete answer to the charge, but in the meantime only wishes me to state, in the strongest possible terms, that he is now, and always has been, a lover of his native country and his purpose in all he has done, however mistaken he may think some of it now, has been, not to injure this country but to serve it.'

Whether he felt any interest in this protestation the magistrate did not show. He said only in the same low conversational tones, 'Michael Townes, you are committed to take your trial next sessions at the Central Criminal Court.'

Thereupon the big stout gaoler, with the tunic shaped like a cathedral bell, put a huge palm on Michael's back in an almost fatherly way—such was his native kindliness—and said, 'Come on, cock,' gently but loud enough for Harry to hear. Michael started at the touch, made a polite bow to the magistrate, and stepped from the dock into the custody of the gaoler and a covey of senior officers. Harry watched him being guided away by these his new fathers.

CHAPTER TWO

AFTER the committal Dick had risen and said, 'Sir, my client's father and mother are in court. May they see him before his removal to prison?'

'Oh, certainly,' said the magistrate with his mildest smile. 'Subject to the usual regulations.' And he directed his friendly little bow straight at Harry and Ida in their corner—which was remarkable because it showed that he had guessed, or known from the beginning, who they were.

Dick, familiar with these places, led them along a passage to a waiting-room. It would be Ida's first meeting with her son for six years, and Harry's first for eight years. The bare brown room was empty, and Harry, not a little apprehensive of this meeting, in such a place and such circumstances—indeed as nervous of it as his son almost certainly was—walked to a window rather than stay still, and looked out. He saw only the grey station yard, with the barred cell windows on two sides of it, and police cars parked around it, and a big blue police van waiting. And a strange car with drawn blinds, also waiting.

Steps on a hard floor—and he turned. Michael was coming in, followed by a young detective sergeant, a man no older than his prisoner and therefore with a career before him as full of promise as Michael's was purged of hope.

Michael was pale and, though trying to show courage, was obviously ashamed of his position and unsure of his reception. But Ida rushed forward and embraced him, saying, 'My darling, my darling,' and 'It'll be all right. It'll be all right.'

The detective sergeant, who had moved tactfully apart, did nothing to stop this embrace, but scanned it carefully.

Harry had put forth his hand to grasp his son's, but as Ida still held the boy, he dropped it to his side again. Michael was answering his mother with a grin, 'Be all right? I don't know about *that*,' but she maintained, 'Oh, yes, it will. And it's wonderful to have you back—wonderful to see you again.'

When the embrace was over Michael looked at his father as

if in doubt about his welcome there. But Harry put out his hand again, and Michael flung his own hand into it. Not for years had Harry been able to show Michael by gesture or word his feelings for him, but now he managed to bring his other hand over and lay it upon his son's, so that Michael's hand was encased in both of his, and there pressed—pressed very tight. 'Look, Michael, old boy,' he said. 'Everything I've got is yours, see. I've told Dick so, haven't I, Dick. Dick's going to see to everything for you.'

'I don't want you to spend all your money on me, Dad.'

'Never you worry about that, son. Every stiver of it is yours. Eh, Mother?'

'Why, of course, of course.'

'It's wonderful of you, Dad, but I've cost you enough already. Dad, I'm sorry I've brought all this on you. I can realise what you must feel about it, thinking as you do——'

'I understand, son. I understand all you've done. I understand much better than a lot in that court, I think.'

'The funny thing is, I can hardly understand some of it myself now. . . . How's our Beth?'

'Beth wanted terribly to come and see you today, but she stayed at home so that the old people could come.'

'That's Beth all over.'

'Yes, she's a good girl,' said Ida, for something to say; then, for something more: 'She sent you all her love.'

'Give her all of mine, Mum. I'm glad, Dad, that one of your children wasn't an absolute washout.' And he tried to grin again.

'Nonsense,' protested Ida; and Harry, changing the subject, said, 'That Prescott man was a gentleman.'

'Yes, Dad, he was. He was decent from the beginning. So were quite a few of the others, after a time.' Mention of Prescott seemed to remind him of something. 'I'm so glad the old Lord of Wensley's still going strong. I was afraid I might have sunk it for you, and I was a lot unhappy about that—truly I was. But Uncle Dick tells me that it is still booming.'

'Yes, the old pub's all right. It's still afloat.'

'Everybody stuck to you in spite of me, did they? Good. I hoped they might. . . . Dad, I know now that I was an idiot to shoot off to Germany like that, but I did try to believe I was doing it for the best. Only nothing turned out as I expected—nothing at all.'

'I understand, son.' Harry repeated it, standing erect and quite still behind Ida, while he raked in his mind, helplessly, for words that would be worthier of this day of reunion.

'I know it didn't—of course it didn't,' Ida comforted, stroking his arm, while the detective watched. 'It was all that Dermot's fault. Why did you ever meet him? Why did he ever come into our lives? I blame it all on him.'

'Oh, no, Mother. I shall always believe I got more good out of Dermot than harm. We had great days together—once. And anyhow he's dead now. Let him rest. I'll take my blame on my own shoulders.'

'He killed himself like a dog in a ditch,' said Harry.

'No, it was not quite like that, Dad. It was better than that. I don't want to hear anything against old Dermot. He was the best friend I ever had.'

'That's right; you be loyal to him,' said Ida, changing her ground at once, and still stroking his sleeve.

Harry walked to the window and looked out at the grey station yard while he gathered courage to say something he wanted to say. 'You've got him now for a brief moment,' he was telling himself. 'Make the amends to him. Be quick—quick—your chance is going—make amends.' But it was a long minute before his courage was ready. Then, slowly, he came back.

'It's ghastly, sitting in that dock and being unable to speak a word while they're saying filthy things about you,' Michael was declaring, with heated cheeks, and trembling limbs, to Ida and Dick. 'They misunderstand half the things you've done, and are blind, absolutely blind, to most of your motives. There were a thousand things I was bursting to say, but couldn't—it's maddening, because you know you're not as bad as they imply.'

He paused breathlessly; and Harry seized the moment to speak his amends. 'I guess it was all partly my fault,' he said.

'Yours, Dad? Oh, no. Why?'

'Oh, I dunno. Dick always made out that I was too heavy-handed with you, and bullied you sometimes, and I dare say he was right. He's much cleverer than I am.'

'You never bullied me, Father. Got hot sometimes, but who doesn't?'

'Yes, but . . . I don't know . . . I dare say . . . what I mean is——'

'Please don't think that, Dad. It can't be your fault if I was three parts of a fool.'

'Well, anyhow, I'd like you to know this, Mike, if it's any comfort to you. Naturally I think you were hopelessly wrong in continuing to back your Nazis after you'd learned what they were like, but I'm damned if you were wrong about those bloody Russians——'

'Harry!' rebuked Ida, glancing quickly at the police officer.

'For Christ's sake don't interrupt!' he shot at her. He was finding it difficult enough to say these things, without being interrupted by her. 'And I can't see, Mike, that appealing to your country to stop the war—though I didn't agree with you for a second—was quite so terrible a crime as they make out.'

'Thank you for saying that, Dad.'

'I meant it, son.'

'Of course it wasn't,' echoed Ida. 'I never heard the like.'

The detective officer came forward quietly to Dick. 'I think they'll be wanting to take him back to Brixton very shortly now, sir.'

'I see, sergeant. I see.'

'I'd rather the lady and gentleman went first.'

Dick nodded, guessing that, after that kiss and those strokings by Ida, the officer had a mind to give his prisoner a 'rub down.' 'Harry, I'm afraid we must end this now. You will have other opportunities of seeing Michael. Mike, they're waiting for you, but your father and mother must go first.'

'Okay, Uncle Dick. I'm ready.' He said it almost jauntily, as if he knew that his face was white and strained and he wanted to belie what was written there. 'Good-bye, Dad.'

'Good-bye, son.'

'And, Mum . . . don't worry too much. Don't let her worry too much, Dad. I can take whatever's coming to me. And I shall only be in Brixton Prison, Mum. That's not so far.' Now it was Michael who was comforting her, with a hand on her back and her sleeve. It was a courageous effort, because his limbs were trembling again. Ida, as always when comforted, abandoned herself to tears and, with handkerchief at mouth and head shaking, hurried from the room.

§

They were back in the Lord of Wensley, Harry, Ida, and Dick. It was after three, and the house was shut. Harry took Dick into the living-room and closed the door.

258

'Now I can ask you, Dick—I wasn't going to speak before Ida in the van—sit down, old boy, and be comfortable—Dick, what is this "answer to all the allegations" that you spoke of? There is no answer.'

'There could be one.' Dick had sat down and was looking up at Harry, who stood before him.

'But *what*, Dick? They've got his broadcasts. You don't dispute they're his. Well, that's the end. There's no defence anywhere.'

'Just one.'

'Well, what the hell is it?'

'That he was a naturalised German citizen.'

'Michael a German citizen! What're you talking about?'

'He says he was.'

'Good God! Oh. . . .' This was a sigh of momentary relief —relief unforeseen and therefore shaking. Shaking, too, because in conflict with dismay. 'But my boy a German citizen! *My* son!—oh, no! Still . . . still . . . if it's of help to him, I'm glad. He can be a naturalised Chinaman for all I care, if it'll save him. Can he prove this?'

'No. His story is that he destroyed the certificate of naturalisation along with all his other papers when he was afraid of capture by the Russians.'

'But, Dick, don't you have to live years in a country before you can be naturalised? He was only there a few months before the War began. Do you believe this story?'

'No, Harry.'

'Oh, but wait. He didn't broadcast till May, 1940——'

'That's no help.'

'Why not?'

'Because it's treason to become the naturalised citizen of a country, once the King's at war with it. That's the Law.'

'And dam-silly law too. If a man wants to be a German instead of an Englishman, he's a double-dyed idiot, but it's not a case for shooting him. Might as well say that if you've once played for Surrey and are fool enough to change your home and play for Middlesex——'

'It's not as simple as that, Harry.'

'Well, it seems so to me. But *could* he have got naturalised in time?'

'I should doubt it. I've found cases of British naturalised as Germans in September, 1940, which looks as though they hurried things up, but if he's an hour later than eleven on September 3rd, 1939, the defence is worthless.'

'Is there any means of finding any proof of his tale in Germany? If so, send somebody to search the records. Spend what you like.'

'We'll do all we can, but he argues that there's little hope of finding anything, because almost everything in Berlin was destroyed.'

'Ah . . . yes . . . I see. Clever! Too clever. Any jury's going to shake their silly heads over that. And any counsel's going to chew it up unless we can find some corroboration for him. Look, Dick—listen—you're a good man; I'm not—I'll go cheerfully into that box and take that blasted oath and swear by Almighty God that he wrote to me and told me he'd done it. That he asked me to try to understand and forgive it— see? It makes quite a likely tale, don't you think?—and I'll tell it in the most convincing way; and if Almighty God likes to strike me dead in the box, well, that'll be that.'

Dick only looked at the carpet. And there saw written that, as a solicitor, an officer of the High Court, he couldn't be a conscious party to deceiving the court.

Harry began to walk up and down. 'You don't like the idea? But it'll be my perjury, Dick; not yours. You're so damned honest. What is a lie compared with a boy's life?'

'I'll do all I can with his tale, Harry.'

'But that's to say you're using *his* lie?'

'I don't *know* that it's a lie. It's my business to try to believe my clients.'

'But you don't really believe him?'

'No.'

'Why, Dick?'

'Because when I asked him at what date he got his certificate of naturalisation, he answered carelessly, "Oh, some time after the war started;" and when I reminded him that then it would be no good, he turned white and tears came into his eyes——'

'Oh, Mike—poor Mike.'

'—and he thought a bit and said, "I meant, after it was obvious that war was coming. Yes, they hurried things up for us then."'

'And anybody could see that he was lying,' agreed Harry with sad nods. 'No, Mike, that won't wash. You're just wriggling. We're not fools. And juries are not fools—at least not all twelve of 'em. Oh, great God, Dick, where are we? What are we to do?'

'He won't save himself with that tale. If he persists in it, we'll have to do what we can with it, but it'll fail, and then I can only hope for one thing.'

'And that is?'

'It is small, but—if we can persuade the court that he at least *applied* for naturalisation before the War, it might increase his chances of a reprieve.'

'A reprieve! Dick!—is there any hope of that?'

Dick's eyes were bent upon the carpet again. 'There might be. A faint hope.'

Harry's eyes had brightened with this hope. 'Oh, yes . . . surely they may feel some pity for him. If he were a big and important person, I wouldn't give twopence for his chances, but he's only the son of a nobody in Balham.'

'But he mustn't persist in this impossible tale of having secured his naturalisation——'

'No, no, they'll see he's a liar then and won't like him, or recommend him to mercy.'

'Unless . . .' began Dick.

'Unless what?'

'Unless counsel could persuade them that he was not a very bright boy, and——'

'Mike was one of the brightest——'

'—and that he somehow believed that his police passes amounted to acceptance as a citizen.'

'There was nothing in his statement about naturalisation.'

'No, alas! the statement as it stands is a petition to the King for death. That was why I was fishing to find out if we could somehow discredit it by showing that he was in no proper condition to make it or to understand what to say.'

'I see. I couldn't grasp what you were after, or what hope there was, anywhere. I thought you were just fighting for the sake of fighting, and I liked you for it. Just going down fighting. General Gordon's last stand.'

'No . . . if . . . if we could only persuade them that he'd applied——'

'Well—to hell, Dick!—I'll go over to Berlin and bribe some dirty German to fake the necessary document; they've been experts at producing false papers all through the War; I'll give

him a hundred pounds—a thousand—anything you like . . .
but, no, I suppose you'll never fall for that. No. I've a low-
class soul. You've not.'

'He'd have to swear to the document, and if I knew it was
a fake——'

'Yes, yes,' Harry sighed. 'Enough said. I understand. I
won't ask anything dishonourable of you, old man. There's
enough dishonour lying around . . . already.'

'Harry.' Dick had looked up, and was looking straight at
him. 'I want to ask you something.'

'Fire away, old boy.'

'You think—as I do—that Michael's been a pig-headed young
fool in all this dreadful business, but you don't think he's been
a coward?'

'No, I don't think that. No, thank God. It was the other
fellow who was a coward. He ran away.'

'So on that score you can still be proud of him?'

'Yes.'

'Well, Harry, if all this naturalisation tale is a lie from
beginning to end, do you want him to lie?'

Silence; till Harry answered with all that he could bring
himself to answer. 'I want him to live.'

'Of course you do,' said Dick gently. And for the time left
his question there.

§

Nearly three summer months had to trail heavily by before
Michael could stand his trial at the Old Bailey. In those
lagging months the doors of the Lord of Wensley opened every
day at the permitted hours, and every day, at opening time,
Captain Townes was there behind his bar. All England might
know that his son was awaiting his death sentence over yonder
on Brixton Hill, but the Captain, after his fashion, would say
to all intimates who were fit to hear, 'My place is on my bridge
though the skies fall' and 'The show must go on' and, as he
went down to unlock his doors at eleven o'clock, 'Beginners,
please' and 'Turn on the beer, Walter. Curtain up.'

There was no lessening of business in his bars. His 'regulars'
were as regular as ever, having agreed, one and all, 'It'd be fatal
to seem to be leaving him now'; and they came at their usual
time and ordered with a studied cheerfulness, 'The usual,

Harry.' For years it had been one of Captain Townes's jests to draw, directly they came in sight, and before they could speak, their usual pint or half pint, or to lever off the crown-cork from their usual light ale. He gave them no less jocose a welcome now, and they would chat together of the war and the peace and the Government—but no one ever mentioned Michael, neither they, nor he. It was the 'casuals' who caused the slightly sinister increase in his custom, and he was well aware that some of them had come for a glass and a glimpse over the top of it at a father whose son was set apart to die. Outside his doors the traffic of the High Road went hammering and hooting on, and he guessed that the people in the buses and the men on the lorries were pointing out his house to one another. Nor did he doubt that some of the buses shed passengers here who had a fancy to see the house and family of Michael Townes; but he served one and all alike, with never a hint of his thoughts. He would often share a joke with the company, laughing almost as loud as any of them, and then quote in a whisper to Walter at his side, 'Laugh, clown, laugh.'

He and Beth had agreed that Ida must not be expected to serve any more. 'Don't worry, Dad,' Beth had said. 'I'll be there to serve all the time. I can do all that Mum would have done.'

'No,' was his reply. 'Better stay with her and comfort her. I don't mind how hard the work is. The harder the better. You look after your mother and I'll look after the bar. But come down sometimes to see the boys. Just to let 'em see that we're none of us hauling down our flags, and the show goes on.'

§

Upstairs Ida went about her household tasks, glad, like Harry, to find manual work to do. Beth stayed with her unobtrusively, and her heart was torn by her mother's silences and sighs as she walked from scullery to kitchen or from larder to stove. They were the sighs of one who walked always with hopelessness. Beth would see her looking at some advertisement of outsize dresses 'for the larger figure'—and then leaving it with the usual sigh, as the pain returned after a brief forgetfulness. Then, as she walked about again from table to stove, she might murmur almost aloud, each emit the memory throbbed, 'Oh dear . . . oh dear . . .' or—and this was harder to bear because it was an attempt to be brave—'Oh, well. . . .'

There were times, however, when, in an uprush of misery, she renounced all effort at self-control and broke down in the old way. Then she would sink into one of the deep leather chairs and cry; and Beth, rushing to her side, would kneel there, grasping her hands, or would sit on the chair's elbow with an arm about her shoulders, perhaps pressing her lips upon her brow.

'I forget for a little and keep coming back to it,' Ida bewailed one such time, her head shaking in hopelessness. 'Day after day, and no hope. Nothing but pain. I can take no more, Beth. I've had enough. I don't want any more. I'm tired of it. Tired.'

'I know you are, Mum,' soothed Beth, seated on the chair's arm. 'Naturally, naturally.'

'Why am I given blows like this? Why am I tormented day after day?'

'Good news may come, Mother dear.'

'No, darling. Don't make me hope again. I'm cured of hope. If you start hoping again, the disappointments hurt all the more. I'm better as I am; not hoping; not hoping at all, any more.'

Comforting her as best he could, Harry had described the counsel whom Dick wanted to brief, Sir David Wade-Collins, as 'the finest defender in England. He'll fight every inch of the ground. If there's an inch on which he can stand, he'll stand there and fight'; and then, a few evenings later, needing to share his pain with someone, he had burst into the room with the words, 'This Sir David fellow says that Michael's defence is about as likely to hold water as wet tissue paper,' and, having got this relief, wandered sadly out again, Beth following him to hear more. Ida was standing by the sideboard; her lips shook; her teeth bit on them; but she did not give way till Harry was gone. Nor then—immediately. Like a child who has tumbled and wants a witness for its passionate tears, she waited till Beth returned; then opened upon her the full gush of her misery.

'Oh, Beth . . . my lost boy of whom I had such hopes! Oh—' here she stamped her foot at the world—'give me some more to bear! Tell me some more to break my heart! Go on! I haven't had enough yet. I can take heaps more. Plenty. Plenty.'

'Come . . . sit down, Mum. Come darling.'

She allowed Beth to lead her to a chair, as if Beth were the mother and she the weeping child. 'There, Mum. Sit down.'

'Michael . . . I expected so much of him. People used to flatter me so about him that I began to have incredible hopes. And now I'm writing them all off for ever; and it's so difficult to do. They come back.'

'We don't know what'll happen, Mother. You may be able to hope everything for him again.'

'No, you heard what your father said. What's the good of hoping? They're set on killing him, every one of them.'

'No, no; not all, my sweet. Uncle Dick is fighting for——'

'And what's so awful, Beth, is that they've got me all confused about him. I thought he was a good boy, if silly at times like all young people are—no one's perfect—but now I no longer seem to know if he was good.'

From the Saloon below, barely screened from them by floorboards that were old and parting, came sounds of blended voices, shrieked female laughs, jocose jeering shouts, and doors swinging shut.

'He was good in many ways,' said Beth. 'And in even more ways now, I think.'

'I keep wondering if they're right. And it's like a blow leaving me sick, when I wonder that. I don't know whether to believe them. I no longer know what to think. Someone tell me he was good.'

'I will tell you, darling.'

'Some one tell me, please, please! Not just you—you're bound to say so. Someone else tell me he was good. I must believe that again. They're almost making me lose my love for him, but *I won't let them*! Directly I feel that happening I sit still and think of what he was, when he was kind and sweet. I'll admit he's been very, very silly, and that's all.'

Beth did not answer this because in her heart she could not believe that this was quite all, and, conscience-driven, especially in these dread days, she wanted, for fear of God, to speak only the truth. Under the windows the footsteps went by in an irregular but unbroken chain, with the tremor of the roadway behind them.

Ida was staring in front of her. 'I will look at his room no more. I am tired of pain. Nor if I can help it at any other things that remind me of him. They hurt too much. Oh, the noise from the road! It never stops, never. On and on. Oh, stop it, stop it! I used to like it but I can hardly stand it now.' Closing a fist she suddenly hammered it on her knee. 'I don't need anybody to tell me he was good. In some ways there was no better boy anywhere. Oh, the awful pain when one sits and remembers what was sweet and kind in him—and it's all lost . . . all wasted . . . all to be thrown away, because one thing was wrong in him. Never mind, Michael dearest. They may all hate you, but I love you still. You and I alone, Michael.'

'*And* Beth,' whispered the girl. '*And* Dad.'

§

Another day Harry, unsparing in his pain, came into the room with a stone-hard face to give them, brutally, some more bad news.

He had just seen Dick down in the bar. And Dick had told him that Sir David Wade-Collins had declined to defend Michael.

'Declined?' Harry had cried. 'But isn't that impossible? I thought it was absolute etiquette to accept a brief unless you were full of other work. I thought you said they never returned a brief.'

'He'd never fully accepted it. He insisted on seeing Michael first. And he declares that he completely broke down the boy's defence in examination. He says there's nothing he can do with it.' (Actually, what he had said was, 'It's a dead case, Templer; still-born.')

'But I thought you said he liked that kind of case because he was a fighter. You said that he'd fight till he dropped, and then get up and fight again. That's what you said, and that's what I told poor Ida and Beth.'

'I suppose he thought——'

'Yes? Thought what?'

'That one must have some small foothold if one is to fight at all——'

'Well . . . let him slink off if he wants to. Good-bye and good riddance. Get someone who *will* fight for the lad. Offer him any fee on earth. Offer him ten thousand. I'll find it. I'm only sixty-five, and fit as ten horses. I can go on working for another ten or fifteen years. Ida will too. I know her.'

'Oh, we're not giving up,' Dick promised him. 'I'd go on to the end, if only because I'm getting abusive letters threatening to lynch me if Michael gets off. Therefore I'll do everything for him.'

When Harry inflicted this new blow on Ida, she heard him in silence, with no breakdown or wild outburst. But only a little later, when Harry and Beth were down in the Saloon, Beth noticed a great silence in the house. And, afraid, she hurried up to her parents' bedroom. There she saw Ida lying face down upon the bed. She touched her. 'Mother, darling.'

Ida lifted her face a little way. 'I'm not giving in, dearest. I'll pick up in a minute. But oh, I should like to die and be done with the struggle of living. Leave me alone. I just want to be alone and get used to it. I shall be better soon. Leave me, please. No, I mean it, dear: leave me.'

And, lying there, alone and prone upon her bed—the bed, as she remembered, in which Michael had been conceived—the bed on which he had been torn from her into life—she came, slowly but steadily, face to face with courage. 'It's not decent to go on like this,' she told herself, face down upon the pillow. 'One mustn't give in entirely. It's not fair to anyone. One can give in and let oneself go, just once in a way, but not all the time. That's only making it worse for poor Harry and Beth. I won't go on lying here and behaving like this for ever. No. I'll go down—go down and help them.'

Pleased with this resolve she rose at once to go down to the bars. She thought of it as courage, and was happy in the thought, and proud in it; not perceiving that the resolve was easier for her than for some, because her nature was gregarious, and she was not made to be alone. In reality she did not want to stay up here any longer, alone with her aching sadness. And so at her dressing table she prepared herself for company with powder and rouge and lip-stick, and to the surprise of Harry, Walter, and Old Agnes appeared in the Saloon and took her usual place at Harry's side between cabinets and counter. She began to serve customers and swab counters and wipe glasses. Soon she was making a very fair show of gossiping and smiling and listening to others. And all the company wondered, but in their decency they were careful not to look at her too long or to show any trace of pity. They spoke naturally with her if she addressed them, and smiled if she smiled, because they felt this was best.

CHAPTER THREE

'Harry . . . Harry. . . .'

Harry, standing with his back to the counter and fixing an optic tap to a new whisky bottle on the bar-back, heard Dick's voice. It was half past five in the evening, and the Saloon, though opened, had been empty as he turned his back on it, so this voice of Dick's was unexpected and startled him. He was alone between his counters because there was seldom need for more than one to be on duty at this early hour. The workers were not yet home.

'Harry, can I speak to you alone?'

'Why, sure, old son. I'm alone, as you see. Walter's hared off to the brewery with the van to pick up some bottled stock we're short of. Don't know what's coming over me. Never used to let my cellar run down and forget to order. Getting old. What is it?'

'I'd rather not speak here. Someone might come in.'

'Is it about Michael?'

'Yes. I've just come from him.'

Harry, hearing this, saw Michael in his prison behind the high grey walls and the iron window-bars. 'Okay,' he sighed. 'I'll get young Beth to take over the wheelhouse. Beth! . . . Beth. . . . Where shall we go, Dick? Is it something Ida can hear?'

'Not yet, Harry.'

'She's up there, mooning about the passages, and passing Michael's room with her eyes shut. Okay, let's go out. It's a lovely evening. Beth ducks, assume command on the bridge and keep the old tub off the rocks. Walter'll be back with the van soon. Come on, Dick.'

Harry followed Dick out into the summer evening. At this hour when the shops were shut and the offices emptying, the pavement along the High Road was a tideway of hurrying people, and Harry exclaimed irritably, 'Oh Crikes, let's get away from all these damned people. Out of this stinking din too.' And he swung round the first turning that would lead them to the Common.

'Let's have it, Dick. What is it, old man?'

'Michael told me today that the whole of his story about naturalisation was a lie.'

Harry nodded. And pleaded, 'Go on.'

'I had told him many days ago that Sir David had declined the case, but he only received this news in silence. And he has said nothing till today. But I could see that he was hurt and angry and bitter about it all, and especially today when I told him that his anti-Soviet line was no defence at all, but the opposite. Then he said furiously, "All right, Uncle Dick— thank you for telling me—but if to differ from the majority of my fellow-countrymen is to be guilty, then I'm as guilty as hell. And if they ask me to die for it, right-ho, let me die." I told him quickly to say no more, but he was hot and despairing and miserably angry, and he simply had to go on, "Of course I never even applied for naturalisation; still less received a certificate."'

Harry walked on in silence, lips compressed. 'Did you ever believe he did?'

'No.'

'Nor I. Of course not. Well, what now; what now?'

'I don't know what to do, Harry. You see . . . I feel he told me as his godfather rather than as his lawyer.'

'And it's impossible for the lawyer not to know what the godfather heard. I see. I see. So there goes your "complete answer". Is there any other defence?'

'Others have attempted the defence that they were playing a double game and only pretending to help the Germans; but that's not possible in the face of his statement. Poor lad, he tried to tell the truth—or some of it—in that statement, more or less courageously——'

'And in so doing, loaded the guns against himself. A pretty piece of work. That Raynes fellow said he sharpened a sword against England, but, my God, he's been and sharpened one for his own breast too.'

Dick evaded this. 'Of course he might repudiate the statement.'

'How?'

'Saying that he made it in terror, or when he was sick.'

'I see.'

'Oh, I can think of several things he could say: that he was bullied into making a statement; that he was tired and frightened and almost hypnotised; that nearly everything he wrote was suggested to him.'

'And you would know that he was only exchanging one lie for several others.'

'Yes.'

'And you'd have to try and discredit that poor Captain Gates, who was only doing his duty?'

'Yes.'

'Oh . . . God . . . I dunno . . . I like people to play fair . . . but it's my boy's life.'

They were now walking by the Common; and that tract of worn grass, old elms, and dark, unfriendly gorse was made beautiful by the glow of the evening's fall. Something in the still enchantment, in this brief visitation of a haunting beauty, caused Harry to ask, 'Dick, tell me this: never mind what you would do as his lawyer: what do you want to do as his godfather? As his godfather you must want him to be honourable and brave. It's your job, isn't it, to—' here Harry tried to smile into his friend's face—'to try and save his soul rather than his body. . . . You don't answer?'

'He is your son, Harry; how can I say I want him to tell the truth bravely—and die.'

'But that is what, as a godfather, you must wish?'

'Perhaps. Yes, perhaps; but look, Harry: unfortunately I now know all that he's admitted, but, if you like, I will not know. I could be struck off the roll for being a party to deceiving the court, but, my God, I'll do it for your sake, and his.'

A pause; and when Harry answered, gazing ahead, it was to say, 'Dick, do you believe in a life hereafter?'

'I try to.'

'And do you—oh, *damn*!'

Some boys were playing cricket on the grass, and their shrill bellowings rasped on Harry's nerves like glass-paper. He muttered a painful protest at each new ear-rending shout. 'Oh, to hell! Blast them. That's where Mike and I used to play cricket. He had a natural batting style, and I used to have dreams that he might play for England. Play for England! . . . Go on about the Hereafter. You lost a son.'

'Yes, and, Harry, whenever I think of that splendid intelligence and that eager vision which were Bob at his best, I find it intellectually impossible—or, at least, very difficult—to believe that anything so radiant, so shining with a glow that surely came from the very stuff of Reality, could have suddenly become nothing. Just nothing. It seems as impossible to think as to say that the sun isn't there—or anywhere—when night has intervened.'

'And shall we know them again?'

'Ah, that I cannot say. I didn't say that.'

'Do you remember Padre Chilworth—the best padre the old brigade ever had? Come in here. Come away from these yelling brats. Their shrieks kill me.'

They had reached a ruined garden on the edge of the Common. It was the garden of a mansion which had long been too big for any to occupy in this unfashionable part and so had stood empty and helpless in 1940 when the bombs and incendiaries fell. On that night when Piggy Weyman died it had blazed towards the sky, and Harry, watching from his window, had seen its death crowned on the clouds with an orange and crimson glory that spanned the world from Herne Hill to Putney. The gutted and sightless walls had stood up dangerously till a demolition squad levelled them, leaving nothing but the brick foundations, the tiles of the entrance hall, and the stone-flagged cellars at the back. That was five years ago, and in five years nature had stormed the defenceless site, covering brickwork, tiles and garden with a forest of wild flowers, tall grasses and sapling trees. Here was a rank wilderness side by side with an urban common, a wasteland knit edge to edge with a trimmed public playground.

Its whole expanse this evening was a sea of carmine, yellow, green and purple. The carmine was the tall plumes of the rosebay which loves the places where fire has been; the yellow was the Oxford ragwort which also likes the ashes; the purple was vipers bugloss, milk vetch, spear thistles, and toadflax; and the green was meadow grass and seedling trees.

An airborne enemy had laid waste mansion and garden, but then the airborne seeds, travelling on their own wings or on the feet of birds and men, had garrisoned the ravaged site with this army of wild, barbarian flowers.

'We shall be quiet in here,' said Harry, 'and I want to ask you a terribly important question. Come, there's a stone seat in the garden. It's an antique sort of thing with a bad list to port, so it'll suit a couple of old has-beens like us.'

As they walked towards the seat they could hardly see any more the brick foundations or the old floor-tiles, or indeed the cavernous cellars. Five years since the fires of history blazed about them, and here was Time's way with history.

There was a beaten track to the stone seat, doubtless because lovers had discovered its secrecy among the high weeds. Doubtless too it had known within its stone arms, shaped as recumbent lions, the best and the worst of a young man's love for his girl.

'You remember the old padre, don't you?' continued Harry as they sat down. 'I was thinking of him two nights ago. I had said my prayers before getting into bed where Ida was lying very quietly, as she always does now, poor girl, and just before I got off my knees I remembered him taking a parade service in a meadow behind Ypres. God, thirty years ago now! In *our* war, Dick, which they've all forgotten. We're old men now . . . damned old. Dick Templer seventy! And Harry Townes not so far off. Very sad. Very sad. The old padre preached about prayer—do you remember? You were there.'

'I remember a service in a meadow.'

'Yes, it was while you were there, and while you were still a bad lad, and he said we could pray for everything we wanted, so long as we said after it, "Thy will be done." He didn't tell us this because we were going to attack at dawn next day—none of us knew anything about that—but I suspected it, and Dick, even though I was a loud-mouthed bullying sergeant, I was in a blue funk. I didn't want to die. I had Ida at home, and Beth, a nice kid of eight, and there was a new baby I'd never seen, Michael, so, blimey, old chap I stood there praying in that damned meadow like an old nun at a death-bed. But I did manage to add, "Thy will be done." . . . It's cold tonight. Not too cold for you, sitting here, Dick? No? Good. We're still pretty tough, both of us. . . . Well, two nights ago I had of course prayed that my lad might be saved, and suddenly I saw that scene. The meadow and the trees and the old padre there. It seemed like an answer to prayer. Could it have been an answer? Or do we imagine these things? You can't say? Well, all I know is, answer or not, I just couldn't add "Thy will be done," because I felt so sure that His will must be that the boy should be done with lies and speak the truth bravely. I stayed on my knees—oh, ten minutes, I reckon—before I managed to say it. But I said it— and then—then I seemed to know at once that I no longer wanted Mike to wriggle and lie. I wanted him to be good.

Dick gazed at the wild grasses before him. 'And is that what you want me to tell him?'

'Oh, God in heaven, no! Never tell him I said that. Never say his old dad wanted him to do that. Whatever he does he must do on his own. But you're a better man than I am, Dick, and you understand these things. Could you perhaps guide him gently towards what you think it right for him to do? . . . Or am I shifting my burden on to you?'

'I am here to help you, Harry. Always. You know that.'

'You see, Dick, it seems to me that, no matter what lies he puts up, they won't save him, so . . . I think I'd rather he was good and brave at the last. We could still hope for a reprieve; but if not—well, I'd like always to be able to tell his mother that at the last—Oh God, what am I saying?' He bowed his head in his hands.

Dick laid a palm upon his knee. 'Let me try to handle this for you, Harry . . . if I can. And if you'll trust me.'

Not free of tears, Harry said, lifting his face, 'I trust you as I trust no one else on earth.'

§

Fingers playing with thumbs, head bent in thought, white eyebrows knitting and unknitting, Dick stood waiting by the window of the bare prison room. Steps on the stone floor outside—steps of two persons coming this way—Michael and an officer? An officer bringing the 'body' which the prison had received into its care?

Yes, here was Michael being ushered into the room and directed to his place at the table by a tall prison officer. Like the detective sergeant at Bow Street, this prison officer was little older than his charge. Each was in his early prime, but the officer had a fine carriage within his neat blue uniform, and his skin was clear, and ruddy, his eyes keen and contented; while Michael's blue civilian clothes were crumpled, his eyes unsteady and wandering, and his posture slackened by lack of hope. Nevertheless Michael managed to smile at his visitor. 'Hallo, Uncle Dick,' he said.

'Hallo, Michael. Good evening, officer.'

'Good evening, sir.' The officer closed the door, and they were alone in the bleak, uncharitable room.

It was a large room, and as suspicious as it was unkind. The top half of the door in the corner was thick glass, and the officer sat or stood or mooched behind the glass, watching to see that nothing contraband passed between them, but hearing nothing that they said. The table was very long, and the prisoner must sit at one end and the lawyer at the other, with a foot high glass screen half-way between them, so that nothing could shoot from one to the other except their words. A blank and forbidding piece of joinery, this long table.

Michael did not speak, but sat with hands joined on its heartless wood, and his eyes waiting, a little sullenly, for Dick to speak. It was plain that he was still bitter at being asked to die.

Dick cast a look at the glass in the door and hoped it was really thick enough to halt all words this side of it. No sense perhaps in talking too loud. 'Michael,' he said, 'I want you to tell me exactly all you are thinking and feeling—I'd like you to talk just as if it were, say, your friend Dermot sitting here. I promise you I won't let any knowledge of mine stand in the way of your defence. Whatever defence you choose to adopt I'll put it before your counsel, and he'll do the best he can with it. But just now I want only the truth in your heart.'

Michael also shot his eyes at the officer behind the glass, and he too decided to trust its thickness. Deliberately fixing his eyes on Dick's because he wanted him to see a hard defiance in them, he said, 'I know I'm technically guilty, Uncle Dick, but the more I think of it, the more I feel that, since the Law chooses to be utterly brutal in this business, I am ready to fight it with lies.'

'Only technically guilty?' asked Dick, but with a gentle smile. 'Is there no more to it than that?'

'What more?' Michael repeated a favourite phrase, being proud of it. 'What the hell is treason but an active disagreement with the majority of your countrymen?'

'Don't you think it is more?'

'No. I can't see it.'

'Oh yes, Michael, you can. In the depths of your heart you can. Think, think. Is that human instinct wholly wrong which says that there's some piety due to the country that bred one?'

Michael, looking at Dick without answer, seemed to be searching behind his troubled eyes for the answer.

'Michael: don't you feel a natural bond to mother, father and sister?'

274

'To my mother, yes—yes, certainly—and to Beth. But not in those days, to Father. I hated all he stood for.'

'And yet he felt it. He hated all you did, and he offered me all he'd got in the world to save you.'

There was no doubt that this pierced the boy's armour. He looked down upon his fiddling fingers, and then said, 'But I was trying to believe in the brotherhood of all men everywhere. I didn't see—and I don't see—why all kinship should be cut off by the English Channel. Or the Rhine.'

Dick began a movement of impatience, but arrested it. 'Talk hard sense, Michael, do. Say you had only a little money to spare, and your mother and sister were in grave trouble, wouldn't you spend it all on them rather than on a man across the Balham High Road?'

Michael withheld all answer, eyes down.

But Dick, knowing the unspoken answer was Yes, went on. 'Very well, Michael: and if there are these charities of the home and hearth, are there none of the homeland too?'

'But—Uncle—if, rightly or wrongly one wanted to change one's country, as I did——'

'And the answer to that is: you can resign from membership of your country, but you cannot resign from your debts to it.'

'Debts?'

'Yes. You have received from its long past more than you can ever give back to it. Eight parts, nine parts, of what is good in you has come from your country.'

Michael frowned over this in surprise and doubt and, hardly aware of the action, shook his head.

Again Dick had to overthrow a small impatience. 'But it is *so*. Whatever ideals you have, whatever feeling for honour or courage or kindness, must have come to you from her, or through her. She's like a temple that's been building for more than a thousand years, so that you and I can get grace from her. We don't feel the grace coming into us, but it's there.'

Michael smiled in cynical disbelief and now shook his head deliberately. 'That may be fairly true for someone bred in the beauty of the countryside, but have you forgotten, Uncle Dick, that I was brought up in the Balham High Road? Was there anything beautiful or good about that? Anything to love, and learn good from, in Clapham Common and Tooting Broadway? Take a look at them again, Uncle.'

'Yes, the guilt isn't all yours: I've often said so to your father.

Some of it must rest with those who created Clapham and Balham and all those horrible little roads that go on interlocking for ever, without cohering into anything. Yes, yes . . .' but just then Dick became conscious of the officer seated behind the thick glass panel, and turned abruptly to look at him. Framed as in a picture by the panel, the young man's head had drooped sideways and downwards, and only his three-quarter profile was turned towards the room. His eyes were on the room's floor, or on nothing—on vacancy. It was the picture of a young man dreaming. Trusting Dick fully, and tranced by the silence and solitude behind the glass, he was dreaming instead of watching—dreaming perhaps of love or marriage or future fame. 'Yes, I agree with you there. It must be easier for a countryman to feel what I mean. He has some sort of blind sense that his fields have a sacredness because other generations have loved them and worked them and wanted to lie near them at the end, in a churchyard a thousand years old. It must be easier to fight for the Sussex Weald than for Clapham High Street or the Balham High Road. But, Michael, you have sometimes enjoyed England at its best. I remember you used to come home from some great house in the country where you'd been entertained with your Leader, and you would rave about the village or the downs or the dales. What about the love you felt then? You are capable of fine perceptions. Didn't your country show you a vision then?'

'What sort of vision?' asked Michael, more quietly, because mollified by this flattery.

'A vision of something very dear. Even holy. Many a great man has spoken of seeing it.'

'Holy?'

'Yes.' But Michael's surprise had stressed the boldness of the word, and Dick sought to justify it. 'It's a word they sometimes use.'

Michael, who'd always wanted to be among the great men, pondered this silently. And at last he joined them so far as to say, 'When I flew away from England in 1939, I was excited at what I was doing, but as I looked down from the aeroplane and saw the wooded slopes of the North Downs and the oasthouses and orchards and farmlands in the Weald, I thought she was very lovely . . . and, well . . . I was not altogether happy.'

Dick, nodding understandingly, left him to say more.

'Indeed, I thought I'd never seen anything quite so beautiful, and I turned my eyes away from it, because I wanted to be happy.'

Dick, feeling that this small portion of English ground was won, left it for different places. 'And did you think at all of the freedom she'd given you to speak your heart out?'

'Freedom!' Here Michael saw a way to defend himself and was palpably glad of it. 'Freedom, when all my friends were put in prison without trial——'

'But that was when the War had started. In peace you can stand on the heights and see wonderful visions of universal brotherhood and freedom, but war drives you down into the valleys where your views of honour and duty and freedom must be more limited.'

'Why? *Why?*'

'Because your country's existence is in danger. It's not your rights then, but hers.'

'But are you saying, then, that a man is made for the State?'

'In war, yes.'

'I wonder. . . . That's not true always.'

'Very nearly always, I think. Michael, I'd like to tell you a little experience of mine. May I? Last year I took my holiday in a village under the South Downs. It was August, and England after five years of war, was safe at last. The Allies were sweeping over Normandy; the American armoured columns were said to be ranging outside Paris; and the Russians were over the Vistula. Victory was in sight at last. And I climbed to the summit of the downs and looked down upon England. I remember that the wheat was all in stook, and the stooks threw long blue shadows on the stubble because the sun was going down. The cattle seemed to be hardly moving on their pastures, and it was all so quiet that you could hear the sheep bells in a field. You could even hear the rooks far away as they went flying towards the elms around some old manor or farmhouse. There was a wonderful light over it all and behind the ridge of your North Downs. And, as you say—as you said just now—I thought I had never seen anything more beautiful.'

Michael, eyes on his godfather, sat listening with interest absorbed.

'I remember that the sheep and cattle on the pastures looked like the very picture of the peace that might so soon come again to her. And, Michael, it may have been stupid, but I remember a kind of breathless exultation—an exultation hardly bearable —to think that she was safe.'

'I don't feel it was stupid, Uncle. Why should I? I love her too.'

'Well, I sat there thinking and thinking, and wondering, like you, if this was an emotion one must grow out of. I kept asking myself: Was it a terrible thing to say that I couldn't wholly regret that in our old war, your father's and mine, my son had died for her. And I decided that I wasn't wholly wrong. I seemed to see, first, that the very fact that for hundreds of years fellows had been ready to die for her had done something to all these places for ever. Something . . . but I could hardly say what. And then I remembered how Halifax the Trimmer, in a passage I've always loved, had said—two hundred years ago, I suppose—that for him there was now a divinity in the earth of England, and he would rather die than see a spire of English grass trampled down by a foreign trespasser. And I felt that his words were somehow true. How, I don't quite know. And then, over and above all that, I seemed to see that, until the countries of the world were much closer knit together there were many things in my country that I must and would preserve against any enemy. Can you understand this?'

'Indeed I can, Uncle. And I often think I'm rather like one of those people who've lost their belief in Christianity and yet would love to have the old simple faith again.'

'But, Michael, do you really think that the new and different faith to which you gave all your loyalty and service was something larger and better than these old pieties?'

'I did at first.'

'And now?'

'No; not now. There was much that was good in it at first but as old Dermot used to say, it went bad on us.'

'Then would I be right in saying that for quite a while you chose to be blind to the badness rather than admit you'd been wrong?'

'Yes. Yes, I suppose so. And, worse than that. When I ceased to be blind and saw all, I went on . . . because there seemed nothing else to do.'

'Yes—ah yes—but I can understand that. You were caught.'

'Caught . . . yes.' Michael beat his finger-tips helplessly upon the table. 'Uncle, I know you say you'll put up any defence I give you, even though you know it to be lies—but I just don't want you to do anything you know to be wrong. What . . . what hope is there for me if I plead guilty?'

Dick stiffened his will to speak the truth. 'Very little. No hope but a reprieve.'

'And if I go on with the lies?'

'Little more. But I can't help wondering whether, if the jury accepted your tale of having applied for naturalisation, there mightn't be a recommendation to mercy.'

Dick saw the hope bestir itself in Michael's eyes, and then slowly retreat. 'I'm glad you told me that,' he said, 'because if I decide to abandon the lies I'd rather do it because it's right than because it'll make no difference whether I lie or not.'

Dick did not show his pleasure in this statement because he did not wish, in a matter that was mortal for a young man, the pressure of his influence to be, by a single grain, too strong. He stayed silent, with his eyes on the bare and heartless table.

And Michael said, after thought, and with *his* eyes gazing, as it were, right through the harsh cream walls of the room, 'Uncle, let me ask you this: what would you really like me to do?'

What could he say? How much was right and fair to say? It was the boy's life that was in issue. After staring at the finger nails of one hand, and stroking them one after another with his thumb he said, 'Last evening I was sitting with your father in an old ruined garden by the Common, and we got to talking about Right and Wrong and God, as men do, whether they are young men at a university or—' here he smiled into Michael's eyes—'a couple of old men on a common. And all I could find to say was that I believed that deep down in every man, even the weakest, there was a little struggling seed which was pure and good because it was a piece of the divine, and that if a man, in his anguish or despair, threw himself on that tiny seed, withholding nothing, it would give him always a glimpse of the truth.'

§

Michael, still awake, hopelessly awake after hours of trying to sleep, opened his eyes and saw the long prison ward. While his eyes were shut he had been seeing the places he had known when he was free and happy: Balham High Road, the Lord of Wensley, Tooting Graveney Common, and the Oval with the great men at play on their vast green lawn, between the tenement buildings, and the monster gasholders. Or places where, in close black garments from neck to heel, he had marched with a thousand others—marched to this end. Alone of all that singing, tramping, drum-led company, he had marched to this locked place where he lay with eyes tight shut. Those marches reminded him of the great meetings when the cheers of a massed multitude would escort his Leader, and himself behind him, all the way up the gangway to the platform. Exultant cheers; almost triumphant cheers. Triumph had seemed at no great distance then.

'And we might have won, perhaps—who knows?—if led by decent men. Why did the Leaders abroad turn everything to rottenness and discredit us all?'

And if they had won . . .? But instead, eyes opened, he saw this long ward in the prison hospital. Surely hours had passed since the lights went out and he had begun his angling for sleep. It must be midnight and more; but he could see the ward well enough because a moon was shining through the barred windows and a lamp was burning by the night officer's chair. He could see the beds against the walls, and the pool of lamplight on the shining surface of the officer's table, and the splashes of moonlight on the cold, burnished floor. And he thought, with some self-pity, but perhaps more with an academic interest, that if the years of his life had begun twenty years sooner they would not have marched him into a decade of violent history which had trapped him like this—like a chicken in a crate where he waited to die.

Was he the only one awake? Apparently so; dismally so. Old Nobby Bowen, the greyhead who was 'inside' for the first time on charges of rape and incest had tossed on his bed and cried out, 'Emmy! Emmy!' to his distant wife and 'Di! Di!' to the daughter he had violated, and been cursed for his noise. 'Oh, shut up, mate!' they had muttered. 'Crown him, someone.' 'Turn it off, for gawd's sake!' 'Why doesn't the old screw hit him on the head and put him out?' But even he was quiet now, lying on his back with mouth open, and stertorously breathing. Bill Withy, Michael's young neighbour in the next bed, remanded only on a small charge of larceny but nevertheless under medical observation, lay sleeping happily.

Midnight certainly. The silence in the prison yard beneath those barred windows was the dead stillness of a small hour.

If he glanced through a window into the moonlit night he saw the high grey punishing walls of another cell-block with its row above row of squat barred windows, all darkened now but caging securely the trapped men within.

He dropped his lids again to shut out all such sights. Little hope of sleep because his brain was alight with a question— far more brightly alight than lamp-lit ward or moonlit yard.

'I know what Uncle Dick was trying to do. I could see into his heart clearly enough. And perhaps, as a godfather, it was his job to do it. He wanted to make me get down to what he calls my "best self", and see what happened then. But if I do that, there's only one possible answer: I refuse to lie. One could give up the lies either because one was without hope anyway or because it was the only right thing to do; and only if one did it for this second reason would there be any good in it. That was why it was a good thing that he told me there might be a glimmer of hope if I went on lying. Because now, if I scorn to lie, there'll be something of good in it.'

'If one's got to die, better to die clean.' Coming from Heaven knew where, this sentence phrased itself in his head. But by uttering it was he not calling upon the hopelessness to help him? Almost he could wish that the hope behind the lies was greater than it was, for then his rejection of it would be a better thing.

The Old Bailey in about four weeks time: this would be his last appearance before the world. And Michael who'd always had a feeling for the right pose before an audience began to see a faintly pleasing picture of himself standing erect in the dock, while every eye was on him, and surprising a whole nation by answering his arraignment with a single word, spoken with calm dignity: 'Guilty.'

That there was guilt in what he had done he questioned no more. He had admitted it to Uncle Dick. Perhaps from the beginning there had been more wrong in it than good, because it was so largely made up of vanity and rebellion. 'I can't think there was *evil* in it then, unless it's a mild form of evil to be both a fool and a mule in one's determination to rebel. But it got more and more wrong as it went on because, as I admitted to Uncle Dick, I carried on deliberately after I knew it was wrong. There *should* be a larger loyalty than patriotism, but this was not it; this was a forced and unreal thing. Yes, I admit there was much wrong in it, but I still can't think I'm as wicked as they say. There's no recognition anywhere of what little was good in it, but perhaps one must be content to see that for oneself, alone.'

He lay there with his eyes shut. The grey prison which enclosed him was more than a hundred years old, and it was possible that in all those years the moonlight had never looked through its bars on an inmate more alone, because this man was despised even by the prisoners themselves. All the prisoners in the ward had greeted his entry with hisses and muted boos and mutterings of 'Filthy traitor.' And the whole prison, when it heard that Michael Townes was come among them, had raged against the insult through cell doors and from cell windows. Men charged with crimes of savage cruelty or animal beastliness, with rape and blackmail and grievous bodily harm, had looked down from cell windows as he marched round the exercise yard and cried, 'Gah! Traitor! Swine!' contriving, some of them, to spit into the yard.

This atmosphere of scorifying contempt had cooled a little with the passing of time, and some of the more decent fellows in the ward now spoke with him amicably, but there were still the righteous and unforgiving who rejoiced to hurt him with their scorn.

He was being tenderly nursed in this ward—and why? Because, while his soul might be worthy of all this contempt, his body was not. Not this body in the bed. From the moment they had picked this up from under the trees they had watched over it like a precious thing. It was a body that had to be cared for like a king's. Like a king's for its coronation on a trap-door. . . .

'If I've got to die, I may as well die clean.'

For a few moments he knew some peace in his acceptance of guilt. And for a few moments he felt some pleasure and pride in his picture of a last act which should display before the world both courage and dignity. There was pride in the thought that by a plea of 'Guilty', he would be refusing to let Uncle Dick sacrifice his conscience, and, whether the world named it courage or not, he would be able to hold his head high and have his own praise, if no one else's. 'If it seems good to me to do this, what matter what anyone else thinks? I'll be loyal to myself and to what I see.' So in these moments spoke the old vanity and rebellion, but in better fashion than of old.

But then, hard behind such thoughts, came realisation.

Sickening realisation of what must follow that lonely utterance, 'Guilty.' To seek no mercy! To accept death without a single struggle! Death in a few weeks. The hangman—asleep somewhere now in his home—what would he be like when he came in?—one would know in a matter of days. A matter of days, and then the ghastly torment of pinioned arms, the floor, the rope, and—whatever agony happened when the floor plunged and the rope tautened. His heart as he lay in bed stopped, then quickened in terror, and stopped and quivered and quickened again. Sweat burst from him under the clothes. Brow, neck, and shoulders were wet with it. 'Oh, no, no, no, no! Not that. Oh, please, not that. Let me say something that may save me from that. Any wriggle or twist but that. Surely one may fight for one's life with a lie? I don't want that agony, I can't take it.' He tossed over in his bed. So terrible seemed that death beneath the trap that he must hold—wildly—to the hope which lay behind the lies, and trust it, believe in it. He tossed over again, struggling for hope. Terror had got him in its many arms like a devil-fish in the sea; it was crushing and sucking all strength from him; and he cried through his silence to Heaven as a sinking man might cry through the waters above him. 'Jesus, Jesus, Jesus. Help me.' He cried it yet more passionately, 'Jesus, Jesus, in thy mercy . . . God, my father . . . my father in Heaven. . . .'

CHAPTER FOUR

HARRY, Ida and Beth were approaching Old Bailey and the Central Criminal Court. They came by Cannon Street, through the far-flung areas of green and coloured wilderness that the bombs had created around St. Paul's. Walking past the low walls of brick or board that fenced these acres of wind-sown herbage, they looked down on to tall grasses that grew, somehow or other, from flagged cellar floors, and on to ferns and flowers that sprang from cellar walls. Most of the rubble had long been cleared away from this area of devastation, and only the belfries and steeples rose from the waste, some of them with their gutted and windowless churches beside them like diagrams of disaster. St. Paul's stood among these dead churches like their unconquerable queen, and she and all her martyred subjects seemed to point to the sky and ask for justice.

'What chance for a boy who has to be tried in the midst of the devastation wrought by his friends?' thought Harry. 'What hope of gentle judgment or mercy? None.'

The very ground was crying for his life as its forfeit. It was saying it with flowers.

Strange to look at the top of London's hill and see it as open ground, green with grass and flowers for the first time since the City was built—how many hundreds of years ago? For a brief spell the fertile soil under London had come into its own, and was perhaps all the richer for having lain fallow during the centuries when men preferred to raise money on it rather than flowers. Everywhere among the high grasses the rosebay fireweed lifted its mauve-crimson plumes, loving the place where a second Great Fire had raged on a December night five years ago—that night of incendiary bombs when London had lit a candle before the world to show that it was a City of the Spirit, which would go down in ashes rather than yield.

Some such thoughts were Harry's as he walked towards the arraignment of his son as a traitor. 'The King against Townes.' He looked at the happy hawk-moths that flitted above these carmine sprays.   And he considered the ragwort and the clover, the larkspur and the toadflax, which, along with the rosebay, were all pressing up against the pavements like new and eager friends.

'Where on earth did they all come from?' asked Ida, to hide where her real thoughts lay.   'How ever did they get here?'

'Airborne,' said Harry.   'Like bombs;' and he laughed sardonically.

Ida was dressed in her best; dressed like a *grande dame* in a black suit and white blouse, with a double rope of pearls about her broad throat and a diamanté ornament glistening on one lapel.   As usual, she had given pains to this composition this morning.   The ruling passion was strong in death, and just as the dandies liked to go to the guillotine 'dressed as gentlemen', so she too chose to appear before the people and accept the death of her heart, dressed as a lady.

Harry and Beth had tried to persuade her not to come, but she had snapped at them impatiently, petulantly, even at last with a massive anger, 'Of course, I'm coming   It's a mother's place to be at his side.   I wouldn't be away from him for all the world.'

'But it may be terrible for you, Mother,' Harry had argued.

'I can't help that.'

'And you know how you say that you hate men's courts and things and don't begin to understand them.'

'Can't help that, I tell you!   I know what my place is. How can you ask me not to go?   He must see me there, and I just know that whenever I catch his eye I can make him feel that I love him as I always did and that I'm with him in all things.   That I'll be with him just as long as they'll let—' but these words caused the tightly held tears to twist and convulse her lips as she 'let herself go' a little way towards despair. 'I'll be with him to the end.   To the very end.'

'Okay then, Mother,' he had sighed.

Harry was in his best suit too, a blue serge suit, but since he very seldom wore it because he was usually behind his bars on a Sunday, it belonged to a fashion of twenty-five years before. His bowler hat, however, was of a younger generation, its shape in tune with these present days, and its sheen so fresh that it recorded modestly the brightness of the sky.

Beth, in a flowered summer frock, was a dumpy spot of colour between them.

They came down a path which was once the busy, book-selling

Paternoster Row and now but a causeway across the flowering wilderness. There ahead of them was the cupola of the Criminal Court with the figure of Justice mounted upon it, her scales hanging level from one hand, but her sword, in the other, pointing like the steeples towards the sky.

In Newgate Street a queue of hundreds waited by the grey wall of the Court. Another crowd stood across the road, pressed against the railings of St. Sepulchre's Church. In the street known as Old Bailey the police were shepherding the people back against the taverns and offices that fronted the main entrance of the Court. Other spectators could be seen in the windows and on the flat railed roofs of these buildings. All were gaping at this heavy grey successor of Newgate Gaol, one corner of which had been gouged away by a bomb, so that the place where the day's prisoner must be tried offered its own witness against him. 'Oh, when will you pay me, Say the bells of Old Bailey.'

Harry braced back his shoulders to pass before the people, and Ida did something of the same kind. And they passed before them, unrecognised, but clothed in the dignity of their solitude. Even Beth's dumpy figure bore the dignity of those who walk without hope.

§

They were able to enter past the policeman at the doors because the name 'Townes' cleared a path for them and commanded help and kindness. Guided by a policeman's hand they walked down an arcaded avenue of green marble columns. The floor beneath them was of black and white marble. The whole place seemed a palace for those who remained on the right side of the Law, while the others, the offenders held below, must sit among lavatory tiles. They climbed a fine staircase to another marble corridor and found themselves opposite the words 'Court No. 1.' on a door. Near this door were groups of chattering people: solicitors in dark suits with leather portfolios talking to barristers whose black gowns and dust-grey wigs made them look like ravens with heads gone grey.

One of the chattering lawyers was Dick—so far as Dick could ever be said to chatter—and he saw them. 'Ah, Harry! Come and meet Mr. Alleyne. Bruce, here are Captain and Mrs. Townes, and Beth. Michael's mother.'

He was presenting them to the K.C. who had succeeded Wade-Collins as Michael's counsel: a full-cheeked and full-bellied little man with, surprisingly, a crisp little moustache, grey and soldierly. If Mr. Bruce Alleyne, in wig, gown, and bands, looked like a grey-headed raven, it was a very plump one, with a white breast.

'Good morning, Mrs. Townes,' he said—since what else could he say? 'Good morning, sir.'

'Pleased to meet you, I'm sure,' said Harry—since what else could *he* say?—and he shook Mr. Alleyne's hand somewhat over-heartily, because nervously.

'And "Beth"—was that the name? Good morning, my dear. How are you?'

'Very well, thank you,' said Beth.

'I've been looking forward to meeting you all, but of course it was rather late in the day that Dick instructed me in this case. Have you ever been to the Bailey before? No. Well, I've secured seats for you. Yes, I've kept them for you.'

'It's very kind of you, I'm sure,' said Ida.

'Sure you wouldn't rather stay outside, Mother, and just let Beth and me go in?' asked Harry. 'Or Beth'd stop with you.'

'No, no; I must go in,' said Ida, though her mouth was trembling. 'He must see me there.'

'Very good, Mrs. Townes. Come along, all of you.' Mr. Alleyne beckoned them to follow him. 'You'll be in the City Lands.'

'In the what?' asked Harry, rather because he wanted to speak and sound self-controlled than because he cared for the answer.

'The City Lands. They're seats belonging to the Aldermen and Sheriffs of the City, and they keep them for their friends, but I've got three for you there.'

'It's very kind of you, I'm sure,' said Ida.

'Yes, the Bailey's an interesting old place, Mrs. Townes. It stands just where the old Roman wall used to sweep round the north of the city. When they were rebuilding it on the site of old Newgate Prison they found a part of this wall, and there it still is, quietly underneath us. This way, please.'

His talk, as smooth as his gown, was designed, no doubt, to cover their shames and give them some ease. One felt that, as a fashionable barrister, he was priding himself on his tact and diplomacy. All this was stuff, no doubt, that he'd said many times before.

Like an amiable spaniel out for a walk with the household, he looked round to see that all were following. They were. 'I feel pretty confident that there's been a court on this spot ever since the Norman Conquest, and I like to think that Shakespeare came to it more than once and sat watching a trial. Along here, Captain Townes. There's a line in one of his plays which seems to prove that he used to see the prisoners stretching their skinny hands through the bars of their cells and begging food from the passers-by.'

'Is that so?' said Harry, since he must answer.

'Yes, it was a common sight in those days. You may be surprised but the present cells down below us are a part of Brixton Prison. A pretty long shot, that!'

'It is.'

'Three miles over the river. But there it is. Some of the most famous prisoners in history have stood their trial here: Lord Russell and William Penn, the founder of Pennsylvania, and——' but here he stopped abruptly, lest his diplomacy were failing him.

He led them along a side passage to a side door, guarded by an old gowned usher.

'This is Captain Townes and Mrs. Townes,' he said to the white-haired old man. 'I'm putting them in the City Lands. If there's an adjournment, see that they get their places again.'

'Yes, sir. Certainly, sir.'

The usher opened the door; Mr. Alleyne waved them through it; and they saw the court room before them: a large box of wooden pens on different levels, much as in the police court, though everything here was on a handsomer scale. Today the place had the melancholy atmosphere of a room lit by artificial light at ten in the morning. And this lighting seemed insufficient because the glass roof above the room had long ago been shattered by bomb-blast and its base boarded in, so that the handsome panelled chamber had now only a wooden lid.

The room carried its witness against today's prisoner.

On their left, as they entered, were three tiers of seats filled with people except for some places in the front row.

'Along there,' said Mr. Alleyne, indicating these front places, and smiling his farewell.

Obediently Ida shuffled past the knees of others, but was stopped in her sidling by a young woman's face. It was a face familiar to all the world—the face of a most famous film actress, who chanced to be in London now. And at her side was a

288

man's face hardly less familiar, for it was that of an old and popular British comedian.

Ida, quite shaken by having brushed against greatness, and ashamed of her rude stare, shuffled quickly on to her seat and sank into it. Harry sat himself between her and Beth.

'Did you see who that was?' whispered Ida.

'Who who was?'

'That lady we passed.'

'What do I care who she was?'

But Ida whispered the name, and then he turned to see, and so, momentarily excited, did Beth.

Except for three enclosed areas the big room was busy with people. The three areas were the Judge's dais, the jury's long pen, and the prisoner's glass-screened dock, which was spacious enough to be considered a room within a room. In the well between dock and dais solicitors, clerks, and detectives stood about the solicitor's table; junior counsel were already seated in the counsel's benches, and the Clerk of Arraigns standing by his upraised desk.

Soon there was no more room for spectators anywhere except in the gangways by the dock. Even some of the watching barristers had to be content to stand here, for their brothers had now filled the counsel's benches with four tiers of wigs—wigs grey and old, and wigs very white and new and junior. No case in any other of the Bailey's courts today could compete with this one.

Sitting silently among all these people, Harry, Ida, and Beth heard the woven orchestra of talk, coughs, footsteps, fidgetings, and the rustling of documents. A highly cultured voice behind Harry, 'an Oxford and Cambridge voice,' as he would have called it, murmured, 'We're watching something that may never happen again.'

'Please . . . what do you mean?' requested the rather arch voice of a woman.

'The war's over, my dear—that nightmare's over—and this handsome ceremonial, unless I'm quite mistaken, is the sort of thing that History will soon have done with.'

'I'm sure I'm very silly, but I still don't know what you're talking about.'

'A trial like this, beloved, is one of the last kicks of a divided and dying world. We shall "cast the kingdoms old into a new mould".'

Well I suppose that means something, but it's beyond me.'

Harry, no more than the lady, fully grasped what it meant, but he felt grateful to the man, because he sounded as if his condemnation was tempered by pity.

The spectators in the tiered seats behind the dock dared only whisper; and Harry, sweeping their serried faces, saw in the back row the same half-dozen lads in belted trench-coats and black jerseys that he'd seen in the public area at Bow Street. There in the middle of them was the prize-fighting type with the flattened nose, sorrow-filled eyes, and falling mouth. These same few loyal disciples had come to see the end. And the end of their ardent and once joyous campaign to evangelise Britain was this, that they should watch one of their apostles being passed through the gate to the lions.

§

Suddenly Harry became aware that people were looking at the clock above his head and speaking with curiosity about the delay in starting. Why this long wait? The clock said two minutes to eleven and the court had been advertised to sit at half-past ten. But there was no hint of the Judge's approach. His chair, and the chairs beside it, were empty; the jury box was empty; and the dock too—except when occasionally the jovial face and huge torso of a prison officer appeared above its floor—he having come a little way up the stairs from the cells below, to learn why in Mercy's name the old Smudge didn't come in and do his job.

Gradually this wonder and questioning swelled into bewilderment as the clock neared fifteen minutes past eleven; it became a certainty that something unusual was afoot when Dick appeared in the dock, having come up from below, and leaned over it, just as a prisoner might, to talk earnestly with little Mr. Alleyne, who'd long been in his counsel's seat. Dick's clerk, from the solicitor's table, joined in this colloquy, which the rest of the world watched. Then, very quickly, Alleyne walked into the dock by a side door and joined Dick; and he and Dick disappeared down the stairway to the cells.

'What's happening?' asked Ida. 'Has something gone wrong?'

'No, no. We know what's going to happen. Dick said it's always upsetting. The Judges don't like it. None of 'em do.'

hatty little man who had escorted them to their seats in the City Lands; he was speaking simply and quietly, and not without something like sadness in his voice. 'He instructs me, my lord, only to repeat what was said on his behalf in the court below, that though many of his acts may have been mistaken and wrong, they were not done out of hatred for his country, but rather out of a misguided loyalty.'

To this the Judge gave only a small and apparently impatient toss of his head. 'He fully understands that there can be but one sentence, and that from such sentence there can be no appeal?'

'He understands, my lord. I have explained it to him. He understands perfectly, but he is adamant in his wish to plead guilty.'

The Judge sighed. 'All right . . . very well . . . let it be recorded . . . And there's nothing more to be done. . . . Sir Arthur'—he turned to the Attorney-General—'I shall not need to trouble you.'

The Attorney-General, long, lean, and dignified, rose a little way and bowed. 'If your lordship pleases,' he said, and sat down again.

In a court shocked and hushed the Clerk said, 'Prisoner at the bar, you have pleaded guilty and on your own confession stand convicted of high treason. Have you anything to say why the court should not give you judgment of death according to law?'

In words that sounded strangely boyish Michael answered, 'No, thank you, sir.'

So the Judge's clerk in his solemn morning coat laid the black cap on the Judge's head, and the usher cried, 'Oyez, Oyez, Oyez. My lords the King's Justices do strictly charge and command all persons to keep silence while sentence of death is passed on prisoner at the bar, on pain of imprisonment.'

A charge little needed, so silent the court now. It was like a box, a tank, of sudden and absolute silence. Into that silence the Judge spoke low and slowly as if weary in his ageing body of a task he'd too often discharged. It is possible, too, that he took pride in his quietness.

'Michael Townes, I have read all the depositions from the court below and the various exhibits in this case, and I am satisfied that you knew from the beginning that the acts with which you have been charged were acts of treason. None the less

294

'Michael isn't ill, is he? It wouldn't be that?'

'Gracious, no.'

'But they seem excited about something. Oh, nothing's happened to him, has it?'

'No. What could happen?'

'He looked so pale the other day. He looked like death. Oh, why do they torture him so?'

'He's all right,' Beth comforted.

'Could there have been an accident, coming from the prison?'

'No, sweetheart.' Harry patted her hand. 'He's down there. Dick must have been with him all this time. He'd have told us if there was anything wrong.'

The universal interest and curiosity in the room enabled all to endure the passing of another fifteen minutes. They were like people who'd been given the first part of a mysterious story and were content to wait in some excitement for the solving of the mystery.

The clock ticked on; people sat back and sighed. Perhaps because the boarding-up of the glass roof impaired ventilation, or because so many people had crowded into the room, its atmosphere was now close and musty; human heat was assembling in this box, and Ida, patting back several yawns, had strange ideas of the square chamber as a wood-lined box raised in the air, with infinite space all around it, and stocked and warmed with people determining the death of a young man. These people, inadequately pitiful, had begun to talk more loudly, more carelessly, with less solemnity and more laughter—but then, of a sudden, came a sharp new silence, as Dick and Alleyne reappeared in the dock, and left it to go into a huddled talk with the Attorney-General and the Clerk of the Court. All the rest watched this conference, because in the heart of it must be the secret. A last the Clerk sent an usher through the Judge's door, and all of them, separating, went to their proper seats.

The jury box remained empty.

Three taps on the Judge's door. Three knocks such as, in serious theatres, announce the curtain's rise.

'Silence! Be upstanding,' called the usher.

All stood and turned towards the Bench. The door, opening, admitted a small chain of sheriffs and aldermen in their robes. One of the robed figures, the last to enter, everyone recognised as the Lord Mayor himself. Thus did the ravaged City honour the day when its traitor came to trial.

291

The City officers stood back to greet the Judge as he entered, an old dried man with pendent cheeks and deep-recessed eyes. Small and ordinary he would have seemed without his robe of scarlet and black and his wig of cinder-grey, but that face, pictured so often in daily paper and weekly journal, how familiar and famous it was—with its sagging under-lip, hanging cheeks, and white prickled skin like that of a poulterer's fowl. He passed to his place, carrying in his hand something black and a pair of white gloves.

'All persons,' cried the usher, 'who have anything to do before my lords the King's Justices of Oyer and Terminer and General Gaol Delivery, for the Jurisdiction of the Central Criminal Court, draw near and give your attendance. God save the King.'

After the words 'God save the King' the Judge bowed low to Lord Mayor, aldermen, and sheriffs; to Clerk and to counsel; and in reply all the four tiers of wigs, white and grey, knowing their duty as the public did not, bowed deep and simultaneously like the breaking of a single wave. This courtesy done, all sat down as to some quiet, solemn, ceremonial meal.

The Clerk rose and, after exchanging some words with the Judge, called, 'Put up Michael Townes.'

And now every eye in the room, except the Judge's and the Attorney-General's, turned towards the dock.

An officer in the dock looked down the stairway as if to pass on the cry, but footsteps sounded on the stairs, and he came away. These steps meant a much humbler procession than the Judge's: the prisoner's: just a uniformed officer, a young man in a neat blue suit, and two more officers. They came to the front of the dock. Women at the back of the court half rose in their seats to get a view of the young man.

'Oh!' This was a low gasp from Ida, for the young man was Michael. Michael—and he looked as if sick at the promise of death; the skin over his pleasant features was pale as vellum, his eyes were sunken and shadowed, and his hands, as at the police court, shook as he rested them on the dock's ledge.

Nevertheless, loving correct ceremonies ever since he used to raise his right arm in salute to his Leader, and loving chivalry because that much at least his Leader had taught him, he bowed to the Judge. Should not a man of chivalry salute his conqueror?

'Oh, he's ill,' whispered Ida. 'The boy's ill.'

'Hush,' rebuked Harry.

'But he's ill,' she insisted.

Yes, this was a young man sick with despairs, but holding himself upright and fixing his eyes on his Judge. that his hands were trembling, he put them behind h and held them together there. Possibly he was unawar he kept drawing his lower lip on to his teeth and there on it.

Harry surmised that even the old Judge, as he looked for first time with expressionless face at the prisoner, was fee some dregs of pity for him; and just as he thought this, he s the Judge's eyes swing from the dock to Ida, Beth, and himse as if he'd been told that they were sitting there. His gaze fe on them. It rested on Beth. But on the old face all though remained anonymous.

There was a pause while the Clerk assembled some sheets, and Michael took this chance to glance round for his family. He saw them in the City Lands, and gave them a smile. Reading on Ida's lips the words, 'Hello, Michael darling,' and seeing her look of abject love, he smiled again to encourage her.

'Michael Townes.' The Clerk was standing. He read the indictment. '. . . did traitorously adhere to the King's enemies in parts beyond the seas. How say you, Are you guilty or not guilty?'

One moment of silence—a universal and complete, but charged, silence—and Michael, clearing his throat to make way for his voice, spoke.

'Guilty.'

Guilty?—there came gasps from every corner of the court. Guilty—then this was what had stopped the trial's start. To plead guilty was to ask for sentence of death and to forswear any appeal; and of this the prisoner was clearly conscious because he followed the word with a nervous little smile.

'Stop—wait!' commanded the Judge to the Clerk. 'Do not record that yet.' And he looked at Mr. Alleyne, who rose, small and round and fat, from his place under the dock. 'Mr. Alleyne, I never accept a plea of guilty on a charge for which the only sentence is death, unless I am certain that the accused understands all that such a plea involves, and that his lawyers have been quite unable to persuade him to take another course.'

'Everything has been explained to him, my lord, but none of us have been able to induce him to change this plea.' This seemed a very different Mr. Alleyne from the fresh and rather

you persisted in them over a period of years, while other men of your age were fighting and dying for their country. That you claim these acts were done in a patriotic love of your country is not an excuse that will seem other than repugnant to most people. They can but remember that you took the pay of the enemy to stab your country, not once but a hundred times; and such gross, such wicked perfidy, has always been regarded by an honourable human instinct as one of the most repellent and most execrable of crimes. Our country protects and seeks to preserve our lives in peace and war, but if we attempt its death in war it decrees death for us. And always and everywhere our human instincts have endorsed that decree. A traitor is unfit to live.' At these words a very slight smile, at once self-possessed, derisory and despairing, bent the corners of Michael's mouth, but the Judge, whether or not he observed it, proceeded quietly, 'It may be that your plea of guilty suggests some repentance now, but remorse mitigates no crime. It comes too late. The grievous harm to Society has been done, and the recompense which Society assesses and demands must be paid. The sentence of the court upon you is that you be taken from this place to a lawful prison, and thence to a place of execution, and that you be there hanged by the neck till you be dead; and that your body be afterwards buried within the precincts of the prison in which you shall have been confined before your execution. And may the Lord have mercy on your soul.'

An old bearded chaplain who had suddenly appeared by the Judge's chair, said, 'Amen,' into the silence.

Michael bowed to the Judge. Whether through a sense of satisfaction at what he had managed to do, or in the peace of despair, or in a temporary dullness of mind, his attitude was easier, the effort at dignity more natural. Some colour was back in his face, and the quivering of his hands at an end. Perhaps his fears had been thrust behind him by a lonely pride.

The officers touched his elbow to guide him away, but before going below he turned to look at his family and gave them a smile. His mother smiled back at him with lips tight and unshaking, and eyes that spoke of her love.

Towards his father Michael lifted a hand in gratitude.

Then starting to go below, he faced the back of the court and saw there his six loyal disciples in their belted raincoats and black jerseys. From the midst of them the young pugilist-type with the broken nose and sad, silly eyes even raised his right hand in the beginning of a fascist salute. A few of the others attempted the like. Michael nodded to them, but spread helpless hands and smiled satirically, as if to say, 'All that's a bit out-of-date now, gentlemen, but thank you; and good-bye.'

Then he went below, disappearing for ever from their eyes and from those of the world.

Ida, conscious of many eyes upon her (for many, and not least the reporters, had guessed from the prisoner's glances and smiles who she was) pressed her lips tight indeed before all these people and moving more quickly than Harry or Beth, went *her* way out of the court room, and out of history.

CHAPTER FIVE

WHILE Michael lay in Wandsworth Gaol waiting for the end, Beth visited him almost every day. Authority, now that the payment of his debt was assured by a Court Order, was good to him and allowed him every comfort within its power. Nor, in this prison, was there any such atmosphere of vindictive hate as had beaten upon him in Brixton. Inmates and officers, knowing that he was to be 'topped', let their indignation be diluted with compassion, and instead of saying, 'Dirty traitor. Swinging's too good for him,' or 'It's hard luck on the rope, which might have gone round a decent English murderer,' said, 'Poor bleeder. But there y'are: he asked for it, if ever bloke did.'

Ida could hardly bear the silent, grey, forbidding precincts of the prison, and Harry, keeping his house open, or, as he liked to put it, 'his flag flying, come fair weather or foul,' had little leisure except on a Sunday; so it was Beth who came day by day along the streets of small suburban houses and across the worn, torn Wandsworth Common to the gatehouse of the prison, bringing the parents' love.

It was a long way through the streets and over the common, but she walked the whole two and a half miles of it because she liked to be alone with her thoughts, and with the ejaculatory prayers which, ever and again, remembering the parable of the importunate widow, she sent storming up to Heaven. They were petitions, desperate petitions, for a wisdom to say the right things to Michael.

Head down as she prayed, she would cross the tired Common whose sooty trees were now emptying of leaves, and hardly notice the children at play among the gorse and the birch clumps, because she was so near now to Michael, branded for death, and to the fear that mingled with her love. With God's help the love must extinguish the fear. God help her to show him, while all the world condemned, the quality of a sister's love. And to show the world that if he was a traitor in their eyes he was a brother in hers.

While never having heard the name in her suburban High Road Beth longed to play the part of Antigone.

The best she could do was to tell the pressmen and photographers at the prison gates, haughtily, who she was and to whom she was going.

Some acres of nursery gardens lay like a ragged green carpet before the massive gatehouse of the prison and its high, discourteous walls. In these gardens many of the plants were in good order and flourishing, but others had gone to seed, or blackened and wilted, like the citizens of the gaol that frowned down upon them. There behind gatehouse and walls was this large city of punishment, outspread upon its levels, its long halls with their squat barred windows radiating from a central lantern like the heart of a star; and its old London bricks, once a clay-yellow, now darkened to deep grey by a hundred years of London's smoke. Sometimes on misty autumn afternoons a red, angry sunset hung above and about the prison, and on one such afternoon Beth thought of it as matching the early and angry close of Michael's day. At other times a wash of light from the lowering sun gave back, for a little, their old clay-yellow to the radiating halls and flooded with something like an enchantment this vengeful city of the plain.

An avenue of fine old lindens led between the nursery gardens to the gatehouse and Beth, her heart now quaking and fluctuating, walked steadily towards it through wafted smells of peaty soil and stable manure. The towers of the gatehouse tapered as in an Egyptian pylon. It could have been the gateway to a temple of the Egyptian Osiris instead of to a palace of the English Nemesis. There was no bell anywhere; only a knocker on the little wicket that pierced the huge iron-studded doors. Nervously Beth would knock on this a genteel, middle-class ratta-tat-tat.

§

Once a strange man was loitering by the gates, and she had little doubt who he was because she had seen him talking gaily, laughingly, to a fellow-dawdler with a press camera.

'Excuse me, miss.' He had hurried towards her. 'Would you care to tell us your name, and who you are visiting?'

'Certainly I will. My name is Elspeth Townes—Elspeth Cawdor Townes. And I am visiting Michael Townes, who is my brother.'

'Oh yes?'

'I visit him daily. I asked the Governor if I might and he most kindly——'

'I understand. I quite understand. And your brother is . . . quite well?'

'Yes. He is well.'

'I mean he . . . he bears up bravely?'

'Naturally. My brother has never been anything but brave.'

The man heard this in a silence that might be sceptical and, angered by this, Beth said, 'Is that all you wish to know?' Her hand went towards the knocker on the wicket. 'May I go now? I want to be with my brother.'

'There is a petition for a reprieve, I think. Does that go well?'

'Splendidly.' A lie, but not to be forgone or regretted if it helped save a brother. 'Thousands are signing it. Thousands and thousands.'

'Thank you, miss. I'm much obliged, I'm sure.'

But she could not immediately escape because the young press-photographer, in his dirty fawn raincoat, had hurried to his friend's side and, hearing her name, had raised his slung camera to its action-station.

'Half a mo', lady. Pardon,' he said. 'But would you mind very much if I made a little picture—just a little one—it won't take half a——'

'I shouldn't mind at all.

'Oh, thank you. Thank you, miss. Ta, immensely. So many people refuse to meet us half-way. And it can't do any harm. Might even do good; you never know. Now if you could—say—just put your hand on that knocker, so as to make it an action picture—natural, like.'

Beth laid her finger on the knocker.

'That's right! That's it exactly! Superb!' cried the enthusiast. 'And if you'd keep your face to the camera like you are, but look above it—over my shoulder—perfect! Perfect! Never a better subject.'

She obeyed his every direction, not displeased that this picture should show the world how she stood at her brother's side. So might Antigone, King Oedipus' daughter, have posed for her picture, haughtily, by the tomb of her brother, Polyneices the traitor. Nor was she without hope that the picture might excite sympathy and so help the petition for repreive.

The camera clicked; the picture was taken; and the photographer said again, 'Ta so much, miss.'

With a slight bow that might have been ironic, Beth turned from him and rattled her little V-signal knock on the prison door.

§

Admitted by the gatekeeper, she would be guided by a principal officer, who was always friendly and kind, across a prison yard to one of the long grey wings. Entering this place by a side door, he led her along its cathedral-like hall, between the railed balconies that rose one above another, to a cell—a cell which differed from others only in having a little guichet-window in the thick brick wall that separated it from the next cell. This window was of thick glass with a ribbon of open grating all round it, through which what words you willed— love, reproach, or pity—could pass, but nothing else. Always as she sat on the hard chair before that window, and laid her handbag on the little shelf beneath it, she saw Michael before her, sitting on a bench fixed to the floor of the other cell. Behind him, against the far wall, withdrawn in their courtesy as far as the cell's narrow compass would allow, sat the two warders who must never loose him from their care. Her own officer, who'd come in with her, diverged in a like courtesy to a far corner and sat there on a chair, looking at his finger nails, brushing specks off his blue uniform, or fiddling with the chain at his breast.

Of this company of five only two spoke, the young woman in her hat and walking-out dress, and the young man in his coarse prison-grey, who would never walk out again. And, strange, but it was Beth, the remote, the self-enclosed, the secret Beth, hitherto so shy of him and ashamed of her love—it was she who spoke fluently, naturally and even cheerfully—either because her prayers on the frayed common had been answered and power had descended upon her or because she didn't dare halt or falter lest Michael's brief hour of contact with his family should be spoiled for him.

And so Captain Townes's two children talked through that window, of the past, of their home, of people they knew, of father and mother, and, once, of God. And Beth, so fluently talking, sometimes regarded that thick glass window as the very symbol of something that had always stood between them, blocking her love, blocking her ache to kiss him; but now, though it would never dissolve, and suffer her to take and hug him as she longed to do, it did seem to be letting her get nearer to him than ever before.

She was helped in this because Michael seemed to have put on with his grey prison clothes a new calm—a calm which came, no doubt, partly from his despair and partly from the strength which suffering had wrought for him. He would tell her of his life in the condemned cell, and generally he spoke comfortingly enough, praising the kindness of all; but once he tried to enact before her a fine stoicism by describing 'the C.C.' with a dry laugh as a mortuary on the wrong side of death. 'It's rather funny,' he said, 'to be put in the mortuary before you're dead'; and saw that he had stabbed her to the heart.

Not too often, however, did he thus seek admiration for himself at the cost of pain to her. Usually he tried to ease her position by talking as naturally as possible himself, and by asking questions of her so that she should be rescued from the danger of silence. Speaking of Dermot once, he asked her if she really believed he would 'see the old sinner again in . . . well, in a few days now.'

'Of course we shall all meet our friends again,' she stuttered. 'I haven't a doubt of it.'

'Poor old Dermot,' sighed Michael, musing behind the glass and the grating. 'I shall always think——' but here he stopped as he remembered that 'always' could mean only a short time now—'I do truly think, Beth, that he was a pretty brilliant chap and ought to have gone a long way in the world.'

'I'm sure he was,' soothed Beth.

'Yes . . . yes . . . but it was his destiny to be caught up in one of History's most febrile periods and somehow destroyed in it. . . . Yes, I should say he had exceptional abilities, but somehow they all went to pot in one of Time's paroxysms.'

These were phrases of Dermot's, used without acknowledgment by Michael in the hope, of course, that his sister would apply them to himself both now as he uttered them and after he had passed, in a few days, for ever from her sight.

At times he spoke calmly and ironically of the dreams and hopes which had been his, less than ten years since.

'Ha, Beth dear,' he scoffed one day, his vellum-pale face framed in the square of grating, 'it makes me laugh now, but

I used to kid myself that I was going to do some good in the world and incidentally—and this, I'm afraid, was the more important—*be* something big in the world. You wouldn't believe what I imagined—perhaps girls don't have the same ambitions—but I who had no influence or any real education had a notion I was going to be Chancellor of the Exchequer or Minister of Propaganda or something. Heavens above, I got that wrong! I must have been the world's prize simpleton.'

'Oh, I don't know. I expect heaps of boys have dreams like that in their twenties,' she suggested; and for a second both fell into silence because each had a sudden vision of the pit in which these boyish dreams would come to their end.

Such words led easily enough to a discussion of Beth's belief in God, and Beth poured through that grating round the glass affirmations of her faith which, to her distress and deep worry, were not wholly sincere. Up till these awful weeks, when death was but eighteen, sixteen, twelve days away from Michael, her religion and church-going had been mainly an escape from the disappointments of the world, a somewhat facile escape, remote from any testing; but now she had to speak, as at a death-bed, about eternity, and immortality and reunion hereafter. And she knew that she had no real certainty about these things. Too often she was inclined to believe desperately that death ended all, and that all religion was a cheat. But she could not, would not, admit this to Michael on the eve of his death, and she lied steadily, firmly, while her conscience shook, because here, right up to the end, she was being the secret and deceitful sister.

'And you do really believe that we shall all meet again?' Michael repeated.

'Of course I do. Certainly I do.' And she quoted, glibly, the words of her clergyman to whom she had gone for help and advice as to what to say to a brother condemned to die. 'Death is nothing but a change from one order of being to another. It can't be anything else because, if our life comes from God—and you must believe at least that much—it's indestructible.'

'I don't quite see why. It seems to me that the same argument would apply to dogs and cabbages.'

Here, in a twinkling, he had got her on to a wilderness, or a vegetable garden, for which her clergyman had provided no guide book, and she could only say feebly, 'No . . . it's . . . it's not the same. . . .'

'But why? I don't see why. You're only quoting your parsons. Why is it not the same?'

'Well . . . because . . . because I was talking of the human soul.' Pleased with this answer, since it seemed she had stumbled on to a route without a guide, she went on, 'One must believe that the human soul is of God and therefore immortal.'

'And that's what you really think?'

'It's what I *know*. I *know* it,' she lied, acting passionate conviction, and at the same time doing secret violence to Heaven for a gift of faith, so that these might cease to be lies. Please God, please God, make it true for me, so that I can make it true for him. 'I *know* it, Michael.' Oh, forgive me if I lie. 'I just know.'

'You really do?'

'Yes.'

'Your faith is absolute and unworried?'

'Absolute.'

Some half an hour of the visit had passed as she said this, and the principal officer who might, or might not have listened with interest to this discussion about Eternity said quietly as he rose, 'I'm sorry, miss, but I'm afraid we must make an end for today. The order says "thirty minutes only." But there's always tomorrow. Will you come along now?'

'Oh, must I? Very well . . .'

'Yes, time's up now, but come again.'

'Thank you so much. Well, Mike——'

Michael had not risen from his bench on the other side of the window—perhaps because he needed the assent of his two warders—but he said, sitting there, 'Tell poor Mum that everybody's being very decent to me here.'

'I will, of course, Mike.'

'I'm being looked after wonderfully. And look, Bethy'— never had he used this endearment before—'I want you to tell the old man something. I know him so well: he's a romantic old thing, with tremendous ideas of honour, and I feel this will kind-of please him.'

'What is it?'

'Will you tell him that, no matter who's asked me, from the minute I was picked up to my arrival here, and no matter what their rank was, I've always refused to supply any evidence against the other boys and girls who were with me in the Rundfunk. I feel that's the sort of thing he'd like to know.'

'Of course I'll tell him.'

'And I can't help thinking, Beth, that—' were his eyes a little shifty while he said this, as if he, like she, knew he was saying something which was invented rather than believed?—'that if I'd done something of that sort, it might have helped with the reprieve. Does Dad ever say I did right in pleading guilty?'

'He's always saying it was brave. He keeps on saying it. To everyone.'

'I feel glad if he thinks so.'

'Come, miss.'

'Oh yes—I'm sorry—I'm coming. Good-bye, Mike dear. Till tomorrow.'

Tomorrow, and tomorrow—and then . . .

§

Dick, without hope, had launched a petition for a reprieve, but few were the signatures that he or anyone else could obtain for it. Apart from people who were opposed to capital punishment in all circumstances, no matter how vile its victim, almost the only people who could be persuaded to sign were Harry and Ida's friends. They signed 'for the old guv's sake.' Indeed there was a concerted movement among the regulars of the Lord of Wensley, both among the white collars in the Saloon and the corduroys in the Public; and in both bars the most active and irrepressible collector of signatures was Bossy Jehoram. 'Have you signed yet?' he would demand of white collar or corduroys, when Harry wasn't looking. 'No? Well, go and do it at once, chum. You're not going to let the Captain down, are you? And he'll never ask you himself because he's so damned scrupulous and won't use his bars for a merely personal matter. Merely personal, mind you! Now go and do what your Uncle Oram tells you, and ask for the form. It's there under the counter with the light ales, for anyone who asks for it. He won't say anything or even look at you, but he'll give it you. It's a bit of foolscap: just put your name to it and add your address and your occupation, if you've got either.' An encouraging hand, large and fat, on the man's shoulder. 'Go and get it out of him for his sake and poor Ida's. Never mind if you think his lad was a rather poisonous piece of work and ought to swing—he will, in any case, because this petition

304

hasn't a dog's chance, so you can safely be a pal and sign it. Every blasted signature is a spot of comfort for poor Ida.'

This last argument that a signature was comfort and no more sent any waverer to Harry behind his beer engines, but only when Ida was out of sight, because no one dared speak of Michael in her hearing. 'Come on, Guv,' the man would say, or 'Come on, Captain. Cough it up. That there petition. Hand it over.'

And Harry would do so without a word.

When the man returned to Jehoram, he was probably greeted with, 'Well done, old cock. And now, if you've got an ounce of decency, which I doubt, you'll get a form from old Dick Templer, and go out and collect more signatures. I don't mind telling you that your Uncle Oram's done plenty of that.'

§

It was raining and therefore quiet on the Common when the little Huntingdon van stopped in the avenue of limes between the nursery gardens, its face towards the prison. Harry stepped out and looked towards the drear and beetling gatehouse and the tall, morose walls flanking it. Clouds, heavy and low, had laid a premature twilight upon the world, so that the gatekeeper's arched window beside the huge studded doors glowed with a golden light. Some of the barred cell-windows in the thick-walled wings glowed golden too. Harry sighed and, opening the car door, gave a hand to Ida. Ida stepped out; and Beth, from the heart of the van, followed her. Ida looked at the prison, but did not speak. Nor did Beth. Harry put a hand under Ida's elbow to support her, as a man supports a mother who is walking to the funeral of her child.

Footsteps sounded in the avenue behind them, and Harry, turning, saw a prison officer, scarcely more than a tall, fresh-faced boy, coming towards them in his blue raincoat and peaked cap. He was smoking happily. He came abreast of them just as they reached the wicket in the doors, and, smiling at them as if he would help them on their way, he lifted the knocker and let it fall with a bang, a single knock very different from Beth's polite little ratta-tat-tat. The gate officer opened the wicket, and the young warder stood aside, politely, while they presented their visiting order—was he not one of their hosts?

The gate officer, seeing on the order the name of Michael Townes who would die in a few hours, said, 'Oh yes . . . yes, of course . . .' and then, more softly, as his imagination took command, 'Please step in, will you? I'll get Mr. Crawford for you. Would you care to wait in the waiting room?'

'Oh, no, we're all right here,' said Harry. They were now standing under the archway of the gatehouse between the first gates and the second barrier. This second barrier was not of blind, studded wood like the first but an enormous grid of vertical iron bars. Looking through the bars, Harry saw the forecourt and steps of the Main Hall. 'Don't trouble,' he said.

'No; please don't trouble,' echoed Ida.

'Okay, sir.' And the gatekeeper hurried into the office at his side, presumably to telephone for Mr. Crawford. Then he came out to talk to them while they waited, and to entertain them, like a good host.

'Won't keep you long, sir. Mr. Crawford's on his way.'

'That's all right,' said Harry.

'Mr. Crawford'll do everything for you.'

'It's very kind of him, I'm sure,' said Ida.

'Yes, he'll look after you.' A man not very articulate, he was anxious to do his best in the way of comfort. 'Ah, here he is. He'll show you everything. Yes.'

A man was approaching the bars, and they judged he must be a principal officer because of the gold on his cap and the silver of his hair. With a jangling of keys, which he'd drawn from his pocket, he opened the iron wicket in the grid and, holding it open with the courtesy of a son of the house, said 'Please come in, Captain Townes.'

Evidently he was pleased to be able to address Harry thus, with rank and name, for directly they had stepped through the wicket and it had clanged behind them, he said 'This way, Captain Townes, sir.'

They followed him across the forecourt, up the steps and through one door; then along a corridor and through a second door—always there was this double security. Now they saw they were in a long and lofty wing like a cold cathedral with a tall arched window at its far end such as might have lit the east end of a basilica. But this great window lit only the shining rails of the balconies and the iron-bound doors of the cells which held the prisoners within like valuable securities in the strong rooms of a bank. After the chill air of a rainy autumn dusk the atmosphere of this great cathedral smote them with a dry warmth and a smell of hot pipes and scrubbed stone.

'This way now, Captain Townes.'

Past one cell door, and another and another and another, they went—and it was only years later that Harry knew that his left shoulder had passed the doors, side by side, of execution chamber and two condemned cells before they reached the doors of the room in which they would meet Michael.

Into this room the officer guided them. Plainly it was a room made by the removal of the wall between two cells because there were the two barred windows high up in the outside wall. It was brightly painted in yellow and green, as were all the walls of the prison, since these colours were supposed to have a sedative effect on troubled men. For furniture there was little more than a table about four-foot square and some chairs. The officer bade them sit at one end of the table, and all three obeyed, but Ida began to suffer from an incipient claustrophobia because of the thick bare walls and those barred windows too high to show anything of the human world. 'I feel I shall choke,' she whispered; and Harry, seeing sweat on her forehead, picked up her hand—which was wet too.

Beth, as usual, said nothing.

The principal officer waited with them, and for a little while silence kept all four of them company in that closed room. But ever and again, in this walled silence, they heard the noises of the prison: the ringing of an electric bell, the rattling of keys, the slam of a door, the echoing steps of a warder pacing up and down. No sound came from the exercise yard beyond the windows, but occasionally they caught, far away, the noises from the railway in its deep cutting, or the hooting of cars on the road over the Common—noises from the world of the free, and of those who would live tomorrow.

Now Ida gave a tiny scream, for a door in the side wall opposite them which she had not seen, because it was flush with the wall and painted over, yellow and green, like the rest, opened, and Michael came through it, with two of his 'death watch' warders.

Michael, Michael.

So far as his coarse grey death-cell clothes would allow—his sack-like buttonless jacket, his shirt without tie, his braceless trousers and laceless shoes—he had spruced himself up for this last meeting with his family. Face and hands were pink from washing and fair hair parted faultlessly and plastered flat with water. For a long time in the bathroom-closet which opened out of the condemned cell (its door standing ajar that his warders might keep their watch) he had been smartening face and hands and hair as for an evening party. And he now greeted the family with a bright—a too bright—smile. All day he had resolved to wear before them a mask of cheerfulness and courage, and especially before his father. Though he knew that tomorrow morning the door opening at nine o'clock would send bullets of terror into his heart, yet there must be this tremendous effort before his father because, after the utter humiliation of being proved wrong before him, he wanted him to see him at least as a young man of courage. Many of the words that he would use now he had prepared and conned in his cell. As these first words: 'Well, Dad . . . and Mum darling . . . it's nice of you to come.'

But Ida could only stare at him; nor could Harry speak at once; and Beth did not think it right to speak before her parents; so it was Michael who strove to hold up this visit from sinking into discomfort; and he did it with a show of cheer—too much cheer. 'How did you come? In the old car? Does she really still work? I should have thought you'd have put her out to grass long ago.'

'Yes, the little old van's still going,' said Harry.

'Going great guns, is she?'

'Great guns is just about the word for it sometimes.'

'I'll bet it is. Oh, I'm sorry.' Prompted by his warders, he sat down at the opposite end of the table from his family. 'I sit here, do I?'

After nodding silently, the warders went and stood behind him, as far back as the yellow and green walls would permit. Here in their decency they looked at their boots or the ceiling or their thumb-nails.

'Beth's been wonderful,' Michael continued, trying to help his parents. And saying anything that came into his head, he added words wholly inapt: 'I shall never forget it.'

'I'm so glad,' said Harry. 'I wish I could have come more often myself, but you know how it is.'

'That's all right, Dad. You get on with the work.'

'I'm sorry the petition failed, son. We all did our best with it.'

'Did you ever expect it to do anything else? I didn't. There never was any hope.'

'There should have been,' Ida murmured.

'Well, perhaps, Mum. But there it is: I quite understand. I'm not complaining.'

'It's wicked. I don't care who hears me say so.' She glanced at the principal officer. 'I shall go to my death saying it. Wicked.'

'Well, maybe, maybe, but I can take it.' He shut his lips tight on the words for as he thought of 'it', his traitorous teeth chattered.

'The lads worked wonderfully for the petition,' Harry interposed. 'And Dick too. He did all he possibly could.'

'I know. I've thanked him. I said good-bye to him this afternoon.'

'Michael . . . Michael . . .' his mother began but controlled herself.

'I don't feel afraid of tomorrow, Mum dear,' he said, though at the word 'tomorrow' his hands, joined under the table, shivered. 'I'm getting quite used to the idea. It seems to be just interesting now. It's so funny to think that in a few hours' time one may know the answer to all the mysteries. It's rather exciting, really—like the night before I flew out of England for the first time.'

So he spoke, in a speech more or less prepared, but behind the words he was thinking, 'Death while life is still warm in my limbs and a bright light in my brain . . . This room will be here tomorrow; tomorrow at ten o'clock and eleven . . . In a few hours now.' Though by tight clasping of his hands he held his body still, his heart within it was slowly pounding.

Meanwhile they spoke of many things, since one must speak of something: of Walter and Old Agnes; of friends in the bars; and of schoolfellows and childhood friends who were doing this and that in the world.

And all the time Harry, though often speaking aloud, was assembling the courage to say something which *he* had prepared.

That afternoon he had gone up to his bedroom and locked the door on himself. And he had knelt by the side of the big bed and, putting his face in his hands and burying head and hands in the quilt, he had prayed for help to do properly his paternal duty in this last hour with his son. 'All my life I have failed in my duty,' he had thought, his head pressed into the darkness of his hands. 'When he was changing from a child into a man I was too shy to tell him all that he ought to know.

I left him to find out for himself. And I never taught him anything about religion because I hardly knew what I believed myself, really. I left him to blunder along alone. Let me not fail him now, O God. Give me strength to say to him all that I ought to say. I know I have been a blunderer with him in my pride and hot temper, and now I can never make it up to him. There's no chance any more. Oh, let me do something for him at the end; something to make it up. Forgive me for everything that was my fault, and give me some words for him.'

And now, since time was passing, he must speak his words. 'Michael, son,' he began hesitantly, 'I've told you that while, naturally, I can't think what you've done was right, I do understand how you came to do it. I understand—perfectly.'

'Thank you, Dad.'

'But there's another thing I want to say now. I've never been much of a churchgoer, as you know—never had the time—our Beth's done all that for us—but I do believe in Heaven, Mike—honestly I do. If you've done wrong—and, as I say, I can't help thinking you have—I still think you'll have been punished enough down here, and there'll be no more pain for you up there. That's what I feel. No more pain, see.'

'Perhaps so,' agreed Michael with a smile.

'And one day, not so far off now for some of us, we'll all meet again, see.'

'Oh, yes, *yes*,' breathed Ida, and her hand went forward as if to reach his.

One of the officers took half a step towards them because, in strictness, no touch was allowed. But it was not necessary to complete the step; Michael had not raised his hands from under the table. He was only saying, 'I wish I felt half as sure of it, Mum,' with the same smile.

'But it's true,' declared Beth.

'Are you really so certain, Beth dear?'

'Absolutely,' said Beth, her eyes on the table.

'Yes, and there's one other thing, Michael lad,' Harry went on. 'I've never told you this before, but in my old war, when I knew we'd got to go over the top in the morning, I used to get into a proper funk, even if I *was* captain of the company; and, Mike, I used to pray and pray. I used to stand in the trench before dawn, waiting to blow my whistle and take the boys over, and, though they didn't know it, I was praying off and on, all the time. Praying for enough courage, if you see what I mean. And somehow—it's a fact—this praying used to do everything for me, so that I led the lads without much fear. What I mean, Mike, is: if you pray, it'll give you power to go through everything. It just does; I *know*.'

'Yes, it does, it does,' Beth endorsed emphatically. 'That I *do* know. Absolutely.'

'I'm sure you're both right,' said Michael. 'The padre here's an awfully decent fellow, and he—we've been talking of these things.'

'And you do believe all he tells you, son?'

'Yes,' Michael declared; but just as Beth had said 'Firmly I believe, and truly' for his sake, so he said it rather more for his father's comfort than because it was completely true. 'Yes, I do, Dad. And I shall try to think it. So don't worry any more about me, any of you. Everybody here's been awfully decent to me, ever since I came, and I'm sure they will be tomorrow.'

'And we shall be just outside, your mother and me and Beth.'

'Yes, Michael my darling,' said Ida. 'There'll be only just a wall between us.' Unwittingly she glanced at the outside wall of the room, and gulped. 'Think of us there, all of us.'

'Don't you come, Mother.'

'Oh, but I will—naturally——'

'No, no; I'll tell you what I want you to do. I want you to take an extra dose of sleeping tablets tonight so that you'll sleep and only wake up when it's all over. That's my idea of what'd be best. I told Beth so.'

'I shall be outside, Michael darling, and just as near as they'll let me come.'

'I'm afraid it's time now, Captain Townes.' The principal officer had spoken from behind them. They had forgotten his existence.

They had been together for about three-quarters of an hour. Officially the time allowed for meetings was thirty minutes, but it was understood by the officers that the last meeting of all might go on for forty minutes, or even more—'as long,' they would say, 'as the parties can stand it.' Sometimes it was in mercy that the principal officer put his hand on the guillotine.

Harry turned towards the voice. 'You'll let his mother kiss him. It's her last time.'

The officer bent his head, not consenting, but not forbidding.

'Come, Michael,' said Harry, and, with a hand at her arm, raised Ida to her feet.

Michael came round the table to her while his two warders, pretending not to, watched under their eyes, narrowly. Ida hugged him against her, saying, 'My boy, my boy.'

'Good-bye, Mum darling,' he said. 'Thank you for all you've always done for me, you and Dad, too.' And after a time, very gently, he pressed her from him.

All this time Beth had been staring, staring at Michael with his grey garments and his death-sculptured face, falsely bright, and thinking, 'The last sight of him. I used to dream of him returning to us, and how we would welcome him and how I would fling my arms around him and hug him, as Mother is doing now. And he came back, but it was for this—' and as she thought of this, Beth, for whom no such consent had been sought, defying everybody, took her mother's place and threw her arms around him. She kissed him on cheek and brow, holding him as she'd longed to do all her life, and as she'd managed to do only once before—that other time when he went from them.

''Bye, Bethy, dear,' he said.

When, reluctantly, she yielded him from her embrace, Harry stretched out his hand. Michael took it, and both men, bringing their spare hands over, made of this a double grasp. They did not speak, but pressed their hands together. It was not easily that Harry let his son's hand go.

The principal officer had opened the door in the side wall, and the two warders, touching Michael, directed him towards it. At the door he turned to look again at his family. Ida was near to fainting, and perhaps it was better so; for Harry must give some of his attention to supporting her; the warder too. It was Beth who in her last look at Michael sent with it a passion of love. He smiled back in gratitude and put a brightness into his eyes to give her heart. But even as a warder touched him again and bid him come, she saw the brightness fly from his eyes. His mask had dropped a second too soon.

In the next second the door closed, and the green and yellow wall was smooth and blank. The effect was as if Michael had vanished from the world into nothing. The bang of the door, final as death, stunned for a merciful moment both heart and sense in Beth.

A voice said, 'No. This way, please, Captain Townes.'

CHAPTER SIX

ALL that night there hung a small notice on the great doors of
the prison. It said, over signatures of a Sheriff of the County
of London and of the Governor, that the sentence passed upon
Michael Townes would be carried into execution at 9.0 a.m.
tomorrow. And even before the sun was risen, and while the
barred cell windows were still chequered golden patches in the
prison's long dark halls, the people began to come towards that
small notice. Not in multitudes; by half past-eight two hundred
perhaps were standing in the lime avenue between the nursery
gardens or strolling up and down its pathways, for the autumn
morning was cold. Fifteen minutes later their number was
swelled by perhaps another hundred, and from now onward
the eyes of all lifted again and again to the clock in the gable of
the Main Hall.

The sun, rising from beyond the Common and almost opposite the prison cast a brilliant light on its eastward faces, and
gave precision to their only ornament, the squat barred windows.
It exchanged their garment of sooty grey to one of smoky gold.
At the same time it flung the shadows of the lime trees in long
purple pointers towards the curtain walls, across a floor of pale
gold. Never a brighter morning saluted with its satire the
face of a prison.

Everything was quiet around the waiting people, because
the gardens and the Common were empty, and traffic was still
small on the long Trinity Road that ran between them. Surrounded by this silence the people spoke little; some were too
cold to speak and only walked up and down and stamped. One
or two were pressmen with notebooks; they wandered back and
forth, looking into faces, no doubt in the hope of recognising
them and finding something that would make a 'story'. Others
were press photographers with cameras and flash lamps. The
reporters began to write when a film company's van turned out
of Trinity Road into the avenue, and trained its camera on to
the little white notice. But since there would be no movement

here till someone replaced it with new notices, they swept the camera round upon the people, who at least provided movement and human interest. Film men and pressmen photographed each other, with mutual laughter.

While they were doing this six young men, bareheaded and in belted raincoats, one of them with a battered nose, a sagging jaw, and silly, sorrow-filled eyes, drew quietly away from all such publicity. Keeping together, they went to a place at the back of the crowd.

If some of the people were merely curious, others were virtuous, and these liked to be heard saying quite loudly, 'I got no sympathy to waste on him. No use for blasted traitors, myself. Reckon he deserves all he's going to get.'

'You're telling me,' another of the virtuous would agree. 'Deserves that and a bit more.'

'Yes. No use for any blasted traitor. Reckon the world'll be well rid of him.'

Hearing this, the six young men stepped over the holly shrubs that fenced the nursery garden and stood among some vegetables gone to seed. They stood in a shy group beyond the thick bole of a lime tree and under its branches. Occasionally from this shelter they glanced up at the clock.

Now another van turned into the avenue, but this was a small and insignificant affair compared with the film company's shining new vehicle. It was but a small blue Huntingdon van, dented and scratched and in places rusty. Its driver, seeing many people in the roadway, stopped his car just by the lime tree that screened the young men. The strolling pressmen came down the path and looked in at the van's windows, but they saw only a large portly man in the driver's seat and a woman heavily veiled beside him. In the shadows behind they just discerned another woman on the spare seat.

The nearer woman's veil, almost hiding her face, suggested that they must be relatives of the condemned man, so, as this was very interesting, one of the more pushing and opportunist of them, notebook in one hand, laid the other on the door and opened it an inch to start inquiries, but——

'Go to hell and die there,' said the man within, shutting the door with a slam and locking it.

'Wouldn't mind betting that was his old man,' said the reporter, not seriously abashed, but walking away. 'The old publican. Captain Townes, the landlord of the Traitor of Tooting.'

ey!' said Harry.   'Was it always as noisy as this?'
ln't to notice it,' said Ida.   'One was always too

that we're getting old, Ida ducks?   Old and quiet.'
p of a rich cigar moved between his lips.   Hadn't
a festival in Clapham?   One's old lady wasn't seventy
y.   'We were young then; lord love you, I wasn't
when I gave up.   But I'll say there's more traffic than
ed to be.   And there was quite enough of it then.'
sed to like it when I was working in my kitchen.   It
l friendly.   One never hears hardly a sound in Mitcham
not from morning till night.'
o.   That's true.   Busy, yes.   I'll say we were busy.   No
nder we didn't hear this din in the bars, with all the chaps
lking their heads off.   Those were the days, Ida ducks.   That
vas Life.'
'Yes,' said Ida, and fell silent, because she was remembering
other days.
'There it is!   There's the old place.'
Fifty yards ahead of them they saw the signboard slung above
the pavement: the Lord of Wensley on his battlements surveying
his parcel of England.
'Not a lovelier inn-sign in the whole country than that,' said
Harry.
A little nearer, and they saw the old pilasters of brown marble
and the windows of engraved glass shining in the last of the sun.
'Hope they keep the place nice, young Bob and Eileen,' mused
Harry aloud.   'But they're young, and not all the young have
standards these days like mine were.   Wonder what their
cellar's like.'
'As good as ever yours was, you vain old thing.'
'I wonder.   Steady ducks; slow up now.'
'Shall you go in?'
'No; just let's walk slowly by.   I don't want them to think
I'm for ever hanging around.   Give the young ones a chance.
I'm like a vicar who's retired: it just isn't fair if he comes back
to the old parish too often.   And to tell the truth, I was here
the other day, looking at the old place, and I don't want young
Eileen to glance out and say, "There's that terrible Captain
Townes again, that dreary old man."'
'She'd never.'
'Oh, she might, and anyhow—six o'clock—it's too early for

any of the old boys and girls to be there. And it'd be sad to see the old saloon and think that Dick'd never come in it again. Best friend man ever had—Dick. You know that.' Harry at seventy-five, was getting forgetful and would say to the woman on his arm things that she'd heard twenty times before. 'Yes . . . Dick . . . I'm always proud to think that the only person he wanted in that hospital at the end was old Harry. I guess old Harry's mug was the last thing he saw before he went off. There you are: the good ship, Lord of Wensley, moored up against the pavement as usual, and ready to embark the passengers. It was a happy ship in our day, I think.' He threw the moist end of his festival cigar, now flaking apart, into the gutter. 'Go slowly, Ida; and if anyone should look out, we're just passing by. Anyone may pass by.'

'It looks just the same as ever, doesn't it?'

'Outside, yes; but I doubt if he keeps his dispense as spotless and shining as I used to. That's another reason for not going in. I don't want to see anything that'd hurt.'

'I expect he's quite as particular as you were, you old fuss-pot.'

'Maybe. Maybe. Oh, dear . . . never really wanted to retire. One doesn't—not from a place that's been one's home for thirty years, though things were never quite the same, somehow, after that business . . . always a little sad after that . . . though the boys and girls stuck by us splendidly, didn't they; and the brewers too. People are decent. Awfully decent. Well, there it is, old lady: my little old pothouse: take your fill of it, and move on.'

Ida looked up at the two first-floor windows behind which was the old living-room; and after a moment she said, 'I suffered behind those windows once.'

'I know, pet; I know. But it's funny how, after five years, ten years, things lose their power to hurt any more. All things heal up at last. Apart from that, we had some good times there, old girl. Remember our New Year Eves? "Knees up, Mother Brown", eh? Oh, yes, we've had our times.' He pulled her arm against him and looked down on her with laughter in his eyes to combat the sentiment in his words. 'And see: because that business happened, we mean a bit more to each other, wouldn't you say?—what? The pains get less, but that gets better. Such is life if you're fond of your wife. Hush. Not a sound inside. The fun hasn't begun yet.'

Ida made an unexpected remark. 'Pity we never had more kids.'

'We've got Beth. Golly, and our Beth's almost an old lady now! Close on fifty. Will you only believe it? And it seems only the other day she was a fat little blighter running in and out of that door. If she's fifty, it must be getting very near closing time for us, old dear. Time, ladies and gentlemen. Drink up, Captain Townes, if you please.'

The home-seekers hurried past them as they dawdled along, and Harry felt them like a pressure urging him to proceed faster on his way.

'Come on, ducks. Home to the quiet old street in Mitcham that suits a quiet old couple, and we'll eat the remains of yesterday's feast. Beth'll be getting it all ready for us, bless her. She's spreading the table for us now, I shouldn't wonder.'

They took a last look at the Lord of Wensley and, arm in arm, went on.

39   39